THE ROOMMATE

The Roommate

By the Author

Business of the Heart

We Met in a Bar

The Roommate

Visit us at www.boldstrokesbooks.com

THE ROOMMATE

by
Claire Forsythe

2025

THE ROOMMATE
© 2025 BY CLAIRE FORSYTHE. ALL RIGHTS RESERVED.

ISBN 13: 978-1-63679-757-1

THIS TRADE PAPERBACK ORIGINAL IS PUBLISHED BY
BOLD STROKES BOOKS, INC.
P.O. BOX 249
VALLEY FALLS, NY 12185

FIRST EDITION: JANUARY 2025

CREDITS
EDITORS: JENNY HARMON AND STACIA SEAMAN
PRODUCTION DESIGN: STACIA SEAMAN
COVER DESIGN BY INKSPIRAL DESIGN

Acknowledgments

I thought that finding time to write with a newborn had been a challenge, but writing with a toddler running around? Whole different ball game! Partly because he can skillfully demolish a room within seconds and is able to climb onto just about any surface in the blink of an eye. But also, because he is way too cute and lovable, and I find myself wanting to stare at him in adoration all day long. But books must be written, and I was lucky to have some fantastic people on hand to help me out.

My partner, Mary—I think you already know how much I appreciate you, but here is a reminder anyway. Your help and support mean the world, always. I'm so lucky to have you.

My mum—you have always been my rock, and when I was writing this book was no different. From granny duties to hugs and words of encouragement, you do it all. I truly couldn't do any of this without you.

My dad—another constant support in my life. Always there to help, and nothing is too much trouble. I really am blessed with the best parents—the number of thank yous you deserve could make up a book of their own.

I am also blessed with great friends. Paula—let's just say, if I were to owe you a drink every time you've been there to help me out, it would remain my round for a very long time. As usual, you went above and beyond, and I am more grateful than I can say. This book would not have got written without you.

Geraldine—not only do you graciously let me steal your wife for babysitting, but you are always on hand to make me laugh and offer endless words of support.

Becks—you always check in to ask if I'm okay, make sure I'm not getting too stressed, and do all the things that a good friend does. It means so much.

My editor, Jenny Harmon—thankfully, you're able to point me in the right direction when I can't quite see it myself. As always, a huge thank you to you for all of your help, expertise, and guidance. What you do is truly invaluable, and I appreciate it all.

Thank you to everyone at Bold Strokes Books for making my dream of writing a reality. I feel extremely lucky and honored to be part of the BSB family.

And last, but certainly not least, to you, reader. If you've picked up this book or any of my others, I thank you from the bottom of my heart. I hope you enjoy it.

For my amazing mum and dad,
thank you for your never-ending help,
encouragement, love, and support.
I am so lucky to have you.
Love you always x

CHAPTER ONE

Jess hated weddings. Would it be overdramatic to say that she despised them with every fibre of her being? Because she did. Whenever she told people that, they either laughed at her in disbelief or gaped at her in shock. How could she possibly dislike the most romantic, heart-warming, magical of days? Well, maybe because any weddings she had been to hadn't been any of those things.

Granted, she had only attended her parents' weddings—to other people, not to each other. She had been to the last three of her dad's weddings—yes, three! The first had been to Helen the Hyena who laughed at everything whether it was funny or not. Next there had been Sally the Shrink who liked to psychoanalyse everything and everyone even though she was totally unqualified. And after that it had been Fiona the Flirt who batted her eyelashes at every man she met. Seriously, a real shocker that none of those had worked out.

Jess had been at her mum's wedding to Barry the Bore too, name self-explanatory, not the most exciting or magical event, but at least their marriage had lasted. None of her dad's had, and because he never learned from his mistakes, there Jess was, on her way to wedding number four. She cringed even thinking about it.

When Jess heard the rumbling of the train approaching in the distance, she reluctantly stood up from the bench she had been waiting on and gathered her bags. She had been checking the arrivals board constantly, so she already knew that it was her train. Another glance at the board told her that it would pull into the station in less than a minute, so Jess hurried over to the painted line near the edge of the platform. She wanted to be one of the first people to get on in the hope that she could find a quiet seat away from everyone else. Usually, she wouldn't care, but she wanted nothing more than to be alone so that she could dread her day in peace. Wallow in her own misery. Sulk, basically.

Jess should have been used to her dad getting married by now. After all, it had practically become an annual event—only a slight exaggeration. However, this time was different. It was way worse than any of the times before. Her dad's bride-to-be wasn't much older than Jess's age for starters, and who wouldn't be annoyed by that? And if that wasn't bad enough, Gretchen, said bride-to-be, was also a terrible person and she wasn't even good at hiding it. Somehow, Jess's father didn't seem to notice how awful Gretchen was, though Jess was sure that his bank balance did.

She had aptly named this one Gretchen the Gold-digger. Though, unfortunately, even if Gretchen had the word *gold-digger* tattooed across her forehead, Jess feared that her dad would remain oblivious. Jess had tried to warn him about her concerns plenty of times, but considering she was on her way to the courthouse for their nuptials, she had clearly failed to get through.

She sighed as she looked down to make sure she wasn't rumpling the dress bag that she had draped over her arm. As much as she didn't want the wedding to happen, her dad was her dad, and she couldn't not be there.

When the train screeched to a halt and the doors opened, Jess rushed onboard and found a single seat in the corner, so there would be no chance of anyone sitting next to her. *Perfect.*

As she made herself comfortable, Jess glanced around at the other people filing in looking for their own seats. The train wasn't packed by any means, so there was no shortage to choose from. There was a seat available directly opposite her, but who would want to sit in the corner face-to-face with a complete stranger? But it was only seconds later that Jess realized that someone did, apparently, think it was a good place to sit. Because a woman breezed past her and plonked herself down on that very chair.

Jess let out a sharp breath through her nose. *Seriously?* Though when she breathed back in again a pleasant smell interrupted her annoyance for a few moments. Jess was almost dazed by it. She subtly inhaled again to try and work out what the scent was. Citrusy, for sure.

Not orange. Lime maybe, and was that a hint of vanilla too? There was something else that Jess couldn't identify. Something spicy that shouldn't complement the other scents—yet did. Whatever it was, Jess liked the combination, anyway. At least her unwanted train companion smelled good—that wasn't always the case on public transport.

When Jess looked over at the pleasant-smelling-woman, she was met with a wide smile. A pretty smile. Really pretty. Full lips and perfect, white teeth. Okay, so she smelled good, and she looked good, but why the hell did she have to sit right there? Jess glanced around at all the empty seats that this woman could have taken.

"Oh, I'm sorry, is somebody sitting here? I probably should have checked before I just threw myself down here." The woman gave a cute little grimace—it was the only way Jess could describe it.

And damn, Jess had been noticeably rude. She immediately felt bad. It wasn't the pretty woman's fault that Jess was in a terrible mood, it was Gretchen's. And her dad's, but mostly Gretchen's. Besides, wishing for alone time on public transport had probably been unrealistic anyway.

She attempted a smile to prove that she wasn't quite as hostile as she likely seemed. "No, you're fine." It wasn't like Jess had any right to ask her to move.

The woman's smile returned then. "Great."

Next came the awkward shuffle. The one where each of them moved their stuff closer to their own seat to ensure it wasn't intruding on the other's space. Jess went to move her dress, which she had hung up by the window beside her.

"Don't worry about that, it's not in my way. You'll get creases if you don't hang it up," the woman said. She indicated the dress with a nod of her head. "Is it dry cleaning day? Or are you going somewhere nice?"

How was Jess supposed to answer that question to a total stranger? *I'm actually heading to my dad's wedding, wedding number four, to a twenty-something-year-old money grabber who I can't stand the sight of and who I'm nearly certain is going to drain his bank account, break his heart, and then do a runner. And when she does do all of this, he still won't learn anything from it, and then I'll end up in this same position again, having to go to wedding number five, to God-knows-who next time.*

"No to both," Jess answered. "Unfortunately," she added, to soften her blunt response. Her phone buzzed in her pocket, and she pulled it out, relieved by the interruption.

Jess shot the woman another polite smile so that she didn't seem too rude by cutting off their conversation, and then she swiped the screen to answer the call. Thank God for Austin. At least she didn't have to face the day alone. "Hey, have you left yet?" she asked him. Austin was finishing up a few things at work and then the plan was that he would meet Jess at the ceremony.

"Hey babe. Uh, some bad news. I can't get away today after all," he said way too casually for Jess's liking.

So much for that thought. "What?" she said, a little sharper than she intended. She lowered her voice. "You know that I really need you to be there today. You've known about it for weeks. Months even!"

"I know, babe, I know. And I told my bosses that I need to go be there for my girl. I really tried, but we're working with a major client and something new has literally come up today. They said they can't spare me. You know how I have to keep my nose clean with this promotion coming up."

Jess closed her eyes and tried to come up with a calm response, anything other than any of the expletives she was thinking of. "Well, if the promotion is at stake…" Complete sarcasm, of course, but better than screaming or swearing down the phone.

"Jess, don't be like that. You know how hard I've worked for this. You'll be fine today. You can handle anything—I know you can. I'll make it up to you later, okay? You can tell me all about it."

She was far from over it, but she didn't want a train full of people to overhear her argue with him. "Mm-hmm."

Jess could hear some other voices muttering in the background of the call before Austin spoke again. "I have to get back to it. Everyone's waiting for me. I'll see you later, babe. Okay?"

"Mm-hmm," Jess repeated. *If you've got nothing nice to say, say nothing at all.* That's what she had always been taught.

"That's my girl. Try to enjoy yourself." And with that, he ended the call.

Seriously, *try to enjoy herself*? Jess had only told him about a hundred times already how hard the wedding was going to be for her. Were all men so clueless? She stuffed her phone back in her pocket with more force than necessary. Thankfully, the woman sitting across from her had busied herself with her own phone. She had undoubtedly heard Jess's side of the call, but she seemed to be actively trying not to pay attention, and Jess appreciated the effort.

She turned to look out the window. Sometime during her call with Austin, the train had started moving. She stared out at the trees and the unfamiliar buildings as they passed by.

So, she had to face the worst wedding in the world alone after all. Maybe it was for the best. Austin was a natural mingler, and he would have made Jess introduce him to each and every person there and prolonged the whole thing. At least this way, Jess could keep herself to herself as much as possible and make her escape at the earliest opportunity. Yes, perhaps this *was* better. That didn't mean that Jess wasn't pissed at him anyway. Austin cancelling on their plans was becoming a regular thing, and this one was a biggie.

Jess got that it wasn't easy to climb the ladder, especially in a big law firm like the one that Austin worked for. And she tried to be understanding, but she couldn't deny that his long and often unsociable hours had put a strain on their relationship. Still, Jess wasn't the type of person to walk away just because things had got a little harder. Her parents had been quick to do that, and she had always vowed to never repeat their mistakes.

"Chocolate?"

Huh? Oh. A purple bag was being waved in front of her. Jess raised her gaze to meet the woman's eyes. Blue and sparkling. Pretty. *Why do I keep thinking that?* Probably because when she was looking straight at this woman, it was impossible to ignore that she was beautiful. "Oh. I'm good. Thanks, though." Trust Jess to end up sitting opposite Little Miss Friendly today of all days. She felt in her jacket pocket for her AirPods and pulled them out. "I'm just going to…" She held them up in way of explanation and then popped them in her ears. Nothing wrong with that. Plenty of people listened to music while they travelled.

The woman nodded, and was it Jess's imagination or did her expression fall a little bit too? Probably her imagination. Why would the woman care if Jess wanted to listen to music instead of making awkward chitchat? She was probably relieved.

Jess pulled her phone out from her pocket again and clicked on the first playlist that she found. Some kind of rock tune blasted out from her phone speaker, and she quickly scrambled to tap the screen and turn it off again. She must have forgotten to charge her damn AirPods. A few heads had turned around to check where the noise had come from.

Little Miss Friendly had gone back to scrolling on her phone, but she was grinning. "You know," she said without looking up, "if you wanted me to shut up, you could just have said so."

Jess felt her cheeks flush. "I…um…it wasn't that."

The woman looked at her then, amusement on her face. "No?"

Jess exhaled. She *had* been pretty obvious. "Well, maybe. Kind of. I'm sorry. I'm not usually an antisocial weirdo, it's just really not my day today."

"And let me guess. You got stuck with someone sitting next to you, being all chirpy, interrupting your bad mood?"

She couldn't help but smile at the accuracy. "Something like that, yes."

The woman laughed. "Okay. Sulk. Brood. I'll be quiet. Unfriendly even, if you'd prefer."

"Well, now I feel bad," Jess said.

"You should, you're being totally ignorant. I might even be offended." She smiled that dazzling smile again as she tossed her long, blond hair over her shoulder. She really was very pretty. And witty too, it seemed.

A man in a navy blue uniform made his way toward them, tapping on some kind of tablet as he walked. "Payment please," he said in an unenthusiastic, monotone voice.

The woman smiled at him and lifted her phone to tap it against his machine. Jess really had to set up contactless payments on her phone too. She kept forgetting.

Jess shuffled around in her bag for her purse, but she couldn't see it. She shuffled some more. "I don't believe this," she muttered. She looked up at the ticket clerk with her most apologetic face. "I seem to have forgotten my card."

"I accept cash."

Jess gritted her teeth. "Yeah, none of that either, I'm afraid. It's the whole that's missing." She vaguely remembered seeing it on top of her bedside table, but that wouldn't help her now.

"No fare, you'll have to get off at the next stop," he said impatiently.

That wasn't good. Jess would never make it to her dad's wedding from there. "Can I not, like, owe you?"

The ticket clerk gave her a bored look. "No. You can't, like, owe me. You have to get off at the next stop if you can't pay."

"I've got it," said the woman sitting opposite. She held up her phone again ready to pay for Jess's fare.

"No, I can't let you do that." Jess put a hand out to stop her, but the woman ignored her and smiled as she continued to reach the phone out.

"It's really not a big deal." There was a beeping sound as her phone payment went through. "There. All done."

The ticket clerk flinched, like he wouldn't have minded throwing Jess off at the next stop. Then with a single nod he went about his business, continuing to the next compartment.

"Thank you so much. You didn't have to do that," Jess said. She didn't deserve the woman's kindness. She hadn't exactly been warm and fuzzy.

The woman waved her off. "Don't even worry about it."

Darkness suddenly engulfed the windows, and Jess winced. She hated going through tunnels. She had done ever since she was a little girl.

Nothing to see out of the windows but blackness. Being completely closed in. Not knowing when the train would reach the light on the other side, or if it would. She had also seen horror movies where there were monsters in train tunnels, so there was that—though that part was maybe a bit more irrational. Jess tried not to let her discomfort show—it was just a silly fear, and the tunnels never took long to get through.

But then the train started to slow down.

Jess tried not to panic even though her heart started pounding. "What is happening? Why are we slowing down?" She closed her eyes and tried to take deep, level breaths to calm herself down. That's what they said to do, right? So why wasn't it working?

"I'm not sure, I think they're stopping for some reason. Hey, are you okay?"

Jess felt a hand touch her knee and she opened her eyes. The woman was leaning forward from the edge of her seat, looking at her with concern.

Jess let out a nervous laugh. "This is a little embarrassing, but

I don't really like tunnels. And I definitely don't want to be stuck in the middle of one." Then, in what some people—not her—might call perfect timing, the train came to a stop. "Oh, God." She blew out a long, shaky breath.

The woman slipped off her seat and crouched down in front of Jess. "It's okay, I'm sure it won't be for long. I bet we'll be moving again in a minute or two."

More shaky breathing. Was Jess causing a scene? Were people looking? People were bound to have noticed her practically hyperventilating in the corner. "You think?"

"I'm sure of it. These hold-ups happen all the time." The woman set her hand on Jess's knee again and gently squeezed to reassure her. Shivers shot all the way up Jess's leg. Likely another reaction to her current state of unease, though she wouldn't have described the feeling as unpleasant.

The woman spoke again before Jess had a chance to think much more about it. "I have a game that I sometimes play when I'm travelling. Want to give it a go?"

"A game? Now?"

"No, that's probably silly, um—"

A voice crackled through the speakers. "It appears that we are having some technical difficulties. We're currently working on the problem, and we hope to be on our way again as soon as possible. We appreciate your patience." Static followed the announcement, then it went silent. There were a few moans and groans from some of the other passengers.

"You said that we would be moving soon. That doesn't sound like soon." Jess hated how whiny her voice sounded, but she couldn't seem to control it.

"I'm sure it won't be long," the woman reassured her again. "Don't worry. Nothing bad is going to happen."

"It could," Jess argued. "The tunnel could collapse. Or we could get blown up. Or another train could come hurtling toward us while we're stuck here like sitting ducks." She didn't mention the monsters, but she damn well thought about them.

"I think those things are pretty unlikely," the woman said, clearly trying to hide her amusement. "Another train may have broken down. Or maybe they have to fix something on the tracks."

"Ah. Okay. Tell me about this game." Anything was better than thinking about the train speeding off broken train tracks.

"Hmm?" The woman blinked a few times. "Oh. The game. My game. Yes. Right. Good." She shifted closer to Jess, still remaining crouched down beside her.

Jess got a stronger whiff of that pleasant smell again. She found it surprisingly soothing, but not quite soothing enough to take her mind off her current predicament. If only conquering your fears was that easy.

The woman spoke softly. "What I do is, I have a look at the people around me." She did exactly that. "And I come up with my own stories about them. Who they are, what they do, where they're going. That kind of thing."

"Like people-watching?" Jess wasn't sure how that could be considered a game, but there was a cold sweat running down the back of her neck, and she was prepared to do just about anything to distract herself.

"Kind of. Only instead of just observing, I make things up. For example…" She subtly gestured a man in a suit in the far corner of the compartment. He was typing ferociously on his laptop, a scowl plastered on his face. "He's an author. Thrillers. He's not happy right now because he's rewritten the ending to his latest novel at least a dozen times, and he still hates it. His story is complicated with lots of twists and turns, perhaps too many, because he can't get it to make any sense. At this point he's considering just killing off all of his characters."

"Really? How did you work all that out?" Jess asked.

"I didn't work it out. I made it up. He could be a banker for all I know. He doesn't look happy, though, so that's the reason I'm choosing to go with." She searched for someone else. "See the woman with the pink coat who's staring into space with a look of contentment on her face? She was on a date last night. Met the guy on a dating app that she was forced to download by her pestering friend. She expected it to go horribly, but instead, it was the best date of her life. He even brought her flowers. She's pondering how long she should wait before arranging their second date, but in truth, she doesn't want to play it cool. She would happily go out with him again tonight."

Jess could see how the story fit. "Too bad she won't get a signal in this stupid tunnel to check if he's sent her a text."

The woman threw her a look. "The point of this is to forget about the tunnel. Tunnel mentions are banned."

As if she could forget, but fine, she would try. "What else you got, then? What about that couple over there?" Jess gestured to an older couple who were holding hands, whispering to one another.

She looked over and a wicked grin spread across her face. "Well, I never. They've got a long journey ahead. They're going to visit their son who lives almost on the other side of the country. And he's just whispered to his wife—who he's been married to for forty-nine years, by the way—suggesting that a bit of smooching would be the perfect way for them to pass the time. She's giggling now, look!"

Sure enough, she was. Jess found herself laughing too. "Oh my God, no chance!"

"No? No chance he said that or no chance that it would be a good way to pass the time?"

"He did *not* say that. Sorry to ruin your theory, but they don't strike me as the type of couple who would be into PDAs. But if you ask my personal opinion, kissing is always a good pastime." Why had she told her that?

The woman's gaze flicked down to Jess's lips for a split second, then back up again. "Well, that was going to be my next suggestion, but you wanted to play my game, so…" She grinned.

Jess's heart, which had finally slowed down to beat at a somewhat normal pace, started racing again. Why did the idea of kissing the time away with this woman appeal to her? Excite her, even? She had never even thought about kissing another woman before. It must be her stupid, terrified brain coming up with a distraction. That's all it was.

"I'm going to do you next."

She was? "I'm sorry?" Jess managed to squeak out.

The woman let out a low, quiet laugh. "The game. I'm going to come up with a story about you. Why? What did you think I meant?" She tilted her head, a knowing look on her face.

"The game. Obviously. Yes." Jess didn't dare say otherwise.

"Obviously." The woman let out that low laugh again. "Okay."

Jess tried not to squirm under the woman's intense gaze as she studied her.

"You're an easy one because, well, look at you." The look she gave Jess could only be described as appreciative. "Naturally beautiful, your makeup applied subtly to compliment that. You don't need to try hard. This hair…" She casually reached up and brushed a few strands that were hanging over Jess's face to the side. "Styled to perfection. And it's a gorgeous shade of brown, might I add. You're elegant, poised. It's clear that you're a model, on your way to a big photoshoot, likely for a high-end magazine or something." She pointed to the dress that was hanging up. "This was too fancy to wear for travel, but you'll change in the bathroom when you arrive at the station. Your agent was supposed to meet you at the shoot but is busy with another client, hence the let-down phone call. So, now you're even more nervous because this shoot is huge for your career, and you have to walk in alone. You have nothing to worry about, though. I for one would definitely buy the magazine if you were in it."

Jess couldn't remember ever being complimented so thoroughly. And with such sincerity that she had no choice but to believe the words. "Are you flirting with me?" she asked before she could think about it. In hindsight, it seemed like a dangerous question.

"Just calling it like I see it. That's the game, remember."

"Right." It didn't feel like a game anymore, even though that's all it could be for Jess. She had Austin. And she wasn't interested in women, even though this particular woman was making her feel… things. How was that possible? They had only just met. "It's my turn to play, then." *Bring it back to the game.* "And you weren't even close to the truth, by the way."

The woman smiled. "That's the beauty of it. It doesn't matter whether I'm right or wrong, it's my story. And I already know that the fundamentals are correct." Then the woman leaned back and put a little space between them, as if she'd only realized how close she had been to Jess. "So? Me or a stranger?"

"You are a stranger," Jess reminded her. "But I'll have a practice run on someone else before I come up with your story."

"A woman who takes the game seriously. Admirable." She grinned. "Let's hear it."

Jess looked around for someone to pick. There were a group of teens, each of them scrolling on their phones, but she couldn't think of anything that made any of them unique enough for a story. The same with the middle-aged couple sitting closest to them keeping themselves to themselves. Nothing stood out. She turned her attention to a man with headphones. He was dressed in dark clothing from head to toe, and he even had a pair of dark sunglasses pushed on top of his head. An idea came to mind. "See him?"

The woman nodded.

"He's a spy. And I'm talking super spy, James Bond level stuff here. He's only pretending to listen to music, really there's no sound coming from those headphones. I wouldn't be surprised if he's tuned in enough to hear our conversation. He's trained to listen to everything around him. He wears the dark clothes because he doesn't want to draw any attention to himself. His job is to gather information."

"Oh my God. That's so weird. I was thinking spy for that guy too!"

Jess smiled at that. "Then it must be true. He's not dangerous, though. Well, not to you or me anyway. Only to the baddies."

The woman raised an eyebrow, a look that Jess didn't find attractive at all. Except she really did.

"How do you know I'm not a baddie?"

"Are you?"

"I couldn't possibly say. You'll have to work it out for yourself, and I'm pretty sure you said you would come up with my story next, so you may have to decide quickly."

Jess didn't know how she was supposed to analyse the woman in front of her. Her thoughts were all over the place. She had never felt so at ease with someone she had just met. Not even with Austin. That feeling had only grown through time.

But at the same time as this comforting feeling, Jess felt nervous too. Like she wanted to make a good impression. Like it mattered what this woman thought of her. *No pressure, then.*

Okay, what could her story be? Jess could list a hundred ways that she was beautiful. Those blue eyes, the full lips, the perfect eyebrows, the long hair that was a perfect shade of blond, the toned body with curves Jess would kill for, the amazing scent that she carried. But if Jess pointed out any of those things, then she would be flirting back. And she wasn't going to flirt with this woman. She couldn't. Nor did she want to, Jess reminded herself.

She looked around the train carriage for inspiration. There was a map of the different stops that the train would make along the way. Her stop for the courthouse was seven stops away. What else was at that same stop? She studied the map. The zoo! Jess could work with that. Funny, not flirty. Safe. "I don't think you're a baddie. I don't get that vibe. You work at the zoo, as it happens."

That seemed to surprise the woman. "The zoo," she repeated. She looked down at her clothes. Light-blue skinny jeans. An immaculately clean white T-shirt. White trainers that were equally clean—no mean feat in England's notoriously wet autumn weather. And an expensive-looking black coat.

"Obviously, you'll change when you get there," Jess clarified.

"I see. And what is it that I do at the zoo?"

Jess didn't miss a beat. "Animal relations, of course."

"Of course. And what does working in animal relations entail?"

"Oh, you don't just *work* in animal relations. You're in charge of the whole department. It's your job to make sure that all the animals at the zoo get along. You're kind of a big deal." Jess would have felt ridiculous relaying such a silly story, especially as she was almost certain that animal relations was an imaginary vocation, but the way the woman seemed to be hanging on her every word with clear fascination, and amusement, spurred her on. "Today was supposed to be your day off, hence the casual attire. But you got a call to say that the penguins have been sneaking into the seal enclosure to play pranks, so of course, you have to go in and get them back in line."

"What kind of pranks?" the woman asked with interest.

"The word is, they've streamed toilet paper everywhere. Put washing-up liquid in one of the pools to make it bubble up. Poured cooking oil over the seals' favourite rock, so when they try to sit on it, they slip right off again."

The woman laughed. "Those pesky penguins. Always up to mischief," she said, playing along.

"And after that whole monkey debacle last week," Jess said with a shake of her head.

"Remind me what happened with the monkeys again?" She was obviously enjoying this.

What could the monkeys have done? "Um…flirting." Because what else was in Jess's head right now? "They were flirting with the giraffes. Remember?"

"Ah yes. It's the long, elegant necks, you see. Difficult to resist. I can appreciate a long neck myself."

Jess almost touched her own neck to check its length, but she stopped herself. "Yes. Well, that's your story. How did I do?"

"You're a natural. Nowhere near close to the truth, but I do sort of wish I was head of animal relations at the zoo now. It sounds like a lot of fun, if not a little bit stressful." The woman smiled that full, beaming smile of hers. "And I think it worked."

"What worked?"

"My distraction. We started moving again while you were talking about flirty monkeys, and I don't think you even noticed."

Wow, they *were* moving—still in the tunnel, but moving. Thank goodness! Before she could think about it, she leaned forward and threw her arms around the woman. "Thank you. You might actually be my hero, or heroine." She felt the woman's arms wrap round her to return the hug, and they stayed like that for a few beats before Jess pulled away. "And now I'm embarrassed. Both for inflicting my stupid fear on you and for randomly hugging you. I'm sorry."

"Nothing to be embarrassed about. We all have our own *tunnels*. If there was a clown on this train, I'd probably be curled up into a ball on your knee right now."

The woman stood up from her position in front of Jess and sat back down on her seat. "And as for the hug, please don't apologize. You're an exceptional hugger. Firm but soft—the perfect hugging combo. I liked hugging you. Would totally do it again."

"See, it feels like you're flirting with me again." The truth was, she was giving Jess more compliments on this train ride than Austin had given her in months. Jess couldn't pretend that it wasn't flattering.

"Does it? Huh. Maybe I am, then."

Maybe it was just her personality. "Do you flirt with everyone?"

The woman looked at her seriously then. "No."

"Oh." They looked at each other for a few beats, the eye contact intense and loaded. Jess knew that she should nip it in the bud, but for some reason she didn't want to.

"And then there was light," the woman said, regrettably breaking the moment to look out of the window.

Jess looked out too, relieved that she could see the outside world again, but immediately feeling the loss of whatever just passed between them as she looked away.

"Well, now that you are safely over your tunnel experience, I can leave you in peace to continue your bad mood. I'll not disturb you again." The woman didn't even try to hide her disappointment.

This time, Jess felt it too.

It would be better to end their interaction there. The woman clearly had an interest in Jess that was something more than friendly, and Jess was enjoying it more than she should. Yes, it was nice to feel desirable for a change, and it made her feel good, but that was no excuse.

Then again, it wasn't like Jess had said anything untoward. She had simply been friendly, and really, not even that most of the time.

And the woman had been kind enough to help her in her hour of need. It wasn't like she'd *had* to help Jess. She seemed like a decent human. And Jess was enjoying her company. What harm would it do if they chatted a little more? Two strangers, passing the time of day until they got to where they needed to be. Jess cleared her throat. "I can probably tolerate a few more disturbances. I mean, I haven't even got to hear about these clowns yet."

❖

Sydney smiled so hard it made her cheeks hurt. She hadn't expected to have much to smile about that day, but trains and tunnels clearly had a whole other plan for her.

Out of habit, when Sydney had stepped onto the train, she had rushed to sit where she usually sat when she used to regularly travel that route. The route from her sister's place to hers. Except it wasn't her place anymore, her ex-girlfriend had seen to that. And after she collected the last of her things that day, Sydney would have no reason to go back. She felt a pang of sadness at that, but she quickly shook it off. As her sister, Rachel, kept reminding her, her ex who had been cheating on her for over a year didn't deserve a second of Sydney's sadness. It had taken a while for Sydney to accept that, but now that she had given herself some time to heal, she knew that her sister was right. She was ready to move on.

And things were already looking up, because the seat across from her had been taken by, no exaggeration, one of the most attractive women Sydney had ever seen in the flesh. Sydney's breath had literally caught in her chest in the moment when their eyes had met. She knew how mushy that sounded, but it had. This woman was stunning, there was no other word for it, but it was more than that too. Sydney felt instantly drawn to her. And even though she had initially received the brush-off, Sydney was sure that she wasn't just imagining the connection that they had started to form since then. Though the woman was proving pretty hard to read.

Sydney was just happy that she wanted to keep chatting with her. Hence the ginormous smile on her face that she couldn't stifle despite the fact that they were discussing Sydney's biggest fear. "Why would you want to hear about clowns? They are the creepiest characters on the planet. The make-up, the wild hair, the costumes, the abnormally large feet, the weird voices." Sydney shuddered for effect. "And have you seen those videos where scary clowns chase unsuspecting people to frighten the bejesus out of them? Terrifying."

The attractive woman laughed. "I can't say I have, but I'll take your word for it. I'm scared of just about everything, but not clowns, strangely enough. I don't need anything to add to my list."

"In that case, you can protect me from clowns, and I'll protect you from tunnels."

She kept giving Sydney this look. Like she was trying to work Sydney out, or maybe she was trying to figure out her intentions. Then after a few seconds, the look turned into a sort of shy smile. Sydney really liked that smile. "Deal," she said.

Sydney wanted to know more. "You know, now that we've upgraded our status from strangers to protectors, maybe we should be on a first name basis?"

"Funny, I've heard that's the criteria. It's not nearly as effective when you need saving and have to shout *hey, you!*" She paused for a few seconds, like she was making sure she wanted to share that much information with Sydney. Then she smiled and stuck out her hand. "Jessica. Well, Jess. Literally, only my mum calls me Jessica, so I've no idea why I said that."

Sydney laughed as she reached forward and softly shook her hand. "Amazing to meet you, Jess-not-Jessica. I'm Sydney, never Syd. Everyone says Sydney."

Jess looked disbelieving. "*Amazing to meet me*? I'm quite sure I've been the train companion from hell today."

Impossible, Sydney thought, but she didn't want to come on too strong. There was a fine line between showing a bit of interest and becoming too much. A pest. A problem. She waved Jess off. "You haven't at all. You've been great company."

Jess still looked dubious, but she gave that shy smile again. "Well, thank you, Sydney-never-Syd. You're not such bad company yourself."

"Even though I disturbed your bad mood?"

"Because you made my bad mood a little bit better. That was... unexpected today."

Sydney smiled at the compliment. She wondered what was bad enough to cause Jess to feel like that, but it seemed too personal to ask.

As if reading her mind, Jess said, "My dad's getting married today to the worst person ever."

Ah. That made sense. "That sucks."

"Yeah. It really does." Jess made a growling noise. "I really don't like her. She's so obvious in her bad intentions, you know? My dad either knows and ignores it or is ridiculously unaware. Either way, it's so frustrating." She shook her head. "And she knows that I can see right through her. Doesn't care. Blatantly rubs it in my face, even."

Sydney made a face. "She sounds horrible. I'm sorry you have to deal with that," she said. "Do you want me to crash? Burst through the doors and object?" Sydney suggested only half seriously.

Jess laughed. "Are you my terrible wedding protector now too?"

"I can add it to my duties. Call it a two-for-one."

"You know, I'd almost be tempted to take that offer." She gave a defeated sigh. "But no. When my dad wants something, nothing can stop him. I fear that I would only be stuck wearing heels for longer than I had to, while I wait for you to be escorted out and the ceremony to inevitably continue."

Sydney wished she could say something useful, come up with some profound advice or something, but she couldn't relate. Her parents had always been together, so she had never had to deal with any wicked stepmothers. Sydney was, however, a good listener, so if Jess wanted to rant and get things off her chest, she could help with that. "Is it a big wedding?"

"Thank goodness, no. He's tying the knot at the courthouse, then there's a meal in a restaurant right across the street. A meal I plan to eat quickly before I make my escape."

"If all else fails there could always be a nasty food reaction in your near future," Sydney suggested.

Jess clasped her hands together. "Oh, please, please serve me some pink chicken and let me get the hell out of there. You, Sydney, are full of great ideas."

Sydney wished she could share some more of her great ideas, specifically, one involving her taking Jess on a date to a nice restaurant, where there would be no chance of pink chicken.

She had already tested the waters a little bit earlier when they were playing the game, but she still couldn't gauge whether Jess would have any interest in going on a date with her or not.

Maybe it was better to leave the ball in Jess's court. Sydney could just make it clear that she was open to the idea. "If things get really bad, you could always come and find me at the zoo. It's only down the road from the courthouse, right? You can help me clean up all the toilet paper."

"Wait. Are you really going to the zoo?"

"Of course. Penguin emergency, remember?"

Jess narrowed her eyes at her.

Sydney grinned. "No, I wish I was. As it happens, my day isn't going to be much fun either, unfortunately."

"Oh my God, I'm so sorry. Listen to me going on about my own stupid problems that you didn't even ask to hear about." Jess buried her face in her hands. "I'm the worst. Of course, you've got your own stuff going on. Please, ignore me. Or tell me. If you want to talk about it. You don't have to tell me anything. But you can."

Rambling Jess was cute as hell. Sydney immediately wanted to put her out of her misery. "Don't be silly, I'm glad you told me all of that. To be honest, I'm enjoying getting to know you so much, I had almost forgotten where I was going anyway."

Jess still looked embarrassed, but she gave Sydney a little smile. "You're so nice."

Sydney shrugged. "Just telling the truth. And I'm happy to tell you anything you want to know." She paused. "I'm going to collect the last of my belongings from the house I used to share with my girlfriend— now ex-girlfriend."

Jess gave her the customary look of sympathy Sydney had received so many times since her breakup. "Oh, no. I'm sure that won't be easy, I'm sorry."

She hummed her agreement. "It probably won't be pleasant, no.

We've been broken up for a while now, though. I've been putting off this part because I didn't want to see her."

"Who broke up with who?" Jess quickly slapped her hand over her mouth. "Sorry. That's really none of my business."

Sydney laughed. "You apologize a lot for someone who hasn't done anything to apologize for. I said you can ask me anything, remember? And to answer your question, she broke up with me."

Jess scoffed. "Then she's a fool."

Sydney couldn't help but smile. "How do you know? I could be a terrible girlfriend."

Jess immediately shook her head. "No way. I don't buy that for a second. Look at the evidence."

"There's evidence?"

"Sure there is. You and me. We haven't even known each other for an hour, and you've already paid for my train ticket, helped me get through that whole tunnel incident, and cheered me up about my family drama." Jess swayed her head from side to side. "A little bit, but still more than anyone else has managed. You didn't have to do any of that, you could have ignored me instead. You've been funny, interesting, good to talk to. Oh, *and* you offered me chocolate." She threw her hands out as if that proved her point. "And I'm nobody. So, there's no way that you don't treat your partner well."

"You forgot sinfully attractive," she added playfully.

Jess's eyes widened. "Well, yes, you are, um, pretty. Lacking modesty maybe, but pretty." Her cheeks turned a light shade of pink and she turned and looked out the window. It was adorable.

Sydney chuckled, but inside her heart was doing a little happy dance. "Why thank you, Jess. And I wouldn't say that you're nobody. True that we don't know each other well, but I think you're somebody worth knowing."

Jess opened her mouth to say something, then closed it again. Maybe Sydney had said too much. Or come on too strong. Maybe Jess wasn't interested in getting to know her, which was totally fine. Just because Sydney had this instant crush of hers didn't mean it was reciprocated.

Sydney decided to play it off. "Besides, I don't offer my chocolate to just *anyone,* you know."

Jess laughed quietly, probably relieved that Sydney had lightened the tone of the conversation again. "No? In that case, I should really take one."

"A wise change of mind." She reached the bag forward to Jess, then took one herself. "Chocolate makes everything better."

"No way, that's tea. My mum always used to tell me that was tea." Jess popped the chocolate in her mouth and gave a little hum of appreciation. "But I agree this is good. Imagine, chocolate *and* tea, together. That could be the perfect remedy."

Sydney screwed her face up. "Chocolate and coffee maybe. Not tea."

Jess gaped at her. "Coffee does *not* have the level of healing powers that tea has."

"It does in the morning when I've just got out of bed and my eyes refuse to open. One cup of magical coffee, and poof, I'm like a new woman."

"For argument's sake, if you switched to green tea, it would do more for your energy levels than the coffee."

Sydney shook her head. "No thanks. I need my coffee. Good coffee at that. The main reason that I'm going to collect the last of my things today is because I left my coffee maker there. I could live without most things, but not that."

"Hmm. You know, I think I could live without coffee," Jess said.

"Do you hate coffee? Is that what this is? Are you a coffee-phobe?"

"Not at all, I just don't hold it in as high regard as I do tea. Why? Are you a tea hater?" Jess threw back.

Sydney scrunched her nose up. "A little bit, yeah. I'm sorry."

"How could you?" Jess playfully held her hand over her heart. "Now I don't know if we can be friends."

Thankfully, being *friends* wasn't what Sydney had in mind. Jess was so much more than friend material, but she went along with it. "Sure we can. When I take you out for a hot drink, I'll order coffee, and you'll order tea, and we can share the chocolate."

Jess playfully tapped her finger against her chin. "I suppose that *could* work."

"We could trial it sometime," Sydney said casually even though the suggestion was anything but. "If you want to."

Jess chewed her lip. "Yeah, maybe."

At least Jess hadn't said no.

The train started slowing down on its approach into a station, and Sydney looked out the window to check where they were. She hadn't really been paying attention, but she needed to start, or she was going to miss her stop. "I have to change trains at the next stop," she said. Regretfully. Sydney would have been happy to stay on the train talking to Jess all day.

Jess looked out too. "Oh, wow. I get off there too." She sounded disappointed, but Sydney didn't know whether that was because of the dreaded wedding she was going to, or because their time together was coming to an end. Sydney couldn't help but hope it was the latter.

She knew that was the reason for her own disappointment. "Oh, yeah, the courthouse."

"Do you have much further to go after you switch?" Jess asked.

"Another thirty minutes maybe. It's just outside the city." She put her arms above her head and stretched. "I plan to be in and out of there as quickly as possible." Jess's cheeks went pink again and Sydney realized that her top had ridden up. She held back a grin that threatened and pulled it down again.

"I've already checked and there's a train leaving at seven. I'm planning on making my great wedding escape on time to catch it. Maybe you'll be on the same one? If you have to come back this way, that is?" Jess picked at her nail, as if she couldn't look at Sydney when she asked. "Just in case there's clowns or something. As your sworn protector, I would hate not to be there."

Did that mean Jess wanted to see her again? She must, or else she wouldn't be suggesting meeting up again. Sydney held in the excitement that was threatening to burst out of her and played it cool. "Well, you can't leave me alone with the clowns. And I need to be there for tunnels, so the seven o'clock train it is. You can tell me all about how ungraceful the bride was and how shitty the speeches were."

Jess laughed. "And you can show me this coffee maker you can't live without."

"Deal. And now I've got something to look forward to," Sydney said honestly.

Maybe she could take Jess for that tea when they got back. Only if Jess felt like it. She had already said that the wedding was going to be hard for her, and Sydney didn't want to push it. She was just happy that she would get to see Jess again. That was enough. Whatever happened after, happened.

Unfortunately, it wasn't long until they arrived at their stop. They both stood at the same time to gather their things.

Jess had more bags than Sydney, so Sydney offered to carry Jess's dress off the train for her. Sydney was two or three inches taller, so it was easier for her to carry anyway.

They walked a few steps along the platform to get out of the way of the dozens of commuters who were either boarding or getting off the train at the same time.

"How long until your next train?" Jess asked when they stopped at a nearby bench.

"Twenty minutes. How long until you have to be at your wedding?"

"Twenty minutes."

They both laughed.

"Well, one thing you were right about was that I needed to change once I got here. So, I really need to go do that or I'm going to be late."

"Do you want me to watch your bags while you change?" Sydney asked. "I'll be here waiting anyway."

Jess looked at her like she was pleasantly surprised at the offer. "You wouldn't mind?"

"Of course not."

"You're the best, Sydney. Thank you." Jess took the dress bag from her and gently squeezed her arm. The tingles Sydney felt through her entire body at the simple gesture solidified how hard Sydney was crushing on this woman.

After her breakup, Sydney had decided to stay away from women and relationships for a while. She wanted to give her heart a chance to heal, and she didn't believe in going into a relationship if she couldn't be the very best version of herself or if she couldn't give it everything. Besides, the fact that her ex had been cheating on her for a long time had left Sydney with a very bruised ego.

So, Sydney hadn't even noticed another woman in months. Until that day, seemingly. The very day that she would finally close the chapter on her old life. Wasn't there a saying about closing doors and opening windows? It seemed fitting.

Speaking of fitting. That. Fucking. Dress.

Was Sydney's mouth hanging open? She knew she was staring, but was she gawping? Was her tongue hanging out the side of her mouth like a dehydrated puppy? She decided that didn't care. Because Jess was walking toward her in a tight-fitting dress, deep red, that clung to her hips and plunged at the neck, and she looked incredible.

"You're staring," Jess said when she reached her.

Sydney had to swallow a couple of times so she could speak. Her mouth had gone uncomfortably dry all of a sudden. "Me and most people in this station."

Jess laughed. "Does that mean I look okay?"

"You look *so* much better than okay," Sydney said without doubt or hesitation.

Jess looked down at the dress. "It's probably not classically wedding appropriate. But the bride will be furious, and that's good enough for me." She gave a grin and glanced up at the clock on the wall. "I really have to go. Thanks for…well, everything."

Sydney suddenly felt awkward. Should she hug Jess? "You're welcome. I know it will be awful, but get the awfulness over with, and I'll see you after. You can scream, rant, cry. Whatever."

Whatever Sydney had just said seemed to be the right thing judging by the look Jess was giving her. "Yeah, I'll see you after. And good luck with your ex. Don't leave until that coffee machine has been rescued."

"I wouldn't dream of it." Sod it. Sydney was hugging. She wrapped her arms around Jess, who immediately hugged her back like they had hugged a thousand times before and it was the most natural thing in the world. Somehow, everything felt right. The hug only lasted a few seconds, but those seconds felt important.

"Bye," Jess said with an adorable little wave before she turned and walked away.

"Jess," Sydney called out and Jess turned back around to look at her. Sydney took a few steps toward her to close the gap again. "Whoever is missing out on you looking like that is a fool. You look amazing. And if I was your date, I would be the proudest person in the room." She took another step closer. "Here's the thing. I like you. And even though I know nearly nothing about you, I want to know. I want to know it all."

Jess's lips parted, as if she was affected by Sydney's words.

In a moment of bravery, Sydney leaned in and gently kissed Jess on the cheek. Only for a split second. Then Sydney grinned as she began to back away. "I can't wait to see you again later." And with that, she turned and strolled toward the next platform.

First stop, her past...next stop, her future?

Sydney had a feeling that it just might be.

CHAPTER TWO

C hlo?" Jess called out as the front door clicked shut behind her. She walked over to the console table and dropped her keys into the bowl where she kept them along with two other sets of keys that belonged to her roommates, Chloe, and Freya. Thank God for keyrings so they could tell them apart.

They had even turned it into a competition to see who could find the wackiest keyring. Freya had a huge avocado wearing glasses, and Jess had a bright yellow rubber duck with a cowboy hat on its head. They had tied for second place. Chloe had taken the number one spot for thinking outside the box and ordering a personalized keyring that said *Wackiest Keyring Ever*, with a photograph of her giving a double thumbs-up to rub it in. They had unanimously decided that she deserved the win for effort alone.

Jess dumped her bags at the bottom of the stairs and threw the dress bag on top—at least she didn't have to worry about creases anymore. She hung her coat on a hook by the door. "Hello? Chlo?" she shouted again. "You home?"

"In the kitchen," Chloe called back that time.

Jess headed toward it and pushed through the door. She closed it behind her and slumped against it pretending to sob. She could have easily cried for real, but if she started, she probably wouldn't stop.

Chloe turned around from where she was stirring something at the cooker and pouted. "Aww, Jess. That bad?" She gave the wooden spoon a few bangs against the top of the saucepan, left it down, and came toward her with her arms out. "Do you need a hug?"

Jess pouted back and nodded before stepping into Chloe's arms. Jess and Chloe had been friends ever since they were kids and had started school together. They had been together through thick and thin. Chloe was her rock. And Jess Chloe's.

Jess squeezed her tight. "It was horrible, Chlo. I didn't even get to speak to my dad before it started because Gretchen the Gold-digger purposely sent me to the wrong room to look for him. When I confronted her about it, she just said *oops*, and then she and all of her little posse laughed about it."

"Why would she do that?" Chloe squeezed her back tighter before letting go. "She's almost thirty, for fuck's sake, not thirteen." Twenty-nine to be exact. A reminder that she was only three years older than Jess.

"Probably worried that I was going to talk my dad out of it." Jess let out a snort. "Like I hadn't already tried." She perched herself on a stool at the kitchen table and Chloe went back to her pot. It was almost nine, but it wasn't out of the ordinary for Chloe to eat late. Jess often joined her for ungodly hour dinners, especially if it meant she didn't have to cook them herself. She had enough skills to keep herself alive, but she certainly wasn't a chef by any means.

"Maybe you couldn't prevent it, but you and I both know that there's a short expiration date on this marriage." That was the only comforting factor. It *would* end.

"I know. But I wonder how much poorer Dad's going to be by the time it does expire. Do you know where she's demanded he takes her on their honeymoon? A twenty-two-night Caribbean cruise. In a suite, no less. They leave tomorrow." Jess huffed. "And don't get me started on the reception dinner."

That was Jess's way of saying *I want to talk about the reception dinner*. Chloe knew that. And she dutifully asked, "Why? What happened at dinner?"

Jess leapt right in. "For starters, I didn't even get to sit with Dad. I ended up sitting beside my dad's weird Uncle Peter, who talked to me for two hours about his last eight trips to the doctor, including some graphic details about a rectal exam. All the while, *she* was unbuttoning my dad's shirt buttons and playing with his bloody chest hair." Jess closed her eyes and held a hand up. "I still might vomit."

"I might join you." Chloe screwed her face up. "Did you get to talk to your dad at all?"

"Yeah, eventually. There wasn't a lot to say. I didn't want to put a downer on his big day, so we talked around it. The weather was discussed, his midweek football match, that kind of thing. I know he was grateful that I showed up, though. I suppose that's the main thing."

"At least you weren't on your own. What did Austin think about the whole thing?" Chloe lifted the saucepan and turned the cooker off. "Want any?" She started to scoop some pasta into a bowl for herself.

It looked good, but Jess had struggled to get down what little she did manage to eat at dinner. She was one of those people who couldn't stomach food when she was annoyed about something. "No thanks." She waited until Chloe took a seat. "Austin didn't come," she said quietly.

"What?" Chloe wasn't quiet, or calm. She stabbed her fork into her pasta bowl so it stood up in the middle. "Jess. Why didn't you tell me? I would have come with you! You needed support today."

Jess patted her hand. "I know you would have, but he cancelled last minute. I decided to suck it up and go get it over with."

"Last minute? That's worse. What reason did dickwad give this time? No, let me guess. Had to work?" Chloe said dryly.

"What other reason is there? And don't name-call."

"I'll stop name calling when he starts treating you well. You already know what I think," Chloe reminded her.

Jess did know. It wasn't like Chloe made any secret of it. She thought Jess could do better. That she and Austin had become incompatible and grown apart. That Austin had become a terrible boyfriend. That he was a man-child who hadn't matured in years. And most importantly, that Jess should get rid of him and stop wasting her time.

Chloe's list was endless.

Did Jess understand why her best friend thought all of those things? Yeah, she was sad to admit that she did. Recently she did anyway.

But Jess wasn't a quitter. She and Austin had been together since they were both fresh out of high school—he had just began studying law at university, and Jess had just started style school. Almost eight years. That was a lot of relationship to give up on.

Besides, relationships went through rough patches all the time, and couples managed to get through them. Maybe this was Austin's and her rough patch—admittedly an eighteen-month rough patch. That's how long ago things had started to change. When Austin had changed.

It wasn't like Jess had never thought about giving up, but she had never given it *serious* thought. Not until today. Not until Sydney. Jess had goosebumps even thinking her name.

"I'm getting a glass of water. Want one?" Chloe asked her as she slipped off her stool.

"Could you imagine me ever dating a woman?" Jess blurted, an image of Sydney clear in her mind.

Chloe stopped in front of the cupboard and spun her head round so fast Jess was surprised her neck didn't snap. She stared at Jess for a few seconds, then turned, opened the cupboard, and pulled out two wine glasses. "Fuck the water."

Jess laughed as Chloe went into the fridge and pulled out a bottle of white and poured two generous measures that they would never get in a bar. She carried them over and sat down again, sliding Jess's glass in front of her.

Chloe took a large gulp of hers. "Now, repeat that for me. Because there's no way that you, never-steps-out-of-her-lane Jess, could have said what I thought you did."

That only made Jess laugh harder. "Why's it such a surprising question? I didn't even blink when you told me that you liked girls. And for the record, I'm not saying that I do. I'm just asking. We're in hypothetical territory right now."

"I told you when we were fifteen, basically unshockable, and I had already made it glaringly obvious. I was like the poster teen for lesbianism. I don't think anybody blinked." Chloe took a mouthful of pasta and studied her while she chewed. She swallowed and said, "And no. I can't imagine it, but I can't wait to hear the story that sparked this sudden curiosity of yours."

Jess took a sip of wine and turned away. "I never said there was a story, nor a curiosity for that matter. You know, forget I even asked." The thought of telling Chloe about Sydney had felt a lot easier when she hadn't been sitting in front of her with that scrutinizing gaze of hers.

Plus, talking about it made it real. Jess wasn't sure if she could handle it being real.

"Can't do that." Chloe grinned. "I know you. Something happened, and we aren't leaving this kitchen until you tell me. And I know you want to talk about it, or you wouldn't have brought it up in the first place."

Wanted to talk about it. Past tense. A regrettable idea.

Usually, Jess liked the fact that Chloe knew her better than anyone else, but it meant that Chloe also knew exactly how to pry information out of her. Letting it get to that point would only be delaying the inevitable.

Unsurprisingly, Chloe prodded some more. "I can sit here all night," she said in a sing-song voice. "I'm going to have another bowl of pasta, and there's enough wine. Consider me well nourished, entertained, and equipped to wait you out."

Jess glared at her. "You can sit here if you want to. I'm not."

Chloe laughed. "Oh, come on, Jess. Just tell me. Did something happen at the wedding?"

"No." Jess sighed. Maybe talking about it would help. "It happened before."

Chloe clapped her hands together. "I knew there was a story. Keep going. What happened before the wedding that has you wondering about sweet-lady-loving?"

"You're unbearable sometimes."

"Yes," Chloe agreed. "And you love me anyway."

"Hmm. Questionable." But Jess threw her a grin. She might as well just spit it out. "I met a woman on the train. A charming, sweet, interesting woman."

"Attractive?" Chloe lifted a brow.

Jess had left that part out on purpose, but trust Chloe to jump right to it. "Very." There was no point in downplaying it. Sydney was gorgeous.

"Nice." Chloe took another bite of food and pondered some. "But you meet plenty of attractive women almost every day. You run your fingers through their silky-soft hair. Have you thought about dating any of those women before? Or any others at all?"

"Specific image you've thrown in there of me doing my job." In truth, Jess had already thought about running her fingers over so much more than Sydney's hair, but she didn't want Chloe's head to explode, so she kept that part to herself. "No, never." The truth. It really was the first time Jess had felt anything for another woman. "And I didn't say that I was thinking about dating a woman. Not really. This woman was different, that's all. Made me wonder."

"I think you need to tell me everything. Start at the beginning and don't leave anything out."

Jess did. She told Chloe about how she had tried to ignore Sydney at first—she still felt bad about that part. How Sydney had come to her rescue and paid for her train fare. How kind and supportive Sydney had been when they stopped in the tunnel. How they didn't stop talking for the rest of the journey. And then there was all the flirting that Jess didn't want to stop. The obvious chemistry between them. The innocent touches that led to Jess having not so innocent thoughts. The stolen looks. Most specifically, *the look*—the one Sydney had given her for those delicious few moments before she walked away that had set Jess's entire body on fire. Jess hadn't stopped thinking about it for a second since. She had never felt so completely…*wanted,* in every way a person could want another person. Had anyone ever looked at her like that before? She didn't think so.

Chloe leaned on the table, holding her head in one hand while she sipped from the wine glass in her other. "How come my straight best friend can have this perfect, magical meeting with a woman and I can't? The universe is mean to me."

"Please. You're so in love with Dana, you wouldn't be capable of noticing anyone else even if they landed smack-bang in front of your face."

Chloe gave a slow, resigned nod because it was true. She had been hopelessly in love with her boss for over a year now ever since a brief fling. "Not that she notices me anymore." She paused. "I've decided to take a step back from my unrequited love interest. It's not healthy and proving to be a little too painful for my liking."

Jess leaned over and gave Chloe a supportive nudge. "Something we both agree on, but I'll believe it when I see it." They had been there before, and Dana always managed to find a way to reel Chloe back in—she was in deep, and that wasn't likely to change.

Chloe shuffled in her seat. "Anyway. It's not about me apart from the fact that I'm jealous. You said you arranged to meet her on the way home…what happened? Did you get her number? Are you seeing her again? Are you dumping Austin and giving the ladies a try? Tell me the answer is yes to all of that, especially the dumping Austin part."

"She didn't show." And Jess's disappointment had told her everything she needed to know about her feelings on that. "The seven o'clock train came, and she wasn't there, so I waited thirty minutes for the next one, but…" She shrugged, deflated. "I thought maybe her other train might have run late, but nope. Nothing."

"Nooo, Jess." Chloe tilted her head. "That is so not the way I expected this story to end. And you didn't get her number?"

Jess shook her head.

"Name?"

"Her name?" Jess hesitated. What if Chloe knew her? Or of her? She could be a friend of a friend of a friend. What then? Jess didn't know what she wanted—or if she wanted anything at all.

Maybe Sydney not showing up was a sign. It wasn't meant to be. Shaking up her whole life had been a silly, momentary whim that Jess would probably never go through with anyway. She wasn't going to throw away eight years with Austin, was she? And what? Ask Sydney out if she ever saw her again? Jess wasn't even a lesbian, for crying out loud. Surely, she would have had an inkling by now if she was into women. She wasn't. The best thing would be to let it go. "No. I don't know her name."

"Dammit," Chloe said. "I would have asked around."

Exactly. "Hmm. But like you said. It's not like I would ever date a woman anyway."

"It's not that." Chloe went to the fridge and brought out the rest of the bottle of wine and filled their two glasses. Jess hadn't even realized that she had drained hers already. "It's just not something I'd ever thought about, so it's hard to picture. There's never been so much as a blip when it comes to your sexuality. Until now."

"A blip?"

Chloe nodded. "Something that makes you question the whole straight thing. Lots of people only realize their true sexuality after blips. Maybe you like all genders. Maybe you'll find one that you like best. Maybe it's person dependent."

That made sense, but Jess was sure that if she were inclined to be interested in women, she would have *blipped* before now. "I think it was more likely a reaction to Austin cancelling on me today. I was shown some attention, it was flattering, especially because my relationship hasn't been…easy lately." *Understatement.* "I enjoyed it. Let it happen. Shouldn't have."

Chloe scoffed.

Jess pointed at her. "No. It wasn't right. If I was with anyone other than Austin, you'd agree."

"Just keep an open mind, Jess, that's all I'm saying. Everything happens for a reason."

"If that's true, then there was a reason for her not showing up tonight. Probably a sign to tell me that I should forget the whole thing and get on with my life." Which was exactly what Jess intended to do. She couldn't stifle a yawn. Her day had been emotionally draining, to say the least. "Anyway. I'm going to go to bed and put my shitty day behind me." Jess stood up and gave Chloe a kiss on top of her head, their usual goodnight. "Thanks for the support and the wine."

"Always." Chloe winced. "Oh shit, Jess, there's something else. Do you want me to make an already bad day a little worse or wait and spoil tomorrow?"

"Oh, God. Just hit me with it. Go."

"Okay, whipping the plaster off." Chloe scrunched her nose up. "Freya's moving out. She got accepted into that work placement in New Zealand that she never thought she would get into, and she leaves in two weeks."

"Oh no!" she said. "I mean, yay for Freya. She wanted that so badly, but shit, I'm really going to miss her. Isn't it a year-long contract?"

Chloe nodded glumly. "With a possibility of being extended for another year."

"Damn Freya and her gifted brain. What does that mean for us?" The three of them had lived together for years. Did life together…and, a more practical thought, split all the bills three ways.

"Two options. Either we need to find a smaller place that costs us less, ew, or we need to find a new roommate."

"That second one." Jess didn't even need to think about it, it was their home. Although she knew that they would both end up moving on at some point, most likely when one of them found a partner that they liked enough to live with, now was not that time. Plus, their place was kind of swanky, and Jess loved feeling swanky.

"Agreed. I'll put out an advertisement then, I guess." Chloe made a *yikes* face. "A stranger is going to infiltrate us, Jess."

"Let the stranger come. But make sure they're one of the good ones and that they don't hog the bathroom, because we both know that's my role."

How bad could it be?

❖

Sydney entered the apartment, wheeling her suitcase in behind her. She closed the door as quietly as she could, shrugged off her heavy gym bag, and set the box she was carrying onto the floor beside it. She straightened and rolled her shoulder a few times, reaching up to rub the spot where her bag strap had been digging in.

"Jeez, that must have dragged on. I thought you would have been back hours ago." The room was pitch black, but the sleepy voice came from the sofa area.

"Conscience? Is that you?"

She heard her sister chuckling. "Sometimes I feel like it, but no, just me. I was waiting to be your support system, but I did a terrible job at the waiting part and fell asleep."

Sydney laughed and turned the light on, and her sister groaned in response. "Wakey, wakey." She checked the time on her phone. After ten. Way later than she had expected to be back. "Let's hope you're better at the support system part, because I have had a *day*." She bent down to lift the box from the floor.

Her sister indicated it with a jerk of her head. "I'm guessing you got it back, then?"

Sydney held it up like a trophy. "I had to fight for her, but yeah, she's home." She carried her beloved coffee machine across the living area to the kitchen and set it on the counter. She gave it an affectionate pat and wandered back toward her sister in the living room. "Why the hell was I with her, Rachel? She's awful."

"Because you thought you loved her, were somehow blind to her bad bits, and you were too pig-headed to listen to me anyway?"

All true, but Sydney still didn't know what she had been thinking for all that time. "I must have been in a coma. Are there comas where you're awake? Or maybe I was sleepwalking—for two and a half years."

Rachel didn't look like she bought it. "At least seeing her again seems to have cured your devastation."

"Still partially devastated, but not at losing *her*. Trust me, that ship has sailed and I'm happy to wave it farewell." She waved enthusiastically to prove her point. "I'm just sad that I'm so incredibly unlovable that someone has to have a whole other relationship while they're with me. Can't seem to shake that one."

Rachel grabbed Sydney's arm and pulled her down to sit beside her. She had her serious face on. "Don't you ever say that again. You are *not* unlovable. She's just awful, like you said. I doubt that she's capable of loving anyone except herself."

If only that was so easy to believe. "She already has the new one moved in."

Rachel gawped at her. "Was she there while you were there? A two-against-one?"

"Thankfully no. But I noticed some of her things lying around. And in case I hadn't, I was told under no uncertain terms that I wasn't allowed to go into their bedroom—emphasis on *their*. Anything that I had kept in there had already been conveniently packed up for me."

Rachel gave a snort. "Good of her. Should have known that she would give the knife one final twist."

Sydney hummed her agreement, but honestly, it hadn't really been much of a surprise. They had already shared a bed plenty of times while she and Sydney were together, so why wouldn't they now that Sydney was out of the picture?

"So, what took so long?" Rachel asked her. "I know you'd planned to be in and out of there."

Sydney gave her head an annoyed shake. "Trying to find half of my things that had been mysteriously hidden in random places. Books, clothes, some jewellery. Then when we got to dividing the kitchen stuff, everything became a fight. She even had the cheek to try and say that Beanie was hers." Sydney's fancy coffee machine, which she had unoriginally named, and saved up for ages to buy. "I let her keep loads, but I wasn't leaving without Beanie."

"Most of it was your stuff, Sydney. You should have taken it all."

She shrugged. "I'll buy new stuff."

"You shouldn't have to."

"No. But it is what it is." Sydney exhaled. "Then, when I eventually went to get my suitcase to carry my things, it was already filled with her holiday clothes. Another argument. By the time she took all her clothes out and I packed up my stuff, I had to wait for the eight-thirty train." She slumped back on the sofa. "And now, I'll never see Jess again."

Rachel blinked a few times and squinted at her. "Who's Jess?"

"The girl of my dreams," Sydney said wistfully. She considered that. "Well, might be. I'm learning that I'm a terrible judge of character, apparently."

"The girl of your dreams?" Rachel repeated slowly. "Can we maybe rewind here? How do we know Jess?"

Right. She hadn't got to that part yet. "We don't. I do. I met her today."

"And you have already deciphered today that she is in fact your dream girl?"

"Possibly my dream girl. Keep up."

Rachel stared at her for a few beats, then whispered, "Is Jess a real person?"

Sydney grinned and swatted her on the arm. "Yes, she's real, thank you. I met her on the train."

Rachel laughed. "Well, great. You deserve to meet someone."

"Did you not hear the part where I'll never see her again? We were supposed to meet on the train home, but I missed it." She stuck her bottom lip out. "Jess could have been my one true love, but instead of finding out, I was stuck in a war over kitchen utensils with the ex-girlfriend from hell."

"And you didn't get *the girl of your dreams*'s phone number?" Rachel said.

Sydney groaned. "No, because I expected to get to the train on time to see her again. I didn't even consider that I wouldn't make it."

"Still, you always get the phone number, Sydney. Always. Things happen. People get held up." Rachel sighed. "Did you not even get her last name?"

"No," Sydney replied glumly. "There wasn't the right moment to ask for that kind of info. I couldn't work out if she was even interested in me like that." At her sister's questioning look, she explained every-thing.

When Sydney was done, Rachel gave her a quizzical look. "So, you really don't know if she likes women, let alone you specifically?"

Sydney shook her head sheepishly. "No?"

"And there's a possibility that she isn't even available, based on the phone call she received from this person who let her down for her dad's wedding?"

"Technically," Sydney replied, dragging it out like it was four words. She lifted a shoulder. "Might have been a friend. Or a relative. Maybe she has an annoying older sibling like I do." She sent her sister a sweet smile.

Rachel shot her a not so sweet glare in return.

Sydney laughed. "Look, Jess was the one who suggested meeting on the train back, so she can't have been totally repulsed by me. And that would also imply that she's single, right?"

"Ifs and maybes." Rachel, always the more sensible voice of the pair of them. Sydney was more inclined to get carried away in the moment rather than to stop to assess the details. Maybe that's why her last relationship had been such a car crash. Damn those missed details.

"Well, now I'll never know," Sydney said. "I scrolled through like three hundred Jess profiles on socials while I was on the train coming home. None of them were her."

"Maybe try Jessica?"

"No, she doesn't go by Jessica. It's a whole thing," she said, remembering how Jess had introduced herself.

"Maybe she'll look you up? I'm sure there aren't as many Sydney profiles." Rachel never gave up. Sydney had always thought that it was one of the most admirable things about her sister.

"Why would she? As far as she knows, I stood her up. I wouldn't look for me if I was her."

"Maybe you could give her a shout out on the radio? Are those still a thing? I used to remember hearing them all the time." Rachel gave her a hopeful look but gritted her teeth. Even she knew that she was really clutching at straws.

Sydney leaned her head on her shoulder. "I don't think so, Rach. I think I'm going to have to lick my wounds and forget about this one. London's a big place. How likely am I to run into her again? The chances must be like six million to one."

"Stranger things have happened."

Things like that didn't happen to Sydney. When it came to matters of the heart, Sydney wasn't lucky. She didn't need to look any further than her last relationship for proof of that. But she had to admit that this felt different to anything she had experienced before. It felt like she and Jess were *meant* to meet, like it had been ordained by some kind of cosmic powers above. But if fate had brought them together, why had she missed that train? She couldn't answer that. What she did know was that she had never felt so instantly drawn to someone before, which made the disappointment she was feeling very real.

Still, Sydney was lucky in lots of other ways. She and Rachel had a fantastic, growing business. Tomorrow, they would be back at Makes Scents, making the quirkiest soaps they could come up with to sell to the nation, all with sustainable packaging of course.

She had great parents who were making the most of their retirement and travelling the world as much as they could, resulting in Sydney's collection of T-shirts with place names on them ever expanding. Not a complaint, she could never have enough tees.

She had the most supportive sister in the world who hadn't so much as blinked in hesitation when it came to letting Sydney move in with her after her breakup. And although staying with her sister in her small apartment was a bit of a squeeze, it also came with the best perk. She smiled at the thought. "Rapidly changing the subject from my tragic love life, how has my favourite man in the entire world been today?"

Rachel grinned. "Ben's great. He said to give his favourite Aunt Sydney a huge, squeezy hug and to tell you that he knows the best jokes to make you smile tomorrow."

Sydney, of course, was his only *Aunt Sydney*. She was his only aunt full stop, but she still loved that he always called her his favourite anyway. "I have no doubt that he will do that. He's the best kid." She nudged Rachel. "You sure know how to make them."

"I do, don't I?" Rachel's face took on a very proud mum look any time she spoke about Ben. She had every right to be proud. She had raised a wonderful son basically all by herself. Sydney and her parents helped as much as they could, obviously, but the hard work was all down to Rachel. Ben's dad had never been involved. The second Rachel had told him that she was pregnant he had gone running for the hills, never to be heard from again. Rachel hadn't dated after that, instead putting all her energy into raising Ben, and later into their soap business.

Maybe Sydney should take a leaf out of her sister's book and forget about dating for a while longer. That seemed like a good plan for her. Besides, it wasn't like Jess was going to magically appear on her doorstep, was it?

"Are you bunking in with me tonight or setting up the sofa bed?" Rachel asked.

"I think I'll bunk tonight." The downside to sharing a tiny two-bedroom apartment with her sister and nephew: no space. As much as she loved to be near them, Sydney knew that she needed to find her own place sooner rather than later. Hopefully she could find somewhere close by.

She made a mental note to start looking tomorrow.

CHAPTER THREE

J ess, honey? There's a man out here holding a big old bunch of flowers, and I'm pretty sure they aren't for Pam or me," Violet shouted into the break room.

"I don't think we've received flowers since we opened this place in 1981," Pam added, as she snipped off a chunk of Mrs Stevens's freshly dyed, bright red hair—a daring choice for the older woman.

Jess bit back a laugh at her two colleagues as she exited the break room. She had no doubt the flowers would be for her. Apology flowers from Austin, whom she had been refusing to see since the wedding a week ago. She had texted him here and there, answered a couple of his calls, but she had made herself unavailable to meet up with him in person. She wasn't in the mood to listen to a bunch of excuses and justifications that she had already heard a hundred times before. Jess would get over it like she always did, but she wasn't in a rush.

It came as no surprise to her that the man who was holding the flowers wasn't Austin himself but a delivery man from the florist they had been ordered from. Jess smiled and thanked him and took the bouquet, twisting it around in her hands to find the card. Ah, there it was. *Beautiful flowers for my beautiful gal. I've left this weekend free for me and you. A x.*

Gal, Jess repeated in her head. Not woman, not lady, not even girl. Gal. She shrugged off an ick.

Also, did it count as an apology when the word *sorry* didn't appear anywhere on the card? She frowned and tucked it back into the envelope. At least he was making time for her, she supposed. A full weekend no less, more time than he usually set aside for their relationship these days.

"Austin?" Violet asked as Jess set the flowers down on the counter. She didn't look up from the appointment book that she was studying, her glasses perched halfway down her nose.

"Who else?" Violet and Pam always knew what was going on in her life. Jess had worked with them for almost a decade, and she told them everything. They were like a pair of unjudgmental, unwaveringly supportive grandmothers who always had her back.

"Did his card say that he knows that he has been a rubbish boyfriend, an all-round prick, that he's shamefully apologetic and would do anything for your forgiveness?" Pam asked. "He stood our Jess up for her dad's wedding," she explained in a hushed tone to Mrs Stevens.

Mrs Stevens glanced up from her magazine with wide eyes and nodded in understanding. She threw Jess a sympathetic look in the mirror.

That's what it was like working with Violet and Pam. Everything was discussed honestly and openly, and more often than not, the clients joined in. A private person would hate it, but Jess prided herself on being an open book, and she personally loved the dynamic.

The salon felt like a close-knit family of three, with the clients acting as friends and extended family members who popped in to visit when they could. Violet and Pam hadn't aptly named the salon the Thairapy Room—just Thairapy for short—for nothing. It couldn't be more fitting. "Not even close," Jess said to Pam. She handed the card to Violet, who had her hand out waiting to read it.

Violet pulled it out of the envelope and flipped it open. "No apology. Wants to see Jess this weekend," she said evenly, not openly giving away her opinion.

Another thing about working in a hairdressing salon was the fact that not much went unnoticed. Mirrors on every wall. Jess watched Violet's attempt to be subtle about her eye roll to Pam, who made a not so subtle face in return.

"At least he's making *some* effort, right?" Jess tried.

Violet seemed to measure her response in her head. She was the slightly more reserved of the two ladies. The voice of reason on many occasions. "Yes, at least there's that. But I hope that he doesn't try to sweep his poor behaviour under the carpet. You deserve better than that."

Pam, ever the more outspoken one, scoffed loudly. "You could break your neck on that carpet, there's been so much swept under it." She leaned in closer to Mrs Stevens. "He either needs to be better, or she needs to find better." She gave a sharp nod and snipped her scissors in the air. Point made.

Mrs Stevens looked at Jess for her response.

"It's his job, Mrs Stevens. It seems to take priority over everything else lately," Jess explained. "He works very hard, which is a great quality too." Now she was making his excuses for him. Jess had noticed that she had started to do that lately. And she didn't love it.

"And we keep telling her that you can be good at your job *and* a be good boyfriend," Pam added. "The right man is out there, Jess. I'm just not convinced that you've found him. There, I said it." The fact that Pam said it regularly kind of took the sting out of it.

"Now, Pam," Violet said, "Austin has been a good boyfriend in the past."

Jess nodded quickly, jumping onto Violet's comment. "Exactly. He was great. It's this demanding job of his."

"Is it the job, though?" Pam asked. "People can change, you know. They can turn into different versions of themselves, and not necessarily for the better."

"Just look at my ex-husband," Mrs Stevens said as she flicked over the page in her magazine. She and Pam shared a pointed look.

Pam had a gift for getting a good read on situations, even when she didn't have all the details. She didn't need them. Jess both loved and hated it because she normally wasn't too far away from the truth, whether it was good or bad. She hoped this was one of the exceptions, but she had to admit, Austin had started to act differently. But Jess was sure she could link the timing to his work.

"He's under a lot of pressure. I'm sure that's all it is."

Violet nudged her with her shoulder. "I'm sure it is too."

Jess glanced at the flowers, a reminder of the apology that wasn't really an apology. "I'm not just going to roll over and forget that he let me down."

"Oh, make him work for it," Violet said in agreement. "He should have been there for you that day."

Jess's mind flashed back to a week earlier and the person who *had* been there for her. The plan had been to forget all about Sydney, but for some reason she hadn't been able to. Jess thought about their short train journey together several times a day. Sometimes, she even found herself imagining what it would be like to kiss Sydney, a clear confirmation that she was attracted to her. As if she had been in any doubt.

Although Jess usually did tell Pam and Violet everything, she hadn't confided in them about Sydney. She almost regretted telling Chloe, who had refused to let it go ever since, making it out to be some kind of life-changing, Jess-defining moment.

How could it be? Jess wouldn't see Sydney again.

But Sydney had been there for her that day when Austin hadn't. Maybe Jess was daydreaming about what would never be to avoid thinking about her reality, which was that her relationship needed some serious work.

"He did say that this weekend was all about us," Jess said. "Maybe he's seen the error of his ways."

"Let's hope so," Violet said kindly.

"He better have," Pam added under her breath.

Opinionated or not, those two women had her back. Jess really was lucky in a lot of ways. Great job. Great friends. Great home. All she needed to do was get her relationship back on track and everything would be as it should be. Then maybe she could finally put the whole Sydney encounter behind her.

Decision made, she lifted her phone and fired off a quick text to Austin.

Thank you for the flowers. Can't wait for this weekend x

Yes. That was exactly how things should be.

❖

Austin had arranged to pick Jess up after work on Friday at five thirty. His metallic blue sports car pulled up outside the Thairapy Room at 5:52 p.m.

He leaned across the car's console and kissed her quickly when she got in. "Hey, babe. Meeting ran late."

Did Austin *ever* say the word *sorry*? Thinking about it, Jess wasn't sure that he did, and now she was acutely aware of it. She didn't want to start their weekend on a bad note, so decided to drop it for now. "Has work been okay?" she asked instead.

Austin grinned as he sped the car off, tyres screeching below them. "Oh yeah. They love me in there. I'm going places, babe, high places. Exactly like we planned."

Jess couldn't remember being a vocal part of that planning session, but she was happy that Austin was doing well. At least his hard work was paying off. She smiled at him. "I'm glad. You deserve it. I'm not sure I've met anyone who works as much as you do."

He reached over and took her hand. "Just securing our future."

How could she be mad about that? Maybe it was time Jess showed more of an interest in Austin's job. Did her part in her role of the supportive girlfriend. "Any interesting clients lately?"

"Can't talk about that. Top secret."

That was fair. Confidentiality was a real and important thing. "What about colleagues? Any fun stories about any of them?"

Austin chewed his lip while he thought as he navigated the car through the busy London roads. Nothing seemed to be forthcoming.

"Oh, come on, Austin, there must be something. I haven't seen you in two weeks. Did someone wear a funny tie? Trip over their shoelace? Bring in a nice cake for everyone to share? Anything?"

"Why would I notice the other guy's ties?" He turned around and squinted at her, then turned back to look at the road. "Oh, you know what? There was something. You know Froggy?"

She didn't. "Does he look like a frog?"

"What? No."

"Then why do you call him Froggy?"

"Because his last name's Hopper and his voice is all croaky. He's quite a heavy smoker." He waved a hand to indicate that it didn't matter. "He's told all the guys that he's going to beat my score at golf tomorrow." He laughed. "Beat *me*? Talk about setting yourself up for failure."

"Tomorrow?"

Still laughing, Austin hummed in confirmation. When she didn't say anything, he looked over. "What?"

"Nothing. I thought we were spending the whole weekend together." Jess tried not to sound annoyed or accusing. This weekend was about making their relationship better, not worse with constant fighting.

He gave her hand a squeeze. "It's only a few hours with the guys. I'll see you after for dinner. You're getting wined and dined this weekend."

"Oh?"

He slowed the car to a stop at a red light, and he turned to look at her. "I told you I'd make it up to you after your old man's wedding, didn't I?"

And he was staying true to his word. Jess squeezed his hand back. "The wining and dining's a start." She hoped that conveyed that she appreciated he was trying, but it would take more than a couple of meals to make up for that. Her phone pinged and she lifted it with her free hand.

Chloe. *Four viewings for people interested in Freya's room scheduled for tomorrow. You be home to sus them out with me?*

A silver lining of Austin ditching her for golf. Jess was unexpectedly free. *Count me in. Let's hope they love to clean in their spare time.*

Chlo sent her back the emoji with heart eyes. *And cook.*

She laughed quietly while looking at her phone.

"What is it?" Austin asked.

"Oh, do you remember I told you that Freya's moving out next week?"

His face remained blank, which meant any recognition of that conversation wasn't happening behind the scenes.

Jess mentally rolled her eyes. "Well, Chlo and I have advertised for a new roommate. There are a few people coming to see the place tomorrow."

"Oh? Another girl, orrr?"

Did Jess sense a bit of apprehension? "I'm not sure. Chlo took charge of it. Does it matter?"

He gave an exaggerated shrug and turned the edges of his mouth downward. "I don't love the idea of some dude shacking up with my girlfriend."

Jess didn't mention that Austin didn't love the idea of shacking up with his girlfriend himself, either. It was one of those subjects that they actively avoided. No big deal. He wasn't ready for the next step in their relationship, and if she was honest, neither was she. "Why?"

He looked at her like she should already know the answer to that. "Because the dude might want to sleep with you."

Jess scrunched up her nose and laughed. "And? That doesn't mean that I would sleep with him. I'm with you. And there's also a very good possibility that this hypothetical man wouldn't be interested in me at all."

"I'd still feel more comfortable if it was a chick."

"Don't say *chick*." Jess couldn't let that one go. A thought popped into her head. "And what if *she* wanted to sleep with me?"

Austin gave her a boyish grin. "That's different. That'd be hot." He squeezed her leg.

Jess swatted his hand away. "You're such a bloke sometimes."

He found that almost as funny as Frog, or whatever his name was, beating him at golf.

Jess doubted he would have laughed if he had seen the look that Sydney had given her at the train station last week. And he definitely wouldn't laugh if he knew that Jess had felt that look in every part of her body, then and so many times since. Even now, her heart raced a little bit faster, and heat spread between her legs. She immediately felt guilty and pushed all thoughts of Sydney to the back of her mind.

Once they pulled up at the restaurant, Austin acted like a perfect gentleman, a stark contrast from his lad-like behaviour in the car. He opened the car door for her. Held her hand as they walked to the very nice restaurant that he had brought her to. Pulled her chair out and made sure she was comfortable before sitting down himself.

That was the thing with Austin—as the children's saying went, when he was good, he was very good. But it was also true that when he was bad, he was horrid. No one was perfect, right? And wasn't a relationship about accepting someone, flaws and all?

The conversation throughout their meal had been...fine. Not earthshattering, but pleasant. They talked about their food, which was delicious. Jess talked a little about work. Austin updated her on how all his favourite sports teams had performed that week. They glossed over the details of her dad's wedding. Austin told her about a fishing trip he was planning with the guys. Jess talked about how she was going to miss Freya, and Austin gave her advice on things to ask the potential roommates tomorrow.

When Austin drove Jess home, he pulled up on the kerb outside her house and they made out in the car for a couple of minutes. That meant that Austin probably wasn't planning on coming inside.

"Are you not staying?" Jess asked him when they broke the kiss. She didn't know why she had assumed he would be.

"You know I need a good night's sleep in my own bed before golf, babe." He checked his watch and then flashed her his most charming grin. "I could come in for an hour if you want."

Thankfully, Jess was immune to his charm. *Nice try.* "No, no." She patted his cheek a couple of times and leaned in for a quick, final kiss. "You go get your sleep and I'll see you tomorrow."

As she walked to her front door and turned to wave Austin off, Jess couldn't help but notice that she wasn't one bit disappointed the date was over.

She spent the rest of the night wondering what that meant.

Chloe stared at Jess in horror once she closed the door behind their third potential roommate. The problem was that none of the people they had met with actually had any potential at all. "Is this what's out there? We can't live with any of these people, Jess."

Jess released the laughter that she had been holding in with great difficulty. "Do you think he was serious about naked weekends?"

Chloe still looked the picture of shock. "Deadly serious!"

They both laughed so hard they struggled to catch their breath.

"He *did* say that our participation was optional," Jess managed to say when she got herself together.

"How considerate of him," Chloe said. "What did he say his reasoning was? I think my mind zoned out at that point in self-preservation."

Jess tried to quote the ridiculous reason word for word. "The restriction of conforming to societal standards all week where he is forced to don stereotypical, professional attire for his meaningless office job." She pumped her fist in the air. "He shall not conform on the days he is a free man!"

They threw themselves onto the sofa, still laughing about it.

"Please tell me we're agreeing that he's a firm no?" Chloe asked.

Jess held her hand up. "I have no desire to see that man naked ever in my lifetime, let alone every weekend. It's a hell no."

Chloe wiped an imaginary bead of sweat from her forehead. "At least he forewarned us. That could have been a nasty surprise to witness when I was eating my bowl of Cheerios on a Saturday morning."

Jess got a visual and immediately tried to shake the image from her brain.

Chloe sighed. "Now we need to decide if we would prefer to live with the girl with three pet tarantulas or the guy who only communicates through his puppet."

Jess felt the laughter bubbling up again when she remembered the puppet guy. "I quite liked Leonardo. He was cute." Leonardo was the puppet, of course, not the master.

"He was," Chloe agreed. "But do you really want to feel like you're on a never-ending episode of *Sesame Street*? That just seems like it would be exhausting to me."

"I would prefer it to living with three humongous spiders. I can physically feel them crawling all over me right now. Can you imagine if they were really in this house?" A shiver shot up Jess's spine. "I am *not* living with spiders."

"Hey, you don't need to convince me. I saw a little one in the bathroom last week and I haven't used it since."

Jess gasped. "Which bathroom?"

"The downstairs one. Why do you think I've been going all the way upstairs all week?"

"You could have warned me! I've been in that bathroom like fifty times."

"I didn't want to scare you. And I didn't want you to steal the upstairs bathroom either," Chloe said sheepishly. "The fact remains, neither of us can live with those spiders. So, that's her out—a pity because she did seem nice apart from her unfortunate choice in pets."

She had been nice, but Jess had never been so relieved that Chloe and she shared arachnophobia. "It's going to have to be the puppet guy, then."

Chloe looked at her watch. "Not necessarily. We have one more person to meet today."

"When?"

"In about an hour. She said on the phone that she would stop by as soon as she finishes work. She sounded normal too, though I'll reserve judgement for now."

Jess checked the time too. "Ugh. I have to meet Austin in thirty."

Chloe's eyes widened. "You're leaving me to deal with one of these people on my own?"

"I'm afraid so." Jess gave her a supportive pat on the arm. "You've got this. I'm trusting you to be on the lookout for any creepy pets. Or habits."

"Speaking of creeps…how's it going with Austin anyway?"

Jess glared at her. "Be nice."

Chloe grinned. "No, but seriously, how was last night? I'm interested."

How could Jess explain when she didn't really know herself? She lifted a shoulder. "Okay."

"Just okay?" Chloe asked, more concerned now. That was the thing with Chloe—even though she didn't like Austin, she didn't want things to go wrong for Jess.

Jess thought about it. The truth was, if the previous night had been a first date, there wouldn't have been a second.

But luckily, it wasn't. She and Austin had so much history, and that meant it was worth working on. *I will not walk away when things get a little bit tough like my parents did.* "It was fine. Dinner was nice. A few comments here and there that gave me the ick, but…" She trailed off because there was no point in dwelling on the bad. Besides, there were lots of good things about Austin. He was smart, ambitious, hardworking. He had a successful career. It didn't hurt that he was a dreamy kind of handsome either.

"I thought he was spending the whole weekend with you?"

"Yeah, so did I. But you know that he never says no to a round of golf. Honestly, I wasn't even that disappointed." She forced a smile. "Maybe tonight will be better."

Chloe reached for her hand and squeezed it. "I hope so. And I'm glad you were here today."

"Me too. I wish I could stay," Jess said. "I'm starting to think that we won't be able to find a good roommate."

"If this next one's not right, we can re-advertise. Don't worry, we'll find someone."

Jess reluctantly pushed herself off the sofa. She would much rather stay with Chloe and meet this last person herself, but if she let Austin down at the last minute, then she would be no better than him with his constant cancellations. "Keep me updated?"

"I will shamelessly blow up your phone and not give a shit that I'm disturbing your date. I promise."

Jess playfully mussed up Chloe's hair, then kissed her on the head. "I have no doubt that you will. See you later."

❖

About halfway through a quiet meal with Austin—they seemed to have exhausted everything that they had to talk about the night before—Chloe was true to her word. Jess's phone buzzed several times in quick succession.

OMG! I love her.

And I might not even be exaggerating. I think I have a slight crush. Jess, this is the one!

And don't worry. It's not because I have a crush in case you're worried that it's clouding my judgement. She's just so nice, and friendly, and totally down to earth. We could def live with her. Chatting and she has lots in common with both of us.

She owns a soap company! Imagine the free goodies! I LOVE soap.

I already know that you'll like her.

When are you free to meet her? Tomorrow? Say tomorrow? What if she finds somewhere else and we're stuck with the spiders?

Jess let out a quiet laugh and looked over apologetically at Austin for being on her phone, but he was too busy on his own to notice.

She read through the messages again. Chloe was certainly excited by this one. And she had always thought that Chloe was an extremely good judge of character. Jess trusted her to make a good decision for both of them.

She quickly typed a reply before Chloe's head exploded. *Tell her the rooms hers. I'll meet her when she moves in.*

CHAPTER FOUR

"Why do you have to move?" Ben asked, his big brown eyes shining with unshed tears. It made Sydney's heart hurt even more than it already was.

She crouched down in front of him so that they were on the same level. "Because I can't live with you and your mummy forever, sweetie. You guys need your own space."

"No, we don't. And you *can* live with us forever." His bottom lip popped out and trembled. "I'll be seven next month and you won't be here."

Sydney put her hands on his shoulders. "Of course I'll be here for your birthday. I'm still going to come and see you all the time. And you can come and see me too. Do you know how close I'm going to be?"

He shook his head and sniffed.

"Like a fifteen-minute walk. That's less than an episode of *Paw Patrol*."

He seemed to consider that through a few more sniffles.

Sydney tried again. "That's not very long, is it?"

"No," he conceded in a very quiet voice.

She wrapped her arms around him and hugged him tight. The truth was, she didn't find it easy leaving Ben and Rachel either. Sydney loved getting to see them every day. But she knew that it was the best thing for all of them. Space had already been limited before she moved in. It wasn't fair.

"I hope you're not keeping Sydney from packing, Ben," Rachel said as she joined them in her bedroom. Sydney kept some of her clothes in drawers that Rachel had cleared out for her, but a lot of it had stayed in her suitcases because there wasn't any more space. Rachel had given her all that she could. Although they were going to miss each other, Sydney was sure that Rachel would be glad to get her room back to herself.

"He's helping." Sydney shot Ben a wink.

The corners of his mouth twitched up slightly at Sydney's defence. "Yeah. I'm helping." He still sounded glum.

Rachel picked up on it. "We're still going to see Sydney all the time, bud."

"That's what I was just telling him. And I haven't even mentioned the best part yet," Sydney said.

Ben perked up a little. "What is it?"

"Do you want to tell him, or will I?" Sydney asked Rachel, tapping her lip.

"Oh, I think you should do the honours," Rachel answered, unaware of what Sydney was even thinking.

"You sure?" Sydney asked her, dragging it out some more. She glanced sideways at Ben's expectant face.

"Someone tell me the best part," he said impatiently.

Sydney laughed. "Sleepovers!" She threw out some jazz hands. "You get to come for lots of sleepovers. And we can watch cartoons and eat all the things that your mum doesn't allow you to eat here." She grinned at Rachel, who was disapprovingly shaking her head at her. "Doesn't that sound awesome?"

"Can we build forts and play football too?" he asked, his tone beginning to get brighter.

"Anything you want. *And* there's a playpark right around the corner that we can go to."

His face lit up.

Rachel put her hands on her hips and smiled at him. "Starting to sound better now, isn't it, kiddo?"

Ben did a bad job of pretending not to smile back. "I suppose. Maybe it will be okay having another house to go to."

Sydney held her hand up for a high five, which he immediately gave her. "Too right. And I have two new roommates, so that's two more friends for both of us."

"What are the roommates like?" Rachel asked her.

"I've only met Chloe, but she seemed really nice. She's fam too,

which is cool. I think she said she works some kind of office job."
Sydney would have to get specifics. "I haven't met the other woman
yet, but she and Chloe have been friends since they were kids. I'm
pretty sure Chloe said that she works as a hairdresser."

"I like getting my hair cut," Ben said.

Sydney smiled at him. "Maybe she'll cut it for you when you
come over."

"Do you think so?" he asked hopefully.

Sydney didn't know, but she couldn't imagine that anyone would
mind giving her adorable nephew a haircut. "Sure." Sydney could pay
her. Anything to make Ben happy.

It worked. "Cool."

Rachel cleared her throat to get Sydney's attention. "Any chance
that you and this Chloe…" She raised an eyebrow to insinuate her
meaning. They tried to speak discreetly about some things around Ben,
though he was clever enough to pick up on most of it anyway. He didn't
react this time.

Sydney hadn't even considered it, which meant that it probably
wasn't an option. "I didn't get that feeling."

"Friend vibes?"

"Definite friend vibes." Sydney doubted it would become anything
more, but she was also really happy to make a new friend.

As for dating, she would settle for nothing less than spectacular.
Intense attraction, undeniable chemistry, her world left feeling a little
unbalanced—she wanted all of that. Naturally, Jess from the train
popped into her head, reminding her that she might have already found
it, and lost it again before she could find out. Her heart sank when
she thought about what could have been, but she was determined to
remain optimistic that lightning could strike twice. Sydney would get
that feeling again, maybe not with Jess, but there was someone out
there for her.

"Maybe you'll fancy the hairdresser," Ben said out of nowhere.
So, he *was* following their conversation. Typical.

"I'm pretty sure that Chloe said she was out with her boyfriend
while I was viewing the house," Sydney told him.

"Does the hairdresser have a name?" Rachel asked.

Sydney couldn't remember Chloe mentioning her name, just that
they were close friends. "Guess I'll find out soon." She looked at the

time on her phone. "Very soon, in fact. I told Chloe I'd be there with the first lot of my stuff shortly."

"Are you coming back here tonight or staying there?" Rachel's eyes were starting to look a touch shinier, and it made Sydney well up too.

Sydney pointed at her. "Don't. If you start, I'll start, and I won't be able to stop. I'm going to see you at the scent station tomorrow." The scent station was what they had named the tiny rental unit that they used for creating and packaging their soap products, and generally running their business. Tiny meaning miniscule. It was all they could afford when they had started out.

Sydney and Rachel had talked about finding a bigger unit someday, but the scent station had become home, plus it had everything they needed. Sydney spent the most time in there. She was in her happy place when experimenting with different oils and fragrances, her focus more on the creative side of the business. Rachel helped when she could, but her strengths lay on the business side of things. Rachel managed their online store, which she could do either from the unit or from home while taking care of Ben. She also was great at selling their products to local businesses. They both shared the packing and shipping duties. Together, they were a well-oiled machine.

Rachel blinked away the threatening tears and nodded. "You're right. We'll still see each other most days. I've got used to you being here these last few months, that's all. It'll be weird without you."

"I'm going to be back and forth all week for my stuff. And after that I'll be here because I want to be." Sydney was reassuring herself as much as Rachel. It was a big step going back out into the world without her support system. It had been a while.

"Can I come for a sleepover tonight?" Ben gave her a hopeful look.

"I think I might need a few days to settle in and get to know my new roommates. Once I've done that, we can organize a sleepover for sure."

"And you have school tomorrow." Rachel brought out the big guns—the mum-look. Ben knew better than to argue any further.

"And that. No school nights." Sydney always backed Rachel up on the important stuff. Confident that she had everything she needed for the time being, she zipped up her bag. She lifted it and carried it to the living room, Rachel and Ben falling into step behind her. She put on her coat and turned to them. "We're not making this a big thing," she said, mainly to Rachel. She hugged them both and plastered on a smile. "I'll see you both tomorrow."

Swallowing the lump in her throat, she lifted her bags and gave them a final wave before she walked out the door and headed to her new home.

At least the hard part was over.

❖

"I can't believe you don't remember her name," Jess said incredulously, as they both leaned forward to peek out of the blinds to see if she was coming.

Chloe turned to her and grimaced. "It might be a place?"

"A place?"

"Yeah, like London. But it's not London." She squeezed her eyes closed while she racked her brain. "India? Paris? No. Oh, wait…" She gave her fingers a few clicks. "I think it might be Savannah."

"How sure are you? Because if I say *Oh, hi Savannah, nice to meet you*, and it's wrong, then that's a pretty bad start." First impressions were important, and Jess wanted to make a good one.

"Like sixty percent."

"Not great."

"It'll have to do."

Jess folded her arms and glared at her. "How can you possibly forget the name of the woman we are going to be living with?"

"Because she was hot, okay? My brain got all twisted and turned to mush, and instead of listening, I was staring at her very pretty eyes and daydreaming about kissing her very pretty lips." She tapped her chin. "Was it Brooklyn?"

"You're unbelievable." She moved the blind to the side to glance out of the window again and started bouncing on her heels.

"What's with this energy?" Chloe pointed at her and waved her finger up and down.

"I have to pee, and I'm holding it because I don't want to miss her arriving." Talking about it only made it worse. She squirmed and bounced faster.

Chloe laughed at her. "Just go."

"I can't. She's due any second."

"You're the one who's worried about making a good impression. What's she going to think if she's greeted by Tigger over there?"

Chloe had a point. "Fine. But it means that I have to go all the way upstairs since I know about the eight-legged lodger down here." Jess darted toward the stairs. "If she comes while I'm up here, make it a priority to find out her damned name so I don't embarrass myself."

Chloe saluted her.

"I'll be quick," she shouted as she ran up the stairs, taking them two at a time.

Just as her luck would have it, the second Jess unzipped her jeans, the doorbell rang. "Fucking knew it," she mumbled to herself. Jess listened to Chloe opening the door and the sound of muffled voices. She couldn't make out what they were saying, but she could guess the pleasantries that were being exchanged. Pleasantries that Jess really needed to be a part of. She pulled up her jeans and made sure her zipper was done despite her rush, because that really would be embarrassing. She quickly washed her hands and checked herself in the mirror. She fluffed her hair with her fingers, then laughed at herself. This wasn't a date. Still, first impressions, she reminded herself.

For some reason Jess felt a bout of nerves coming over her as she walked down the stairs, but she reassured herself that it was normal to feel like that when meeting someone new. Besides, from the sounds of things, she had nothing to be nervous about. The conversation sounded friendly, and she heard laughter as she reached the hall. Jess sidestepped the box and two cases that were sitting there.

"Here she comes now," she heard Chloe say.

Jess put on her friendliest smile as she entered the living room. "Hey. Sorry about that."

It felt like everything that happened next happened in slow motion. Their new roommate had been leaning her hip against the arm of Jess's favourite sofa, turned away from doorway where Jess stood. Her long, blond hair cascaded down her back in natural waves. At Jess's voice, she pushed herself off the chair, straightening to showcase her tall, flawless frame. She tossed her hair back over her shoulder as she turned around, in a move that Jess had only seen in shampoo adverts. And then she smiled, and Jess was almost certain that the world stopped. It was a smile that Jess would recognize anywhere, despite the brief amount of time she had known it. The smile that had been invading her thoughts and haunting her dreams. The smile that she had tried so hard to forget but couldn't.

A voice spoke, and Jess barely registered that it was Chloe's. "Jess, this is—"

Sydney, she finished in her head at the same time as Chloe said it. Not Savannah, not Brooklyn. It was Sydney, standing right there, in the middle of her living room. Correction, it was now *their* living room, wasn't it? Because, of all people, Sydney was her new roommate.

Jess was frozen to the spot. Stunned. Staring. Her mouth was hanging open. She was vaguely aware of it but didn't quite have the ability to fix it because she seemed to be in some kind of trance. Any control she had over her reactions had been momentarily lost.

And what was that sound? That thudding in her ears. Was that her heartbeat? Surely, that was too fast to be safe.

This couldn't be happening. Stuff like this *didn't* happen in real life. It was too coincidental, and quite frankly, bizarre. The chances of this scenario? Slim to none. Yet Sydney was right there. If Jess reached out, she could touch her. She wouldn't, but she could.

As for Sydney—who in Jess's memory was the epitome of cool, calm, and collected—she seemed gobsmacked. Those big, expressive, blue eyes revealed that she was just as surprised as Jess was about this turn of events. However, unlike Jess, she collected herself again very quickly, and that initial look of shock transformed into a beaming smile. "Oh my God—"

The sound of Sydney's voice broke the trance, and Jess quickly thrust her hand in Sydney's direction before she had the chance to finish her sentence. Jess could practically see her name resting on Sydney's tongue. "So nice to meet you, Sydney. I'm Jess." Back to her senses again, kind of, she plastered on a smile of her own. Polite and friendly, like she would smile at any new roommate she was welcoming to her home. Nothing strange to see here, no siree.

Sydney glanced down at Jess's outstretched hand and frowned at her in confusion.

Jess widened her eyes at her and sent silent prayers to whatever entity was listening that she would just go along with it and ask questions later. Chloe was standing right there, and she did *not* need to know that their new roommate was Jess's train crush that she had gushed about three weeks ago. It would only end up being awkward for all three of them. Maybe she would have to tell Chloe down the line, but first, she needed to buy herself some time to think. This was a reality that Jess had never expected to face, and she was wholly unprepared to handle it.

Prayers answered, Sydney reached forward and shook her hand. "Nice to meet you too, Jess." Her frown turned to amusement. "Not Jessica?"

Oh, so Sydney was going to play with her. Jess deserved that. She had to bite her lip to stop herself from grinning at the reference to their actual first meeting. "Only to my mum."

"I see. Forgive me, I thought you looked familiar for a second."

Jess was going to have to come up with some kind of explanation to give Sydney for what must seem like really weird behaviour. She couldn't tell her the truth. That would only reveal Jess's feelings. Feelings that had been pushed aside and were now flooding back, but Jess would figure that part out later. "I must have one of those faces."

If Chloe had sensed the tension, she didn't show it. "Maybe Jess cut your hair before. You wouldn't believe how many people we bump into on the street that have had their hair done by Jess."

"Perhaps that's what it is," Sydney said. She wasn't the best of liars. But then again, Chloe had no reason to suspect anything, so it didn't matter.

"Do you want a tour of the house?" Maybe if Jess could get Sydney alone for a minute or two, she could manage to get their stories aligned.

"I already showed her around last week when she came to view the room," Chloe said. All that was missing was *duh* by the end of it because of course she had.

"She did," Sydney said. "I know the important stuff like where the good chocolate and the wine glasses are kept."

Wine never sounded better. "Oh. That's great," she said with forced enthusiasm.

"But I'm happy to have another look around. Can never have too many tours, right?" Sydney seemed to pick on the vibe that Jess was trying to get her alone.

Before Jess could answer, Chloe hooked her arm through Sydney's. "You got it. Another tour coming right up."

Not exactly what Jess had in mind, but Chloe was playing her role of super-accommodating new roommate very well. Too well. Because Chloe had a thing for Sydney. Jess could have slapped herself on the forehead as the realisation hit. She was never going to get Sydney alone because Chloe was like an eager little puppy, wagging her tail and trying to impress. Caught up in the shock of seeing Sydney again, she had briefly forgotten about Chloe's crush. Well, didn't that just multiply the complication level by about fifty?

She's so hot, Chloe silently mouthed to her as she led Sydney out of the living room.

Sydney, on the other hand, just gave her an apologetic look. She'd tried.

Choosing not to tag along on what was supposed to be *her* tour, Jess threw herself on the sofa and used the few moments alone to examine her issues. Deep breath first. Another. Okay, this didn't have to be a big deal. Sydney was a nice person. Jess already knew that. She was probably going to be a great roommate. This whole situation could end up being a really good one where Jess made a fantastic new friend.

The stumbling block? Sydney was the first woman Jess had met that she didn't just want to be friends with. She had fantasized about Sydney a lot over the past few weeks. About what it would be like to be with Sydney. To kiss her. To touch her. As indulgent as it had felt to allow herself to think those things, it had also felt safe, because Jess was never going to see Sydney again. It was like imagining herself sleeping with a movie star—never going to happen, therefore acceptable to think about. And because it was only in the privacy of her imagination, Jess didn't have to analyse what it meant about her either. Her sexuality wasn't in question because it was only a daydream. Now that daydream was upstairs looking at the closet where she stored her bath towels, and those buried questions were swirling around in Jess's brain. She could almost laugh at the irony of it all.

Then there was Chloe. Her dearest, closest friend, Chloe. She hadn't seen Chloe get excited about anyone other than Dana since, well, Dana. Chloe's boss had been basking in Chloe's affections and stringing her along for too long. Chloe gave everything, and Dana gave her practically nothing but always dangled just enough to keep Chloe hooked. Jess had always hoped for the day that someone decent would turn Chloe's head so she could get over her one-sided infatuation once and for all. Sydney could be that someone decent. Jess couldn't get in the way of that. Their friendship came first. Always.

Lastly, there was Austin to consider. Rough patch or not, Austin was very much her boyfriend. What kind of girlfriend fantasized about their roommate, male or female? A lousy one. That's what kind.

And was it even fair of Jess to think of what they were going through as a rough patch? As Austin had said himself, he was only too busy right now because he was working hard to secure *their* future. Maybe Jess needed to cut him some slack and step up and act like the type of girlfriend who deserved all that effort.

It all added up to the same conclusion. The same one that Jess had already decided on after Sydney hadn't shown up to meet her that day.

Jess had to bury any feelings that she may or may not have and forget about Sydney, in *that way* at least. Sydney miraculously winding up in her life now didn't change any of that.

How hard could it be? It wasn't like Sydney knew that she had made such a big impression on Jess. And she didn't need to know. Jess had been receptive to Sydney's flirting, yes, but she had never reciprocated. Jess had been careful of that. She could pass any of their past interaction off as mere friendliness.

Of course, there was a chance that Jess was worrying about all of this for nothing. Sydney probably hadn't given Jess a single thought since the train. She hadn't even shown up to meet her again that day. Jess could be making the whole attraction between them so much bigger in her head.

"You guys keep a really lovely home," Sydney said when she breezed back into the living room past her. Jess got an aroma of something lovely again. Different from the train. Spicier. Still pleasant.

"It's your home now too," Chloe reminded her. She plonked herself down beside Jess, and Sydney took a seat on the armchair opposite. "Jess and I spend a lot of time down here talking total rubbish and watching trash TV. Feel free to join us as often as you like, or if you're happier in your room, we won't be offended either. Right, Jess?"

Act like you would with any new roommate. "Right. Whatever you're comfortable with."

Sydney smiled at her. "I appreciate that, thanks."

"What else do we need to tell you?" Chloe pursed her lips in thought. "My work hours can be all over the place. So, if you hear me coming and going at weird times, that's why."

Sydney nodded. "What is it that you do again? I think you mentioned an office?"

"I'm a personal assistant. So, yes, I do have an office. But my job requires me to be many different places at many different times." Chloe sighed. "Just whatever Dana needs," she added quietly.

"Dana's your boss, I'm assuming?" At Chloe's nod Sydney asked, "And what *is* Dana? Like what's the company?"

"She's a property developer. Very rich. Very powerful. Very smart. She's an impressive woman. Formidable." Chloe cleared her throat. "But she can be demanding sometimes."

Sydney's grin was knowing but she didn't press. "Gotcha," she said simply instead.

Jess was surprised that Chloe was quick to give so much away to someone she fancied, but then again that was the Dana effect. Even when Chloe was trying her hardest to get over her, Dana always had that inevitable hold on her.

"And you're a hairstylist?" Sydney directed the question at Jess. "Possibly *my* hairstylist at one time or another. Who knows?"

Jess appreciated Sydney keeping up the charade, and she hoped her shaky chuckle didn't give away the nerves that she couldn't seem to tamp down. "I am. I work at a salon called the Thairapy Room. My hours are normal, and my bosses are not demanding in the slightest. They're very sweet."

"No wild comings or goings from you, then?"

Chloe chimed in. "No. The only thing with Jess is that sometimes her boyfriend stays over. You might run into him here sometime."

Well, that cat was out of the bag. Jess felt her cheeks heat up, but she forced herself to look right at Sydney. "Yeah, sometimes. Eh, Austin. He stays. Overnight." Really cool, Jess.

Sydney's stare didn't falter. "I see. I think Chloe had mentioned that you were out with him when I was here last week. Your boyfriend." There was no sting in her delivery, but Jess felt it anyway.

"We were at dinner, yeah," Jess confirmed, uncomfortable with the whole conversation.

"How lovely. You two been together long?" Sydney gave her a

taunting look. She could clearly tell Jess was squirming, but that didn't deter her.

"A while," Jess said, opting for vagueness.

"He hasn't stayed over lately, though," Chloe added, oblivious to the tension in the room. "In fact, he hasn't been here in a few weeks, has he?" she asked Jess.

How could Jess justify throttling Chloe when she didn't know she was doing anything wrong? "Um. I'm not sure."

"He hasn't. Not since way before your dad's wedding," Chloe confirmed. "Not that I'm complaining," she added sweetly.

Jess chose to ignore that part. She opened her mouth and closed it again when no words formed. The fact that Austin hadn't stayed over since she had met Sydney was telling.

Thankfully, Sydney continued the conversation, coming to Jess's rescue. Once again. "Well, thanks for the heads-up. If I meet a random guy called Austin in the hallway, I'll not scream or attack him with the coat stand." Sydney plastered on a smile that was far from genuine but no less attractive. Jess could admit that. She had two eyes and a functioning brain—she liked how Sydney looked.

"Feel free to still do that," Chloe mumbled. Jess shot her daggers this time and she laughed it off. "What about you, Sydney? Dating anybody who we should expect to see staying over?" Chloe posed the question casually, but Jess knew the ulterior motive.

Jess couldn't pretend she wasn't curious herself. For platonic reasons only, obviously.

"No, I'm not dating anyone right now. I broke up with my girlfriend a few months ago, which is what led me to renting your spare room. I've been staying at my sister's place up to now."

"I'm sorry to hear that," Chloe said. "Who knows? Maybe you'll find someone worth dating soon."

"Maybe."

Jess didn't miss that Sydney's gaze settled right on her.

❖

Sydney had never been so glad to have unpacking to do. It wasn't that the company was bad. Chloe was a sweetheart and was going above and beyond to make Sydney feel welcome. Jess had been polite, but quiet.

But hold the phone, it was Jess! Her new roommate was Jess! She fired off a text to Rachel because she needed to tell someone.

Two questions. 1.Do you remember the woman that I met on the train? 2.Guess who my new roommate is? I'll give you a clue. Both answers are the same.

Sydney had been delighted to see Jess. Overjoyed. Ecstatic. She had wanted to invite Fate and Destiny for drinks and buy them the really good champagne to say thank you. But what happened next had thrown Sydney for a loop. Jess hadn't been unfriendly per se, but she had acted weird. Pretending she had never met Sydney? What was that about? She must have had her reasons, but Sydney was sure interested in hearing them.

On top of that, there was the boyfriend. Sydney wasn't naïve. She had hoped otherwise, but she had already considered the possibility that Jess was seeing someone. The confirmation left her with an aching disappointment that settled somewhere deep in her chest.

What did it all mean? Had the attraction between them been one-sided? Sydney's gut told her no, but her logical brain was beginning to wonder.

Holy shit, Sydney! A bunch of emojis with exploding heads. *If that isn't meant to be, what the hell is?*

Before Rachel got carried away, Sydney typed a message spilling the evening's revelations. Getting it off her chest made her feel a little better about it. She threw her phone on the bed and continued to unpack.

Her room was nice. It had been decorated in neutral colours, which Sydney liked. It felt like a blank canvas that she could put her own stamp on. She could brighten it up with some bright coloured bedding and cushions and add some pictures to the walls. Maybe she would invest in a new rug. The bed was huge, although any bed would have been bigger than the cramped sofa bed at Rachel's—not that she was ungrateful. That sofa bed had been a godsend. Storage was no longer an issue here either. There were two bedside cabinets, a silver lamp on each. The wardrobe was a good size, and anything that didn't fit would go into the chest of drawers in the corner. There was even a bookcase that she planned to do something fun with. Yeah, she liked her new room. And the house. Her second tour had only made her like it more as she picked up on little details she hadn't before. The heated towel-rail in the bathroom. The quirky lightshade that hung in the living room. The kitchen filled with every utensil she would ever need—a relief, as her ex had held most of hers hostage.

Sydney could see herself feeling at home here, but that depended on how she handled things with Jess. She only had one chance to get that right.

They needed to talk. That was clear. Sydney was good enough at reading the room to know that Jess didn't want to say anything in front of Chloe, so she would have to wait until it was just the two of them. The thought of being alone with Jess again was as exciting as it was necessary.

Her phone buzzed again. *The lie is probably linked to her having a boyfriend. Maybe she freaked out. Are you okay?*

Yes, I'm fine, she lied. Kind of. She wasn't not fine. Confused, yes. Disappointed that a reality she had hoped for didn't exist. And still a tad shell-shocked because, seriously, what the fuck? But above all of that, she was still riding the high of unexpectedly finding Jess.

There was a soft knock at her bedroom door and her heart skipped. It could just be Chloe checking to see if she was settling in okay. Or it could be Jess.

"Come on in," she said, raising her voice enough to be heard through the closed door.

Jess. "Hey," she said softly as she leaned against the doorframe.

Sydney hadn't had long to wait after all. "Hey, yourself."

"Are you busy? Can we talk?"

"Sure." Sydney gestured for Jess to come in. "It feels weird giving you permission to enter a room in your own house."

Jess gave a half laugh. "Our house," she corrected her. "And it's fine. This is your private space. I'd feel weird not asking." She hesitated, then slowly took a few steps into the room.

"So…" Sydney said on a breath, but she stopped there. The ball was in Jess's court here.

"So," Jess repeated. A pause. "You're probably wondering why I did that."

"Haven't thought about much else since," she said honestly.

Jess nodded her head a few times. "It's silly really, but"—she ran a hand through her dark hair, tossing it back and letting it fall back around her face—"I thought it would be awkward for Chloe, if she found out that we already knew each other. And I didn't want her to feel like the odd one out, you see. She was so excited about us both getting to know you." Her eyes darted around everything else in the room except Sydney.

Sydney could handle most truths, good or bad. Lies, not so much. She folded her arms. "Uh-huh. But you two both knowing each other, and me being the odd one out. That's different? More acceptable?"

Jess blinked a couple of times. "Huh. I never thought about it like that."

"Jess," Sydney said to get her to look at her. When she did, she eyed her and said, "*Come on.*"

"What?"

Sydney laughed because it was ludicrous. "That's just some wishy-washy reason that you made up because you don't want to tell me the truth." She shrugged. "If you want to stick to that ridiculous story, then okay, I'll go with it. Whatever. But do you want to know what I think happened?"

Jess didn't speak, but she stared, clearly waiting for Sydney to continue.

Sydney took a few steps closer to her because this was too important to say from across the room. She stopped just shy of touching distance. "I think you freaked out," she said, mirroring her sister's words from a few minutes ago. "You panicked when you saw me because of the attraction between us a few of weeks ago. You don't seem like a terrible person, so I'm guessing there's some guilt there regarding your boyfriend. Maybe you're worried that I'll say something to him. Or, if Chloe finds out, that she will, although I'm getting the impression that Chloe doesn't like him that much." She paused, then gave her head a shake and held her hands up. "You know what, that part's none of my business. But back to my point, lying to protect yourself is at least understandable. I don't love it, but I get it. But do me the courtesy of being up front with me. I'm quite a reasonable person, most of the time, I think."

Jess's face, which had been so flustered and easy for Sydney to read before, suddenly gave nothing away. "Attraction between us?" she said evenly.

Where was this going? "Yes."

"I'm not sure what you're getting at."

"What I'm getting at is that we met. We clicked. And there was a spark. I have no shame in saying that I was very attracted to you, and I felt a connection between us." *Am* very attracted. That part hadn't changed but it seemed like an inappropriate time to say so, especially under the freshly revealed circumstances.

Jess did the hair thing again, definitely a nervous habit, but her face remained impassive. "That's...kind of you to say. And I enjoyed your company that day too. I'm still grateful for how lovely you were to me." She drew her bottom lip into her mouth and let it go again. "And I agree that we got on well, but it was more a friend level thing for me."

Uh-oh. "Friend level?"

"Yes. Uh, I mean, I guess I did sort of know that it was more than friendly for you. You said some really nice things and I was flattered."

"Flattered?" Apparently, Sydney had lost the ability to think of words herself.

"I was. Truly. But it was, um, different for me. And I do have Austin." Jess's nostrils flared, the first chink in her newly found armour. "I'm also straight, if I didn't already mention that. Probably important."

Sydney hummed. "Probably." She clasped her hands together and tapped them against her chin. "But was it not you who arranged to meet up with me after?"

"Friendlily," Jess challenged.

"Right. Because I meet women all the time and decide to be their friend and meet up with them instantly." Sydney refrained from rolling her eyes.

"It's kind of irrelevant anyway," Jess said. "You didn't show."

"No, but—"

Jess waved a hand at her. "It's fine, Sydney. Really. I was relieved you didn't. After I left, I worried that me suggesting meeting up was only leading you on anyway. It was my mistake. An unfair one. I apologize."

Well, that one hit. And hurt. "So, that's all that day was to you then? A mistake?" Sydney hoped her voice didn't crack.

Another pause. "No, I don't mean...Look, I was down, and you made me feel better. It was good for my ego. So, I maybe didn't make my situation clear to you at the time when I should have. That was the mistake."

Sydney had heard enough. Humiliation flooded through her. "I'm so happy to hear that I was able to cheer you up and *massage your ego*. Now, if you'll excuse me, I'm in the middle of unpacking." She gestured the door with her head, getting the sudden urge to hide from this whole situation. How had she been so wrong? "Thank you for clearing everything up for me."

"Sydney," Jess said with a regretful look. "I want us to be friends."

"And maybe we will be, but I think I'm all friended out for tonight. I just want to get this unpacking done and get some rest. Moving has proved to be kind of draining."

Jess sighed and left the room. She turned from the hallway. "I'm sorry."

"There's nothing to be sorry for. It was entirely my misunderstanding. Goodnight, Jess." Sydney gave a final curt nod before Jess closed the door gently behind her.

Sydney suddenly didn't feel like unpacking anymore. Instead, she took a seat on the edge of her new bed and replayed the conversation with Jess on repeat.

Either Jess was massively in denial, or Sydney had picked up on the signals all wrong that day. One thing was for sure, if Jess had been interested in her before, she certainly did not seem to be interested in her now.

CHAPTER FIVE

Jess had been out of line, and she felt terrible. She had gone to bed feeling terrible, she'd woken up feeling terrible, and she'd been preoccupied all through work that day, still feeling terrible. Pam and Violet had both noticed how quiet she had been, but they put it down to the fact that she and Austin were still having issues.

Yes, telling Sydney that she hadn't felt anything for her had been a downright lie. The hurt look that had crossed Sydney's features had replayed over and over in her head as punishment. But Jess had managed to justify it to herself that the lie was for the best. For everyone.

For starters, Jess would be happy. Her safe, comfortable life would keep going the way it was. There would be no upset with Austin, so he would remain obliviously happy. Chloe would be unknowingly happy, given that she fancied Sydney. Who knew, maybe that would go somewhere, and Chloe and Sydney would end up living happily ever after—all thanks to Jess's lie. And lastly, Sydney would be happy. Initially annoyed, sure, but she would be much better off in the long run. Just because Jess had had a few fleeting thoughts about what could be didn't mean that she would ever act on them. She just wouldn't. So admitting feelings would only result in stringing Sydney along for something that could never and would never happen.

Jess *did* regret how she had gone about it. She had practically dismissed Sydney's feelings and almost belittled them, hence the feeling terrible.

So, she went home laser-focussed on a mission to make amends and become friends with her new roommate. That's what she would do if it wasn't Sydney, so there was no need to approach it any differently just because it was.

Jess found Sydney in the kitchen mixing something up in a bowl. Her long blond hair was tied up on top of her head in a messy bun, a few strands that had escaped hanging down to frame her face. She was singing along with the song playing on the radio and humming the tune when she didn't know the words. She hadn't spotted Jess yet, so Jess took the chance to really look at her for the first time since yesterday.

Relaxed Sydney was a really good look, Jess decided. She wore an oversized, baby-blue sweater with the sleeves rolled up. She was looking down, engrossed in her task, but Jess already knew it would bring out the blue in her eyes. Her jeans were blue too, and form-fitting Jess noticed as Sydney swayed her hips in time to the music. Jess found herself smiling at the sight.

Then Sydney looked up at her, put her hand to her chest, and let out a quiet laugh. "How long have you been standing there?"

"Long enough to appreciate your little performance over there. I'm very impressed."

Sydney grinned. "Oh, you should be. I can murder just about any song. It's a talent. And a necessity while I'm baking."

Jess took a few steps toward her. "I've heard way worse, mostly from my own lips." She leaned over the table and peeked into the bowl. "What ya making?"

Sydney leaned the bowl toward her to show her the contents. "I call these apology cookies." She gave her a soft smile that indicated they were for Jess.

That made Jess feel even worse. "Sydney, you don't have anything at all to apologize for. It should be me making you cookies. Although I doubt that mine would be remotely close to edible."

Sydney continued stirring up her mixture. "No, I overreacted."

"I was rude and inconsiderate."

"But I was assuming and jumped to conclusions."

"And I made it easy for you to come to those conclusions because of the way I acted," Jess countered.

"Well, I was judgemental and argumentative."

"I argued more than you did."

They both stopped and looked at each other, then burst out laughing at the same time.

"Why don't we agree that we're both idiots, and call a truce?" Sydney suggested.

Jess tilted her head from side to side. "I wholly agree to the truce, but I remain of the opinion that I'm the bigger idiot here." She held a finger up when Sydney tried to argue again. "Nope. The truce is now in effect."

Sydney gave her head a soft shake and banged her spoon on the edge of the bowl.

"What kind of cookies are these?" Jess asked, partly to change the subject to something normal, and partly because they looked really, really good and she needed to know more.

Sydney thought about it for a few seconds. "I'm calling them bitta cookies." She gave a sharp nod, clearly proud of the name.

"Bitta cookies?"

"Yeah. Bitta this, bitta that." Sydney laughed. "They've got white *and* milk chocolate chips. Peanut M&M's. Marshmallows. Fudge. Reese's Pieces. I raided the local supermarket."

Jess peered in at the mixture again. "And that's all in there?"

"I was going to make a few different types, then decided on a super-cookie." She shrugged. "I tend to make it up as I go along. When I was experimenting with different scents at work today, I came up with a cookies and cream soap. I guess this was inspired by that."

"Inspiration is very much welcomed in this house," Jess said.

Sydney put on a smug look. "See, I knew this would be a good way to make my new roommates like me."

Jess watched Sydney spoon a couple of blobs of her mixture onto a baking tray. "I already like you," she said quietly.

And then came the problem, because Sydney looked up at her and their eyes connected. For how long, Jess didn't know. Could have been a few seconds, could have been several minutes. It didn't matter. What mattered was that the air around them sizzled. Noticeably. And loaded moments like those made it much more difficult for Jess to hide from the fact that she felt something for Sydney. It was glaringly clear. It had been the day they met, and despite her denial, it was still clear as ever now.

Jess cleared her throat. "The cookies help, though," she said in the hope that it would lighten the heavy moment.

Sydney put the tray into the oven and tapped her phone. "In that case, I'll become very popular in approximately twelve minutes."

"Do you mind if I stay here and wait?" Jess asked.

Sydney smiled. "On the contrary. I'd like it if you did."

Jess felt her stomach flip-flop, but she ignored it. She had to. "Did you say that you experiment with different scents at work?"

"I did. It's my favourite part of the job," Sydney replied.

"Do you remember that day we met? On the train?" It probably wasn't a good idea to bring that day up, but Jess pushed on rather than focussing on it. "Do you remember which scent you used that day? I remember thinking it smelled good." Understatement. Sydney had smelled irresistibly divine.

Sydney thought about it for a second or two. "I mostly try my experimental ones myself to work out if I like them enough to sell or not. Can you remember what it smelled like?"

Jess shrugged, pretending like it wasn't a big deal and she couldn't really remember. Lies. "Lime or something. Maybe vanilla. I don't know."

Sydney squinted one eye and nodded slowly. "Kind of rings a bell. Definitely an experimental one, though. I can't remember exactly what was in it."

"Damn," Jess said. "I so would have bought it."

"Are you saying that you like the way I smell, Jess?"

Jess felt her cheeks heat up. "I'm saying that your soap is nice."

Sydney laughed that low laugh of hers. "Maybe I still have some, but I don't label my experiment bottles. If you smell me wearing it again, tell me and I might be able to recognize exactly what I used."

"So, sniff you?"

"Basically."

They both laughed.

Jess cast her gaze around the kitchen, and she spotted a shiny silver machine in the corner of the kitchen that hadn't lived there before. "Ooh. Is that the infamous coffee machine?"

"It is." Sydney grinned. "Meet Beanie." After a few seconds, her grin faltered. "Beanie's pretty much the reason that I missed the train that night, you know. I didn't mean to be a no-show."

Jess hadn't known. She had spent a lot of time telling herself that Sydney had missed the train because she just wasn't interested in Jess. But she couldn't dwell on that now. "Well, I did tell you to make sure that you rescued it," she said lightly. What was the point on going over the fact that Sydney hadn't stood her up, but simply got held up. It wouldn't change anything anyway. "Does *Beanie* make good coffee?" Deflection was required.

Sydney narrowed her eyes like she knew what Jess was up to, but then she softened after a few beats and went with it. "The best around. Much better than anything you would get out and about. Good-quality coffee can be really hard to find."

"You sound quite annoyed by that."

Sydney smiled like she had been busted. "It's my pet peeve. Bad coffee."

A knock at the front door interrupted their friendship building.

"Are you expecting anyone?" Jess asked.

"No, no one."

"Huh, me either. I'll go see who it is. You mind the treats." Jess already felt much better than she had done all day and walked to the door with a spring in her step that hadn't been there earlier. She pulled it open. "Austin. Hi." Why was he there?

"No need to look so shocked, babe," Austin said. He pulled off his sunglasses and held his arms out. "No hug?"

She stepped into his arms automatically. "Of course. I just wasn't expecting you."

He let her go and stepped inside. "I thought I'd surprise you. Maybe meet this new roommate of yours. Introduce myself."

The thought of Austin and Sydney in the same room made Jess feel a bit sick, but it was going to happen sometime. Apparently, that was going to be sooner rather than later.

"Is it not a good surprise?" he asked when she didn't answer him.

"Always," Jess said, making sure to smile. Austin used to surprise her all the time, but it had been a while since he had stopped by out of the blue. She wasn't used to it anymore. That's all it was.

"I knew you'd be happy." He clapped his hands together. "So, the new roomie home?"

If Jess was a cartoon, she would have visibly gulped. "In the kitchen."

Austin led the way and burst through the door bellowing, "You must be Sydney."

Jess wished she could hang back and avoid the entire scene, but God knows what he would say, so reluctantly she followed. She just hoped that Sydney wouldn't think this was some grand plan of hers to prove a point. Things were starting to go so well between them.

"That's me," Sydney said to him. "And I've been told if I run into any strange men in this house that it could only be one person, so I'm going to make an assumption here and say that you must be Austin."

"The one and only." Austin laughed and turned to Jess. "I like her already."

"Good to meet you," Sydney said politely.

"Believe me, the pleasure is mine."

Jess mentally shook her head at him. She was used to Austin turning the charm on to just about any woman he met. It was who he was, but it seemed more cringeworthy when Sydney was the subject of it. "Sydney has just put the most amazing cookies I've ever seen into the oven," she said to move him swiftly on.

"If you're hanging around you might get one," Sydney added.

Austin rubbed his hands up and down his stomach. "And ruin the best shape I've ever been in? No thanks." He nudged Jess. "Make sure you don't eat too many cookies either." He winked and grinned, trying to disguise it as a joke, but it wasn't the first time he had said something like that to her. Austin was an extremely looks orientated guy.

"Or, alternatively, eat as many as you want." Sydney looked away, but her words had been sharp. Jess could tell.

Austin wrapped an arm around Jess's shoulder. "She knows I'm kidding. Don't you, babe?"

"He is," she agreed to defuse the situation.

Sydney frowned at her but seemed to back down. "Tell me, what is it that you do, Austin?"

"As little as possible," he joked again. He probably shouldn't go into comedy.

"Oh? I thought you worked a lot," Sydney said. "Or so I've heard."

"No, I do. I'm a lawyer. Working my way up nicely through a pretty big firm, I must say. Takes a lot of work, long hours, that sort of thing." He waved a hand as if he was bored talking about it. "And what is it that you do, Sydney?" He took a seat, seemingly settling in for a chat.

"I run a business with my sister."

Jess leaned against the counter beside him. At least he was taking an interest and starting to behave himself. "Sydney makes the most amazing soaps."

Austin nodded. "Nice. Your own business, eh? Excellent. Does it do well?"

Sydney lifted a shoulder. "We're happy with it."

He indicated Jess with his head. "See, I keep telling this one that she needs to work for herself. Open up her own salon. But she's too sentimental about those two little old ladies she works with."

Jess felt her cheeks heat up. Now Sydney was going to think she didn't have any ambition, which wasn't true. Jess just loved her job. And she loved Pam and Violet. As far as she was concerned, there was nothing wrong with that.

"In my opinion, loyalty can only ever be a good thing," Sydney replied instead. "As long as Jess enjoys it, it doesn't really matter where she works, does it? I'm sure you only wish for her to be happy."

Jess wasn't used to seeing Austin flustered, but she couldn't pretend she didn't enjoy it a little bit. Jess knew he was just showing off, trying to impress the new person, but she hated it when he did it at her expense. Jess also felt her heart skip at the fact that Sydney was standing up for her.

"That is the main thing," Austin grudgingly said then, trying to act like that was what he had meant all along.

Chloe burst into the kitchen. "What am I missing, good friend and new friend?" She froze when she saw Austin. "And non-friend. Well, well, well. Long time no see."

"Chloe," Austin replied simply.

It used to bother Jess that they didn't get along, but she had learned to ignore their little jibes and digs. They were both grown-ups, and Jess refused to be stuck in the middle.

"I thought maybe we'd seen the last of you, but Jess told me that's not the case. A girl can hope, though." Jibes like that one.

Austin gave Chloe an insincere smile that bordered on patronising. "Always happy to burst your bubble."

Chloe gave him her sweetest smile in return and pretended to pop a bubble in the air. She turned away abruptly. "What's that amazing smell?"

"Sydney has made the most decadent cookies I've ever seen. They're nearly ready, and I've positioned myself close to the oven so that I can snatch the first one." Jess could feel her mouth beginning to water.

Chloe laughed. "That's what I get for not beating you home from work. Second place for cookies."

"How was work?" Jess asked.

Chloe picked at a bit of dough that was stuck to the counter. "Work itself was same old. But, in better news, Dana asked me to stay and help her tonight and I said that I couldn't. Proud of me?"

"Very," Jess said. Usually when Dana felt Chloe starting to pull away, she came up with some extra tasks for them to do together to remind Chloe that she needed her, and to reel her back in. Chloe rarely ever refused.

"Dana wasn't very impressed. But what can she do? I finished my work for the day. I'm allowed to have plans, and now I know that my plan is eating cookies."

"Finally giving up on pining over a woman you can't have?" Austin said.

Jess nudged him to shut up. Not getting involved didn't mean that she would let either of them take it too far. "Don't be mean."

"Coming from the invisible boyfriend," Chloe bit back. "Don't mind if I don't take it to heart."

He laughed it off. "What about you, Sydney? Has a good man snatched you up? Can't imagine a pretty girl like you being single."

Sydney had been very quiet, taking in the scene, up until then. To say she looked unimpressed would be an understatement. Her brow had furrowed on more than one occasion. Jess had been watching. It probably wasn't a great first impression meeting Austin when Chloe was present. They didn't exactly bring out the best in each other.

"That would be a good lady," Sydney corrected.

"Oh shit, I didn't mean to presume—"

"It's fine. Most people still make those kinds of assumptions all the time. But to answer the core question, no. Still waiting to be *snatched up*, as you say."

"What about Chloe here?" Austin said with a smirk. "She's available and no longer lovesick, seemingly."

Chloe rolled her eyes. "Don't even entertain him, Sydney."

"No, I don't mind. I think Chloe would be a fantastic prospect for anyone," Sydney said. "I'd be lucky to be with her. But I'm giving dating a rest for a while." She leaned toward him and lowered her voice. "Besides, I'm a real sucker for brunettes." She glanced over at Jess and then winked at him.

Chloe let out a loud laugh, and Jess felt like someone set her cheeks on fire.

Sydney patted Austin's hand. "Kidding, of course."

"Should have seen your face, though," Chloe piped in. "You mustn't have liked sharing your toys as a child."

Austin wrapped a possessive arm around Jess. "For once you're right, Chloe. I don't share what's mine. Ever," he said coldly.

"She was joking," Jess said, attempting to keep her tone casual, because she knew that Sydney hadn't been joking at all, no matter how she played it off. Jess could feel Sydney's eyes on her, but she avoided her gaze.

"Hmm. Funny," Austin said without laughing.

Sydney and Chloe shared a furtive look, and Jess sighed internally. Not the most successful first meeting with them all together.

Silence descended over the kitchen—the awkward kind. Luckily, Sydney's phone timer went off to indicate the cookies were ready.

"Who wants cookies?" Sydney asked with forced enthusiasm as she lifted the tray out using oven gloves.

"Me, for sure," Jess said.

"And me." Chloe never turned down sweet stuff.

Austin didn't answer, instead keeping his focus on his phone.

It baffled Jess that Austin could be so charming and polite with work colleagues or even strangers, but when it came to her friends, he was a nightmare. Honestly, Jess couldn't even blame them for not liking him.

As she ate not one but two of the best cookies she had ever tasted, Jess couldn't help but wonder what Sydney thought of Austin.

❖

"He was a complete and utter douchebag," Sydney said as she passed a stack of empty boxes to Rachel. "You know, I don't think I've ever met someone who I've taken such an instant dislike to before."

"And you don't think it's just because you're jealous?" Rachel asked as she carefully placed a bottle of one of their most popular scents—Sun, Sea, and Lemonade—into the first box along with a fifteen percent off voucher and their personalized business card.

Sydney lifted her own stack of boxes and cards and started do the same with the next batch.

Admittedly, when Austin had breezed in like he owned the place with his perfectly coifed dark hair, expensive polo shirt with designer sunglasses hanging from the collar, and smug smile, Sydney had initially bristled. And yes, she was aware that most of that disdain had been a result of her own envy. She wasn't proud of it, but she was only human. Still, she had managed to shake it off. It wasn't the guy's fault that he was inconveniently with the woman she liked.

But it was the guy's fault that he was an asshole.

"No," Sydney said assuredly. "He's not a nice guy. There were so many things." She listed them. Austin's sleazy comments. The body shaming. The career shaming. The sly comments to Chloe. Thankfully, Chloe seemed to give as good as she got.

Sydney had previously wondered why Chloe disliked Austin so much, but now she understood it. What baffled her was how Jess *did* like him.

Rachel scrunched her nose up in disgust. "Okay. I get your point. He does sound like a piece of work."

"He *so* is, Rach. Seriously, why is Jess with him? Why would anyone want to be with a guy like that?"

Surely Jess wasn't shallow enough to be swayed by a handsome face, a well-paid job, and a fancy sports car. And the reason that Sydney knew that Austin had a sports car was because he told her about seventeen times. Sydney had managed to zone out of the conversation by the time he had started bragging about his expensive new alloys.

Rachel shrugged. "Maybe she likes douchebags. Or…maybe she is one. They might be like Mr and Mrs Douchebag."

Sydney shot her a glare.

"What? She didn't exactly showcase impeccable behaviour the

other night when you moved in, did she? And don't forget she blanked you at first when you met her."

Sydney immediately leapt to Jess's defence. "She had her reasons for that. Anyone can have a bad day."

Rachel didn't look convinced. "Whatever. I'm just saying, maybe you should take some time to get to know her better before you decide she's worth all your time and brainpower."

"But I really do think she's a good person. I have this wrenching feeling in my gut that she is. And I've seen glimmers of that side of her too."

"Remember when you thought that your ex-girlfriend was a lovely person too?" Rachel said.

"Okay. Ouch." Although it was probably a fair comment. Sydney had thought her ex hung the moon once upon a time, and look how wrong she had been about that one.

Rachel at least attempted to look somewhat apologetic.

"Are you saying that you think I've got this one wrong too?" Sydney asked.

"I'm not saying anything. I've never met the woman," Rachel said. "I'm telling you to keep an open mind, that's all."

"Keep an open mind?"

Rachel smiled kindly at her. "It's early days. Time will tell whether Jess is a decent human worthy of your affections. At the minute, she's just a pretty girl who you *think* you had some kind of connection with a few weeks ago."

"Sometimes when you know, you know, Rach. The fact that we somehow ended up living in the same house, out of all the houses in London—you don't think that's fate?"

"I admit, it's highly coincidental. Fate?" Rachel lifted a shoulder. "We'll see."

"Well, hopefully I won't be *seeing* much more of that Austin guy," Sydney said.

"Try to avoid him. He can't annoy you if you're not in his company."

Sydney screwed her face up. "Not true. The knowledge of his existence as Jess's boyfriend annoys me." She paused. "Did I tell you that he blatantly suggested that Chloe and I should date? Because why wouldn't we? Two single lesbians—it's a given that we must date each other."

"Ew. Old-fashioned guy mentality right there."

Sydney grinned. "He didn't like it so much when I told him that Jess was much more my type."

Completely her type. And Sydney was positive that time would only confirm it.

Chapter Six

"You know the way I'm totally kicking ass at this whole getting over Dana thing?" Chloe said as she pushed herself up to sit on the kitchen counter. Four chairs, and three stools, and still more often than not, Chloe opted for the sterile work surface.

"I do. And I'm beyond proud of you for it." Why did Jess sense there was a *but* coming?

"I know you are. I was proud of me too, and I really thought I was moving on this time, but..."

And there it was.

"I'm obviously not over her, nor have I moved on as far as I had hoped. I'd imagined that I'd moved to, like, Mexico when in reality, I've just been floating about Wales or somewhere else not too far from London." She frowned for a few seconds, then shrugged it off. "You know my geography skills aren't the best, but you get the gist."

"I think I understand the metaphor. And are you saying that you have now made the short trip back from Wales?"

Chloe nodded. "On the express train. Bought a return ticket, as it turns out."

Jess leaned against the counter beside her. "Forgetting about transport analogies for a minute, as inspired as I think they are, what happened?"

"She's going on a date tonight." A tear rolled down Chloe's cheek, and she reached up a hand to wipe it away. "And she made *me* book the table at the restaurant."

"Oh my God, Chlo." Jess strolled over to the table and plucked a few tissues out of the box and handed them to Chloe. "That's low even for her."

Chloe dabbed her eyes and blew her nose. "It's a new one, that's for sure." She sniffled.

"It's another way of toying with you, Chlo. You know that every time she feels you pulling away, she does something to keep you interested. She literally basks in your attention."

Chloe looked at her with tearful eyes. "How does her dating someone else keep me interested?"

"Because your focus is back on her."

"I thought maybe she made me book it as some kind of punishment because I didn't stay when she asked me to the other night."

"She never did like you saying no."

Chloe ducked her head. "Is there something wrong with me?"

Jess pushed herself off the counter and wrapped her arms around Chloe. "There's nothing wrong with you," she said, stroking her back. "You can't help who you fall for." Wasn't that the truth. "Even if it does mean you have terrible taste."

Chloe playfully pushed her, but she smiled at least. "Like you can talk anyway. Was Austin on some kind of jerk steroids the other night, or is his bad behaviour generally escalating?"

"I knew you were going to bring that up."

"As if I'd ever let it slide." Chloe grinned. "Sydney got him good, though, didn't she? Did you see his face when she said she likes brunettes?"

Jess gave her a look. "Stop. You and Austin are both as bad as each other sometimes. I wish you would just get along." She also didn't want to think about Sydney's comment too much.

"Some wishes don't come true. Believe me, I would know." She looked into space and narrowed her eyes. "Do you think Sydney meant it?"

"Meant what? To annoy him?"

Chloe laughed. "No, I'm positive she meant to do that. I mean the brunette thing." She lifted a lock of her own blond hair and studied it. "Do you think that's more her type?"

"Oh, um, I don't know. Who can really say they only have one type?" Jess's own type seemed to have taken a major swerve lately.

"I do like Sydney."

"Like, like her, like her?"

Chloe considered it before she answered. "I think she's hot and funny and a nice person, so I guess, yes?"

Jess had expected Chloe's crush to turn into something more. It had been inevitable, really. Sydney was a catch. But she hadn't expected to feel so nauseous about it.

"She has to be better than Dana," Chloe added.

"Anyone would be nicer than Dana." Jess ran her hands through her hair. "So, what? You're going to ask her out?"

Chloe shrugged. "Why not? We're both single. Worst case, she says no. Best case, we fall madly in love and live happily ever after."

The nausea intensified. "Do you think you're asking for the right reasons, though?" It came out higher pitched than usual, and Jess cleared her throat to try and mask it.

"The right reasons being that she's a woman I'm very attracted to? Yes."

Jess tilted her head to look at her. "The right reasons being that you're no longer affected by Dana and are truly ready to be with someone else." Weird nausea and blatant jealousy aside, she couldn't condone it as a good idea when Chloe had literally been crying her eyes out over Dana just minutes before.

Chloe stuck her tongue out at her. "Why do you have to be so sensible?"

Jess smiled at her. "One of us has to be. Besides, didn't Sydney say she wasn't dating right now?"

"So, you're saying no? Don't ask her out?"

"I'm saying that it's bad timing. And what's the rush? It's not like she's going anywhere." There. Jess had managed to give impartial advice that had nothing to do with it being Sydney who they were talking about.

"You're probably right. But if the right moment presents itself, I'm going for it."

Jess nodded quickly. "If it happens, it happens." *But please not yet.* Jess wasn't quite ready to let go of her Sydney fantasy yet. Burying feelings was a process.

"Speaking of Sydney. We're having a movie night tonight. You in? Or is Austin going to be here? If he's coming over, then I officially uninvite you. I want to enjoy my TV time after the day I've had."

Only because of that day, Jess didn't bite. "Austin's working on a new case, so I likely won't see him all week."

"You'll hang out, then? You and Sydney could use some bonding time—youse are a little tense around each other."

Chloe had noticed? "We are?"

"It's likely just a new roommate, getting to know each other thing. It takes some people longer than others." She patted Jess on the shoulder. "You'll gel, don't worry. But movie night is mandatory."

❖

At least *bonding time*, as Chloe had called it, meant that Jess was around to make sure that Chloe didn't make any hasty moves. Jess's own feelings aside, it really wasn't a good idea when Chloe was emotional and hurting.

The living room had a much more romantic feel than it usually had when it was just the two of them for a movie night, or when Freya had joined them in the past. Chloe only had one lamp dimmed in the corner, and she had even gone to the effort of lighting some candles.

Thankfully the film that Sydney had chosen wasn't a romance. Jess would have really felt like she was third-wheeling on a date. It was bad enough that Chloe and Sydney were sharing a sofa, a blanket, and a bowl of popcorn. Jess took a handful of her own popcorn, popped it into her mouth, and ignored the fact that she wished she was in Chloe's position. She watched the actress on the screen instead, who was beating up about five baddies at once. Unrealistic but entertaining.

"If I was a teenager, I'd put her poster on my wall," Chloe said to Sydney. She crunched some popcorn and lifted a shoulder. "I still might."

"Tell me about it," Sydney said with a smile.

Jess zoned out while Chloe and Sydney continued to discuss their famous crushes. All of Jess's posters growing up had been of boys. She'd never fancied a female actress or pop star. She did appreciate how beautiful some were. She had looked up to a few and wanted to look like them. She had copied their hairstyles. Dressed the same way. Admired them, sure. But crushes—she didn't think so.

As for the actress on the screen, Jess could see that she was gorgeous. The supple moves of her body while she ran and punched and kicked were impressive. She understood why people would fancy her. But did that mean she did too? Jess had never thought about it that way before. It seemed more like an innocent appreciation to her.

"There's no point in asking Jess who her favourite is," Sydney said.

At the sound of her name, Jess pulled her attention back to the conversation. "Hmm?"

"Hot celebrities. Women."

"Oh. No, I'd have no idea." Jess played off her discomfort with a laugh. She indicated the screen with her head. "I suppose she's pretty."

"She most definitely is," Sydney said with an amused grin. "Although I don't think *I suppose she's pretty* really counts as high praise."

Jess swallowed. "Um…"

Sydney laughed. "Don't worry, Jess. I know it's not your thing."

"Oh, I wouldn't be so sure about that," Chloe said with a mischievous glint in her eye.

Oh shit. Alarm bells started blaring. Sirens were going off. Lights were flashing. All at the same time. "Chloe," Jess said in a warning tone.

Chloe held her two palms up. "I'm just saying. Maybe it's not *completely* not your thing. That's all."

Jess shot her a look to convey *that better be all.*

"What do you mean by that?" Sydney asked. Why did she have to ask?

"She doesn't mean anything," Jess said quickly. "She's just kidding around, aren't you, Chlo?" She widened her eyes so much they probably could have rolled out and across the floor. She wished they had, because at least that would have given them something else to talk about.

Chloe's smile was still showing as she took a sip from the straw that was in her drink, which was pink gin and lemonade, Jess realized. Oh no. Chloe couldn't be trusted not to be a chatterbox when she drank gin. It always went straight to her head. That's why she was blabbing. "Yeah, of course," Chloe agreed though it was thoroughly unconvincing.

Sydney didn't look like she bought it either, but she smiled anyway. "For a second there, I thought Jess had some secret female celebrity crush that she was keeping from us."

Yes, the benefit of the doubt. "No, I don't. Sorry to disappoint."

"Not a *celebrity* crush," Chloe said with a giggle and a hiccup. Yep, Chloe was drunk.

"Chloe, please stop," Jess said almost pleadingly now.

"It's only Sydney, Jess. Sydney's, like, the nicest person ever. She will sooo get it, wait till you see." She swivelled her head toward Sydney. "Jess got all hot and bothered over a woman she met on a train a few weeks ago."

And there it was.

Just like that.

Jess closed her eyes. Chloe had really come right out and said it. To the woman from the train herself. When she dared to open her eyes again, she met Sydney's gaze, which was glued on her. Of course it was.

"What do you mean hot and bothered, Chloe?" Sydney asked, her eyes still on Jess.

"Jess, you tell her. It's your story."

Jess swallowed a couple of times. "I'd rather keep that story private."

"Nooo, don't be silly," Chloe said waving her hand. "I'll tell it, then," she said when Jess stayed quiet. Chloe hit her chest with her fist a couple of times and cleared her throat, like she was about to make an announcement. Well, she had already done that part. "Jess was on the train going to her dad's wedding." She shot her head round to Jess, suddenly side-tracked. "He back from his honeymoon yet, by the way?"

"What? Oh, I think so," Jess said, her brain not really focussed on that right now.

Chloe shrugged. "Anyway, she met this mysterious, sexy woman. Came home with a real thing for her. She even said she was thinking about what it would be like to be with a woman. *That woman.*"

"I see," Sydney said. She licked her lips. "And what happened to this woman? How do you feel about her now, Jess?" She threw Jess a challenging stare.

Thankfully, Chloe answered so she didn't have to. "She stood poor

Jess up. She was very disappointed." She turned to face Jess again. "You were very disappointed, weren't you, Jess?"

Jess ran her hands down her jeans to get rid of any crumbs of popcorn and, basically, for something to do. "I think you're exaggerating a bit there, Chlo. But, hey. It's all for the best." Jess flashed a smile that probably looked as fake as it was. She stood up. "I just realized the time, so now that you've had your gossip, I'm going to go to bed."

Chloe covered her mouth with her hand. "Oh dear, you're mad at me. Is my mouth really, really big?"

"The biggest." Jess shook her head. "But no, I'm not mad at you. I'm just tired." And a little mad, but she would talk to Chloe about it when she sobered up. She walked over and kissed her on the top of the head. "Night, Blabbermouth. Night, Sydney." Jess didn't dare to look at Sydney as she passed, but she sure felt Sydney's eyes burning into her back as she scarpered out of the room.

CHAPTER SEVEN

"If that's how you want to play it then you've really left me no choice," Sydney said under her breath as she typed into the search bar on her phone.

She didn't know it could be so easy to avoid somebody you lived with, but Jess was making an art of it. Almost two days had passed since Chloe had come out with that *revelation* during their movie night, and Sydney hadn't laid eyes on Jess since.

It wasn't like she hadn't tried. Sydney had knocked on Jess's bedroom door that same night and got nothing but silence. Jess had either been sleeping or ignoring her—more likely the latter given the way Jess had fled the living room like it had been on fire. The following morning, Sydney had tried knocking again, only to be informed by a very hungover Chloe in the hallway that Jess had left early to go to the gym before work. Sydney didn't hear Jess come home that evening either, which meant she must have slipped into the house either very late, or very quietly.

That morning, the same again. So, halfway into the afternoon, Sydney decided to take matters into her own hands.

"Sorry? Did you say something?" Rachel asked, peeking up from her laptop at the small desk in the corner of the scent station.

Sydney glanced up from her phone. "Just talking to myself. Hey, I've finished mixing the new batches of Fireside Mallow and Cinnamon Buns, and orders are prepped. You okay if I skip out early today?" She knew Rachel wouldn't mind, but they always did each other the courtesy of checking.

"Of course. I'm just processing these new orders and updating the stocks, then I'll be done too. Where are you going? Anywhere nice?"

Sydney tapped on the phone number that she had searched for and held the phone up to her ear. "I think I need a haircut."

A woman answered. Not Jess. "Hello, the Thairapy Room. How can I help you today?"

"Hi there. I know it's very short notice, but I was wondering if Jess had any appointments available today? I only need a quick trim." She crossed her fingers and ignored the dubious look that Rachel was giving her.

"Hmm, I'm not sure. Jess is very popular. Let me have a look here." Sydney could hear pages being flipped. "Oh! You're in luck. She has a small slot free in thirty minutes. Would that suit?"

Sydney grinned. "That would be perfect."

"Great. Can I take your name, please?"

"My name? Oh, yes, it's…Rachel." That earned her an even more suspicious look, and a head tilt from the real Rachel.

"Okay, Rachel. See you soon," the woman said in a warm, friendly tone that would make anyone look forward to visiting the Thairapy Room.

"What the hell are you up to?" Rachel asked her the second she ended the call.

What *was* she up to? "Jess has to speak to me if I'm a client. She can't avoid me forever."

"But showing up at her work, Sydney. And under a false name. That's a bold move."

"If I gave my real name, she could dodge me again. I'm not showing up to embarrass her, I'm trying to make things right between us. She must be feeling awkward if she's avoiding me so much. I want her to know that she doesn't have to feel like that."

Rachel didn't look convinced, but she relented. "As long as you know what you're doing."

Sydney slipped her coat on and put an arm around her sister and squeezed. "Don't worry. It will be fine." She smiled and held her thumb and forefinger together. "And maybe a little bit fun."

That confidence had transformed into nerves by the time Sydney arrived at the Thairapy Room. She checked the time, and she had ten minutes to spare. Jess had been a mere twenty-minute walk away from the scent station the whole time. To think, Sydney had worried that she would never see her again. That seemed almost laughable now.

From the outside, the salon looked well kept. The Thairapy Room name was lit up on the black, white, and pink sign above the window. There were beautiful hanging baskets filled with flowers and greenery which hung down at either side. The window was partly frosted, with large image of a hairdryer and a pair of scissors.

Before she could change her mind, Sydney pushed through the door. A bell jingled above her head, and she was hit with a comfortable warmth—very much welcomed given the chilly October weather outside.

There were six hairdressing stations in the salon, three at each side of the room, and two more seats with sinks in the corner. Sydney stopped at a small, tidy-looking counter just a few feet from the front door.

There were three clients already seated in the salon, and two ladies who obviously worked there. There was no sign of Jess.

"Hi. Take a seat and we'll be right with you," the taller lady said with a friendly smile. Sydney recognized her voice from the phone.

"Thank you." She looked to her left and found three more seats lined up against the wall beside the front door, and she took the one on the end.

Less than a minute later, the taller lady leaned in and said something to the woman whose hair she was styling and walked toward the counter. "Now, then." She glanced at a notebook. "Rachel?"

"Um, yes." Sydney hated lying.

"Great. I'll grab Jess for you now." The lady strode toward a door at the far side of the room and poked her head through it. Sydney could just about make out her voice saying, "Your next appointment is here." She turned and flashed Sydney a smile before rejoining her client.

Seconds later Jess emerged from the room with a smile on her face which faltered the moment she clocked Sydney. She froze for a second, then continued to approach Sydney slowly. "What are you doing here?" she asked quietly when she reached her, looking around the salon to see if anyone was listening. It wasn't that big, so they probably could if they wanted to.

Sydney pointed to her head. "I heard you do haircuts. I need one."

Jess folded her arms and gave her an impatient look.

Sydney lowered her voice to a whisper. "You're avoiding me, and I wanted to talk to you."

"Here?" Jess narrowed her eyes. "Rachel."

"My sister's name." She gave a shrug and a sheepish look. "It's not like I had this well planned out or anything. I improvised."

"Well, your unplanned plan sucks because we can't do this here."

"What? You can't do my hair?" Sydney flashed her a sweet smile. "I have an appointment."

"Seriously?" Jess sighed and shook her head slowly. "Fine. Come on then." She reached over to a hook beside the counter and tugged a black gown off it. "Please just don't say anything," she whispered.

"I won't mention anything about you liking me." At Jess's horrified face she added, "Again."

Jess huffed out an annoyed breath through her nose and held the gown open.

Sydney stepped into it and felt Jess's warm breath lightly caress the back of her neck. Then Jess leaned in to position the gown around her shoulders, and Sydney could feel every soft touch of her fingertips through the thin fabric of her top. Shockwaves travelled right down her body, and Sydney had to resist shuddering at the simple pleasure of it. Under normal circumstances with anyone else, it would have been a completely innocent move that Sydney wouldn't even have blinked at. But it wasn't anyone else, and the way her body responded was a clear reminder her attraction to Jess hadn't faded. If anything, it appeared to be stronger than ever.

Jess must have noticed their close proximity too, judging by the way she practically leapt backward to put some space between them as soon as she had tied the gown. "Um. Okay, come sit over here." She quickly turned and led Sydney over to the chair furthest from everyone else in the salon.

"Do you two know each other?" the shorter of the two women asked as Sydney sat down.

"This is my new roommate," Jess said with more geniality than she probably felt in that moment.

The taller lady looked puzzled. "I thought you said that your new roommate was called Sydney."

"She is." Jess shot Sydney another glare in the mirror but played it off with a smile that was clearly for their benefit rather than Sydney's.

"I wanted to surprise her," Sydney explained to both women, who were watching her with interest. It was kind of the truth.

It seemed to appease the taller woman, who smiled. "Isn't that lovely. It's very nice to meet you, Sydney. And as Jess obviously hasn't thought to introduce us two old dears yet"—she frowned at Jess in a way that couldn't have been less threatening—"I'm Violet. And this is Pam." She indicated the smaller woman, who gave a little wave. They both seemed adorable.

"My bosses," Jess added. She fixed Sydney with a pointed stare. A second warning for Sydney to behave.

Violet shook her head. "We don't do all that boss stuff in here. We're colleagues. And friends."

"Well, it's good to meet both of you," Sydney replied.

"Likewise," the smaller one, Pam, said. They both smiled at her and continued with their clients, curiosities obviously satisfied for now.

"So," Jess said, positioning herself behind her. "What were you thinking?"

"So many things," Sydney replied.

"About your hair," Jess almost squeaked. She stared at Sydney like a deer caught in the headlights.

"Relax." Sydney grinned at her through the mirror. "Just trim the ends off."

Jess began to frown as she studied Sydney's hair.

"You'll probably have to touch it to cut it," Sydney whispered after a few more seconds of staring.

Jess glared at her again. "I was just thinking that it looks like it's already been cut recently. The ends are in perfect condition."

Sydney feigned innocence. "It has, but my usual hairdresser didn't take off as much as I wanted."

"You're unbelievable," Jess said with a shake of her head, but she dutifully lifted a chunk of Sydney's hair and started to smooth it out between her fingers.

Getting her hair cut had never felt particularly sexy, but Jess stroking through her hair with her fingers was a whole new experience. Sydney shifted uncomfortably in her seat. *Not the point of this.* "Did you enjoy the film the other night?" It was an innocent question to unknowing ears, and technically she wasn't mentioning the forbidden subject.

"It was fine," Jess replied, focussing all her attention on Sydney's hair as she measured it out between her fingers and started cutting off the ends.

"I found it really enlightening myself." That earned her another glare. If looks could kill, Sydney would have died in about seven different ways already.

"What film did you watch?" Violet asked. An indication that no conversations were private in the small salon.

When Jess didn't answer, Sydney filled her in on the action flick that they were talking about. "But I don't think Jess liked it too much. She didn't stay up to watch it until the end."

"No?" Violet asked. "Not your cup of tea, Jess?"

"I think it grabbed my interest at the start, but it didn't hold it for very long," Jess said, as she snipped away at Sydney's hair. Sydney had a feeling it was going to be a quick cut.

She chuckled at the hidden meaning in Jess's words. "You admit that you *did* like it in the beginning, though?"

Jess dropped the section of Sydney's hair that she had been holding and fumbled to pick it up again, the only slip in her composure. "I thought it was okay for an action flick. But I'm much more of a comedy girl at heart." Sydney didn't miss the ghost of a smile on Jess's face as she regained the upper hand.

"Just because you've always liked comedy doesn't mean that you couldn't find an action movie that you really enjoy. There are some good ones out there."

Jess scrunched her nose up. "I'm sure there are, but I prefer to stick to things that I already know I like, and I've always liked comedies."

"I would argue that an action film could give you so much more excitement and exhilaration than some comedy that you've already seen a hundred times. Maybe you're just used to it."

"And I would argue that, yes, although comedy might be a safer and more comfortable choice, it's the one that makes me most happy."

"Does it really make you happy though?"

"Yes," Jess snapped.

"I'm not totally sure that it does," Sydney threw back at her.

"And I don't think it's any of your business. I—"

Someone cleared their throat and Sydney and Jess both turned to see Violet, Pam, and the other three clients all watching them intently.

Pam in particular looked utterly amused. "I don't think I've ever seen such a passionate movie genre debate."

"You should see us when we discuss music." Sydney mimicked an explosion going off and everyone laughed. Well, almost everyone. Jess didn't seem to see the funny side.

Violet shrugged. "I like a good thriller myself."

"Or anything with Denzel," Pam said.

"Ooh. Now you're talking." Violet's eyes lit up, and the women all giggled away to themselves in agreement.

Jess still looked somewhat startled, and Sydney started to feel bad. "Maybe we can talk more about cinema choices at home. Tonight?"

"Fine." Jess shook out Sydney's hair and measured the ends against one another. She took a couple more snips with the scissors and stood back. "We're about done here anyway."

Sydney checked her reflection in the mirror. "I love it. Thank you."

"I didn't exactly do much," Jess said with a look that said *obviously.*

Sydney stood up and removed the gown herself to give her overly eager libido a break from Jess's innocent yet highly effective touch. She passed it to Jess, who then led the way back to the counter. "It was lovely to meet you," Sydney said as she walked past Violet and Pam.

"And you, Sydney," Violet said.

"Please, come back and see us again. Anytime," Pam added.

"How much do I owe you?" Sydney asked Jess when they reached the counter.

"Don't worry, I've got you covered. I practically did nothing." Sydney went to argue, and Jess stopped her. "Honestly, it's fine. I'll see you in a couple of hours. We can talk then." Jess hovered for a few seconds like she was going to say something else, but then she muttered a quick *bye* and scurried back into the salon area.

Sydney offered a final wave before she left. She didn't know what she would do while she waited for Jess to get home, but she definitely wasn't in the mood for comedy.

❖

"Vi, have we got a knife?" Pam asked.

Violet looked up from the appointment book on the counter,

glasses perched halfway down her nose as usual. Violet always ended the day by studying the next day's appointments. Pam was brushing up, and Jess was tidying, putting everything back in its designated place. "There's probably a knife in the kitchen, why?"

"I could have used one earlier. That's all," Pam replied.

"What for?" Violet asked.

"To cut through all that sexual tension in the room when Jess's friend was here."

Jess snapped her head round. "Sexual tension? Me? With Sydney? You're out of your mind."

"Am I?" Pam held the brush up and leaned on it. "Then why were you so twitchy?"

Jess scoffed. "I was not twitchy."

"Vi?"

Violet gave her an apologetic look. "You were a little bit twitchy."

"Have been ever since too," Pam said.

Jess threw her hands up. "I'm not twitchy and there wasn't any sexual tension. Sydney and I hardly even know each other. She's my roommate, for crying out loud. And did I mention, she's a she."

"Well, *she* was certainly into you." Pam waggled her eyebrows at Violet. "Did you see her looking at Jess like she was some kind of snack?"

"I don't think I would put it quite like that, Pam." Violet pursed her lips. "But I did notice the odd look of longing."

Jess wrapped a cord around one of the hairdryers, pretending not to look as interested in that as she felt. "Really? There were looks?"

Violet nodded and looked back down at the appointment book. "From both of you."

Jess dropped the hairdryer, and it clattered on the floor. She quickly bent to pick it up again and checked it wasn't broken. It wasn't, thankfully.

"See?" Pam said smugly. "I'm not wrong about this. We might be old, young lady, but we recognize desire when we see it."

"Old and senile more like," Jess muttered.

"Watch it, you," Pam said, pointing the floor brush at her.

"Oh no. Not the brush." Jess held her hands up. "Please! Don't attack." Jess and Pam winding each other up was nothing new. It was part of their dynamic. Violet's role was more like the slightly disapproving aunt who secretly found it all very amusing and triumphed over them both with her clever one-liners when she decided to get involved.

"Take it back, then," Pam said, keeping the brush raised.

"You take back all this nonsense about sexual tension," Jess countered.

"Can't do that. I saw what I saw."

"Well, I don't know what either of you *thought* you saw, but I was not looking longingly at Sydney, and I doubt she was looking at me like that either."

"What was that whole fiasco over the film about then?" Pam never did let things go easily. "I know a coded conversation when I hear one."

"Coded conversation? Who do you think I am? Jane Bond? It was a disagreement over movie preferences. Nothing more." Jess held her palms up. "Sorry to disappoint."

"If you say so," Pam said, lowering the brush. "But don't expect me to believe you."

"Enough, you two. If Jess wants to keep her head in the clouds about the pretty young woman, then that's up to her," Violet said. "I myself thought Sydney seemed very nice. As a roommate, or a friend, or whatever. I don't see the problem."

"There is no problem. She is nice," Jess agreed.

"Then why were you so prickly?" Violet asked.

"It was because of the *sexual tension*," Pam said slowly, emphasising her point again.

Jess let out an irritated sigh. "I wasn't prickly, and can you *stop* with the sexual tension?" Her phone rang and she held it up. "Oh, look. It's my *boyfriend* calling." She swiped to answer it. "Hey. I've been thinking about you."

"Overcompensating," Pam mumbled.

Jess gave her a dirty look and turned her back to continue tidying. She held the phone up to her ear with her shoulder as she pulled some hair out of one of the hairbrushes.

"What exactly have you been thinking?" Austin said in a suggestive tone.

"Now, that would be telling," Jess said with a soft laugh. From the background noise, she could tell he was driving. "Are you finished work already? What time are you coming over?" Jess had hoped to get

THE ROOMMATE

the conversation with Sydney out of the way before he arrived. Usually, he didn't finish work for at least a couple more hours.

"Um…" Nothing else followed, which was never a good sign.

"Austin?"

"I, um, I don't think I'll be able to make it tonight, babe."

Another cancellation. Why was Jess not surprised? "Uh-huh. Why?"

"I know we had plans, but I said that I would go out with a couple of the guys from work. Some of the higher-ups are going too. I couldn't say no."

She sighed.

"I know, you probably want to kill me. But I knew that we weren't doing anything major and—"

"That doesn't matter. It's all the time, Austin."

"I know, I know. I'm just so desperate to impress that I say yes to everything. It's pathetic, really." He let out a self-deprecating laugh.

"Look, I get it. I really do. You want to look good." Supportive girlfriend box ticked. "I just wish you were as committed to our relationship as you are to this job." Reality check box ticked.

"Don't say that, babe. You know that I'm doing all of this for us. For future us."

"But it's really starting to affect present us, don't you think?"

She could hear his sigh loud and clear. "You know what? I'll cancel. I'll come over."

Jess wanted him to come and see her because he wanted to, not because he had to. Plus, she didn't want to be *that* girlfriend. "No, it's fine." She needed to sort things with Sydney anyway. "Just, please keep it in mind and try a bit harder from now on."

"You're the best, babe. And I will. You have my word," Austin said in a noticeably brighter voice.

"Okay. Well, enjoy your night with the guys."

"Will do, babe."

Jess hung up the call. *Bloody typical Austin.* When she turned back around, Violet was giving the appointment book her full concentration, and Pam was brushing the same spot on the floor repeatedly. They were such bad actresses, Jess had to laugh. "I think that's clean now, Pam." She snuck up behind Violet. "And July was quite a while ago. We're in October now."

"I was just checking something," Violet said, her pitch raising a couple of octaves.

"Well, I was listening into your conversation," Pam said as she threw the brush into the cupboard. "He let you down? Again?"

Jess nodded. "It's fine. Well, it's not, but..." She shrugged.

Violet reached forward and gave her forearm a squeeze. She smiled sympathetically.

"I'm fine." Jess reached for her jacket. "I'll see you both tomorrow?" They went through their usual end of day routine with hugs and goodbyes.

Just before she opened the door to leave, she heard Pam say, "I bet Sydney wouldn't cancel plans."

Jess gave Pam another look and threw the door open to leave. Sydney was next on her list of things to deal with.

❖

When Jess reached home, she stormed into the house both dreading the impending conversation and looking forward to getting it over with. No matter how hard she tried, she couldn't hide from the truth forever. And maybe once everything was out in the open, Jess would finally be able to move on.

She found Sydney waiting for her in the living room. She jumped to her feet as soon as Jess walked in.

"Is Chloe here?" Jess checked. Because they couldn't do this in front of her.

Sydney shook her head. "She's still at work. Jess, I'm—"

Jess held a hand up to stop her. "What was that?"

Sydney looked surprised. Like she wasn't expecting Jess to be as irritated as she was. "You wouldn't speak to me. I had to do something."

"So, you thought it was a good idea to come to my work? Where everyone listens in to every little detail of every conversation?" Jess exhaled loudly. "We live in the same house. Do you not think this would be a better place to have a private conversation? *In private?*"

"That's been a bit hard to do when you've been avoiding me like the plague. I've been trying to talk to you ever since the other night."

"We would have run into each other eventually. Could you not have waited? Did you *have to* confront me at work? Now I've got Violet and Pam on my back about this…apparent"—Jess gestured between them—"sexual tension between us."

"And what does that tell you?" Sydney said. "There is something between us, Jess, whether you want to admit it or not. Why didn't you just tell me that you felt it too? Why did you lie?"

"Because I *can't* feel something for you, Sydney," she said, becoming exasperated. "I have a boyfriend, or did you forget that part?"

"Oh, believe me, I could never forget about him, especially after that excellent display he made of himself the other night."

"What does *that* mean?"

Sydney opened her mouth to speak and closed it again. She held a hand up. "Never mind. I shouldn't have said that."

"No, go on. Say whatever it is you want to say." They might as well put all their cards on the table.

Jess braced herself for a full-scale attack, but then Sydney looked at her and softened. "Why are you with him, Jess?"

That question, coming from Sydney, in the almost compassionate way that she asked it felt like a thump right in the middle of Jess's chest. Especially when Austin's latest let-down was still so fresh. And the biggest problem was that Jess didn't have a straightforward answer to give. "Because…I…" She honestly didn't know why lately. "You know what? It's none of your business." *Oh, yeah. Great response, Jess. Very convincing.*

Sydney remained undeterred. "I know it's not," she said gently. "But I can't wrap my head around it. I don't understand how you can be with a guy who treats you like that. Some of the things that he said to you the other night were bang out of order."

Jess folded her arms. "He's not always like that." At least, he didn't used to be.

"But he is sometimes?" Sydney pushed.

"Look, Austin's a good guy. He is. And besides that, who I choose to be in a relationship with is irrelevant. The point is, I *am* in one, and that's what we need to remember." *That's right, Jess. Deflect from the issue like you always do.*

"Right." Sydney nodded in reluctant acceptance. "Consider it etched into my brain."

"Good." Now she just sounded like a petulant child. She cringed internally.

"Look, can we sit down for a second?" Sydney asked calmly.

Jess hadn't realized until then that they were both still standing in the middle of the living room looking like they were about to go ten rounds. "Sure."

"We still need to talk about the thing that Chloe said." Sydney said quietly once they sat on the sofa.

Did they really? Jess thought they had been skirting around it rather nicely. "As I'm sure you guessed already, Chloe doesn't know that it was you on the train that day. I'd rather keep it that way. I don't want things to get awkward."

Sydney gave her a look.

"Any more awkward than they already are," Jess corrected.

"I won't say anything. But we still need to talk about it."

"Does it really matter? It won't make any difference."

"Yeah, it does matter to me," Sydney said. "I want to understand what's been going on between us."

There was no way of avoiding the truth. Jess hated the fact that she had lied to Sydney in the first place. "Fine. I was attracted to you, okay?" There. She'd said it. And as far as Jess was aware, the world still seemed to be spinning.

"You could have told me."

"No, I couldn't have, because see"—Jess pointed—"see that hopeful face you're giving me? Now I have to crush it."

"Why?"

"Because I do, Sydney. Because I have a life that I happen to like, and whether you like him or not, I have Austin. So I can't even think about you and me, let alone do anything about it," she said.

"But when we met?" Sydney's voice trailed off then, like she didn't even see any point in asking.

"Yes. I liked you," Jess said truthfully. "And for a brief moment, yeah, I wondered..." She could feel her face burning up at the admission, but she continued, "But you need to understand, that brief moment should never have happened." She closed her eyes and lowered her voice almost to a whisper. "And honestly, I've been struggling with it since. That's why I lied to you about it before. I think I was trying to lie to myself too."

"Struggling? In what way?"

"In lots of ways. Guilt. Confusion. Shock. Those feelings

happening out of the blue threw me for a complete loop. I've been questioning everything, including myself. But after the train, I didn't think I would see you again, so I thought I could let it go. That the feelings and questions would fade away until I forgot about them and got on with my life as normal. Then you showed up here, and I had no idea how to handle it. So, right or wrong, I tried to hide how I felt—like if I pretended my feelings didn't exist that they would magically disappear."

Sydney nodded slowly. She seemed to take a few moments to take it in before she spoke again. "You know, it was a shock for me too. I had no idea you lived here when I took the room."

"I know." Jess had never thought otherwise.

"And since we're being honest with each other, I should probably tell you that it wasn't an unpleasant shock for me. I'd thought about you a lot since that day. I was really happy to see you. I still am."

Jess felt a twinge of guilt at that. She had been obsessing so much over her own feelings she hadn't really stopped to consider Sydney's. Jess had gone about this all wrong, from start to finish. Not her finest behaviour by a long shot. "It wasn't that I was *un*happy to see you. Not at all. Just a bit…thrown."

"And what about now? Is me living here going to be a problem for you?" Sydney's blue eyes were big and expressive, and Jess could tell she was worried about the answer.

"No. Of course not," she said immediately to put her at ease. "I never meant to make you feel like you weren't welcome. This is a total me problem. It's not you. And I'll get over it. Like I said, it was a shock, and I guess I'm still adjusting."

Jess couldn't tell if Sydney was disappointed or relieved. Maybe a mixture of the two. "But our feelings…if we both still have them—"

"Nothing can happen between us," Jess stated firmly. She stood up before Sydney could argue or question her. She had done all the explaining she could do, and she was more than ready to make her escape to the safe solitude of her bedroom. "We're roommates. We have to leave it at that."

CHAPTER EIGHT

"Good morning, Sydney," Chloe said chirpily from her spot at the kitchen table as Sydney entered the room.

"Morning, Chlo."

"You look really nice in that top." Chloe cast her eyes down to Sydney's black top, then back up, and grinned.

"Oh." Sydney looked down. "Thanks. I got it online. I'll WhatsApp you the link if you want." She rounded the corner to get to her coffee machine and almost bumped right slap bang into Jess. "Oh, sorry, I didn't know you were there." She offered a friendly smile. "Good morning."

Jess gave a tight smile and a polite "Morning."

Sydney gestured the empty cup she was holding. "Do you want me to make you some coffee?"

Jess blinked and looked down at it. "Oh. No, thank you."

"You sure? I'm making some for myself anyway. Or I can make you tea if you'd prefer? Green tea?" Sydney hadn't forgotten Jess's preferences.

"You know, I actually didn't realize the time." Jess set the cup down on the counter. "I better get going. I told Violet I'd be at work early today."

"To, what? Count shampoos?" Chloe asked.

"Ha ha, very funny." Jess walked over and kissed the top of Chloe's head. "I'll see you later, smartass. Have a good day." She glanced back over at Sydney and gave her another tight smile before she turned and rushed out of the kitchen.

Sydney sighed as she pressed the button to spark Beanie into action. It had been like that between them ever since their talk a couple of weeks ago. They spent little to no time together, Jess either opting for her bedroom when she was home, or Sydney staying in hers to give Jess some space. Anytime they did find themselves in the same room together, they exchanged polite pleasantries and nothing more. Well, Jess didn't offer anything beyond that. Sydney sometimes did try to extend their interactions, but the result was always much like it had been this morning, with Jess quickly coming up with excuses to leave. "Do you want coffee, Chlo?"

"I've already helped myself." She sipped from her cup and let out a long, satisfied *aah*. "God, I love Beanie."

Sydney laughed. "She's my pride and joy." She waited for her own coffee to finish pouring.

"Speaking of joy," Chloe said, "or should I say, lack thereof? What the hell's going on with you and Jess?"

"What do you mean?" Sydney asked, acting as if she had zero clue what Chloe was referring to.

Chloe pinned her with a sceptical look. "Come on. You must have noticed that anytime you walk into a room, Jess can't get out of it fast enough."

"She said she had to work."

"Right. And last night she had to catch up on her washing. The day before she had to go out for milk when there was already plenty in the fridge. I know because I checked. She's started going to the gym more than I've ever known her to. And Jess bloody hates the gym. Calls it a necessary evil."

Sydney forced out a chuckle. "Maybe she's just keeping herself busy. Some people go through phases like that."

Chloe narrowed her eyes, studying her. "No. There's more to it than that. Have you had some kind of disagreement or something?"

"I can't think of anything," Sydney lied. She took a long sip from her cup to avoid Chloe's stare. "Maybe we just don't click."

"That's what's so strange about it. Jess gets along with everyone she meets."

"There's a first for everything."

"Hmm." Chloe tapped her fingertips on the table. "I'm worried that it might be my fault."

"How would it be your fault?"

"Because she's been acting strangely around you ever since I let it slip about that woman she fancied." Chloe gritted her teeth. "A perfect example of why I should never drink too much gin."

Sydney laughed it off. "None of us should."

"But she was fine with me after, so I don't know why she would be acting off with you. Embarrassed maybe?" Chloe chewed her lip. "I don't know."

"If you think Jess is uncomfortable with me living here, maybe I should look around for a different place." The thought had been in the back of Sydney's mind ever since Jess and she had talked.

Yes, Sydney liked the house and all the touches she had made to her room. She liked the neighbourhood, the location, and that it was easy travel distance to both her work and her sister's place. And she liked her roommates—both of them. Chloe had quickly become someone she would call a friend, and even though things currently weren't good between Jess and her, she still wanted the chance to be around her. To get to know her. But not if that was at the expense of Jess's happiness. If Jess didn't want her there, then Sydney would leave.

"Don't even say that," Chloe said, wrapping her fingers around her cup. "For starters, you can't take Beanie away from me."

"You could visit Beanie in my new place."

Chloe stuck her fingers in her ears. "Stop. I'm not listening to you talk about new places. You're not leaving."

"But Jess clearly doesn't want to be around me—"

"So, you *did* notice. I knew it." Chloe gave Sydney a self-satisfied look. She shuffled forward in her chair. "Look, I'll speak to Jess. I'll threaten her with the naked guy coming to live here if she doesn't start playing nice. That should solve it."

"Naked guy?"

Chloe waved her off. "You don't want to know. My point is, you're staying. I like you living here. In fact, I…I like you, full stop."

Sydney would have thought it was a simple, friendly statement if Chloe's cheeks hadn't turned such a deep shade of pink. Chloe liked her? If anything, that made the situation even more complicated. "Aww, thanks, Chlo. I like you too, you're a good friend," she replied tactfully.

If her response disappointed Chloe, she didn't show it. "Yeah. That's what I mean, you are too." She cleared her throat. "So, you can't leave. Jess will come round, just give it some time."

Nice dodge. Sydney nodded. "I'll give it a bit longer, but if she doesn't want me here, maybe we'll have to revisit the idea of me moving out again. I like it here, but the last thing I want is to make anyone feel awkward."

"It'll not come to that," Chloe insisted.

Of course, Sydney knew there was more to the story. Which meant that it could very well come to that. But she hoped it didn't. "We'll see. For now, though, I have a favour to ask."

"Shoot."

"My nephew, Ben, has been begging me for a sleepover ever since I moved in. Would you mind if he comes to stay at the weekend? I'll check with Jess too."

"Sydney, this is your home too. You don't need to ask us for permission. We'd be happy to have him stay."

"Great. He'll be so excited." And to be honest, Sydney was excited to spend some time with him. She had missed seeing his little face every day.

But Sydney tried not to dwell on the fact that it might be their first and last sleepover in her new house. How had she got everything so wrong?

❖

"But why did you give her your credit card, Dad?" Jess pinched the bridge of her nose. "You must have had some idea that something like this was going to happen. Gretchen's obsessed with expensive things. Look at your honeymoon!" She refrained from adding *That's why I call her Gretchen the Gold-digger*. Probably better to leave that part out rather than kicking her dad while he was down.

"I told her to treat herself to something new to wear. I didn't tell her to buy out the whole bloody shop." Jess could imagine her dad pacing frantically, waving his arms about while he was talking to her.

He might have been shocked. Jess, however, was not in the least bit surprised to learn of Gretchen's latest spending spree.

Jess fumbled around in her bag for her keys. She would at least try to *sound* sympathetic, even though she had warned her dad about stuff like this a million times already.

"That was very kind of you, Dad. But maybe you're going to have to ease up on the gifts for a while. You've been more than generous already."

"But what if she gets bored of me?" he asked, suddenly sounding vulnerable.

"If she has to max out your credit cards to remain interested in you, then I think that speaks for itself." Jess found her key and let herself in through her front door.

"What's that supposed to mean?"

He knew exactly what Jess meant. Sometimes she wondered which one of them was the child and which was the parent. She kicked her shoes off at the bottom of the stairs and padded into the living room. "I just mean that—"

She stopped. A child looked up at her from the middle of the living room floor. A boy, with big dark eyes and floppy, dark blond hair. She glanced around, but there was no one else around.

"Dad, I have to go. I'll call you back later." Jess hung up despite the sound of his protests. She could deal with him later. "Hi there," she said to the boy.

He blinked a few times and stared up at her in silence.

Okay. Um… "I'm Jess. What's your name?" she tried.

He grinned then. "Are you the hairdresser?"

He knew who she was? Why didn't she know who he was? "Yes. I mean, I'm not sure if I'm *the* hairdresser, but I am a hairdresser."

"Cool. I'm Ben. Do you want to watch TV with me?"

Jess glanced at the cartoon on the screen. "What are you watching?"

Ben looked at her like she was stupid. "Pokémon."

Obviously. Silly Jess. She'd heard of it, but she had never had the pleasure of watching it. "Is there a grown-up here with you?" That seemed like a nice way of asking who the heck the kid belonged to.

"She's getting snacks from the kitchen. You can share them, but you have to sit still to watch TV. That's the rule."

That sounded reasonable, but still didn't clear up who Ben was. Jess was sure that after all this time she would know if Chloe had a relation called Ben, so she ruled that out. That left Sydney. Or else there was an intruder in their kitchen. "Who's getting snacks?"

Judging by the look on his face, Ben was clearly unimpressed that Jess wasn't keeping up. "My Aunt Sydney."

Ah, *Aunt* Sydney. That made sense. "I see. Well, I don't want to interrupt you and your Aunt Sydney's, um, Pokémon time. Thank you for offering, though."

"Is it because you don't like my Aunt Sydney?"

"What? Why would you think that?"

"Because I heard my Aunt Sydney tell my mum that you don't like her very much."

"She said that?"

He nodded and made a show of thinking about it. "She said that you can't stand to be in rooms with her, and that my mum shouldn't be surprised if Aunt Sydney has to move back in with us." He shrugged. "I really hope she does move in with us again, because I miss her."

"Oh." Sydney was considering moving out? That was news.

It wasn't that Jess couldn't stand to be in the same room as Sydney, she just didn't know how to act around her. Especially after recent events. But Jess thought she had at least managed to keep things civil between them. "Well, I'm not sure why she said that, but I like your Aunt Sydney just fine."

"Then why don't you want to watch TV with us?"

"It's not that I don't want to, I, um—"

"Okay, we've got jellybeans, jelly babies, fizzy strawberries, chocolate buttons, and some kind of cheesy crisps." Sydney walked into the room with her arms filled with bags of snacks. "Oh, hey," she said when she saw Jess.

"Hey," she replied.

"Yes!" Ben raced over and pulled some of the bags from Sydney's arms. "I want all of them."

"Take your time, buddy. Just pick one for now. You don't want to make yourself sick." Ben clearly had selective hearing because he threw himself on the sofa and immediately started to tear open all the bags.

Sydney shook her head at Jess and smiled. "I take it you've already met Ben, then."

Jess smiled back. She obviously needed to work on being friendlier. "I have. I didn't know you had a nephew."

"There are a lot of things you don't know about me." Sydney gave her a charming grin.

See, it was smiles like that one that made Jess want to grab Sydney's face and kiss her into next Tuesday and all kinds of inconvenient thoughts. That's why Jess had felt it was imperative to avoid Sydney and not linger in the same room all the time, torturing herself. If they were only going to be roommates, she needed to steer clear of that smile. This newfound inner lesbian of hers could not be trusted to behave.

"He's very cute," Jess said, sticking to the safe topic of Ben and purposely not addressing anything to do with Sydney's flirtatious comment.

"Way too cute. Makes him impossible to say no to." Sydney looked at him fondly as he tore into the sweets. "You don't mind him being here, do you? I cleared it with Chloe, but I didn't get a chance to check with you."

"No, of course not. This is your home," Jess said. "This *is* your home now, isn't it?"

Sydney gave her a questioning look.

Jess glanced at Ben to see if he was listening, but he seemed engrossed in the TV show and jellybeans. She lowered her voice anyway. "Is it true that you might be moving out?"

The flicker of recognition on Sydney's face confirmed it. "It might have crossed my mind."

"Because of me?"

Sydney gave her a sheepish look and shrugged. "I don't want to make you feel uncomfortable."

"Sydney, I don't want you to move out." Jess hoped she sounded as adamant as she felt about it.

"No?"

"No. Not even slightly." And she meant it. The thought of Sydney not living there anymore left a sinking feeling in the pit of her stomach.

"I know you said that, but I thought maybe you were just being nice, and it would be easier if I left and—"

"Sydney. No." Jess regarded her seriously. "Stay."

Sydney studied her face for a few seconds then nodded. "Okay."

"What are you two whispering about?" Ben asked loudly, breaking into what had probably been the sincerest moment between them since Sydney had moved in.

"If you were supposed to know, then we wouldn't be whispering," Sydney said to him playfully. "Nosy."

He stuck his tongue out at her, and Jess couldn't help but laugh.

Then he said, "I asked Jess why she doesn't like you," like it was the most casual thing in the world.

Sydney gaped at him. "Ben!" She turned to Jess. "Don't listen to him."

"She said she does like you," Ben said with a shrug. "I asked her to watch TV with us, but she said no." He shoved a handful of jellybeans into his mouth. This must have been what people meant when they said that kids have no filter.

"I wouldn't want to intrude," Jess explained so that Sydney didn't think she was being unfriendly.

"Don't be silly. You're welcome to join us."

"Yeah, come watch TV with us," Ben mumbled with his mouth full of sweets. "Pleeease, Jess." He smiled, revealing a gap in his front teeth which only added to the cuteness.

"I see what you mean about him being hard to say no to," Jess said to Sydney. She threw her hands up and let them fall to her sides. "Okay, I can stay and watch for a little bit."

"Yay!" Ben shouted, bouncing enthusiastically up and down on the sofa. He patted the spot beside him. "Come on, Jess. You can sit beside me, and I'll tell you all the Pokémon that are my favourite."

"Lucky you," Sydney said to her with a sly grin.

Jess laughed. "I don't mind. I've never had a Pokémon education before."

Sydney took a seat on the armchair beside them. "Well, you're sure about to get educated now."

Wasn't that the truth. They made it through four episodes, or had it been five? Jess had lost count. But Jess certainly wasn't a novice after that. "And they're huge rivals? Right?" she asked him about the two characters on the screen.

"The biggest," Ben said, his eyes still glued to the TV.

Jess glanced over at Sydney, who had a massive grin on her face. "What?"

"Nothing," she said, but her grin grew bigger.

Jess squinted at her. "Sorry? Are you amused by my newfound interest?"

"That. And a touch relieved that I'm not the one getting tortured today."

"Hey!" But Ben started to giggle. "At least Jess doesn't forget all the names like *somebody* does." He rested his head on Jess's shoulder. "I'm glad you're here, Jess. You can hang out with us all the time. Can't she, Aunt Sydney?"

Jess melted on the spot.

"Yeah, she definitely can." And that, paired with the soft smile Sydney gave her, made Jess's heart turn from melted to pure mush.

Ben suddenly jumped up off the sofa. "I've got the best idea in the whole wide world." He ran over to Sydney and cupped his hand around her ear to whisper something.

"I don't know, buddy," Sydney said. "She might be busy."

"But can I ask her? Please?"

Jess had a feeling that she was that *her.*

"You can ask," Sydney said.

Ben immediately raced back over to Jess. He bounced on his heels in front of her, a sweep of blond hair covering his left eye. "Jess. Are you busy next weekend?"

Jess made a show of thinking about it. "Well, that depends. Which day next weekend?"

Ben turned back to Sydney. "Which day," he whispered loudly. Jess couldn't help but chuckle.

"Sunday," Sydney whispered back.

He turned back to Jess. "Sunday," he said confidently.

"Hmm." Jess made a show of thinking about it. "You know, as it happens, I don't think I am busy on Sunday."

Ben's beaming smile confirmed that she had answered correctly. "Do you want to come to the zoo with us? Aunt Sydney is taking me for my birthday treat. It was only s'posed to be me and her, but I want you to come too."

"The zoo, huh?" Jess automatically thought back to her zoo conversation with Sydney on the day they met. Judging by the knowing smile on Sydney's face, she had too. Allowing herself memories of that day was dangerous. Maybe it wasn't such a good idea after all. "Perhaps your Aunt Sydney just wants it to be you and her that day. If it's for your birthday treat."

"No, I'd like it if you came with us," Sydney said. "I mean, only if you want to," she added quickly.

Between Ben's pout and Sydney's hopeful face, Jess was well and truly screwed. "I guess I'm going to the zoo, then."

CHAPTER NINE

A re you sure she's coming?" Ben asked, gripping Sydney's hand tightly in anticipation as they made their way toward the zoo entrance. "I don't see her."

Sydney quietly laughed to herself. It seemed she wasn't the only one whom Jess had made an impression on. "She's coming. She said she would meet us at the gate." Secretly, Sydney was just as eager to spend time with Jess, but luckily, she was much better at playing it cool.

"Where is the gate?" Ben asked impatiently.

"Just a little bit further." Sydney craned her neck to see if she could see it.

She had to admit, she had been surprised when Jess had agreed to go with them. Sydney suspected that it was more for Ben's benefit than for hers, but whatever. She would take whatever she could get.

And thank the heavens, things had been better in the house all that week too.

It wasn't that Sydney and Jess had spent a lot of time together—mainly because Sydney had either been working or helping Rachel get ready for Ben's surprisingly high-maintenance birthday, which had gone down yesterday without a hiccup. But any time she and Jess had ended up in the same room, things had been way more amicable than before. Jess didn't up and leave, for starters. Dare Sydney say that some of their exchanges had even bordered on friendly?

Even Chloe had noticed the new and improved, harmonious household. Long may it continue for all of them.

"Are we there yet?" Ben asked. That old cliché.

"Nearly." Were they? Yes, Sydney could make out the entrance now.

She automatically reached up to fix her hair with her free hand, then scoffed at herself. There was no point in trying to impress Jess, was there? Jess had made it abundantly clear that nothing was ever going to happen between them. At best, they would become friends, and Sydney didn't need to fix her hair or look particularly good for friends. Though she may have overlooked that when she changed her outfit four times that morning, eventually settling on the jeans that she knew made her bum look good.

God, navigating a crush on an unavailable straight girl wasn't easy.

What made it even more difficult was how unbelievably hot Jess looked leaning against the railings waiting for them. No one had any right to look that good.

"There she is," Ben shouted excitedly. He whipped his hand away from Sydney's and took off running toward Jess.

Sydney held back and gave herself a moment. Just a couple of breaths to steady herself, and then she followed.

Jess was already smiling and laughing with Ben as she approached. She looked up at Sydney and their eyes met, and for just a second everything stopped. Jess's dark gaze bored into hers, her freshly glossed lips parted slightly. Dark hair hung loosely around her face like its whole reason for existing was to frame the sheer perfection of it. Maybe Jess had styled it that way on purpose. Her outfit was simple—tight black jeans, white T-shirt, black leather jacket, grey scarf—the result was not.

She looked incredible, but Sydney wasn't going to focus on that part. She wasn't going to let her crush sabotage a potential friendship between them.

That meant that she also refused to wonder what Jess was thinking as she blatantly looked Sydney up and down, giving her a once over of her own.

Sydney put on her game face. "Well, hello there." No interest here. Nope. Just a friend greeting a friend.

"Hello back." Jess beamed. She held a hand up to shield her eyes from the winter sun.

It did seem extra bright that day. That wasn't a complaint. Any sunshine was a welcome change from their usual rainy November weather. But Sydney was glad she had remembered to bring sunglasses so she didn't have to squint all day.

That, and they made it easier to sneak glances at Jess without getting caught.

Just because she couldn't be with Jess didn't mean she couldn't look at her, did it? It was like being on a diet but still being allowed to look at the menu.

Ben tugged on the sleeve of Jess's jacket, hurrying her to go in. Jess broke eye contact with Sydney to smile down at him. "Well, someone's excited."

"I heard that sometimes you get to see the zookeepers feed the lions," he gushed. "Do you think we'll see that?"

"Let's hope so. Failing that, I hear the penguins are always up to all sorts." Jess shot Sydney a grin.

It was the first time Jess hadn't shied away from referencing the day they met. Their platonic relationship really was progressing, though the platonic part remained a pity.

"Let's not forget about the philandering monkeys," Sydney added.

"What does phil-an-der-ing mean?" Ben asked, drawing the word out slowly.

Jess looked at her, covering her mouth with her hand to hide her smile, which turned into a laugh when Sydney gave her a panicked look back. The shaking shoulders gave her away.

"Um…" Sydney paused to think.

"I think it kind of means mischievous." Thank goodness for Jess and her quicker brain than Sydney's.

Sydney looked at her gratefully and nodded. "Yes. That's exactly what it means."

Before Ben could ask them to elaborate or come up with any more questions, Sydney ushered them forward to join the short queue at the ticket desk.

Sydney bought all three of them their tickets, ignoring Jess's protests. "Today was my treat for Ben, remember?"

"Yeah, but that didn't originally include me."

Sydney leaned in and lowered her voice. "You'll just have to find a way to make it up to me." She purposefully walked away without waiting for a response, amused enough by the dumbfounded look she had left on Jess's face.

Maybe she could still have a little fun, even with the friend thing.

It didn't take Jess long to catch up, and they all gathered around the map that Ben had insisted on being in charge of. Sydney didn't mind one bit. She hated carrying those things around. Unfolding it, studying it, folding it back up, putting it in her pocket. Only to need it again two minutes later. No thanks.

Rather than following the recommended route, Ben decided to make up his own. It would likely take longer, but Ben would make sure that they didn't miss anything, even though it meant that they would be zigzagging all over the place to take it all in.

Rachel probably would have taken control of the map and insisted on the recommended route if she were there, but she was fun Aunt Sydney, and this was Ben's day.

He gleefully informed them that their first stop was going to be the farm animals, and they headed that way.

"Jess, come and feed the horses." Jess didn't seem to have much choice in the matter, with Ben pulling her by the hand, but she also didn't seem to mind. Jess was good with Ben. Another box ticked in her favour.

"What about me?" Sydney called after them, feigning offense.

Ben turned back and tilted his head at her. "Obviously, I want you to come too. You don't need an invite. You're my favourite Aunt Sydney. We're besties."

Okay. Ben's innocent charm won her over as usual. Sydney smiled and trudged along behind them ready to feed some animals. She was glad she had opted for a pair of her older trainers as she stomped through the mucky ground.

They took turns at feeding and playing with all kinds of different farm animals. The lambs were Sydney's favourites, jumping and skipping around in their field.

Ben was highly entertained by a pig who was putting on an excellent show rolling around in the mud and hay.

And Jess got very attached to a baby chick which had curled up into a tiny ball in her hand. She had been reluctant to put it down again, so Sydney suggested they spend an extra few minutes there.

What was the rush?

Sydney took her phone out a few times to snap some photos. It was shaping up to be a day she knew she would want to look back on. Significant somehow.

While Ben quizzed one of the zookeepers about every animal in the farm exhibit, Sydney and Jess stopped to wait for him by the gate. They leaned over the bars, side by side.

"He's so adorable," Jess said, watching him intently.

"I'm sure that guy won't think so by the time he finishes answering thirty-five questions about cows." Sydney chuckled. "His mum will be happy, though, when he comes home having learned a bunch of new facts."

"What about his dad?" Jess asked. "Neither of you have mentioned him."

"Not in the picture. He never was. The asshole took off the minute he heard Rachel was pregnant with Ben." Sydney hated even thinking about him.

"That's terrible."

Terrible was one word for it. "Some men really suck."

"Yeah, I can't argue with that. They really do," Jess agreed wistfully, her tone implying that she wasn't only referring to Ben's non-existent father. Her head shot round in panic when she realized that she might have revealed too much. "I mean…pretend I didn't say that. Some men are great." But it was too late to save the statement.

Sydney grinned at her. "I can pretend, but you definitely did." Maybe Jess didn't think Austin was all sunshine and roses after all. That's what Sydney took out of it.

How interesting.

"Anyway," Jess said pointedly, moving on from her slip-up. "It's his loss. The dad's. Ben's a really great kid."

"Yeah, he is." Sydney looked over at him. Her heart swelled up with love and pride like it always did.

Eventually, when Ben ran out of questions, they did move on from the farm, slowly making their way around all the different exhibits.

"Whoa," Ben said when they reached the lion enclosure. His jaw dropped as he watched the huge, majestic animals through the safety glass. "He's so cool."

"At least the enclosure isn't tiny," Jess said quietly beside Sydney.

Sydney nodded her agreement. "It's the pro versus con thing about zoos, isn't it? Con, even a massive enclosure can never compare to these animal's natural environments. Not even slightly."

"Yep. But pro, they do help in conserving endangered species that wouldn't survive otherwise. Some of these animals need protection. From humans especially."

"Exactly." She paused. "I don't agree with whales in tanks, though. Not under any circumstance." Not that there were any whales at the zoo, but it was something that Sydney was passionately against. She used to watch *Free Willy* all the time as a kid, and it had stuck with her for life.

"God no. Me either."

They looked at each other in acknowledgement that they were both on the same page. It was a pity they weren't on the same page about other stuff. Specifically about each other.

Their day together wasn't doing much to tamp down Sydney's feelings. If anything, they had intensified once again. But she nudged that thought away.

"I think we'll go to the penguins next," Ben said. He whipped out his map and studied it again. "There's an underwater viewing tank."

Sydney smiled at his animated face. She mussed up his dark blond hair, which was the exact same shade as Rachel's. Sometimes Ben reminded Sydney of her sister so much. "Well, that I have to see," she said, trying to match his enthusiasm.

They set off again, this time in search of penguins.

"Jess?" Ben said as they strolled along the path. "Why aren't you Sydney's girlfriend?"

"Ben!" Sydney was a couple of steps behind, but she could still hear them. "You can't go about asking questions like that."

"Why not? She would be the perfect girlfriend for you. And you told Mum that you fancy her." He seemed genuinely confused about what the problem was. Bless him.

Sydney shot Jess an apologetic glance, then leaned down to get on Ben's level. "You shouldn't listen in to people's conversations." She tapped him gently on the chest but gave him a small smile to show she wasn't really angry. She didn't think she could ever get angry with Ben. "And not everyone wants to be my girlfriend, believe it or not."

He frowned. "But why?"

"Because I already have a boyfriend," Jess interjected.

"You do?" he said in horror.

My feelings exactly, kid.

"I'm afraid so." Jess scrunched her nose up. "So that means that I can't go out with your Aunt Sydney, even though I think she's great."

Sydney managed to keep her face neutral, even though she didn't enjoy hearing the rejection any more than she had the first time. "Exactly. Sometimes two people are just supposed to be friends."

"Well, I think that sucks." Ben stormed off, but not quick enough that they couldn't keep up with him. Which they did.

"Is that what we are, then?" Jess asked, looking ahead as they walked side by side a few steps behind Ben. "Friends?"

"Well, I know you said we could only ever be roommates, but I think it's okay to be friends with your roommates. People do that. Right?"

"I've heard that kind of thing is universally accepted. Yes."

Sydney gave a nod. "That's settled then. I'll be the best friend you've ever had." She paused. "Bar Chloe, obviously. I don't want to step on any toes."

Jess laughed. "Maybe you could just be an adequate friend. You know, to keep Chloe's toes safe and all." She regarded Sydney seriously. "And because I'm trying to like you less, not more."

Sydney couldn't resist. "So, you still like me?"

"Sydney," Jess warned.

"What? You're the one who brought it up."

"I'm trying to be honest. Isn't that what the problem was before? My lack of transparency?"

"Okay then. Honestly, do you still fancy me a little bit?"

"Sydney!" Jess said, louder this time. "Can you be serious for one second?"

Sydney laughed. "I am being serious."

Jess shook her head, but she seemed more amused than annoyed. "See, this…this is stepping over the line."

"There's a line now?"

Jess nodded. "An adequate friend line." She sliced through the air with her finger.

Sydney grinned at her. "I was always terrible at staying inside the lines."

❖

"You're trouble," Jess said, glaring playfully.

Sydney laughed again and perched her sunglasses on top of her head. "So I've been told."

Once again, they were in dangerous territory. Flirty territory. And what was worse was that Jess was enjoying it.

A few hours in Sydney's company and the walls she had spent weeks building around herself came crashing right back down again. They might as well have been made of paper.

Because her attraction to Sydney was irresistible.

And Jess didn't know what to do about it.

Ben stopped up ahead and waited for them as they reached the entrance to the penguins.

"Come on. Let's go see what the penguins are up to," Sydney said, leading the way. "I wonder if they've been teasing any seals today."

Jess's gaze dropped to Sydney's bum, and not for the first time that day—something kept drawing her eyes to it, probably the fact that it looked like it had been carved by the gods themselves. It was, however, the first time that Sydney had turned around and caught her looking.

Shit.

Jess felt heat rush to her cheeks at the same time as a slow grin spread across Sydney's face, but she didn't comment, thankfully.

Jess cursed herself, then tried to shake it off as best she could. After a few seconds, she regained her composure and approached Ben and Sydney, who were already looking through one of the huge, circular underwater windows.

Jess took a few steps forward to join them. At least thirty penguins were swimming around in a stunning display. "Wow. They're beautiful." She had never really thought of penguins as beautiful before. Cute, yes. Snuggly. But all together like this, gracefully swimming around the turquoise water in sync, beautiful was what they were.

"Yeah. They really are," Sydney said softly, not taking her eyes off Jess for a second.

Jess knew it, but she didn't dare turn round. Turning around would only lead to another moment, and Jess wasn't sure how many more of those she could take. Her resolve had already started to crumble.

She kept her gaze fixed firmly on the glass and wondered if the penguins could hear the thumping bassline that was her pounding heart. They said that some animals had excellent hearing, far better than humans.

"Hurry up, you two. There's loads more penguins up here."

Sydney let out a long, wistful sigh beside her and stepped away in the direction of Ben's voice. "Coming."

Jess let go of the breath that she had been holding and followed, trying to ignore the roll in her stomach that remained. Wanting a woman for the first time was intense. Especially when it was obvious that the woman wanted her back.

It can't happen.

Ben managed to drag out their visit for another two hours. Not that Jess minded. She couldn't remember the last time she had enjoyed herself so much. And the fact that it wasn't with Austin wasn't lost on her. Jess couldn't remember the last fun day out she had spent with her boyfriend.

Eventually, they reached their last stop. The gift shop. "Okay. I still have to get you a birthday present, so pick anything you want," Jess said to Ben.

His eyes lit up. "Anything?"

"Anything at all."

"You might regret that," Sydney said to her as he ran toward the shelves at the opposite end of the shop, the ones packed with toys and stuffed animals. "You don't have to get him a present, you know."

"I want to."

"Well, thank you. And thank you for coming with us. It made Ben's day," Sydney said.

"Just Ben's day?" Jess asked playfully, then she mentally kicked herself. They were supposed to be abstaining from flirty comments like that. Her own rule. And there she was, letting them roll off her tongue so easily.

Not that Sydney seemed to mind, judging by the warm smile she was giving Jess. "No. Not just his." She seemed to consider something. "I'll be back in a second."

"Just Ben's day?" Jess quietly mimicked to herself in a silly voice

as Sydney walked away. Apparently, Sydney wasn't the only person who had trouble staying in the lines.

Jess distractedly browsed some of the shelves while she waited. A couple of minutes later, Ben reappeared beside her holding a huge stuffed lion. Jess chuckled. She *had* told him he could have anything. "This one?"

"Yeah! He's going to live at the end of my bed."

"I think that's a great place for him," Jess replied. "Come on, let's go pay for this." She scanned the room. "Have you seen your Aunt Sydney?"

"She said she would meet us out front."

"Oh. Okay." Jess led Ben over to the checkout desk.

Once she paid, she handed the lion over to Ben to carry. He had inaptly named him Poodle by the time they had reached the exit. Poodle the Lion.

Sydney was waiting outside for them, just as Ben had said. Her eyes widened when she clocked the huge lion. "Wow, buddy. Did they not have any bigger lions?"

Ben shook his head earnestly, the sarcasm lost on him.

Jess laughed. "Where did you disappear to?"

"Nowhere." The guilty look on her face said otherwise. What was she up to?

"I don't want to go home," Ben said sulkily before Jess could challenge Sydney about it.

"You have to, buddy. You have school tomorrow. And your mum is waiting to hear all about your day," Sydney told him.

"Plus, Poodle needs to go and settle into his new home," Jess added, nudging him gently. "Doesn't he?"

Ben considered that, then nodded, hugging the lion tighter to his chest. "That's true."

"The lion's called Poodle?" Sydney leaned over and murmured to her.

Jess shrugged. "His choice."

"Are you coming home with us, Jess?" Ben asked.

"I wish I could, but I can't tonight. I have to have dinner with my dad." Jess adored her dad. But she wasn't looking forward to hearing about how miserable Gretchen was making him. It made her blood boil.

The issues in their marriage had happened even sooner than Jess had predicted they would. The words *told you so* fluttered through her brain, but that's where she would keep them. No one needed to hear that.

"But I want to show you my bedroom," Ben whined.

"Ben..." Sydney put on her stern aunt voice that Jess had only heard once or twice throughout the day. "Jess has plans. She'll come and see your room another day."

There was something sexy about authoritative Sydney. Who was Jess kidding? Everything about Sydney was sexy.

Thankfully, Ben's puppy dog eyes broke that thought. "Promise?"

"I promise," Jess said, pushing aside all thoughts of Sydney seductively telling her off. God, she was screwed. "I would love to see your room another day. And that way, I'll get to see you *and* Poodle again too."

Ben seemed happy with her answer.

"Are you getting our train home?" Sydney asked.

"Oh, our train, is it?" Secretly, it was the exact same thought that Jess had when she got on the train earlier to meet them. "I am. But I'm meeting Dad first at a restaurant near the station."

"We're going that way." Sydney pointed her thumb behind her. The opposite way, sadly.

"Ah. Okay." Jess shuffled on her feet. She was suddenly unsure of what to do with her hands. It felt like the end of a date, and she wasn't sure whether she was going to get a hug or a goodbye kiss—or neither. "I'll see you at home, then."

"You will." Sydney paused, drawing the moment out longer. "I hope dinner with your dad goes well." Maybe Sydney wasn't sure how to act with Jess either. They were in new, unfamiliar territory.

Ben, on the other hand, unabashedly threw his arms around Jess's waist. "Thank you so much for Poodle and for coming with us to the zoo, Jess."

Jess grinned and hugged him back. "Thank you for having me. I loved it." When she let go, she smiled at Sydney. "See you later?"

"Aunt Sydney," Ben said in a hushed voice that was probably even louder than his normal voice. "Hug her."

It was one of his better suggestions, though probably a very bad idea. The last thing Jess needed was any form of physical contact with Sydney. No, she absolutely did not need that.

But she wanted it.

So when Sydney gave her an uneasy smile, Jess took the initiative and stepped forward, pulling Sydney into her arms without hesitation. She slid her arms around Sydney's body, and gasped when Sydney did the same. Did Sydney hear her? Could she tell that Jess's body was on fire everywhere that they touched? Hopefully not.

Jess breathed in Sydney's scent and sighed. "You always smell so good," she whispered. Did Sydney really have to smell that good *all* the time? Was it necessary?

She felt Sydney's low laugh vibrate against her shoulder.

Reluctantly, Jess pulled back to look at her. "Seriously. What is with that? It's always a different smell, but it's always amazing." Though Jess still hadn't noticed Sydney wearing the scent she had worn on the train that day. It was Jess's favourite, but that was probably more to do with the associated memories than the smell itself.

"I make soap, remember?"

"Right. That makes sense."

Sydney winked. "'Tis the name of my company."

Jess hadn't even thought about it like that before. Makes Scents. She laughed. "Oh my God, that's so clever." How had she missed that?

"I thought so."

"And what's today's Makes Scents scent?"

"Another experiment. It's not officially on the market. Not yet, anyway. It's Freshly Baked Scones with Jam." Sydney shrugged. "I wasn't sure about it."

"Sell it. You smell good enough to eat." Oh Christ, did Jess really say that? Out loud? Oh shit, she had.

And Sydney was grinning at her in sheer amusement.

Jess, on the other hand, was gaping back at her like an idiot. She couldn't help it. "I didn't mean it like…not like…" She closed her eyes. Holding a hand up, she said, "I'm just going to go."

Jess started to walk backward toward the path. "Thank you both again," she said, giving them both a final wave before she turned and walked away as fast as she could, taking her big mouth and undoubtedly red face with her.

"What's wrong, Aunt Sydney? Does Jess not like scones?" Jess heard Ben say to Sydney as she set off down the path.

Oh, Ben. That was the problem.

Jess really fucking did.

CHAPTER TEN

K iddo, over here." Jess's dad stood up from the table and waved as she entered the restaurant.

Jess smiled. She was a grown woman, but she was still *kiddo* to him, and probably always would be. She weaved around the other tables until she reached him. "Sorry I'm late."

"You're always late," he said good-naturedly as she sat down opposite him.

It was true. Nine times out of ten, she was.

"What kept you today? Anything fun?"

"Actually, yes." Jess poured two glasses of water from the jug in the middle of the table and passed one over to him. "I was at the zoo with my new roommate and her nephew, and it turned out to be a really nice day. It was Ben's birthday yesterday, he turned seven. He's an extremely cute kid."

"Yeah?" He smiled. "I keep wondering when you're going to give me one of those."

"A nephew? I think I might have to teach you how a family tree works, Dad."

"You know what I mean. A grandchild. Someone I can teach football and bad habits to and take to the zoo." He sipped his water. "You and Austin should get to work on that, for your old man's sake." He grinned to show he was only half serious. Her dad wasn't the type of parent to put pressure on her about those kinds of things.

Besides, Jess would have to have sex first. She couldn't remember the last time that she and Austin had. A quick, unsatisfying—for her anyway—fumble a couple of months ago sprang to mind, but nothing since.

She certainly hadn't slept with him since she met Sydney.

Why had *that* come to mind?

Jess took a large gulp of her water like it would wash away the thought. "There's plenty of time for that."

Her dad laughed. "I know, kiddo. I'm just messing with you. How is Austin anyway? Still working far too hard?"

That was a tolerant way to put it. "You know Austin."

"He's a good kid. And he's going places. He'll be able to look after you."

Jess wanted to say that she didn't need someone to *look after her*, but it wasn't the time or the place, so she let it go. "Speaking of looking after people, how's Gretchen?"

Her dad's face changed immediately, worry lines galore gathering on his forehead. "I asked her to give the credit card back."

Jess winced. "Let me guess. It didn't go down too well?"

He shook his head gravely. "An understatement. She went ballistic. Screamed, yelled, threw things. I nearly lost an eye with the TV remote." He sighed. "I'm starting to think she's only with me for my money."

Oh, Dad.

"She only came round when I bought her a new gold bracelet to make up for it."

Again. Oh, Dad.

He let out a long sigh. "Can I tell you a secret?"

"Of course," she said patiently, already knowing exactly what the secret was. It was always the same one.

"Sometimes I really regret not making things work with your mum."

There it was. It was a reoccurring theme. Anytime there was a failing marriage, there was a regretful dad. "I know you do, Dad."

"Let me give you some advice."

Okay. Advice was new. Usually, he just spent a few minutes reminiscing and wallowing in self-pity.

"Don't waste your time looking for something *more*," he told Jess. "Me and your mum had a good relationship back in the day. Not perfect, because none are, but good. And instead of letting myself be happy and content with what I had, I kept thinking, what if there's something better out there?"

Unfortunately, Jess's dad had got caught looking for something better in the next-door neighbour's pants. It wasn't her favourite, but Jess knew the story.

"There isn't," he concluded. "Or if there is, I haven't found it in all these years."

It was all his own doing, but Jess couldn't help but feel a little bit sorry for him. Thankfully, her mum had eventually found happiness and faithfulness, albeit with Barry the Bore. Her dad hadn't.

"Well, thank you for the advice, Dad. I'll remember that."

"Not that you'll need it. You and Austin are a match made in heaven. You wouldn't be silly like your old dad and let a good thing go."

Wouldn't she? Jess had thought about it more times than she could count. Especially recently.

Was Jess all that different? She too was in a relationship, imperfect, but fine. Yet all of her thoughts lately were taken up with someone else.

Panic started to bubble up inside her. Was she looking for something better?

Oh, God. Was she just like her dad?

"Anyway, enough doom and gloom for the evening. How's work? Are Pam and Violet behaving? And Chloe? How's she?" Her dad sat back, all ears.

Fortunately, the waiter chose that moment to come over and take their order, giving Jess a couple of minutes to get back onto her equilibrium. She was nothing like her dad. Because unlike him, Jess would make wise choices. She wasn't driven by hormones or lust. And that's what made her different.

As always, they both ordered the steak, and Jess filled him in on the basics of her life. Work good, Pam and Violet good, Chloe good. That was the gist of it. "I think that's everything."

Her dad cut a chunk of his steak. "No. You still haven't told me about your new roommate. Sydney, isn't it? What's she like?"

Jess had left Sydney out intentionally in the hope that her dad wouldn't ask. No such luck. "She's nice."

"Nice? That's good. Anything else?" He made a rolling gesture with his hand.

"She's around my age, or maybe a year or two older. Owns a soap company with her sister. Tidies up after herself." Jess shrugged. "That's all I can think of."

"Did you not say that you were out with her today? There must be more to her than her just being tidy."

Her dad was right. There was so much more to Sydney than her neatness, but Jess didn't trust herself when she focussed on all the things she liked about Sydney.

"I'm still getting to know her. She's a friend."

An adequate friend, and there was a line. Jess would not cross it. She could *not* end up like her dad.

❖

Jess let herself into the house, relieved by the quiet she was met with. Sydney and Chloe were either out or in their own rooms.

After her emotional roller coaster of a day, silence was exactly what Jess needed. She went into the kitchen and helped herself to a glass of water, then slipped quietly up the stairs to her own room. She shut the door gently behind her and let out a long exhale.

What a day.

Not that it had been a bad day. Not at all. If Jess was honest with herself, she couldn't remember the last time she had enjoyed herself as much. That wasn't the problem.

And it also was.

She sighed and threw herself down on her bed, landing on something soft but lumpy. Frowning, she arched her back to remove whatever it was she had lain down on.

To her surprise, it was a penguin. Stuffed, not real, obviously. She turned the soft, fluffy toy in her hands, breathing out a laugh when she noticed it was wearing pink earmuffs. There was a piece of paper sticking out from under its wing. Jess pulled it out and unfolded it.

Fun facts about Penguins.

Do you know that penguins mate for life? I didn't until Google told me.

Oh my God. Do you know how they commit themselves to one another? One penguin searches for the perfect pebble, the prettiest and smoothest one they can find, and presents it to the penguin of their affections. How cute is that?

Wait, I'm still looking.

Jess! They sing love songs to one another. They touch their beaks to kiss or say I missed you. Aww.

They perform synchronized swimming—well, we saw that today.

Oh, and they express delight through doing fun little dances. Apparently, they co-parent really well too. Go penguins.

I was not expecting to learn all that.

Anyways, I know you liked these little guys (plus it reminded me of the day we met), so I thought I would get you your very own penguin as a memento and to say thank you for making OUR day today.

Please name it something better than Poodle. Honestly, that kid!

Sydney xx

Jess was *stupid* grinning. The biggest, goofiest of smiles.

So that's where Sydney had disappeared to earlier. To buy her a present. Jess read the note again, and another time after that, and then she clutched it to her chest and closed her eyes. She felt like a teenage girl who had found a love letter stuck in her locker.

Jess's heart was doing backflips.

Sydney regularly made her heart do all kinds of gymnastics. Thanks to Sydney, it could probably perform in the Olympics.

Jess folded the note back up. She opened her bedside drawer and lifted out her favourite book. She pressed the note in between the first page and the cover to keep it safe and closed the drawer back up again. She hugged her new penguin and let out another sigh when she lay down again.

Why did Sydney have to be the sweetest person on the planet? It was wildly inconvenient when Jess was trying so hard to resist her.

Her dad's words from earlier echoed through her brain, acting like some kind of warning that Jess didn't ask for. *Don't waste your time looking for something more.*

But what if Jess wasn't looking for something more?
What if she had already found it?

❖

"Jess? What are you doing here?" Sydney asked as she sat up in her bed.

"I couldn't stay away any longer," Jess replied in a tone that Sydney was sure bordered on seductive. She leaned against the doorframe in Sydney's bedroom. "Can I come in?"

Sydney nodded quickly, staring at her in a mixture of surprise, curiosity, and wonderment. "Of course. Please. Come in."

Jess entered the room fully, pushing the door closed softly behind her, like she didn't plan on leaving anytime soon. "I needed to see you. I couldn't wait." The steps she took were agonizingly slow as she approached Sydney's bed. Each one added to both Sydney's anticipation and impatience.

Sydney swallowed. "Did you like your present?" She wasn't sure whether buying Jess the stuffed penguin was a good idea or if it broke the rules of their newfound friendship. But she had decided it was worth the risk if there was a chance it would put a smile on Jess's face.

"I loved it," Jess said. "That's why I'm here."

"It is?"

She nodded. "I wanted to give you yours."

"Mine? You want to give me a present?" What kind of present could Jess possibly have to give her in the middle of the night? She was still wearing the same outfit she had worn at the zoo that day. Maybe she had only just got home? That must have been it.

"If that's okay?" Jess asked, suddenly hesitant.

"Yes! Yes, it's more than okay," Sydney reassured her quickly. If Jess had something to give her, Sydney wanted it. She just hadn't been expecting any of this.

"Good." The grin Jess gave her made Sydney gulp. "Are you not going to ask me what it is?"

"What is it?" Sydney asked, her voice barely audible.

Jess climbed on top of the bed and swung her leg over Sydney's waist to straddle her. "Me."

Holy shit.

"I haven't been able to stop thinking about you, Sydney," Jess said softly.

She hadn't? Was this really happening? *"I haven't stopped thinking about you either."*

Her whole body thrummed and pulsed, and so much heat gathered between Sydney's legs it almost ached.

Sydney didn't think she had ever been more turned on in her entire life. In fact, she knew she hadn't.

Jess seemed to notice how affected she was too, because she pushed her hips down firmly against her to apply even more pressure.

Sydney moaned as a wave of pleasure ran through her body.

Then Jess placed a hand at either side of Sydney's shoulders and leaned herself down. Their faces were so close they were just shy of touching, and Jess's breath was hot against her lips.

Jess flicked her gaze from Sydney's eyes, down to her mouth, and back up again. She slowly ran her tongue over her own lips. *"I want you, Sydney. I can't ignore it anymore. Say I can have you."*

"Oh, Jess. I want you too," Sydney whispered. "Do you not know by now that I'm yours?"

"And I'm yours."

Sydney had never wanted to hear words more.

But where had those words come from? Shut up, brain, and let me enjoy this.

But her brain wouldn't stop. Suddenly Jess was hers? Just like that? What had changed in the last few hours? What happened to being friends? To Jess being unavailable?

"But what about Austin?" Sydney found herself asking. Damn moral compass.

"Yeah, what about me?" Austin's deep voice came from beside her.

Sydney woke up screaming, clutching on to her bed sheets for dear life. She shot up into a sitting position, her breath coming in fast, ragged gasps.

She darted her eyes around the darkened room, barely able make anything out. She blinked a few times to let them adjust. One thing was for sure, Jess was not on top of her. Nor was she in Sydney's bedroom.

Much to Sydney's relief, neither was Austin. Oh, thank God for that—it was only a dream.

It had felt so real. Sydney's heart was practically jumping out of her chest. She placed her right hand over it and blew out a slow, heavy breath to calm herself. With her left hand, she reached over and tapped her phone on the bedside table to check what time it was. She groaned. Two forty-four a.m., literally the middle of the night.

She reached for her water bottle. Had she only screamed in her dream? Or had she screamed out loud? Sydney wasn't sure, but either way, her mouth was bone dry.

And her bottle was empty. Typical.

With another groan she swung her legs out of the bed and headed downstairs to the kitchen to fill it. She could do with a cold shower too, but a cold drink would have to do.

Still sleepy, Sydney lifted her hands to rub her eyes as she walked into the dark kitchen and ended up colliding with something in the middle of the room, causing her to scream out again.

Only this time, the thing she collided with screamed back at her. Sydney scrambled over to the light switch and flicked it on. "Jess?"

"Sydney? Oh my God, you scared the shit out of me."

"Me? *You* scared the shit out of *me*!" She clutched her chest again. Any more surprises and Sydney was going to end up in heart failure. "What are you doing up at this time?"

"I'm assuming the same thing as you." Jess held up a glass. "Getting a drink."

"In the dark?"

"Well, the plan was to slip in, fill my glass, and slip straight back to bed again and sleep. I only woke up because I thought I heard someone yelling. I probably dreamt it."

Speaking of dreams, funny story. "Yeah, that might have been me. I had a bit of a nightmare." Well, the Austin ending had been. The part where Jess came to her bedroom to seduce her had been more enjoyable.

"Oh no. Do you want to talk about it?" Jess asked, sweetly concerned. "Sometimes talking helps to rationalize it."

No, Sydney absolutely did not want to talk about it. "It's okay. I can hardly even remember what it was about now." Liar, liar, pants on fire. "Thanks, though."

"That's a good thing. There's nothing worse than having a dream that you can't forget and end up playing in your head over and over again."

Oh, Sydney was sure she would replay this one a few times.

Jess turned to get another glass from the cupboard, presumably for Sydney. It was only then that Sydney noticed what Jess was wearing. Or more accurately, what she wasn't wearing. There was a serious lack of clothing going on.

She averted her eyes quickly to stare at the ground.

That didn't last long.

Her gaze snagged that Jess was barefoot, and from there started to travel slowly up her smooth legs. Toned. Defined. All those trips to the gym clearly showed.

And, side note, could Jess have found any shorts shorter than the grey ones she was wearing? A lot of leg was on show. Sydney could even make out the exact spot of Jess's thigh that she would start running her tongue up if she ever got the chance.

She shouldn't be having thoughts like that.

She should look away.

She couldn't.

Sydney blamed the dream.

Instead, Sydney's gaze shifted upward to the sneak peek of Jess's midriff that her cropped T-shirt allowed. Unlike the shorts, it didn't reveal much. But enough. Sydney could picture herself placing open-mouthed kisses on the soft-looking skin right beneath Jess's belly button. And lower.

Still rising, Sydney's gaze took in how the T-shirt generously bulged at Jess's chest. Was she wearing a bra? Sydney didn't think so, but she couldn't be sure. What she wouldn't give to find out, though. To run her hands under that top and upward, feeling the swell of Jess's breasts against her palms, the hardening of her nipples beneath her fingertips.

Then she could pepper kisses across that smooth collarbone. Let her mouth linger on that sensitive spot, the one right between Jess's shoulder and the base of her neck. Run her lips gently up the length of Jess's neck.

And she would finally reach those lips. Those perfect, full lips, begging for Sydney's to touch them with her own.

As Sydney pictured it, they parted slightly, and Jess let out a sharp gasp, which made Sydney's eyes snap up to meet hers, their final destination. Sydney could get so lost in those eyes and not care if she was ever found again.

They stared at each other. If all the moments that had led up to this one had been charged, they were now on the brink of explosion.

Loaded. Intense. Still, neither of them looked away.

Sydney dared to take step closer. "Jess," she said in a breathy voice, the longing in it clear even to her own ears, revealing exactly what it was she wanted.

Jess's breathing gave her away—her chest rising and falling quickly—she knew what Sydney wanted. There was a subtle twitch in her throat as she swallowed. Her gaze moved down to Sydney's lips. She frowned as she stared at them—was Jess really considering kissing her?

Then, suddenly, Jess snapped her head away.

The brakes slammed on the moment so abruptly, Sydney feared she might have emotional whiplash.

"Jess," she said again, this time with a hint of desperation that she hated herself for showing.

Jess ignored her pleas and strode over to the sink. "Do you want some water?" she asked casually, like the last minute and a half hadn't just happened. Jess carried on filling the glass without waiting for Sydney's answer.

"Jess," Sydney said loudly, for a third time.

Jess glanced up at her then, probably because they had the safety of an island between them. Literally. They were standing on opposite ends of the kitchen island. "Sydney, stop," Jess warned.

"But—"

"Adequate. Friend. Line."

Sydney groaned. "Seriously? Are you still going on about that silly line?"

Jess set the glass of water down and stuck her hands on her hips. "It's not silly, it's necessary. And I wouldn't have to go on about it if you didn't bloody cross it."

"I didn't."

"You almost did." Jess pinched her thumb and forefinger together. "You were this close."

"How?" Sydney gave her a challenging look.

Jess stuttered a few times. "You…you…you were looking at me with that look on your face."

"What look did I have?"

Jess gave her a knowing glare. "The one like you want to rip my clothes off."

"To be fair, there aren't many clothes to rip." Sydney gave her another quick look up and down.

"Don't. Cross. The. Line."

"Wear. More. Clothes. Then." Sydney grinned.

A ghost of a smile crossed Jess's face too. "In my defence, it's not like I was expecting much kitchen traffic at three a.m."

"Neither was I." Sydney looked down at her own pink pyjama bottoms, baggy, but cuffed at the ankle, and her white tank top. "But I still managed to remain decent."

"From now on I'll wear a onesie. Now, can we change the subject, please?"

Sydney laughed. "If we must." She put her elbows on the surface of the island and leaned forward. "What do you want to talk about?"

"The gift you left on my bed." Jess's pinched expression softened into a smile. "Thank you. That was really sweet of you."

Sydney's brain flashed back to how dream Jess had wanted to thank her, but she did her best to ignore it. "Yeah? Didn't cross any lines?"

"If it did, I can let it slide." Jess paused. "Did Ben and Poodle get home okay?"

"Both delivered safe and sound to my sister. Poodle's job is now to guard Ben's bedroom from monster attacks. Apparently." They both laughed. "He had a lot of fun today. *We* had."

"So did I."

"And dinner with your dad? How did that go?"

Jess chewed her lip for a second. "It was…" She paused. "I needed it."

Okay. Cryptic. Sydney knew when not to push a subject, so she moved on. "Have you given the penguin a name yet?"

"I have." Had Jess started to blush? "I've, um, named her Pebbles."

Ah. Sydney's note. The pebble proposal. So, Jess *was* a romantic— Sydney had hoped she would be.

Jess cleared her throat. "Right. I'm off to bed." She hurried past Sydney to the door at a lightning pace.

"Oh, Jess. One more thing," Sydney said.

Already halfway out the door, Jess froze and poked her head back. She really wasn't going to give Sydney another glimpse of that outfit, was she?

She smiled broadly. "I was just wondering. If that's what you wear to bed during winter, what do you sleep in during summer?"

Jess audibly growled and turned to storm out. "Goodnight, Sydney."

Sydney chuckled. And what a good night it had turned out to be.

Sydney stretched her arms up above her head and let out a loud yawn.

"Why are you so tired today? That's like the tenth time you've yawned in the past twenty minutes," Rachel said, peeking her bobbed-blond head out from behind a wall of boxes she had been building.

Makes Scents had received a ton of orders over the previous couple of days, and Sydney and Rachel had been in a race against time to get them all packed up and ready for the distribution company they used to collect for shipping.

Not that having a load of orders was ever a bad thing. It just meant an extra-busy day. Thankfully, they were almost done, and with thirty minutes to spare. They really were the best team.

"I didn't sleep much last night." Sydney had been fine all morning, but once the afternoon had hit, the tiredness seemed to have caught up with her.

Sydney hadn't managed to get back to sleep at all after her middle-of-the-night rendezvous with Jess in the kitchen.

Her mind had been in overdrive for the rest of the night.

She had lain in bed willing sleep to come, but it never had. Mainly because Sydney couldn't stop going over all of her interactions with Jess, trying to analyse the meaning behind every look Jess had ever given her.

Basically, torturing herself.

"Something on your mind?" Rachel asked.

There were so many things on Sydney's mind she didn't know where to start. "I'm just trying to work out how to do this whole friend thing with Jess."

"Ah. Jess-insomnia. I should have known." An email dinged from Rachel's laptop, and she visibly winced. Rachel, aka Queen of Organisation, as Sydney liked to think of her, was the type of person who liked to keep on top of her dings, and there had been about eight in the past hour that she hadn't been able to get to.

Understanding her constant need for order, Sydney said, "Why don't you go get caught up with the admin and I'll finish these. There's not many left to do."

Rachel didn't hesitate. "Thank you, thank you, thank you," she sang as she practically skipped over to the desk, six feet away. A smile spread across her face as she tapped her laptop to life.

Sydney breathed out a laugh and kept boxing.

"The Jess stuff, then?" Rachel asked, so much more relaxed in her happy place. "Do you want to talk about it?"

"There isn't much to say. We're supposed to be trying to be friends, and all I want to do is kiss her like my life depends on it. It's exhausting."

"I get that," Rachel said, her eyes never leaving the computer screen. "Do you think that maybe the more time you spend together as friends, the more you'll start to think of her as one?"

"No," Sydney said grumpily.

Rachel laughed. "Ben loved her. He didn't stop talking about her all last night and this morning."

"That's because Ben has fantastic taste."

"He also thinks that Jess fancies his Aunt Sydney every bit as much as Aunt Sydney fancies her."

"And smart too." Sydney grinned but it faded quickly. "Pity about Jess's annoying, stupid boyfriend."

"Ben said that too. God, you two are alike."

"In that case, you are welcome for my superb influence," Sydney said proudly.

"Hmm." A few seconds later, Rachel looked up from her screen and gasped. "How about we kidnap the boyfriend?"

Sydney blinked a few times. "Well, that was out of the blue, random, and frankly, a little scary."

"I just read an email advertising an escape room."

"Ah."

"Think about it. We can keep him in here. Feed him, obviously. But he'll be out of the picture, and you can swoop in and be with Jess." Sydney had to laugh at her straight face and nonchalance.

Anyone who didn't know Rachel would probably think she was being serious.

"I think you should go ahead and delete that email, maybe stop watching so many true crime documentaries, and also refrain from trying to get me arrested."

Rachel waved her off. "We'll let him go, obviously."

"Yeah, I'm still going to go with no."

"Fine. But don't say I didn't come up with solutions." Rachel shrugged and went back to her emails, but there was an amused look on her face. She had always had an odd sense of humour.

"This is interesting," Rachel said, already right back in business mode. Sydney knew because she had her serious work face on.

"What?"

"We've been short-listed for some small business award..." Rachel squinted. "In the Creative Products category." She popped out her bottom lip.

"Oh?" Sydney said, pleasantly surprised. "That's good. Right?"

"It's great." Rachel narrowed her eyes at the screen. "It's really soon too." She looked at the desk calendar. "Three weeks from now. Wow. They didn't give much notice, did they?"

"Oh, come on. What would we be doing in our exciting lives anyway? We're always available for last minute plans." Sydney smiled. "We'll get to dress up."

"We will. Oh, shit." Rachel frowned at the calendar. "I can't go. Ben has a parent teacher thing that evening." She eyed Sydney. "You'll have to go without me."

"Alone?" Sydney shook her head. "Nope. I don't think so."

"Invite one of your friends." Rachel's expression brightened. "Ooh. Why don't you ask Jess to go?"

"Ooh. Because that's a very bad idea."

Rachel held up a finger. "Hard disagree. I think it's an excellent idea. Imagine it…you two getting all dressed up, looking fabulous. A nice, fancy dinner. Some champagne. It will be just like a date."

"Yeah exactly. That's the problem."

"Why?"

"Because it would be a date that isn't really a date, because it's not allowed to be a bloody date. Talk about a mind fuck."

Rachel moved her mouth to the side as she stared at the email. "There are a couple of extra tickets. You could invite your other roommate too? That way you and Jess won't be alone, therefore no date vibes, *and* you'll be guaranteed to behave. Who knows, maybe it will bring you all closer together as friends. Win-win."

Sydney considered it. She would love the opportunity to get all dressed up and go out with Jess. And it would be the perfect excuse. That wasn't the issue. The issue was how much she would love it.

Would it not only get her hopes up? Bring them closer together? Add to Sydney's heartache?

But. If Chloe was there to act as a buffer, the three of them could potentially have a nice time. And there was no way that Sydney could show up to an event like that alone, so at least she would have people.

"Do I absolutely *have* to go to this thing?"

Rachel scrunched up one eye. "One of us should really be there, yes. And it can't be me. Sorry, Ben's more important."

Sydney waved her off. "A hundred percent. I would never think otherwise." She thought about it. "I guess I *could* ask Chloe and Jess." Odds were they both already had plans anyway.

She stuck a message into the roomie group chat that Chloe had created a few days before. She had said it would come in handy, which it had—like when they had run out of chocolate the day before. A true emergency.

Hey! Short notice but Makes Scents has been shortlisted for some kind of small business award and there's a whole evening do. It's a bit fancy. Rachel can't go, and I was wondering if you both wanted to come? She read over the message and added, *Would be good to get all three of us together to do something fun.* Sydney felt the need to reiterate that point.

Before she could overthink it or back out, Sydney pressed send. As an afterthought, she added the date and time in another message.

They probably needed to know when in order to know if they were available.

Sydney saw that Jess started replying right away, then stopped again. That happened a couple of times. Maybe she was struggling with the idea as much as Sydney had been. Understandable.

A minute or so later, a reply popped up from Chloe. *Sounds like fun. I'll be there!!!*

Great. At least Chloe was in. Sydney wouldn't have to fly solo.

The question of Jess still remained.

Sydney watched the screen again as Jess typed and stopped. Typed and stopped. It was another couple of minutes until the reply appeared.

I'm in.

Sydney sighed with happiness.

Sydney was in too.

In way over her head.

CHAPTER ELEVEN

T onight's the big night." Pam did a little shimmy with her shoulders. Jess rolled her eyes. "It's not a *big* night. Just a night out with my two roommates. A normal sized night."

"The lady doth protest too much, methinks."

Jess let out an amused snort. "Okay, William Shakespeare." She glanced at Violet. "That is Shakespeare, isn't it?" she whispered.

Violet smiled and nodded. "*Hamlet*, if I recall."

Mrs Morton, who was in for her usual weekly appointment, confirmed it. "The very famous line spoken by Queen Gertrude."

Jess was surrounded by literature buffs. Who knew? "Could be handy to know in a pub quiz."

Mrs Morton laughed. "And what are you protesting, dear?"

"That she has the hots for her gorgeous roommate," Pam broadcast. Not quite as Shakespearean that time.

"Oh?" Mrs Morton looked the picture of surprise. "What happened to your boyfriend, Jess?"

Pam piped in again. She was on a roll. "Oh, he's still around. But he's turned into a bit of a so-and-so."

Mrs Morton gave an understanding nod. "It can be very difficult to find the right man nowadays."

"Or the right woman," Violet said quietly.

Jess whipped her head round to see Violet's overly sweet smile that nobody was buying. Jess glared back at her. "I expect comments like that from her." She jerked her head in Pam's direction. "But not you!"

Violet pushed her glasses up and held her hands up, palms forward. "I'm simply reminding you it's an option. That's all."

"Only it's not an option. We've already been through this."

"Your roommate's a woman?" Mrs Morton asked, like it was the gossip of the century.

"Yes, she's a woman. And no, I don't have the hots for her." Because her feelings ran so much deeper than a simple physical attraction. Not that Jess was going to tell Mrs Morton that, nor was she ready to discuss it with Violet and Pam. She was still hoping that it would miraculously fizzle out somehow, and she would never have to discuss it with anyone.

"Vi's just saying, don't completely rule out a *Mrs Right* even if it's unlikely. You might change your mind someday. Stranger things have happened," Pam said.

Violet grinned and snapped her fingers at Pam. "Exactly. Well put, P."

"Well, thank you both for clarifying my options for me," Jess said dryly. "Can we change the subject now?"

"Why? There's nothing wrong with dating a woman, you know," Pam said.

Jess stared at her. "I know there's nothing wrong with it. My best friend is a lesbian, as you know."

"Then what's the problem?"

"There is no problem," Jess said. How had the conversation taken this turn? "Just because I'm not going to date a woman doesn't mean that I have any issues with it."

"My granddaughter is a lesbian," Mrs Morton interjected. "I could put in a word."

Jess gaped at all three of them. Now she was being set up with Mrs Morton's granddaughter? "Um, thank you, Mrs Morton. I'm sure your granddaughter is great, but I think I'm going to stick with Austin for now."

Not that Jess had seen much of Austin lately. Three times in as many weeks. Twice for dinner—both times had been pleasant enough. They had caught up on each other's weeks, ate nice food, then Austin had opted to stay at his own place because he had to be up early the following morning.

Perhaps it wouldn't be everyone's idea of the perfect relationship, but not living in each other's pockets seemed to work okay for them. Besides, it was only short-term until Austin got promoted, then he would be able to cut back on his hours and they would spend more time together.

The third time Jess had seen him was a few nights ago when he had landed on her doorstep unannounced with an easy smile and big ideas for a sleepover. It had been a shame about the terrible headache Jess had come down with. The sleeping part was all Jess had been able for.

Mrs Morton just shrugged and went back to her magazine.

Violet strode over and wrapped a supportive arm around Jess's shoulder. "So! Are you looking forward to tonight?"

"Yeah, yeah. Suck up to me now, troublemaker." Jess leaned in and gave Violet a quick hug anyway. "And yeah. Kind of. It will be nice to get out with my friends." She made sure she emphasized the word *friends*.

A second later, Jess's next client, Margot, pushed through the door. A gust of cold air burst in behind her. Thankfully, Margot was quick to close it again. "Brr. It's absolutely freezing out there." She rubbed her hands together to warm them up and gave them all a friendly smile. "How's life in Thairapy? What hot gossip am I walking in on today?"

Pam, clearly still enjoying herself, didn't miss a beat. "We're just telling Jess that it's okay if she wants to date a woman." Because apparently there weren't enough people involved in this conversation already.

Margot beamed as she shrugged her coat off. "Excellent. I dated a woman once. There's nothing quite like it." She leaned toward Jess and waggled her eyebrows. "Trust me, you'll love it."

Jess didn't know what she was expecting, but it wasn't that. There was no point in going over the same argument again, so she plastered on her widest smile as she took Margot's coat. "Good to know, Margot. Shall we get you gowned? Tea? Coffee?"

"Oh, tea please." Margot followed her to the chair beside Mrs Morton, and Jess attached her black gown and towel round her shoulders before gesturing for her to take a seat.

Thankfully, they were much too busy for the rest of the afternoon to talk about Jess's night out, or Sydney, or anything at all really. It was only once the Thairapy Room closed for the day that Jess had time to think about the awards ceremony.

"How about an up-do?" she said, grabbing a handful of her hair and holding it on top of her head while she posed in the mirror. Jess turned her head from side to side. "What do you think?"

Violet appeared behind her and nodded. "I think it would work."

"Show me a picture of the dress again," Pam said, sidling up beside them.

Jess swiped through her phone until she found it. She held it up to show them and studied it again herself.

Pam took the phone out of her hand and tapped at the screen. "How do you make it bigger again?"

Jess laughed. "What are you trying to do? Zoom?" She took the phone back and did it for her.

"That's better." Pam let out a low whistle. "That dress is gorgeous. You're going to turn heads tonight. Mark my words."

Secretly, that was the plan. "You think? I've only worn it once." Jess made a face. "Dad's third wedding. I always liked it, though."

"It's stunning. And you can't go wrong with black. You're going to look fabulous," Violet reassured her. "What are Chloe and Sydney wearing?"

"You know Chloe wouldn't be seen dead in a dress. She's got black dress trousers and a shirt. And, um, I'm not sure what Sydney's wearing."

But Jess couldn't wait to find out.

For platonic reasons only, of course. Jess had always been interested in fashion and how people presented themselves. She was in the style business, after all. Objectively, she knew that Sydney's flawless body would look incredible in a dress.

Who was she kidding? She really didst protest too much. There was nothing objective about the way she thought about Sydney.

Jess had initially decided to decline Sydney's invitation.

The friends thing had been going well for them, but Jess knew better than to push the boundaries.

Case in point, their day at the zoo. It had been good, but maybe a little *too* good. That underlying attraction between them that constantly brewed and bubbled under the surface had almost boiled over. Their strong connection from the day Jess had met Sydney had not only returned, but grown.

That was when Jess had decided to cut back on situations where she might find herself weak and vulnerable around Sydney.

Situations like fancy evenings out.

But when Chloe had texted and agreed to join Sydney, Jess's stomach had rolled.

She refused to analyse why she had felt that way, but she also refused to ignore it. Ergo Jess was going on the fancy evening out.

Now, here she was. The day of. A bundle of apprehension, nerves, excitement, and anticipation. Wanting to look her absolute best, for someone she shouldn't want to notice. But, oh, how Jess wanted Sydney to notice.

Jess had tried on every dress she owned. All with one thought in her head. *What would Sydney think of me in this?* None of the dresses had been right. They had been good enough for nights out in the past. Maybe for parties and special occasions. But they weren't good enough for Sydney. She had considered wearing her red dress—after all, she already knew that Sydney liked that one.

Then Jess had remembered the dress she had worn to her dad's wedding to Fiona the Flirt. She had stored it right at the back of her wardrobe after Austin had thrown a fit over Jess receiving a few looks from some other guys at the wedding. Jess had laughed about it at the time and even found his jealousy quite sweet. It wasn't like Jess wanted attention from other men.

Now she just wanted attention from one certain woman.

Ugh. That was bad, wasn't it? Jess wasn't a bad person. But she was a very confused person right now. Confused about what she wanted, who she wanted, who she was. Everything she was feeling was so new.

Jess could hardly deny the fact that she was interested in women any longer. Her attraction to Sydney was only intensifying. Was she bisexual? Maybe so. Had she been bisexual this whole time and not known it? Her interest in women remaining dormant until she met the right one? Perhaps. But how would she know for sure? And what would that mean for her relationship with Austin? Did she even still love him? She was beginning to wonder.

"I'd say Sydney is the dress type," Pam said.

Jess gave her a wary look. She wasn't sure if Pam was still on the wind-up or not. But that was Jess's guess too. She just didn't know what kind of dress Sydney would choose.

"Well, I want pictures of all three of you," Violet said. "London won't know what hit it with three beautiful ladies having a night on the town."

"I can't get pictures on my phone," Pam said.

Violet held up her iPhone. "That's because your phone is old as the hills. You need one of these so you can download WhatsApp."

"What's up?"

"WhatsApp," Violet repeated, more pronounced. "I'll get you a new phone for your birthday."

"Don't bother. I don't want to live on my phone like these young 'uns. I can type in a number and speak to somebody when I want to, and that's all I need."

Jess couldn't hold in her laugh. Those two really were too much sometimes. She adored them. "When you're done arguing about technology and its evil existence, could one of you please do my hair?"

"I'll do it," Violet said, taking her place directly behind Jess. "That dinosaur can make the tea."

"You're four months older than me," Pam argued, but she stomped into the kitchen anyway.

Violet threw Jess a wink and began brushing her hair. She lowered her voice. "Seriously, how are you about going to this thing tonight?"

Jess hesitated, then decided not to lie. "A bit nervous. And desperate to make a good impression." She didn't explain why.

Violet didn't ask. "You know, it's okay to be happy, Jess. You might have to make some tough decisions to get there, but you have people on your side. Always remember that."

Jess blinked up at her. Sometimes Jess felt like Violet knew her better than she knew herself. "Thanks, Vi."

It took four attempts, many pins, and a ton of hairspray to eventually get Jess's hair the way she wanted it. It was a good job Violet and Pam were patient with her demands. With hugs, and no further teasing—Jess suspected that was because Violet had words with Pam—Jess made her way home to finish up getting ready.

She still needed to shower, and somehow manage not to ruin her hair in the process. Put her fancy makeup on—a slightly different routine to her normal one. And get into her dress that she hoped would both fit and look half decent. Sydney and Chloe better not hog the bathroom.

As Jess reached the front door, her phone pinged with a message, and she stopped to check it. Maybe Pam had been right about young people and phones—she probably could have waited until she got inside. Oh well.

It was Chloe texting into the roommate group chat. *Bad news guys, demanding Dana strikes again. I have to work so I'm not going to be able to make it tonight. You two have a blast though! I'm sorry for flaking, Sydney. Win big!!*

No, no, no. It couldn't just be Sydney and Jess alone.

If Chloe wasn't going, then Jess wasn't either. She couldn't.

She let herself into the house and threw her keys into the bowl. Sydney's were already there, and she smiled at her attempt to win the wacky keyring competition—an Elvis style potato. A solid effort, though Chloe still insisted she was the winner.

Sydney herself came running down the stairs wearing a dressing gown and a towel wrapped around her head—clearly in the midst of getting ready. "Did you see Chloe's message?"

Guilt ate at Jess when she clocked the worried look on Sydney's face. How was she supposed to tell her that she wasn't going now either? She swallowed. "I did."

"I was so looking forward to it being the three of us," Sydney said. "But at least you'll be there. We'll have fun, right?"

Jess stared at her, trying to think of an explanation as to why she couldn't go. One that wasn't the truth.

Sydney stared at her apprehensively. "Jess?"

"Yeah?" She coughed to clear her throat. "I mean, yeah. Yes. We will. We'll have fun." There was no way Jess could cancel now. The look on Sydney's face was like a knife through her chest. Jess couldn't let her down.

Sydney's smile showed her relief. "Good. I've finished in the bathroom because I knew you'd need it for the next hour."

Jess laughed at how well Sydney already knew her. "In that case, I better go and prepare myself."

In more ways than one.

❖

Jess blew out a long breath as she checked herself one more time in the mirror. She was going on a date with Sydney.

She needed to stop calling it that, but ever since Chloe had cancelled, those were the words that had swirled round and round Jess's brain on repeat.

It wasn't a real date. Jess knew that. And neither of them would call it a date, not out loud.

But that was exactly what it felt like.

And she needed to meet Sydney downstairs for their date in precisely two minutes' time. *Argh, not a date.*

She spritzed a final squirt of perfume on her neck and wrists, touched up her lipstick, and grabbed her handbag before she could change her mind and hide out in her wardrobe instead—wouldn't that be appropriate in her situation?

As she walked down the stairs where Sydney was waiting, Jess died. She must have because her heart seemed to have stopped beating and she had forgotten how to breathe.

When Sydney turned to face her, Jess had to grab hold of the handrail to steady herself. As their eyes met, Jess's heart began to pound. Not dead then.

Realizing that she had stopped moving, she continued down the stairs, feeling very much like Kate Winslet in *Titanic* heading toward Leonardo DiCaprio. Only Sydney was a much prettier Leo.

She was exquisite.

The deep shade of pink of Sydney's dress looked amazing on her. Jess could never get away with that colour. There was a slit that started just below Sydney's upper thigh, giving Jess a great view of Sydney's long legs. Jess tried not to let her gaze linger there for long. Sydney's hair was down and straight. And the beaming smile she was giving Jess was everything.

"Permission to cross the line? Just once," Sydney asked as Jess reached her.

"I'll grant it. Just once." Like Jess hadn't crossed it so many times herself in her mind.

Sydney unabashedly looked her up and down. "You look so fucking beautiful it should be a crime."

Jess bit her lip and looked down at her dress, suddenly feeling self-conscious under Sydney's appreciative stare. "Thank you," she said softly. She forced her gaze back up. "And you look…" Jess searched for the right word, but none of them did Sydney justice. "You're…" Still nothing good enough came to mind.

Sydney grinned. "I'm going to go ahead and take your lack of words as a compliment."

Jess smiled back at her. "Do."

"Shall we?" Sydney held her arm out for Jess to link hers through.

Jess couldn't help but laugh at her chivalry. She threw Sydney a look that said *seriously?* but stuck her arm through Sydney's anyway, ignoring how her body responded to the contact. If the simple gesture of touching Sydney's arm turned Jess on, what would she be like if she touched her… *Stop.* "Let's do this."

The Uber ride to the event was quiet, but not uncomfortably so. They both watched out the window, the lights of the city flying by. If Jess had to guess why Sydney wasn't saying much, she would say that she was every bit as nervous about their non-date date as Jess was.

A few minutes later, when they arrived at the hotel where the awards ceremony was being held, they were each greeted with a glass of champagne. Jess held hers up. "Oh. This really is a fancy event. You were right about that, big-time businesswoman."

Sydney chuckled. "Hardly big-time."

"You must be kind of big-time. Look at all this." Jess made a sweeping motion around the room that had been decorated with no expense spared. Lots of people were milling around dressed in their best. It all screamed success.

"Rachel is more the brains behind the business. I prefer trying out different smells until I come up with something that I like." Sydney shrugged. "I basically play around for a living."

"Is this award not because of your creative products that you *play around* to make and sell to thousands of customers?"

"I guess."

Jess grinned at her. "See? Let's go and find out where we're sitting, Big Time."

She heard Sydney laugh quietly as she followed Jess to the dining area. There must have been thirty or more tables all draped in white linen tablecloths and laid out with shiny cutlery, ready for the evening ahead. Everyone had an allocated seat, and Jess scoured the different place cards to find theirs.

Sydney found them first. "Here we are." She stopped at a table beside what looked to be a small dance floor. Jess wondered if there would be dancing.

Sydney held up a card with her name on it. Jess and Chloe's name cards were laid on the two spots to Sydney's left. Chloe would have been in the middle had she been there, and Jess beside Chloe.

Jess reached over and swapped those two cards around. After all, it would be weird to leave a gap between Sydney and her. "And we have a spare seat for our handbags thanks to Chlo. Silver linings."

"That's maybe not the only silver lining," Sydney said. Then she seemed to catch herself. "I mean, it's handy to have some, um, space around us."

The thing was, Jess agreed. She couldn't deny that she was having a nice time with Sydney, just the two of them. She had quickly gone from being concerned about Chloe not joining them to being glad that she hadn't.

As they took their seats and sipped their champagne, Jess took in some of the people around them. An idea sprang to mind, and she leaned over to whisper to Sydney. "You see those three men with the matching waistcoats and haircuts?" She subtly gestured to them.

"Mm-hmm."

"They're brothers. They run a second-hand car business. The taller one thinks he's the boss of the group even though they are all supposed to be equal. And the one on the right doesn't know a thing about cars and blags his way through every day."

"Yeah? Do you know them?" Sydney asked.

Jess gave her a look. "No. It's the game, remember?"

The memory must have dawned on Sydney then, and she smiled. She scanned the room herself, ready to play. "The man and woman sitting at that table over there, beside each other but almost facing in opposite directions?"

Jess nodded.

"They're actually business competitors. In advertising. Both of them refused to help out with the advertising for this event, so the organizers thought it would be funny to stick the two of them at the same table. To say they're unimpressed would be an understatement. Especially after that one-night stand they had last year. Though it's never talked about."

"Maybe it'll teach them to be more helpful in the future," Jess said with a grin.

They played the game until the dinner began. Then it was course after course of delicious food and polite small talk with all the other people at their table.

"And what is your business, Jess?" the man sitting opposite—Ted, she had learned—asked her. She had also learned that Ted was in the early stages of launching his own sportswear brand.

"Oh, I'm not here for an award. I'm here to support Sydney and her fantastic business, Makes Scents. I'm a hairdresser myself."

"And a brilliant hairdresser at that. I'd recommend her to anyone," Sydney said, smiling first at Jess, then over at Ted.

The comment warmed Jess right through. Sydney had a way of making her feel important even when she didn't feel it herself.

"You should leave some business cards. Everyone needs a good haircut," Ted suggested. He cut into his chicken. "And how long have the two of you been together?"

"Oh, we're not..."

"Jess and I are just friends." Sydney smiled again, though its sincerity had significantly faded along with its wattage. Jess could tell.

Ted let out a grunt of a laugh. "You could have fooled me. You two have couple written all over you."

Jess tried to come up with an appropriate response, but again Sydney took the lead.

"Why, Ted, I'm flattered that you could think that I'm with a woman as beautiful as Jess, but no. She's already spoken for."

Jess smiled politely, hoping that her cheeks weren't too pink and the conversation would shift onto something else.

It did, thankfully. Ted began to quiz the woman sitting on the other side of Sydney, who ran a dog-grooming business.

The award ceremony itself turned out to be extremely boring. *Long* and boring at that. Jess had to stifle several yawns, much to Sydney's amusement. She only perked up when the spokesperson announced the Creative Products category that Sydney's business was competing in.

He read out the names of the six businesses up for the award, including Makes Scents, and Jess felt Sydney shuffle in her seat beside her, bracing herself. She was bound to be on edge. Jess would be a nervous wreck if it were her.

Ignoring all the reasons not to, Jess reached over and took Sydney's hand in hers. Sydney's fingers immediately gripped hers tightly, and Jess gave her a squeeze of support.

"And the winner is…Lorraine's Luscious Lollipops!"

Well, that wasn't how that was supposed to go. Jess deflated immediately, but when Sydney removed her hand from hers to applaud, Jess politely clapped as well.

She shot Sydney an apologetic look and resisted sending Lorraine a dirty one as she took to the stage to accept her award.

It's fine, Sydney mouthed to her. She smiled to show she wasn't disappointed, though Jess was sure that she must have been. Jess was gutted herself.

"Your soaps are so much better than stupid lollipops," Jess said to Sydney as soon as the ceremony concluded.

Sydney laughed. "I appreciate that, but I really don't mind. I didn't even know we were up for an award until Rachel told me. Besides, I've had the loveliest time tonight. That's so much better than winning some silly award."

"I have too. Apart from Lorraine the award stealer," Jess joked. Kind of. She was clearly much more indignant than Sydney was about the defeat.

"Are you two getting up to dance?" Ted asked as he trotted past them with some of the worst dance moves Jess had ever seen. So, there *was* dancing.

"Wanna?" Sydney asked her.

Jess checked out the dance floor. They were playing some upbeat party tunes, and nobody seemed to be taking themselves too seriously. Jess could get on board with that kind of dancing. "Sure."

They boogied to "Y.M.C.A." and Wham's "Wake Me Up Before You Go-Go," before the inevitable ballads began and people started to couple up for a slow dance.

Sydney looked at Jess in silent question.

This was probably where the line should be drawn, only Jess didn't want to think about lines right then. Would one dance really be so bad? People danced together all the time. It didn't have to mean anything.

Jess gave Sydney a small nod and took a step toward her. Sydney wrapped her arms around her, and Jess followed suit.

Their bodies melded together perfectly. Jess already knew that from the handful of times they had hugged, but there was something much more intimate about dancing together. Sydney was slightly taller than Jess, which meant Jess could comfortably lean her head on Sydney's shoulder as they swayed in time to the music. She felt Sydney's arms tighten around her waist.

They fit. In more ways than one.

Jess stroked her hand down Sydney's back in a move that felt completely normal. She didn't miss Sydney's sharp intake of breath as she moved her hand lower, dangerously close to Sydney's bum. Did Jess want to touch Sydney's bum? Had she made that move intentionally? Jess's mind was in such a jumble, she didn't know. And in that moment, she didn't care.

In response, Sydney pulled Jess even closer, and their breasts pressed together. The feeling was delicious. Jess felt her nipples ache as they strained against the material of her bra. Did Sydney's nipples feel the same? Did she long for Jess's mouth around them as much as Jess longed for Sydney's? Just picturing it made Jess ache elsewhere, and she had to resist the urge to push her hips further into Sydney.

Dancing with a woman felt so different than dancing with a man. Exhilarating. Softer. Better. And far more natural than Jess had expected. She liked the feeling.

When the song ended, Jess literally had to peel herself away from Sydney. There was no way she could keep control of herself if they danced for another song. She was already struggling after four minutes.

Without looking back to see if Sydney was following, Jess made her way back to the table and took a slug of champagne.

"Jess. Wait up." Sydney had followed. Jess heard her laugh. "Where's the fire?"

When Jess turned to meet her eye, Sydney was already right beside her, reaching across Jess to grab her own glass from the table.

How easy it would be for Jess to just reach out and touch her.

To pull her close. To join their bodies exactly like when they had just danced a minute ago—the thought both terrified and excited her.

If Jess kissed Sydney, would Sydney let her? Jess was sure that she would. How would Sydney respond? Would their kiss be light and delicate? Slow and intimate? Or would passion take over as soon as their lips crashed together?

Jess could find out.

All she had to do was lean in. Ever. So. Slightly.

"Oh, thank God. You're both still here. I thought it was a risk showing up so late, but I wasn't too far away from the venue and figured, why not?"

Jess lunged back like she had been shot. Chloe. She turned toward her, trying to keep the panic off her face and probably doing a terrible job of it. "I had an eyelash," she blurted.

Chloe scrunched her forehead. "What?"

"Just then. Sydney was trying to get an eyelash out of my eye."

"Okay," Chloe said as if Jess had just told her something totally inconsequential. "Did she get it?"

"What? Oh, I think so." Jess made a show of blinking a few times. "Yeah, I think it's gone now." Sydney gave her an odd look which she tried to avoid—she was probably puzzled by Jess's sudden bizarre behaviour and the eyelash that never was.

"Well. Great," Chloe said.

"I'm so happy you made it," Sydney said then, reaching forward to hug Chloe. She looked the picture of normal and unfazed. Why wouldn't she? Sydney had no idea that Jess had been seconds away from kissing her.

"Did you win?" Chloe asked Sydney, her face hopeful.

"No. Lorraine's Luscious Lollipops are supposedly more creative than my soaps."

Chloe tutted. "Fuck Lorraine and her lollies." She glanced at Jess. "You okay, Jess? You look like you've seen a ghost."

"Me?" Her voice came out higher than she would have liked. No, Jess was very far from okay. She was the definition of *not* okay. Because if Chloe hadn't interrupted, there was a very real possibility that she would currently have her tongue inside Sydney's mouth, and that wasn't even in the fucking realm of okay. Or was it? *Argh.* Jess didn't know anymore. When it came to Sydney-related matters, she was beyond confused.

And while Jess was facing her major inner dilemma, Sydney was just…fine. Chatting to Chloe like nothing had happened. Which it hadn't. Not for her. Sydney hadn't been the one about to screw up her relationship and change the course of her entire life with a single game of tonsil tennis. Nope—that had been all Jess.

She needed to get out of there. To think things through. Again.

"You know, I'm not feeling the best. Too much champagne, I think. I'm going to head home now that you're here to keep Sydney company." Jess reached for her bag. "Meet you both there?"

She didn't wait for them to answer as she literally turned and fled the scene, feeling like some kind of slutty Cinderella.

What the hell had she been thinking?

CHAPTER TWELVE

If there was one meal that Sydney was good at, it was stew. She made a mean Irish stew. A nice, normal winter meal. Sydney needed some normal right now.

She cooked her meat and onions, then lifted the vegetables that she had already peeled and chopped—potatoes, parsnips, carrots, and leeks—and bunged them into the huge pot on the cooker. She added her jug of stock, a touch of salt and pepper, and left the stew to do its thing.

Thanks to Rachel being a total whizz on orders with her that day, Sydney had been able to leave work an hour early, and she wanted to do something nice for Chloe and Jess to thank them for supporting her. Especially Jess, who had been cagey around her ever since the awards a couple of nights ago. Hence Sydney trying to get things back to normal. Maybe the stew would be a good start.

Sydney wasn't quite sure what had happened. As far as she had been aware, she and Jess had been having a nice time. They'd laughed, and chatted, and okay, they had danced—but it was only one song, and it wasn't like she had snogged Jess in the middle of the dance floor or anything. There had been a few intimate touches, sure, but none had strayed far enough to overstep the mark—although a couple may have come close.

The only thing Sydney could think of was the moment right after they had danced. Sydney knew desire when she saw it, and maybe it was the dance that had sparked it in Jess. That, and the way Jess had shot back when Chloe arrived, rambling about a non-existent eyelash, all but confirmed it.

Jess must have wanted Sydney.

Still, nothing had happened between them—sadly, in Sydney's opinion—so why the reaction? No lines had been crossed. Which made Sydney wonder, how close had Jess come to crossing it?

Very, she suspected, if it warranted Jess freaking out so much.

Sydney didn't know whether to be happy about that, or totally frustrated. She let herself feel a mixture of both. Obviously, she wanted Jess to want her back. It was pretty much all she thought about these days. But on the flip side, if Jess truly did want her, then why did she refuse to do something about it?

Two hours later, Sydney was ready to confront Jess with that very question when she walked into the kitchen. It fell dead on her tongue when she saw Austin appear behind her. "Oh. Hey." She refrained from a lip curl.

"Hey," Jess said semi-normally, except for the fact that she couldn't make eye contact with Sydney. "We were just coming in to make some dinner, but we can come back when you're done."

Jess turned to leave again, but Austin must have had other ideas and took a seat at the kitchen table. It just had to be the spot that Sydney usually sat at, didn't it? Maybe she was becoming too petty.

"I actually made dinner for all of us." Sydney almost had to grit her teeth to get the next part out, but her mum had brought her up to have manners, so she had to. "I didn't know you were coming, Austin, but there's enough for you too if you want some."

"I'd love some. That's really kind of you. Thanks, Sydney."

Great, he was being pleasant. It was so much easier for Sydney when Austin was acting like an ass whom she could despise.

"Oh. How long will it be until it's ready?" Jess asked, shifting uncomfortably from one foot to the other. All of them sitting around eating dinner together like the Brady Bunch probably hadn't been in Jess's plans.

Sydney peered into the pot. "It's ready. The longer it's left, the better it tastes, but we can eat now. Though maybe we should wait for Chloe." *Please wait for Chloe*—preferably in a different room. Reinforcements were required for this level of awkward.

Jess shook her head immediately. "No, we don't have to wait—"

"It's fine, Jess. We can wait," Austin said. "I'd only get the blame if we didn't." What had him on his best behaviour all of a sudden?

Sydney sent up a silent prayer that Dana didn't have anything for Chloe to do that would keep her past her normal working hours.

Austin patted his knee, beckoning for Jess to sit on it. Seriously? Did people really do that?

Thankfully, Jess declined and pulled up the seat next to him instead. Sydney was sure her lunch from earlier would have made a swift reappearance if Jess had opted for the lap.

So, they were all going to wait for Chloe together. How cosy.

"I hear commiserations are in order for the other night," Austin said to Sydney. "Those award things can be tricky."

"It's fine. It was a good night in lots of other ways." Sydney glanced at Jess, who was keeping her eyes fixed firmly on the kitchen table in front of her. "Your girlfriend was excellent company."

"That's my girl." Austin wrapped an arm round Jess, who immediately leaned into him like it was the most natural thing in the world. It seemed like an automatic response. Probably because it was. Austin was Jess's person, after all. Not Sydney. "She's the best."

They remained like that, cuddled up, as Sydney hovered awkwardly beside the stove. "Do you guys have any plans after dinner?" she asked as means of small talk. An attempt to fill the silence.

"I'm staying over," Austin said pointedly. He glanced over at Jess. "Finally, some quality time with my girl." He bit his bottom lip and grinned at Jess, while his gaze dropped to Jess's mouth, or maybe it was lower. Sydney didn't let her eyes linger for long enough to be sure.

And she didn't need three guesses to decipher what *quality time* stood for. She practically shuddered. Had someone just thrown a bucket of ice water right over her head? She felt cold and shivery all over. Not to forget nauseous—that was a major feeling in that moment.

Sydney needed to distract herself. She grabbed a spray bottle and a cloth and started to wipe everything on the counter. Beanie was about to sparkle.

Unfortunately, images of *quality time* still flashed through her brain. *Argh.*

It was fine. Sydney just needed to think about nicer things—mind over matter. Cocktails in the sunshine. Cute little puppies with their tongues hanging out. A full week off work. A long, hot shower on a freezing cold day.

"What's wrong with your neck?" Sydney heard Jess ask Austin. She kept wiping with her back turned to them.

He groaned. "It's my neck and my shoulders, babe. I've been leaning over my desk all week and they're killing me." A pause. "Ooh. Maybe you'll get some oil out later. Say yes." They both started to laugh. There was shuffling. Was he tickling her? Sydney refused to look. "Yeah?" Austin said through their giggles. "Yeah?"

Sydney closed her eyes. Clear blue skies. The first bloom of flowers in springtime. The first coffee of the day from Beanie. A hug from her nephew.

"Austin, stop," Jess said, still laughing quietly.

"Say you'll rub my shoulders later and I'll stop."

"No."

A big bar of milk chocolate. The feeling when her new soap sold out. Hyde Park in autumn.

"Say it." More laughter.

"No!"

"Say it."

Sydney whipped around. "Oh my God, please just fucking say it!" *Oh, shit.* She clasped her hand over her mouth.

Both Austin and Jess froze and gaped at her.

Sydney froze too. She opened her mouth to explain, but no words came out.

Then Austin's face relaxed into a lazy grin. "See? Even Sydney thinks you should say it."

Jess, on the other hand, didn't relax. At least she had the decency to look embarrassed. She nudged Austin to shut up.

Sydney plastered on a smile, not caring how false it must have looked. "Shall we just go ahead and eat?" Acting like a little piece of her didn't die inside every time Jess was with Austin was exhausting, and she could only keep it up for so long—the cracks were already starting to show with that outburst.

Jess nodded quickly. "Yes."

"What's the rush?" Austin asked. "And why are you two being weird around each other?"

"We're not," Sydney and Jess both said at the same time.

Austin glanced between them in confusion. Then he started to smile. "Oh, I see."

"See what?" Jess asked.

"I've heard about these little tiffs when girls live together." He lowered his voice. "Too many hormones flying around."

Oh, there he was. The real Austin. The ass Sydney loved to hate.

Jess gave him a slap on the arm. It was slightly comforting to know that Jess wasn't ignorant to his chauvinist comments; however, why she chose to endure them remained a mystery to Sydney.

"You're imagining things," Jess said. "There's no tiff."

But there *was* silence. And it seemed to drag on forever.

"Hey, guys. I'm home," Chloe called from the hall what felt like hours later. Sydney had never been so happy to hear her voice.

"In here," Sydney shouted back. If she could have got away with it, she would have followed up with, *"Hurry!"*

Chloe appeared through the kitchen door like a guardian angel in office wear. "Oh goody. We're all here." She threw a sarcastic smile in Austin's direction. "What smells so good?"

"Sydney's cooking. She's been kind enough to make dinner for all of us." Jess offered Sydney a small smile then. Of thanks? Of peace? Of apology for flaunting her boyfriend in Sydney's face? Was she trying to prove to the room that things were fine between her and Sydney after they had been called out?

Chloe held a hand up to her heart. "For us to eat together like one big, happy family? Yay!" She laughed at her own sardonic humour, then came over to join Sydney. She leaned over and peered into the pot. "Seriously, though, that looks amazing. Thanks, Sydney."

Did it? Sydney had lost her appetite.

She took a deep breath. All she had to do was get through one meal, then she could lock herself away for the night and pretend that Jess wasn't lathering Austin with oil and doing God knows what in the next room.

Easy, right?

It was no surprise that sleep didn't come easily to Sydney. She tossed and turned, and hoped with all her heart that she didn't hear any unwanted noises coming from Jess's bedroom.

She didn't, but that didn't stop Sydney's torturous, overactive brain picturing things that she really did not want to picture. Things that turned her stomach and made her want to hurl.

If that wasn't bad enough, on top of Sydney's repulsion, there was an aching feeling in her chest. An ache like that could only mean one thing.

Sydney had let her heart get involved.

She hadn't meant to let this thing with Jess get any bigger than an attraction, a few feelings that would fade with time—because she knew the risks. There were too many obstacles, and when she couldn't overcome them, she would get hurt.

But it *had* got bigger. And now Sydney was falling for a woman who was unavailable, uninterested, and unwilling to change.

She grabbed her phone and googled *how to sleep with heartache.* She scrolled through results.

The first one was to stay away from screens. Sydney breathed out a laugh. It was too late for that. What other suggestions were there?

Sleeping tablets? No. Left her too groggy the next day.

Meditation? Sydney did enjoy meditating. She wished she could switch her mind off long enough.

Chamomile tea? She didn't love tea, but that could work. Sydney had spied some chamomile teabags in the kitchen cupboard. They must have been Jess's, but Jess owed her. After all, it was her fault that Sydney couldn't sleep.

She swung her legs out of bed and headed downstairs to the kitchen. Remembering how she had bumped into Jess the last time she had got up in the middle of the night, Sydney switched on the light immediately so there wouldn't be a repeat.

Mercifully, there was no one else there. Good. Sydney wasn't in the mood for any late-night chats with Jess.

She waited for the kettle to boil, dropped a teabag into a cup, poured in the water, then quickly fled the kitchen.

As she turned the light out and headed toward the stairs, Sydney heard movement coming from the living room. What was it with this house at night-time? Did people not sleep?

On further inspection, she could see light coming from the crack underneath the living room door. She edged closer and heard a muffled voice. A deep muffled voice.

Which meant it could only be Austin.

Who was he talking to? Sydney tried to listen, but she couldn't hear anyone else. He must have been talking to someone on the phone. Who would he be talking to in the middle of the night? It must have been well after one a.m.

Sydney shook her head. Not her problem.

When she turned to leave, and she turned too quickly, hot water swished over the side of her cup and right over her hand. "Shit."

"Hello?" Austin said from the living room, obviously hearing the commotion. He mumbled something quickly, then appeared at the door before Sydney had a chance to flee to the safety of her bedroom.

"Oh. Hi," Sydney said, attempting to sound blasé, like she didn't realize he was there. Because she wasn't trying to listen into Austin's conversation. Nope. Not her.

Austin smiled at her, but there was something off about him. Shifty even. "What are you doing down here?" he asked. Sydney could tell that he was uneasy. What had she almost witnessed?

"I could ask you the same thing," she said.

"Oh." He looked behind him into the living room and pointed. "That? That was a work call." He made a point of rolling his eyes. "You know us lawyers. On call twenty-four seven."

"Right." Sydney didn't believe him for one second, but she wasn't going to argue. *Not my problem*, she repeated to herself.

"You didn't hear anything did you? You know, confidentiality and all that."

Why did Sydney suspect that the confidentiality had nothing to do with his job? "No, I didn't even know you were in there. I was in the kitchen." Not a complete lie.

He nodded. "Good. Good."

Sydney forced a smile. "Well, goodnight, Austin. I'll let you get back to your...work call." She went to pass him, but he put out an arm to stop her.

"So soon? We only started to chat."

Sydney glanced at the outstretched arm that now blocked her path. Not ideal. "Yeah, I just came down for some tea." She held up her cup as evidence. "If you'll excuse—"

"Why don't you drink it down here? We could, um, get to know each other better." Austin cast his eyes downward, and...wait. Did he just look down Sydney's top? No. She must have imagined it.

Still, she tensed up even more. "Where's Jess?" she asked. *You know, your girlfriend.*

"She's in bed. Jess sleeps like the dead, don't worry." Austin grinned. "Come on. Come sit down in the living room. It'll just be us."

"Why would we just want it to be us?" Was Austin hitting on her?

"No reason. But I thought it might be nice. The two of us haven't had a chance to get properly acquainted...yet." Austin ran his gaze over her again, and this time Sydney was in no doubt that he was checking her out. There was no mistaking the predatory look in his eye.

She stared at him in horror. "I think you might be barking up the wrong tree here."

He looked momentarily confused, but then his face relaxed into a smirk. "Oh. You mean the lesbian thing?"

Sydney let out a bitter laugh in disbelief. "I mean the you have a girlfriend thing. One who happens to be a friend of mine. What exactly do you think you're doing here?"

"What are you talking about?"

"I'm talking about you coming on to me. In your girlfriend's house, Austin? Really?"

"Whoa, whoa, whoa. That's not what I was doing." He held his hands up.

Sydney took the opportunity to start to slowly edge away from him. "No?"

"Of course not. You're clearly imaging things."

"I don't think I was."

Austin glared at her for a few seconds, then let out a nasty chuckle. "This is what I get for trying to be nice. It's not my fault you got it so twisted." He sneered. "You girls are all the same."

Sydney backed away toward the stairs. "Stay away from me, Austin. Jess might not realize what kind of an asshole you are. But I see you. And I'll be very happy when Jess does too."

He pointed after her. "Don't you even think about poisoning my girlfriend's head with your silly, made-up stories."

"Maybe you should have thought about that before."

"Yeah?" Austin smiled smugly. "And who's she going to believe? Her loving boyfriend? Or some delusional girl she's only just met?"

"The only delusional one here is you." Sydney turned and walked up the stairs, ignoring what she was sure were the words *fucking bitch* being muttered behind her. She felt like sprinting, but she refused to show Austin any weakness, so she forced herself to keep a steady pace.

She could feel Austin's eyes on her the whole way.

It was only when Sydney reached her bedroom and shut the door that she dropped the composure. She leaned against the door and gasped. Had that really happened? It had, hadn't it? What a creep.

Sydney already disliked Austin, with his condescending remarks and superior attitude. In fact, she couldn't stand him. But she hadn't realized that he was such bad news.

Did Austin hit on women all the time? Was he a cheat?

Sydney didn't know, but she did know one thing.

She needed to talk to Jess.

❖

Sydney waited until she heard Austin leave the following morning. She couldn't bear to look at his smarmy face for even a second. If she never had to lay eyes on him again, that would do her just fine.

As soon as the front door banged closed, Sydney made her way downstairs. She spied that Jess's keys were still in the bowl, so she hadn't left for work. And Chloe's keys were gone, which meant they could talk in private. Good. Sydney didn't want an audience. She didn't relish the thought of telling Jess that her boyfriend was an untrustworthy, unfaithful pig. But she had to. Jess deserved to know.

As soon as Sydney entered the kitchen, Jess practically leapt in front of her. "Sydney, I need to talk to you."

"You do? That's good because there's something I need to talk to you about too."

"I think I already know what it's about," Jess said, pushing her fingers through her hair. "Austin was really upset this morning."

Did Sydney hear that right? "Austin was upset?"

Jess nodded. "He said that you two had a bit of a misunderstanding last night, and he's really annoyed about it today."

"Okay." *This took a turn.* "Did he tell you what this misunderstanding was about?"

"He said that he was trying to be nice to you and that you might have taken it the wrong way." Jess winced at her, like Sydney was the one who had made a mistake.

"He was trying to be nice to me?" Sydney repeated in disbelief. "He blatantly hit on me, Jess." There was no point in sugar-coating it, especially seeing as Austin had already tried to do that for himself. "I assure you, there wasn't a wrong way to take it."

"Hit on you?" Jess frowned and shook her head. "See, that's what Austin was worried about. He said that you might have misinterpreted his intentions."

"Did he? Tell me. What exactly did he say happened?" Sydney couldn't wait to hear how Austin had spun things.

Jess frowned in concentration as she recalled what he had said. "He told me that he came out of the living room after an urgent call with a client, and he saw you in the hallway holding a cup. He told you that you were welcome to drink it in the living room, and you didn't have to leave just because he was there." Jess grimaced. "But he said that he got the impression that you took it as an invitation. Like he was trying to get you alone or something when really, he was only being polite."

Funnily enough, polite wasn't a word that Sydney would have associated with Austin, nor with much of his behaviour. Did Jess really believe that bullshit story?

"I see." Sydney rolled her lips in and bit down on them to stop herself from blurting out any of the furious responses in her head. She composed herself and proceeded to tell Jess the truth. "So, he didn't mention that he stopped me from leaving because he thought that we should...how did he put it? Oh yes, 'get to know each other better'?" she said, doing air quotes with her fingers. "And that it would be 'just us' because you were asleep? Or how about that he didn't take his eyes off my chest while he was talking to me? He didn't tell you any of those things?"

"Austin would never—"

"Austin *did*, Jess! That's what I was coming here to tell you this morning. Why would I make that up?"

Jess began taking things in and out of her bag for no obvious reason. "Well, you obviously don't like Austin." More fidgeting. "And, I mean, we've already established that you *do* like me, so..." She trailed off, leaving Sydney to work out what she was insinuating.

Which Sydney did. "Seriously? You really think that I would pretend that your boyfriend came onto me, in, what? Some kind of ruse to get you to be with me?"

Jess flung her hands in the air. "No, I don't really think that. But how am I supposed to believe that he would do something like that? What kind of a girlfriend would that make me? Yet I…" She paused and abandoned her handbag, looking up toward the ceiling instead. "Forget it. I don't know what to think right now."

Jess wasn't naïve. She had to, on some level, know that Austin was capable of some questionable behaviour. Sydney hoped that deep down Jess also knew that Sydney would never lie to her. Part of her wanted to console Jess. But as much as Sydney had no desire to make things any worse than they already were, she needed Jess to learn the truth.

"Who has work calls in the middle of the night?" Sydney pushed on.

"What?"

"Austin's a junior lawyer, Jess. He's not the bloody prime minister."

"So? What's your point?"

Sydney took a breath. "That I seriously doubt that he was whispering down a phone on a work call at that time of night."

Jess glared at her. "Well, now you're grasping at straws. What do you think? That my boyfriend is seeing someone else, and I wouldn't realize it? I would know if Austin was cheating."

"It doesn't reflect badly on you if he is. Most cheaters are great at hiding it. Until they aren't."

"Well, Austin isn't a cheater."

"You're sure? Even though he had no qualms about chatting up your roommate in your own house?"

"What are you trying to achieve here, Sydney?" Jess asked.

"Me? Nothing." Sydney let out a long sigh. "This wasn't supposed to be about me, or you and me. I just thought that you had the right to know what happened."

If Jess wasn't prepared to listen, there was nothing she could do. Sydney had told her the truth. What she did with that was up to her. They stood in silence for a few minutes, neither of them able to look at each other. Sydney focussed her attention on the tap that dripped every three seconds.

Jess was the one who broke the silence. "Look. Even if Austin was…more flirtatious than he told me…" She paused, like she was trying to come to terms with that part herself. "He's a renowned charmer. Not that it's okay at all, it isn't, but maybe that's what it was."

"Well, his *charm* certainly made me feel uncomfortable." Sydney would never get a better moment to tell Jess what she really thought. "You deserve to be with someone who treats you better than that. I've heard the way he speaks to you sometimes, Jess. It's gross. And last night…was just the icing on the cake."

Jess stared at her. The mask of defiance that she had been wearing seemed to soften into something more vulnerable. "So, what would you have me do? Leave him? Over some stupid remarks and him checking you out? Don't you think that would be kind of hypocritical of me?"

"What do you mean?" Sydney asked, genuinely confused.

"Well…" Jess hesitated. "Am I not guilty of doing something similar? Of being attracted to you?"

Sydney scoffed. "No, Jess. It's not similar at all. In fact, it couldn't be any more different."

"Really? How?" Jess asked quietly. "How am I any better than he is?"

"Because you and I have feelings for each other. Actual, real-life feelings. Yet we aren't sneaking around, having some seedy affair. We aren't doing anything! Nothing can happen between us because you're with him. *You've* put boundaries on us, and I agree with them. I do. I've been cheated on before, and I never want to be the cause of anyone else's pain." Sydney paused. She had to be delicate. "But it's almost like you stay with him as a shield, even though you're unhappy. Like you're using your relationship to hide from something real. From something that could potentially be amazing."

Jess looked at Sydney wide-eyed. "Are you suggesting that I leave Austin? I leave him, and you and I be together instead?" She shook her head quickly. "Sydney, I've never dated a woman."

"I know. I'm not saying that I have all the answers here. All I know is that we do like each other."

"I do like you." Jess tilted her head slightly and gave Sydney a smile that could only be described as regretful. "I like you too much to let you be my experiment."

"Sometimes experiments work out." If only Jess would give them a chance, Sydney would happily take the risk.

"And sometimes they go down in flames." Jess reached for her bag. "I better get to work."

Sydney swallowed down the lump that was forming in her throat. "Wait. What about the thing with Austin? What he did last night wasn't cool, Jess. You and I aside, you still deserve better."

Jess pushed a strand of hair behind her ear and cast her gaze down. "Is there any chance you were mistaken?"

"None," Sydney replied surely.

Jess sighed and nodded. "Okay. I'll speak to him. Whatever happens, I promise, you won't be made to feel uncomfortable again."

Sydney nodded. "I appreciate that, but honestly I'm more worried about you."

Jess waved her off. "I'll be fine."

"I know you will. But I'll still worry because I care," Sydney said softly. "How about us? Are we okay?"

Jess cleared her throat. "Of course. We're good."

Sydney felt instant relief. She hated being the bearer of bad news. "I'm sorry that I had to put all this on you."

"No, I'm sorry for Austin's terrible behaviour."

"Totally not your fault. He's the one who should be sorry."

"And he will be," Jess replied.

❖

Jess wasn't an impulsive person. Normally, she took her time to think things through before she acted on, well, anything. She always tried to consider all the different angles and possibilities before coming to her own conclusions.

Only this time, Jess didn't need to think.

Even when Austin had spun his story to her the very second that she had opened her eyes that morning, Jess had felt like something was off—she just hadn't realized *how* off. There had been something different about Austin, about his demeanour, but Jess couldn't put her finger on what it was. She put it down to him being upset about what had happened during the night. But when she heard Sydney's side of things, it began to click.

Austin had been acting strangely because he had got caught.

Jess knew in her gut that Sydney was telling her the truth. Not that she had wanted to believe it. Who wanted to believe that their partner was capable of being unfaithful? But the more it sank in, the more sense it made. And now Jess had a ton of questions, and Austin had a lot of explaining to do.

Jess had thought that her day was going to drag like a month of Sundays. That was always the way, wasn't it? When you had somewhere to go or something to do, time seemed to slow down. But surprisingly, her workday flew by, and before Jess knew it, she was headed in the direction of Austin's office. He had told Jess that he would be working late for the next few days, so she knew exactly where to find him.

Rather than arriving unannounced, she took out her phone and called Austin's number. No answer. No shock there. Lately, Jess had spoken to Austin's voicemail more than to the man himself.

Unannounced it was, then. Jess was sure that Austin would be able to spare her ten minutes considering it was their relationship on the line.

The weirdest part was, Jess wasn't nervous. She was going to confront her boyfriend of eight years about him hitting on her roommate, and she felt strangely calm about doing so. Probably because deep down Jess had known that their relationship had been struggling for a while. She just hadn't wanted to face it before. But now that she couldn't *not* face it, Jess was ready—whatever the outcome.

The street that Austin worked on was nice. Among the multitude of varied office buildings there were a bunch of trendy bars and restaurants that were always bustling with people. A good sign. Jess took her time to look through each of the windows to see which places she might want to try sometime.

She was peering through the window of a fancy-looking Italian restaurant when she found herself having to do a double take because she could have sworn that she had spotted Austin inside. When she scanned the restaurant again, sure enough, Austin was sitting at a table opposite a woman. A very attractive woman, Jess noted.

No big deal, she told herself. It could very easily have been a work thing. Maybe the woman was a colleague, or a client. But as Jess watched Austin reach over and top up the woman's wine glass, then take the woman's hand in his, she dismissed that thought.

Wow.

Fearing it was true had been one thing, but watching it play out right in front of her eyes was a whole other ball game—Austin really was cheating on her. And look how easy it had been to find out.

How had she been so stupid?

Jess tore her gaze away and leaned against the wall next to the building. She didn't know whether she wanted to laugh, scream, or cry. She felt like she was a cocktail brimming with feelings and emotions. Shock. Hurt. Disgust. Embarrassment. Foolishness.

But strangely, mixed into that cocktail, Jess also felt relieved, in a way. Because the doubts and questions were all gone. She finally knew for certain that her relationship was over, and she suddenly had total clarity about what she needed to do next.

And there was no time like the present.

Before Jess could think better of it, she pushed herself off the wall and marched straight into the restaurant. Was she sure that it was a good idea? Nope. But she was doing it anyway.

She strode over to Austin's table with as much confidence as she could muster, making sure she kept her head held high.

Austin was still reaching across the table caressing the woman's hand, the woman completely engrossed in whatever charming story he was telling. It took a few seconds for him to notice that anyone, let alone Jess, was standing beside the table. Judging by his lack of reaction, he mistook her for waiting staff at first, but the second that he realized it was Jess, his face dropped. And so did the woman's hand, hitting the table with a thud as Austin quickly let it go.

Jess plastered on a smile. She didn't care how fake it obviously was. "Austin! Imagine running into you here." She had to admit, she enjoyed watching all the colour drain from his face.

"I...um...this..."

"Can we talk in private?" Jess asked, keeping the smile glued to her face. She was sure that Austin would prefer to speak less publicly. Jess looked over at the woman, who was staring at her like she had three heads. Apart from that, she really was very pretty. "Hi, so good to meet you. And I'm sorry to disturb, but you don't mind if I steal your date, do you? This will only take a moment."

The woman looked the picture of bewilderment, but she nodded. "Sure."

Austin nearly jumped off his seat. He grabbed Jess by the elbow and ushered her away from the table. "What are you…how did you…" He was spluttering. "Look, this isn't what it looks like."

"No? Because it looks like you're on a date with another woman."

"I can explain." Austin paused, and Jess waited. "It's a work meeting. I work with that woman," he ended up settling on, his shifty eyes betraying him. The same shifty eyes that Jess had seen that very morning.

Did he really think Jess was so gullible? "Aww, a meeting? Silly me. Okay, you can introduce me, then."

Austin froze. He clearly hadn't thought that lie through.

"No? Tell me, do you hold hands with everyone you work with?" Jess dropped the niceties then. "Save it, Austin. You're a liar, and you're a cheat. And you've got caught." She let out a humourless laugh. "And to think, all this time. All the excuses I've made for you. And all along, you've been having an affair. Or several affairs, I don't know. And you know what? I've just realized that I don't even care."

"This is the first time, I swear," Austin conceded, his tone turning desperate. "It's a mistake. I've made a mistake, Jess."

"Oh really? The first time?"

"Yes."

"Then what was last night when you hit on Sydney? Was that the first time too? Another *mistake*?"

"I already explained what happened to you this morning."

"Yeah," Jess said. "You lied to try and save your own ass because you realized that you'd fucked up when you hit on *my* friend, in *my* home."

He scoffed. "Like I would ever do that."

"But you did. I know you did. Sydney told me what really happened, and I believe her. You want to know why?" Jess didn't wait for an answer. "Because Sydney is one of the kindest, most genuine, and honest people I know, and she cares about me. And you—well, you're nothing but a lying sack of shit."

"Now, wait a minute. She's the one who's lying—"

"Austin. The evidence is right here." Jess pointed toward the woman sitting at the table waiting for Austin to return to their date. "In this restaurant. If I needed any confirmation, I got it tonight."

"I told you—this is just a mistake. I don't even know what I was thinking. I wasn't thinking, I—"

"Stop." Jess blew out a heavy breath. "Please stop with all the lies and the excuses. Let's face the truth, Austin, shall we?"

"What do you mean? What truth?"

"That me and you are over. And we've been over for a long time." God, it felt good to finally say it out loud. Like a weight had been lifted off Jess's shoulders. Like in some way, she was being set free.

He shook his head. "No."

"Yes, Austin. We are."

Austin leaned in closer to her, flashing his charming grin. Only Jess didn't find it charming at all. Not anymore. "Come on, baby. You don't really believe that, do you? Maybe we can do something. Fix this. Yeah?"

Jess took a step back. "I doubt it. But even if we could, I don't want to." She kept her voice steady, determined to remain calm and composed. "I'm done. I've been done for a while now."

His grin faded quickly. "So, that's it? Just like that? Even with all our history, and all our plans for the future, you're ending this?"

"Yes. If you cared about our history, or our plans, or about me at all for that matter, you wouldn't be seeing other women, Austin. At some point over the years, you changed. Hell, maybe I've changed too. But I don't think that we work anymore, and I think it's time that we both move on and try and find our own happiness. Separately. And despite everything, I do hope that you find yours."

"You're seriously just going to walk away? From *me*?" He laughed. "You'll come crawling back."

Jess's brain was starting to get dizzy from going around in circles. She had said what she needed to say. "That's exactly what I'm going to do, and no, I don't think I will." Jess made a point of turning and giving Austin's date a wave. She didn't look happy. "Say bye to your date for me. Word of warning, from the look she's giving you, I think she's worked out what's going on. Goodbye, Austin."

And with that, Jess turned on her heel and left the restaurant without looking back. It was only when she stepped out into the fresh air that she stopped to take a couple of shaky breaths.

Had she really just done that? Had it been the right thing to do?

Jess knew that it was—she just couldn't believe how much had happened in the space of a day. *One day.* That's how long it had taken for her whole life to change.

Her heart started to hurt like hell, but it didn't hurt for that guy— she never wanted to see that guy again. No, Jess's heart ached for an Austin who had faded away a long time ago. In truth, there weren't even glimpses of the man who Jess had once thought she would spend the rest of her life with anymore. And that made her sad. It was baffling how much people could change.

Jess felt her phone vibrate in her pocket and she pulled it out. It was Sydney.

Hey, just checking to make sure you're okay.

Of course Sydney texted precisely when Jess needed it.

I will be, she typed back. Then she realized how vague that sounded, so she added, *I broke up with Austin.*

Sydney's reply came seconds later. *Oh my God. Are you okay? Where are you? I'm home, but do you want me to meet you? Do you want Chloe? I can call and summon her. What do you need?*

No summoning required. I'm on my way home.

I'll get some tea ready. Someone wise once told me that tea makes everything better.

Despite everything, Jess found herself smiling at that. That's what she had told Sydney when they first met. And Sydney had remembered. The simple gesture comforted Jess immediately.

And in that moment, although she no longer knew what her future held, Jess just knew that everything was going to be okay.

Chapter Thirteen

Y our side needs to go higher," Jess said, holding one side of a string of metallic green tinsel.

Chloe struggled to reach. "Did you ever consider that maybe it's your side that needs to be lower?"

"No, it's definitely yours." Jess grinned. "Go on. Big stretch."

"I hate you." Chloe groaned as she got up on her tiptoes and stretched up to stick the tinsel to the wall. "If you want it up any further, you can do it your damn self."

Jess laughed. "I suppose it will do. Short arse."

"Oh, because you're *so* tall with your average five-foot-five frame." Chloe stepped back a few steps to assess their work. She gave it a nod of approval. "You know who should be helping with these bits? Sydney. She's like, what? Five-eight?"

Jess usually tried not to focus on Sydney's body too much—not an easy task. "Yeah, she's tall. Did you tell her we're decorating today?"

"I messaged her earlier to ask if she would be home to help. She said that they were swamped with Christmas orders and that we should go ahead and start without her. She hopes to be home in time to help us decorate the tree."

Jess hoped so too. She liked it when Sydney was there. "Maybe Sydney can do the star, then."

Chloe clasped her hands together. "Thank God for that. No more Pilates for me."

Jess held up her forefinger. "Hold that thought." She bent down to rifle through one of the storage boxes. She gathered up three more wall decorations including a long banner. "I think that wall over there is looking kinda bare. Don't you?"

Chloe glared at her. "Sometimes I wonder why we're friends."

Jess chuckled and threw over a ball of Blu Tack, which Chloe skilfully caught. "They say Pilates is good for you."

"Yeah, yeah, yeah," Chloe mumbled. "I don't remember it being this much like hard work last year. Did Freya do the stretches?"

"No, Austin did." Jess looked down and focussed on the Blu Tack she was holding. She ripped a piece off and rolled it between her fingers. Since the break-up, Jess had tried not to think about Austin too much. She hated that it still hurt weeks later, especially considering how things had ended up. But Austin had been a big part of her life for a long time, and Jess guessed that it was only natural that it would take some time to adjust to life without him.

"Ew. That's probably why I'd forgotten. I tend to block out such precious memories as those."

"Exactly what I'm trying to do."

They were silent for a few moments, then Chloe muttered, "Wanker."

Jess found herself laughing because as blunt as Chloe was, it was true. She couldn't have said it any better herself.

"Seriously, though, how are you with that?" Chloe asked with genuine concern. "Are you doing okay?"

"Getting there, I think. I know that I did the right thing. Even besides the cheating, I hadn't been happy with him for a while. Ending things was inevitable."

"So, no regrets?"

"God no." Jess shook her head. "Honestly, I only regret that I didn't do it sooner. I put up with so much. I wish I had listened to you. I feel like you hated him forever and I stayed oblivious for too long."

Chloe seemed to consider that. "I wouldn't say I hated him forever. No, we were never best buddies or anything—for a long time he was just your boyfriend who I said hello to now and again when I saw you together. I don't think I really had *any* opinion of him. Until I did. So don't beat yourself up. He wasn't always terrible."

"Just for the past...?" Jess posed it as a question.

Chloe squinted as she thought. "Year. Definitely." She gritted her teeth. "Probably nearer two in all honesty. But I never dreamt that he was a cheat. Simply a self-absorbed, snide, pompous prick—but he even managed to exceed my expectations of his awfulness."

"Tell me how you really feel," Jess said jokingly, though she agreed with all those things now too. There was nothing like seeing a person's true colours to highlight all the flaws you'd been overlooking.

"Oh, I will. I'm allowed to now."

"Not that it ever stopped you before."

"It didn't, did it?" Chloe chuckled. "You'll be fine, Jess. Better, in fact, without him. I promise."

Jess nodded. "I know. It's just taking some getting used to. I haven't been single in, well, ever. Not since I was a teenager."

"So, enjoy it. Look after you. And when you're ready to be with someone again, I'm in no doubt that you'll find the right man."

"Man. Woman. Whatever," Jess said before she could catch herself.

"Women? Seriously? Are you still on that?"

Jess shrugged to try and remain casual. "Maybe I should leave my options open."

Chloe gave her a doubtful look. "I'm still pretty sure you'll end up with some clean-shaven dude who wears a suit every day and folds his underwear."

Jess wondered if Sydney folded her underwear. Then she got a shiver just thinking about Sydney's underwear. About Sydney in her underwear, about Sydney out of her underwear. *Stop.* That was the problem, though. Jess didn't seem to be able to stop thinking about Sydney. Even more so lately since it was, technically, no longer forbidden. But she shouldn't, because even with Austin gone, the other reasons remained. Didn't they? Plus, Jess was literally only out of a long-term relationship. Rushing into anything else, especially something unknown, wouldn't be wise. "How about you and Dana?" Jess asked, ready to change the subject.

Chloe ran a hand over her face. "Nothing to tell. Not really. She's being lovely to me again—professionally. Making sure that we work closely together and acting like I'm the most valued employee ever. Like I'm her oxygen and she can't possibly manage without me." Chloe held up a hand, palm forward. "And before you say it, I know what she's doing, but God do I love it."

That was Jess's cue to roll her eyes.

"I know, I know. I'm a sucker and she knows how to play me. But I'm embracing us working harmoniously together, with the full knowledge of what Dana's like. So, basically, I'm taking it for what it is, and I'm covered emotionally. Sounds healthy, right?"

Jess moved her head two and frow. "Healthier than before. But I still see the glimmer of hope in your eyes."

"As it happens, the hope in my eyes is glimmering for someone else these days." Chloe thought about it. "Well, maybe there's still some glimmering for Dana too."

"Oh, yeah? Who?"

Chloe looked at Jess like she had just tried to add up two plus two and come up with sixty-seven. "Sydney." She lifted her eyebrows. "Did you see her at that awards ceremony? She looked am-az-ing."

Ah, yes, Jess had seen her all right. Jess had thought about Sydney in that pink dress at least ten times a day since. Apparently, so had her best friend—one of the very big Sydney obstacles that still remained. Jess couldn't disregard Chloe's feelings. She tried to laugh off her discomfort. "So, you're replacing your hot boss fantasy with a hot roommate fantasy?"

"No. I do think that Sydney is gorgeous, but I also think she is an awesome human being. I happen to like her a lot."

Jess couldn't agree more. "Is it a good idea, though? To date someone you live with? It could end up pretty awkward if things didn't work out." Maybe Jess was reflecting her own worst-case scenario.

Chloe gave her a funny look. "I'm starting to think that you don't want me to go out with Sydney."

Jess avoided Chloe's gaze by focussing on hanging the snowman wall plaque in her hand. "Why would you think that?"

"Before when I first talked about it, you told me to wait until I got over Dana. Now you're saying that it's a bad idea because she's our roommate."

When Chloe put it like that, maybe it was kind of obvious that Jess was against the idea. Because, selfishly, she was. In all honesty, even the thought of watching Sydney and Chloe together felt like torture. But although she hated the thought, maybe it was the medicine that she needed to get over Sydney once and for all.

And who was Jess to stand in the way of her best friend's happiness anyway? She would never. No, she needed to back down. "I'm just highlighting the risks. Ignore me."

"Some things are worth the risk, Jess."

Were they?

If only Jess was brave enough to take some risks herself, her life could be very different. But the reality was that her best friend could potentially end up with the one person Jess truly wanted but was too scared to take a chance on.

Life could be cruel sometimes.

Putting her own feelings aside, the bottom line was that Jess wanted Chloe to be happy. And Sydney too. And if they could make each other happy, then great. She had to support it, not condemn it. Right?

Jess plastered on a smile. "So, what's the plan, then?"

"Plan?"

"Are you going to ask Sydney out? Write her a love poem in a Christmas card? Sing her an out-of-tune version of 'All I Want for Christmas Is You'?"

Chloe clasped her hand to her chest. "I'll have you know that my Mariah is excellent."

"I've heard you murder the theme tune to *Friends* every time you watch it, and you think you're up to Mariah?" Jess snorted.

"My vocal ability is an acquired taste, I'll have you know." Chloe paused. "Maybe I won't have to rely on my musical prowess." She shuffled around inside one of the boxes and pulled out a sprig of green mistletoe. "Ta da."

Great. Jess was going to have to avoid her feelings *and* bloody mistletoe for the remainder of December. "That's one way to get the ball rolling."

Chloe raced over and hung it above the living room door.

"You didn't seem to struggle much with stretching that time," Jess teased.

"If it means that these lips get to touch Sydney's"—Chloe puckered—"I'll do all the stretches you want."

"Great. You won't mind holding the end of this banner, then." Jess threw one side over and Chloe caught it. "I'm thinking of draping some lights on the curtain pole too."

Chloe sighed. "Sydney better be a really good kisser."

Jess longed to know too.

Maybe it would be safer if that mistletoe miraculously disappeared. For everyone's sake.

❖

"I hope you guys don't mind, but I brought reinforcements," Sydney said, as Ben charged past her and straight into the living room.

"The more the merrier." Jess pointed to a large box labelled *tree decorations*. "We have to get *all* of these decorations onto the Christmas tree, and there's a lot of them. We need all hands on deck."

"I can help," Ben said enthusiastically. "I like decorating the Christmas tree. I have a big Christmas tree in my living room and a little Christmas tree in my bedroom."

"Yeah? That means you should be a pro," Chloe said to him. "Let's see what you've got. Whoever hangs the first five wins."

Never one to shy away from a competition, Ben took off straight away, giggling, and Chloe followed behind. They both grabbed a handful of baubles and raced toward the tree.

Sydney approached the spot where Jess was standing and leaned against the wall beside her. "Do you think they would notice if we stood and watched, then swooped in and hung, like, two at the very end?"

Jess laughed. "Oh, Chloe would. Believe me, after all the work I've had her doing today, she's going to pay me back. Chloe's very bossy when it comes to the tree. My vision lies more in room décor." She swept her arm to gesture around the room.

Sydney looked around at the various decorations. There were twinkly lights everywhere. The walls had an array of different plaques and banners—Sydney smiled when she read one that said *Welcome to our Ho-Ho-Home*. There were different ornaments and stuffed Christmas teddies on the bookshelves and around the fireplace—everything from Santas, to elves, to snowmen, to reindeer. An impressive-looking village had been constructed and lit up on one of the tables. "If your vision was Winter Wonderland, I think it paid off."

"As it happens, that's exactly what I was going for. With a touch of Santa's grotto."

"Well, you nailed it. The room looks great." They shared a smile that warmed Sydney right through.

"I won!" Ben shouted. He was jumping up and down, pointing at the tree. "Chloe's only done four and I've done five. Look, Aunt Sydney!"

"So you did, buddy. Way to go!"

Chloe hung her last decoration and gave him a round of applause, which he bowed at. "I think you might be a tree decorating ninja."

"I think you're right," Ben said smugly, strutting over to the box to lift out some more ornaments.

Chloe laughed, then looked over at them and stuck her hands on her hips. "Are you two going to stand around chatting all night or are you going to hang some decorations?"

Jess gave Sydney a conspiratorial look as she pushed herself off the wall. "See what I mean? Drill sergeant."

It took almost an hour and a half to get the tree looking the way they—well, Chloe—wanted it. Jess wasn't wrong; Chloe did not mess around when it came to the Christmas tree and barked orders at them all throughout the decorating process.

Sydney delegated the job of putting the star on the top of the tree to Ben, and she lifted him up to reach as he proudly did so.

They all stood back and took a moment to admire their hard work. Sydney had to admit, they had done a pretty good job. The tree looked amazing.

Christmas had arrived at the Black-Price-Fletcher house.

Sydney pondered if she and Jess ever got married, whether they would double barrel their surnames or not. She had always liked the idea of double barrelling. Sydney Black-Fletcher? Or Sydney Fletcher-Black? She quickly pushed that notion out of her head. Sydney had been thinking too many thoughts like that recently, ever since Jess's shock breakup with Austin. Maybe she had gleaned a little hope that things could change with Austin out of the picture, but she was being silly. Jess had already made it clear that nothing was going to happen. They were just friends. Sydney would likely remain Sydney Fletcher forever, as her terrible luck with love would have it.

Chloe saying, "You guys are under the mistletoe," pulled Sydney from her wonderment.

Sydney looked up to see if she herself was standing under any mistletoe, then she realized that the mistletoe was above the door where Jess was leading Ben out to the kitchen to make hot chocolate.

"Yes!" Ben said, pumping his fist. "You have to kiss me, Jess."

Sydney breathed out a laugh. Lucky Ben. Why hadn't she offered to help Jess with the hot chocolate? An oversight Sydney might now always regret. "How do you know about mistletoe?" she asked Ben.

"It's in my Christmas book. Come on, Jess." He stood on his tiptoes, closed his eyes, and puckered up.

At least Jess looked to be amused about the whole thing. "Don't push it, mister." She leaned down and planted a quick kiss on Ben's cheek.

"Hey! Not fair. That's not a real kiss." But Sydney still noticed how red his little cheeks turned.

Jess laughed and ushered Ben out of the living room. Sydney heard him continuing to complain the whole way down the hall.

"He makes me laugh so much," Chloe said, walking over and taking a seat beside her.

Sydney nodded her agreement. "There's never a dull moment, that's for sure."

"Beware of mistletoe, huh? Who knows who'll be next."

Sydney sensed that undertone of flirting from Chloe again, and she tried to sidestep it. "I'm pretty sure Ben will try and drag you and Jess both under there whenever he can now that he knows it's there."

"I was kind of hoping to get caught under there with someone else," Chloe said. Definitely flirting. Sydney was right.

She didn't want to walk into the trap of asking who Chloe meant, so she laughed it off. "At least there's no risk of being caught under it with Austin anymore."

"Thank God," Chloe said, sticking her tongue out in disgust. "Poor Jess, though."

"Right?" Sydney and Chloe agreed on that one.

Chloe sighed. "It sucks being single at this time of year." She paused. "Do you not miss it? Having someone?"

Sydney had to tread carefully with this topic. The last thing she wanted to do was to either hurt Chloe or lead her on. "My last relationship was a bit of a disaster. I certainly don't miss that."

"Not all relationships end in disaster, though," Chloe said.

"True. But I don't think it would be fair for me to get into a relationship with someone when my heart's still somewhere else, you know?" Of course, Chloe would probably assume Sydney was talking about her ex-girlfriend, even though the truth was that Sydney's heart resided a little closer to home these days.

Chloe gave her a playful nudge. "Did you never hear the expression that to get over someone, you should get under someone else?"

Sydney let out a nervous laugh. "I have heard that. Though it's never really been my style."

"What's never been your style, Aunt Sydney?"

Oh, thank God for Ben and his impeccable timing. Sydney could have hugged him as he marched toward her. "What have I told you about eavesdropping?" she asked him good-naturedly.

"Not to do it," he said, smiling. "But that's no fun."

Sydney laughed. "We were just talking about how we decorate Christmas trees." She gave Chloe a look to go along with it.

She seemed to pick up on it. "We were. I was advising your Aunt Sydney that she might want to try a new approach. Maybe to get her tinsel out of the way first instead of waiting too long."

Sydney nearly choked. She'd meant to change the subject, not use innuendos. "Why aren't you helping Jess with the hot chocolates, buddy?"

"Jess is on the phone," Ben said. "And you told me not to listen in to other people's private conversations, so I came back here to listen to what you were talking about instead."

Sydney tussled his hair. "You're too much of a smart-butt." She stood up and passed him an empty box. "Make yourself useful, then. It's tidy time."

Ben groaned but started to gather up the pieces of paper and packaging to put in the box. Sydney grabbed an empty box herself to help him. That way she wouldn't be a sitting target for Chloe's advances if Ben disappeared back to the kitchen again.

"Well, Christmas is officially ruined," Jess said as she re-entered the living room. She held up her phone. "That was my mum. It seems that Barry the Bore has booked for the two of them to go away on holiday. A surprise gift, apparently. They won't be back until the day after Boxing Day." Jess threw her phone down on top of the sofa and slumped herself down beside it.

"Oh, no." Chloe said, frowning at her. "Does that mean—"

"Yep," Jess said, seemingly already aware of the question. "I'm going to have to spend Christmas with Dad and Gretchen." She let out a pretend sob.

"You could come to my brother's house with me," Chloe suggested.

"There's already so many of you. It'll be cramped as it is," Jess said.

Sydney felt a pull on the arm of her sweater and looked down to see that Ben was tugging on it. Sydney gave him a questioning frown, and he beckoned for her to lean down.

He cupped his hand over her ear. "Can Jess come to our house?" he whispered.

"I don't think she would want to, buddy."

"Why not?"

"Because she probably wants to be with her own family on Christmas."

"But she just said that her mummy's going on holiday and that she doesn't want to go to her daddy's house." He blinked. "Can I ask her? Please…" he asked, dragging it out.

"You can ask once, but if she says no, don't argue." Sydney knew what Ben was like. He would rhyme and rhyme at Jess to try and wear her down. Though, she had to admit, she would bite someone's hand off for the opportunity to spend Christmas with Jess.

On second thought, maybe Sydney could tolerate a small amount of rhyming.

Ben beamed and ran over to the sofa. "Do you want to come to my house for Christmas?"

Jess gave him an affectionate look. "Oh, thank you for asking, that's very kind of you. But I think I'm going to go to my dad's house."

"No," Ben whined. "Come to my house instead. Aunt Sydney is coming to my house. So are my granny and granda. And my mummy too, but she already lives there."

Jess smiled at him. "That's already lots of people. There probably wouldn't be any room left for me."

"There will be. I'll make room. Please come," Ben asked again.

"Ben," Sydney warned. "Don't be pushy."

"I'm not," Ben said quietly. "I'm just telling Jess that there's lots of room. Isn't there, Aunt Sydney?"

Sydney pictured Rachel's shoebox apartment and tried not to flinch. "There's...some room."

Jess glanced between Ben and Sydney, her gaze settling on Sydney. "I wouldn't want to intrude on you and your family."

Sydney felt a feeling in her chest, and she realized it was hope. "I mean, I'm not going to be pushy like my darling nephew here"—she gave Ben a look which he ignored—"but you wouldn't be intruding if you wanted to join us. You're very welcome to come."

Ben started to bounce up and down. "See? And you said before that you would come to my house someday. That can be my Christmas present."

Sydney watched as Jess had an internal debate. She understood it. It wasn't like Sydney and Jess were just normal friends. There were probably a hundred reasons why they shouldn't spend Christmas together, especially from Jess's point of view.

"At least you wouldn't have to spend Christmas with Gretchen," Chloe said to Jess. Sydney could have hugged her, but it probably wasn't a good idea considering their earlier conversation. She didn't want to encourage any more flirtation.

"Please." Ben stared up at Jess with some of the best puppy-dog eyes Sydney had ever seen. Apparently, Sydney had a secret weapon in the form of a three-foot-ten cutie pie.

"Seriously, how do you say no to this guy?" Jess asked Sydney. She dragged Ben in for a hug. "You're too adorable."

Ben shrieked with excitement. "Does that mean you'll come?"

"Okay." Jess nodded. "I'll come." Ben took off cheering and running around the room, and Jess looked at Sydney. "Looks like we're spending Christmas together."

Maybe Santa really did exist.

CHAPTER FOURTEEN

What time is it?" Sydney asked. She didn't really need to because she looked at the clock on the wall herself.

Rachel laughed. "That's like the fourth time you've asked that in the past thirty minutes. I think somebody needs to chill." She glanced down. "Even your clothes say so."

Rachel was referring to Sydney's choice of Christmas jumper—black, with a fluffy penguin wearing a Santa hat, and the words *Have a Chilled Christmas*. She had chosen it on purpose, given her and Jess's penguin affiliation. "Ha ha," she deadpanned. "And you're right, but Jess is going to be here any minute and I'm stressing out. Why does every plan we make feel like a date? We live together. We literally see each other every day. Yet we do something outside of that, and boom. Date vibes."

"I think they call that wishful thinking," Rachel said. "Unless circumstances have changed, and you haven't told me."

"First off...brutal." Sydney glared at her, though Rachel remained undeterred and a little amused. "And secondly, no. Nor do I expect any changes. She's still getting over her breakup. Even without Austin on the scene, we're just friends who have inescapable but very inconvenient feelings for each other and sometimes fight about it."

"Sounds like any relationship I've ever been in."

Sydney laughed because it was true. None of Rachel's relationships had been plain sailing by any means, hence her decision to remain single ever since she had Ben. "Please, just don't be all...meddle-y today."

"I think the word you're looking for is meddlesome, and would I ever?" Rachel put on her most angelic expression. "I can't speak for Ben though. Or Mum."

"Oh, God. I hadn't thought about Mum. What have you told her about Jess and me?"

"Nothing. What do you take me for? I just told her that your roommate is joining us for Christmas dinner."

"Hmm. Mum's like a bloodhound. She always sniffs out when there's something more to the story."

"Then you better be on your very best, *just-friendliest* behaviour." Rachel said, right as the apartment door knocked. She nodded in the direction of it. "You gonna get that? Might be your girlfriend."

"What did I *just* say?"

Rachel held her hands up. "That was the last one, I promise."

Why had Sydney thought everyone spending Christmas together was such a good idea? Because in that moment, she couldn't remember. As she approached the front door, Ben charged past her yelling, "I'll get it."

He swung the door open before Sydney even had a chance to answer him. "Jess!" he said excitedly. "Did you know that the best way to spread Christmas cheer is singing loud for all to hear?"

Jess hesitated for a few seconds, probably unaware of the reference. "I didn't, but it sounds like a good tactic."

Sydney approached the door to save Jess from being *Elf*ed by Ben. "Ignore him. He's watched *Elf* like twelve times this week."

A look of recognition passed over Jess.

Ben glanced up at Sydney. "I think it was more times than that."

"Probably." Sydney lovingly tussled his hair, then turned to Jess, who was looking adorably festive wearing a green Christmas jumper with Rudolph on the front, visible under her unzipped coat. "Merry Christmas! Come on in. Welcome to my sister's humble abode." Sydney stood aside to let her pass.

"And mine," Ben said.

"And Ben's humble abode too," Sydney added. "Can I take your coat?"

"Thank you so much for having me." Jess shrugged her coat off and handed it to Sydney along with a gift bag. "I wasn't sure what to bring, so I went with wine and chocolates thinking that you can't go wrong with that combo."

"You thought right, but you didn't have to bring anything."

"Of course I did." Jess reached another bag to Ben. "And this one's for you."

"Another present?" Ben said in disbelief. "But you were the present. Remember?" he said sincerely, though, Ben being Ben, he was already tearing it open anyway. "Pokémon! These are the coolest. Thanks, Jess." He glanced up at Sydney excitedly. "Look!" He held up the boxed figures to show her.

Sydney smiled at him. "Wow. Very cool."

"I'm gonna go put these in my display. I can't wait to show Poodle our new toys." Without any further ado, he took off running to do that.

"Kids on Christmas," Sydney said in amusement to Jess. She jerked her head. "Come sit down."

"That's what it's all about." Jess said, following Sydney to the living area. "I take it Santa came?"

"Oh, he made it all right, along with his elf, who ate way too many cookies and even chewed on Rudolph's carrot." Sydney rubbed her stomach. She had stayed over the night before so she could help Rachel with Santa duties.

"One of the perks of being Santa's helper, right?" Jess's gaze followed Sydney's hands down and she grinned knowingly. "Nice jumper."

Sydney held it out by the hem. "Well, as we have already discovered, there's a lot to like about penguins. They're fast becoming my favourite animal."

"Mine too." Jess leaned in closer to Sydney and lowered her voice like she was giving away a guilty secret. "Did you know that I sleep with Pebbles every night? We even snuggle."

Lucky Pebbles. If only they could trade places. Sydney would love to know what a Jess snuggle felt like.

"I didn't know that." Sydney's voice came out huskier than she intended. Jess slept with the penguin Sydney had given her. That had to mean something, right? She cleared her throat. "But I'm happy that you do."

Jess's cheeks turned a subtle shade of pink that most people wouldn't have noticed, but Sydney noticed everything about Jess. She looked down, turning her attention to another bag she was holding and passed it to Sydney. "I got you something too."

"You already gave me a bag with booze and sweets."

"That was for your whole family. This one's just for you." Jess held a hand up. "It's nothing big."

"You shouldn't have." Sydney opened the silver gift bag and pulled out a box and a pack of something. She gently ripped the tissue paper to reveal an electric coffee roaster and a bag of green coffee beans—from El Salvador, she discovered on further inspection. Sydney bet they were good ones. "Oh my God. Jess…" She was officially lost for words. And that didn't happen to Sydney very often.

"Well, you said that it can be really hard to find good quality coffee, so I did some research on coffee beans. Then I thought, what better quality than roasting your own, then giving them to Beanie to work her magic on." Jess glanced at Sydney. "You're not saying anything. Was it a stupid gift?" She grimaced. "It's fine if you don't like it."

Sydney immediately reached out and gave her arm a reassuring squeeze. "It's the most thoughtful gift anyone's ever given me. I love it, and I can't wait to use it. Thank you." She shook her head in disbelief. "I can't believe you remembered I said that."

"I have a good memory," Jess said. But they both knew that it was more than that.

Sydney pushed herself up off the sofa. "I've got something for you too. Wait here." She quickly headed to Rachel's bedroom, where she'd stashed Jess's gift the night before. She hadn't even been sure whether she was going to give it to Jess or not, but what had she got to lose? She rejoined Jess on the sofa and passed her the box that she had wrapped in red Christmas paper.

"Thank you. You didn't have to, either." Jess was a careful present unwrapper. Unlike Ben, who would have torn it right open, Jess carefully opened each fold, which only added to Sydney's anticipation.

Would Jess like the gift? Would she think it was too personal? Did it cross the line? When Jess pulled the Makes Scents box out of the paper, she sent Sydney a cute little frown-smile, was the only way Sydney could describe it. Sydney's heart started thudding as she pulled the bottle out of the box and read the label—one which Sydney had made and printed especially for this one special fragrance.

Jess gasped. "No way! Is this what I think it is?" She wasted no time unscrewing the lid. She held the bottle up to her nose and slowly inhaled the smell inside. Her face mellowed into the softest smile as she did, followed by a wistful sigh. "Sydney! That's it. Oh my God, that's exactly it."

Sydney glanced down at the bottle in Jess's hand that she had, in her opinion, aptly named The Day We Met.

It had taken Sydney a while to recreate the exact scent, because it wasn't one of their Makes Scents signature smells. Rather one of Sydney's many experiments. There had some trial and error with using different oils to replicate what she had used before. But Sydney had been pretty confident that she had managed to nail it in the end. And she had. The happiness on Jess's face confirmed it.

"Yeah?" Sydney suddenly felt insecure. "I remember that you said you really liked that smell, so…" She trailed off, self-conscious.

"I think it might be my favourite smell in the whole world." Jess inhaled the aroma again. "It brings me back too," she said quietly. "If I close my eyes, you and I are sitting on that train again."

"Some scents are like that. They can bring back memories. Good or bad, I guess."

"Meeting you could only be a good memory, Sydney," Jess said quietly.

They shared one of their secret smiles. One that portrayed all of the feelings that they weren't supposed to have.

Then Rachel's voice broke the spell. "You must be Jess," she said as she left the kitchen and walked toward them with a friendly smile on her face. Sydney appreciated the niceties, but did she really have to come out at that very moment?

Sydney managed to bite back her frustration and remember her own manners. "Jess, this is my sister, Rachel. Rachel, Jess."

"It's so good to finally meet you," Jess said, standing to shake Rachel's hand. "Thank you for letting me crash your Christmas dinner."

"No problem." Rachel brought her in for a hug instead. "It's great to meet you too. I feel like I already know you, with the amount Ben and Sydney talk about you."

Sydney shot Rachel daggers as she retreated from the hug.

Rachel balked. "I mean, Ben mostly. Obviously. Sydney, doesn't, um, talk about you. Much."

Oh, because that was so much better. Sydney rolled her eyes.

"Oh, look. Was that the door? I'll get it." Rachel scurried toward it.

Sydney tried to ignore the knowing smile Jess was giving her. "That'll be my parents," she explained, as Rachel let them in.

Everything suddenly felt like it was happening at once.

"Ah. My girls," her mum said like she hadn't seen them in months, throwing her arms around Rachel. Her dad followed behind with a beaming smile even though he had been lumbered with the job of carrying all the bags.

Her mum turned and headed in Sydney and Jess's direction, arms outstretched. "Sydney, my darling! And you must be Jess!" She hugged them both. "Sydney, why didn't you tell me your friend was so pretty?" Her eyes lit up. "Are you single, Jess?"

"Mum," Sydney exclaimed.

It could turn out to be a very long dinner.

❖

"I need to ditch my family more often," Jess said. "That was the best Christmas dinner I've ever had."

"Rachel kicks ass at Christmas dinner." Sydney suspected it had something to do with her flawless organisational skills. Everything was cooked to absolute perfection.

"Well, she didn't learn it from me," Sydney's dad said, looking lovingly at her mum.

Sydney's mum waved him off. "Flatterer. Can you cook, Jess?"

"Not as good as this," Jess said. "You know, Sydney's a great cook too. The quality of my meals has significantly improved ever since she moved in."

Her mum threw Sydney a knowing look. There had been a few of those moments over dinner where Jess had given Sydney some kind of innocent compliment and Sydney's mum had read into it as more than simple politeness. *Bloodhound.*

"You'll have to let me do the washing-up," Jess said.

Sydney's mum stood up and started to clear the plates. "Nonsense. You're a Fletcher family guest. Me and Sydney are on clean-up duty."

That was Sydney's cue to start clearing too. Sydney knew that without even a look from her mum.

Rachel held her hands up. "I'll not argue. Come on, Jess. We have wine to drink."

Sydney's dad gasped. "Do I get to share this wine?"

"Fine. You can come too," Rachel said. "But none for the helpers until they've got all the work done and my kitchen has been left gleaming. If it's more gleaming than it was to begin with, even better."

Sydney stuck her tongue out at Rachel and followed her mum into the kitchen with as many dishes as she could carry.

The second Sydney pushed through the door, her mum was on her like a shot. "Why didn't you tell me you were seeing your roommate?"

"What? I'm not!"

Her mum pointed at her. "Don't you lie to me, young lady."

"I'm not," Sydney said. "What makes you think that?"

Her mum laughed like it was obvious. "Oh, I don't know. Maybe it was all of the secret smiles across the table? The longing looks when each of you think the other one isn't looking? The eye sex you were having during dessert?"

Sydney couldn't hold her laugh back at that one. "Eye sex? Seriously, Mum?"

"Call it whatever you want. But the bottom line is you're into that girl."

Sydney sighed. There was no point in arguing. "You're right. I am, but we're not together. Nothing's happened bar this apparent eye sex you speak of."

"Well, why the hell not? She'd be lucky to be with my daughter."

Sydney smiled. Mums really were the best cheerleaders sometimes. "For starters, Jess had a boyfriend until a few weeks ago. They had been together for a long time. She's healing."

"Okay. Understandable. And do you think when she heals, maybe you two might…?"

"I don't know. There's other stuff too. I'm not exactly Jess's type."

Her mum scoffed. "You could have fooled me. That woman is every bit as smitten with you as you are with her."

"You think?"

"Think? I know. She can't take her eyes off you for longer than a minute, and when she does look at you, it's like you're the most intriguing thing ever put on the planet. During conversations, she hangs onto your every word. And whenever you smile, she smiles with you, like your happiness makes her happy too. So, yes. Jess is one hundred percent smitten. Trust your mother."

"Yeah?" The knowledge both pleased Sydney and saddened her. "Then why isn't it enough?"

"Only Jess knows the answer to that," her mum said softly. "But let me tell you something. You are enough." Her mum took the dishes out of Sydney's hands and set them beside the sink, then she took Sydney's hands in hers. "You are more than enough. Don't you doubt that for a second just because that horrible ex-girlfriend of yours couldn't see it." Her mum knew better than anyone how much that break-up had knocked Sydney's sense of self-worth. "And if Jess can't see it, or if she chooses to ignore it, then it's her who isn't enough for you. You understand?"

Sydney nodded. A pep talk from her mum turned out to be just what she needed.

"Look after your heart. Sometimes we want something or someone so badly that we settle for whatever they give us, even if it's just a crumb. Don't settle for less than you deserve."

"It's not like that. We're trying to work out how to be friends even though we like each other. Jess isn't stringing me along or anything. This is hard for her too."

"Yes, but I'm not worried about Jess. I like her, she's a lovely woman. But my worry is for my daughter. Always."

"I can't help having feelings for her, Mum. Trust me, I've tried. They won't go away."

Her dad bustled into the kitchen with another stack of dishes. "What are you two in here chinwagging about? And not even a dish washed either," he teased.

"Sydney and Jess," her mum said simply.

"That they fancy each other?" Her dad nodded like it was already old news. "Fair enough. I'll leave you pair to it. Your mother's much better with matters of the heart than I am."

Sydney gawped at him as he casually breezed back out of the kitchen. "Even Dad noticed?"

Her mum smiled. "I told you, darling. You two are clear as day."

❖

"You didn't have to come home with me, you know? You could have stayed with your family," Jess said to Sydney as they arrived back at their house.

"Do you know how long a game of Monopoly lasts with my family? If I didn't come home now, I would never make it back."

Jess smiled. She wasn't stupid, she knew that the real reason Sydney had come home with her was so that Jess wouldn't be alone on Christmas. Sydney was thoughtful like that. She had been everything Jess had needed after her breakup—ever since the night it happened.

The original plan had been to make a brief appearance at her dad's house before heading home, but he'd texted to warn her that Gretchen had invited all her friends over, and that did not sound remotely like a merry Christmas to Jess.

As soon as Sydney had realized that Jess was going straight home, she had started to gather her things to come with her.

"What would you like to do?" Sydney asked, then hesitated. "If you want to hang out, that is. I didn't mean to assume that *we* would do anything. I can give you some space if you'd prefer—"

"I'm not ready for our Christmas to be over yet," Jess said quickly to put her at ease.

"Really?" Sydney beamed at that, and it did funny things to Jess's heart. "Me either."

"Good. Then I vote we watch a movie?"

Sydney nodded. "I second that. With wine? Or hot chocolate? Ben said that you're the queen of hot chocs."

Jess laughed. "A crown I wear proudly." She moved her head from side to side while she weighed up her decision. "But I'm thinking wine tonight."

Sydney looked like she agreed. "Red?"

"Duh. PJ's?"

"A given."

Jess grinned. "Okay. Let's get changed and rendezvous back in the living room in ten minutes."

"Deal. I'll pour the wine when I come down."

"I'll pick the movie, then, and you can change it if you don't like it." They really did make a good team, didn't they?

They both climbed the stairs and headed to their respective bedrooms. Jess got changed into her new pyjamas that Chloe had bought her for Christmas—their gift to each other every year. This year's were pink and grey with puppies on them.

Jess hesitated before wiping off her makeup, then continued. She told herself that was because she wasn't trying to impress Sydney, but the truth was that she was comfortable enough around Sydney to be herself. When Jess was with Austin, she didn't take off her makeup until right before she went to bed—another telling sign that she had overlooked.

She felt herself smiling as she returned downstairs and turned on a couple of lamps in the living room. Christmas Day had been lovely. Jess had woken up that morning feeling nervous, but Sydney's family were great, and they had pulled out all the stops to make her feel welcome. Jess shouldn't have been surprised at that—Sydney was pretty great herself. Why wouldn't her family be every bit as awesome?

The heating was already switched on, so the living room was quite warm, but Jess grabbed a blanket from the ottoman and threw it onto the sofa. Just in case.

Then Jess curled up on one side of the sofa, tucking her legs underneath her bum. She flicked through the channels on the TV to see what was on. They always played good movies at Christmastime.

Sydney held up a bottle of wine as she entered the room to join her. "I brought the bottle and two glasses so I don't have to get up to do refills."

Jess chuckled. "Wise move."

"I thought so. Did you pick a movie yet?" Sydney asked as she poured each of them a glass, then settled on the other side of the sofa Jess was on. She left a considerable gap between them that Jess pretended she wasn't disappointed about.

"I did." Jess gestured the TV screen with her head, where *Die Hard* was playing. "It's literally just starting."

"An action movie? I thought you didn't like action movies?"

Jess could feel Sydney's gaze on her, but she kept her eyes glued to the screen. She lifted a shoulder. "Maybe I'm warming to them," she said, aware of the double meaning. Slightly daring, but she hoped Sydney didn't ask her to elaborate.

Luckily, Sydney didn't. "Wanna share the blanket?" she asked quietly, after a few seconds.

Jess could feel herself starting to smile. It was the real reason she had left it there, wasn't it? To cosy up with Sydney. "Sure." *How nonchalant.*

Sydney draped it round them, shuffling a little bit closer so they both fit under it. As Jess sipped her wine, everything about her felt warm inside. It was the effect of everything. The wine, the blanket, the day, and the biggest factor of all, the company.

They didn't talk much during the movie, but somehow Sydney remained aware of everything Jess needed without words. She topped up Jess's wine when her glass was almost empty. She gave Jess more of the blanket when she started to feel a bit cold. She went and fetched them some snacks seconds before Jess was about to suggest going to get them herself. And of course, the snacks that Sydney brought consisted of all Jess's favourite treats.

If there was such a thing as a perfect night in, Jess was having it. The only thing missing was the feel of Sydney's arms wrapped around her. She couldn't have that, but oh how Jess longed for it.

Craving any kind of contact with Sydney, no matter how small, Jess stretched her legs out. Without looking away from the screen, Sydney lifted Jess's foot and set it on her lap—once again instinctively knowing exactly what Jess needed.

By halfway through the movie, they had shifted pretty close together. Jess's skin practically tingled in every spot where her body was touching Sydney's—especially the spot just above her knee where Sydney's hand rested. At one point, Jess felt Sydney's gaze on her, and she wondered if Sydney could feel it too. The profound effect of their innocent contact. Jess didn't dare turn around because she knew what would happen if she did. Her resolve would crumble away to nothing—though she was starting to think that might not be such a bad thing.

They didn't speak much during the movie—not until the credits started rolling on the screen.

"Do you think it's a Christmas film?" Sydney asked her. "It's an age-old debate, isn't it?"

"It's set during a Christmas party, so I think that's why it counts."

"Well, it's a good film anyway. That's a good enough reason for me to consider it as a Christmas tradition."

"I think that's actually the first time I've ever watched it at Christmastime."

"Maybe it could become a new tradition, then," Sydney said softly, the suggestion behind her words obvious.

Jess nodded non-committedly. She didn't trust herself enough to speak. Her words could give her away so easily.

"I think I'm going to go to bed," Sydney said.

Reluctantly, she pulled her legs away from Sydney, feeling the loss immediately. She pushed herself off the sofa too. "I didn't realize how late it was."

"Time flies when you're enjoying yourself," Sydney said, shaking out the blanket and folding it back up.

Jess busied herself by turning off the lamps, causing the room to descend into darkness. Luckily, she knew the layout of the room well enough that she didn't need the lights on anyway. She padded to the door, totally unaware that Sydney was going the same way. Their bodies crashed together as they both tried to walk through it at the same time. Jess gasped, more a reaction to feeling her body pressed against Sydney's than shock. They both turned so they were facing each other fully, and Jess could feel Sydney's chest heaving against her own as she breathed.

"Is, um, the mistletoe still up there?" Sydney asked huskily.

"I took it down." A decision Jess was now very much regretting.

"Right. Probably for the best." Sydney still didn't move.

Neither did Jess. "Probably." She could just about make out Sydney's tongue moving slowly across her lips. Her gaze followed it before lifting to look into Sydney's eyes, which somehow still glimmered blue, even in the dark.

"You know," Sydney whispered. "Maybe there's a rule that...if the mistletoe *was* there...that it still counts. After all, it's Christmas."

"Good enough for me."

Before she could talk herself out of it, Jess leaned forward and pressed her lips to Sydney's. Someone whimpered, probably Jess, or maybe they both had. Jess didn't care. Sydney's lips were so soft. They felt like warm velvet against hers.

The kiss only lasted a few seconds, more a brief, lingering touch of lips than a kiss, but Jess had never felt more alive in her life. When she pulled away, Jess reached up and covered her lips with her fingertips. How had such a simple kiss made her lips feel like they were on fire? "Sydney, I'm sorry, I shouldn't have—"

"I know. It's fine. You don't have to say anything," Sydney replied, her voice even huskier than it had been. "Merry Christmas, Jess."

"Merry Christmas, Sydney."

Once again, Jess felt the loss as Sydney slipped away from her and headed up the stairs to her bedroom. Jess waited, frozen to the spot, until she heard the click of Sydney's door close behind her.

What had Jess just done? Why had she liked it so much? How could something that she had been sure was so wrong for her feel so incredibly right?

Questions flooded her brain as she headed to her own bedroom, her heart thudding in her chest as she bypassed Sydney's room to get there. Part of her felt like knocking, but the more sensible part of her kept her feet moving until she reached her room.

Jess climbed straight into bed and pulled Pebbles in close to her chest like she did every night. She couldn't believe that she had admitted that to Sydney too. Christmas really gave Jess loose lips, didn't it? In more ways than one.

She replayed the kiss in her head. There had been nothing spectacular about it. It hadn't been a passionate kiss. She had basically given Sydney a peck on the lips that lasted a couple of seconds longer than polite. Jess had given Chloe a peck on the lips before, several times.

What was different about it was the way it made Jess feel. Like everything in the world had shifted right into place the second their lips had connected.

Jess spied the Makes Scents box on the bedside table where she had left it earlier. She reached over and opened it, smiling at the The Day We Met label that Sydney had made especially for her. She lifted the bottle to her nose, once again inhaling the sweet aroma that she associated with Sydney. It was Jess's favourite smell—because it *was* Sydney.

That's the reason Jess loved it.

CHAPTER FIFTEEN

I can't believe you're sitting alone on New Year's," Rachel said, frowning through the screen of Sydney's phone. "You should be over here, with us."

"I'm fine. You know I don't care about New Year's Eve. I'm perfectly happy eating my body weight in chocolate and watching trash TV."

"Uh-huh. And it has nothing to do with you moping about Jess kissing you last week, then never mentioning it again?"

"Nope. Nothing to do with any of that. Besides, it was barely a kiss. Two blinks and you would have missed it. And I haven't mentioned it to Jess either. It's like an unspoken agreement that we don't or something." Maybe Sydney should have been sitting around obsessing over the kiss, but she wasn't. Why? Because it hadn't changed anything. The simple fact of the matter was that Jess wasn't prepared to change her life to be with Sydney. And Sydney wasn't going to waste any more time hoping that she would. So, Sydney was done with hope. *That* was her New Year's resolution. No more hoping. From now on, whatever happened, happened.

"Uh-huh," Rachel said again, giving her a sceptical look.

"Stop worrying about me. I am fine." To prove it, she plastered on her biggest smile, showing all her teeth. "See?"

"I can see that you look like Jaws. I'll possibly have nightmares." Sydney laughed. "You're always so good for my self-esteem."

"I know, I try." Rachel grinned. "Where is Jess tonight anyways?"

"Her mum and stepdad's annual New Year's Eve party." Jess

hadn't been looking forward to it, but her mum had talked her into going.

Rachel sighed. "Are you sure that you're not sad and lonely?"

"Yes, I'm sure. Stop worrying."

Rachel seemed to accept it that time. They chatted for another few minutes and then said their goodbyes.

Sydney hadn't realized that she had fallen asleep on the sofa until she heard the front door banging shut. The noise startled her awake, and she blinked a few times to adjust.

The bang was followed by the sound of giggling. Of Jess giggling. Sydney could tell.

There were a few more clattering sounds, like things were being knocked over, followed by Jess making a loud shushing noise.

Sydney pushed herself off the sofa to go and see what was going on. When she entered the hallway, she found a very drunk-looking Jess slumped against the wall.

"Sydney!" Jess said overenthusiastically. She threw her arms up in the air and almost lost her balance in the process. Luckily, she had the sense to grab onto the stair banister to save herself. "Wow. This room is so spinny tonight," Jess slurred.

"Spinny?" Sydney repeated, folding her arms. She couldn't help but smile. "I suppose it can be spinny if you've drank enough."

"I might have had some champagne."

Sydney laughed. "I can tell. How did it go?"

Jess groaned. "I'm so glad to be home." Then she suddenly brightened and clapped her hands. "With you! Jess and Sydney. Sydney and Jess. Roomie One and Roomie Two." Her eyes widened. "Oooh, how about Jessney? Sydsica! What will we call us?"

Sydney started to laugh. "Whichever one you like best. I'll let you pick."

Jess pushed herself off the banister and tried to walk. An image of a baby deer taking its first steps sprang to Sydney's mind. "See, you're so thoughtful like that. You—" Jess stumbled, and Sydney quickly lunged forward to grab her before she fell onto the floor.

Then they were practically in an embrace. Somehow, they always managed to end up in a situation where their bodies were touching. Either they were both very clumsy, or some higher being enjoyed messing with Sydney and testing the resilience of her libido.

Jess stared up at her with a frown and glassy eyes. "You saved my life," she said with such sincerity, Sydney had to stop herself from laughing.

"I think you're giving me too much credit. I don't think your life was ever at stake, but I possibly saved you from a bruise." Determined to be a responsible human, she linked her arm through Jess's and led her to the kitchen. "Come on. Let's get you a big drink of water before bed."

"Water? Pfft. Get me more champagne."

"Maybe later," Sydney lied. "Let's see if you can drink some water for me first."

"But you said that you were taking me to bed after the water. Am I going to drink my champagne in bed?" Jess gasped. "Are you coming to my bed too?"

"Only to tuck you in," Sydney said. She eased Jess down onto one of the kitchen chairs and went to the fridge to see if they had any bottles of water. They did. She pulled out two—probably ambitious. She would be doing well to get Jess to drink one. "Here. Drink this and I promise you'll thank me tomorrow."

"Why? What's happening tomorrow?" Jess asked with a confused look on her face.

"A very bad hangover, I'm imagining."

Jess groaned and held a hand to her forehead. "I don't want one of those." She gave Sydney a vulnerable look. "Are you going to look after me?"

Sydney pushed the water toward her. "Already trying to. Now drink."

"I like bossy Sydney." Jess leaned forward and gave her a big, drunken grin. "Are you *always* bossy?"

Sydney smiled back. "Maybe. But mostly when I need drunk people to drink their water."

"I'm not drunk," Jess said defiantly. "Tipsy, maybe. But not drunk." But she lifted the bottle to her lips and took a few generous gulps. "Oh, yummy. How did you know I was thirsty?" She greedily drank some more, and water dribbled down her chin.

"A lucky guess." Sydney grabbed a napkin from the table and passed it to her.

"What's this for?" Jess threw it back at Sydney and giggled.

Sydney shook her head in amusement. She lifted the napkin back up and reached forward to dab Jess's chin with it softly. "A little bit of water must have jumped out of the bottle."

Jess burst out laughing. "Sydney. You're so silly…water doesn't jump. Are you drunk?"

Sydney laughed too. "Nope. Still just you."

When she finished wiping and dropped the napkin onto the table, Jess leaned forward and pressed a finger to Sydney's chin.

What is she doing now?

"You're so pretty." Jess dropped her gaze to Sydney's mouth and slowly ran her finger along Sydney's bottom lip. "I love your lips. Did you know that?"

"You do?" Sydney swallowed. "I mean, no. I didn't know that."

"Well, I do." Jess remained focussed on them. "I always have. Even when we first met, I imagined what it would feel like to kiss them."

"Really?"

Jess nodded. She traced her finger upward, and along Sydney's upper lip. "So soft," she whispered. "But I already found that out the other night under the mistletoe."

Sydney stopped herself from reminding Jess that they had kissed in spite of the fact that the mistletoe had no longer been there. A minor detail that really should have been the last thing on Sydney's mind—Jess had finally mentioned the kiss!

"Remind me again why it's such a bad idea to kiss you?" Jess continued.

It isn't. Kiss me! But Sydney had to remain strong. "You have your reasons."

"Stupid reasons." Jess let out a long sigh. "I think about you more than I should."

Begrudgingly, Sydney reached up and pulled Jess's hand away from her mouth. They couldn't have this conversation when Jess had been drinking. It gave Sydney an unfair advantage, and she couldn't live with that. If Jess was going to admit her feelings to Sydney, it would have to be in cold, sober, light of day.

"I think about you too," Sydney admitted. "Now, drink more water," she added to rapidly change the subject.

Luckily, drunk Jess was easily swayed. "You're such a water dictator." But she drained the rest of the bottle.

Sydney took it from her and handed Jess the other bottle she had pulled from the fridge.

"Why do you not have to drink any?" Jess complained.

"Because you're thirsty and I'm not. Here's an idea. Why don't you take it up to bed with you?"

Right on cue, Jess gave a wide yawn. "I am a little sleepy," she admitted.

"Come on, then." Sydney pulled Jess up from the chair and linked her arm through Jess's again to lead her up the stairs.

When Sydney got Jess to her bedroom, she faced the conundrum of what to do next. She didn't feel right taking Jess's clothes off, but she also didn't want to put her to bed in her dress and heels. She could deal with the heels first, she decided. Removing footwear was pretty unintrusive.

Sydney led Jess over to the bed and sat her down on the edge of it. Then she leaned down and easily slipped the shoes off Jess's feet. "Um, where do you keep your pyjamas?" she asked when she stood back up again.

Jess thought about it for a second, then shot her arm out and pointed to a drawer where, sure enough, Sydney found a selection of different nightwear. She lifted a pair of blue pyjamas that were folded on the top of the pile and passed them to Jess.

"Do you think if I leave the room for a minute, you'd be able to change into these?"

"Duh. I know how to put on clothes," Jess said, already reaching to pull off her dress without a care in the world.

Sydney quickly turned around and wasted no time in leaving the room. "I'm just going to use the bathroom."

"'Kay," Jess shouted casually behind her.

Sydney waited for a few minutes before returning to Jess's room again. She made sure to knock first. "You finished changing?"

"I guess you'll have to come in and find out," Jess called back playfully.

Sydney eased the door open slowly and peeked her head round, ready to avert her eyes if she needed to. She started grinning when she spied Jess on the edge of the bed, her pyjamas on back to front, trying to remove her makeup with a wipe and doing a pretty poor job of it.

Sydney took the wipe from her. "Here. Let me."

Jess didn't argue. She turned to face Sydney and closed her eyes. Sydney wiped as gently as she could, tracing every part of Jess's face with care. Sydney wished she could lean in and kiss every inch of her soft skin, but she forced that thought away. "All done."

"I love it when you touch me," Jess said as she opened her eyes. Then she froze, like she had realized what she'd said. "I think I better shut up now."

Sydney smiled even though her stomach was doing somersaults. "Probably best."

Jess gave a sharp nod. "Okay, shutting up. What's next? Oh, I know! My teeth. And I have to pee. But pretend I didn't tell you that because, hello? Embarrassing."

Sydney laughed. She waited until Jess stumbled to the bathroom and back. She pulled back the duvet on the bed and motioned for Jess to climb in.

"Pebbles!" Jess called out. She threw herself down and pulled the stuffed penguin in for a hug. "I love Pebbles. Did you know that I love Pebbles?"

Sydney smiled as she fixed the covers around Jess *and* Pebbles. "You told me. I'm glad." She straightened and took a breath. "I think you're all good now. There's water beside you."

"Wait. You're not staying with me?"

"I'm only up the hall."

"But...but...up the hall is miles and miles away."

"It isn't. And you're going to be asleep anyway."

Jess threw the corner of the duvet back down the bed. "I've got a better idea. Why don't you sleep in here with Pebbles and me? We can all cuddle." She patted the mattress.

How Sydney managed to resist the best offer she had possibly had in her whole entire life was a mystery. But she did. She dutifully pulled the duvet back up again. "Because it probably isn't as good an idea as you think it is." She tucked it in around Jess's shoulders. "Goodnight, Jess."

"Night, spoilsport."

Sydney ignored her and switched off the light. She walked toward the door.

"Sydney?" Jess said quietly.

She froze. "Yeah?"

"Thank you."

Sydney looked back over her shoulder. "For what?"

"For being here. For helping me."

"I like looking after you."

She smiled at that, before leaning her head back down on the pillow. "Night, Sydney. Oh, and happy New Year."

"Happy New Year, Jess." Sydney pulled the door behind her, leaving it slightly ajar so that she could check on Jess without waking her. Though she was pretty sure that once Jess crashed, she would be out for the count until morning.

Sydney's New Year's Eve had turned out to be rather eventful after all. Perhaps that was a sign that her year would be too. Was that hope that she was feeling?

Who stuck to their new year's resolutions anyway?

❖

Ouch. Jess's head hurt.

She tried to sit up, but that made it hurt even more, so she slumped back down again. Her mouth felt like the Sahara Desert too. Jess reached out one unsteady hand and grabbed the bottle of water from beside her bed.

The bottle of water that she vaguely remembered Sydney had left there for her.

After she had come home from her mum's New Year's party absolutely trashed.

Jess gasped as she started having flashbacks of the night before. She concentrated. She could remember the party. Jess had been bombarded with questions from nosy family members about why Austin wasn't there. Then more about why Jess and Austin had broken up. She was so ready to never talk about Austin or the break-up ever again.

That was when Jess had begun tearing into the champagne, gulping it back like it was fruit juice. In hindsight, maybe she had torn into it a little too much. She winced at the hammers banging around in her head.

Jess continued to search her foggy brain, trying to remember how she had got home. Oh, yes. She had got a taxi. She remembered talking to the taxi driver when he dropped her off. Jess had always been a chatterbox after a few drinks.

Then she faintly recalled Sydney telling her to drink water. Jess may or may not have called her bossy. And had Sydney put her to bed? She must have, but all of that part was blurry.

Ugh. There was only one way to find out.

Jess caught a glimpse of herself in the mirror as she got up to go downstairs. She must have remembered to take off her makeup, which was surprising, but impressive. She glanced down at her pyjamas, which she was wearing back to front. She quickly took them off and put them on the right way round before she ventured downstairs.

She let out a groan as she did. Even walking felt like it required maximum effort.

Jess smelled something cooking in the kitchen, and she was conflicted between feeling hungry and wanting to throw up as she went to investigate.

"Good morning," Sydney said to her with a knowing smile as soon as she walked in. "How are you feeling?"

"Not good." Jess fitted Sydney with the best glare she could muster in her current state. "You know too much."

Sydney started to laugh, and the sound of it instantly made Jess feel a tiny bit better. "You weren't that bad."

"What did I say?" Jess might as well get the embarrassment over with.

"You don't remember?" Sydney asked. She turned her focus back to whatever she was cooking.

"Not a lot. I remember you making me drink some water, which I appreciate because I would probably feel a whole lot worse right now if you hadn't."

"See? I told you that you'd be thanking me this morning."

"You were right and I am. Thank you."

"You're welcome." Sydney moved across the counter and poured some hot water into a cup. She stirred it then passed it to Jess. "I didn't know whether to make you tea or coffee, but I went with tea to see if your theory that it makes everything better works on hangovers." She held up a finger. "However, I have been playing with my fancy new bean roaster, so I also have some coffee good to go if you need that too. Just say the word."

Jess wrapped her fingers around the warm cup and smiled. "You're like the hangover fairy."

Sydney grinned. "Oh, you better believe it. I've also made you a very greasy breakfast, which yes, you probably hate the thought of. But if you eat even a little bit of it, I guarantee that you'll start to feel better."

Jess scrunched her nose up. "What is it?"

"Bacon, sausages, lots of bread to soak up that champagne. And I'm going to make some eggs now."

"You're right. I do hate the thought of it."

"Trust me, you're going to thank me after. It'll be like the water all over again."

Funnily enough, Jess did trust Sydney. And just being in her company automatically made Jess feel better. Sydney had fast become her comfort place. "You still haven't told me what I said or did last night."

"There's nothing to tell. You were a very charming drunk."

"Charming?" Jess hid her face in her hands. "How charming?"

Sydney laughed as she cracked an egg into the frying pan. Then another. "You worry too much. I just mean you were pleasant. Nice. Talkative. And a little amusing at times."

An image of her fingertips touching Sydney's lips shot through Jess's brain and she nearly dropped her cup. She grasped it tighter. There were definitely things that Sydney wasn't telling her—it was probably for the best that she didn't.

"How was the party?" Sydney asked while she started to plate up the food.

"It was...not the greatest. I mean, it was good to see my mum, but I swear, if one more person asks me about Austin or I hear his name again, I'm going to explode."

"Nosy neighbours?"

Jess nodded. "And aunts and cousins." She sipped some hot tea, which felt lifesaving as she felt her dehydration begin to fade. She decided to be honest. "As far as I can remember, the highlight of my night was coming home to you."

Sydney looked round at her then. "It was?"

Jess nodded.

"It was the highlight of mine too," Sydney replied softly, and Jess's heart soared.

Sydney tossed the eggs onto the plates and turned off the cooker. She brought two plates over to the table, one for each of them. "Try it."

Jess's stomach rolled, but she refused to be ungrateful after Sydney had gone to so much effort, so she took a hesitant bite. Then another. And another. "This is actually really good."

"Told you."

Before Jess knew it, she had managed to clear the plate. Her head still hurt, but Sydney was right. She didn't feel as sick anymore. "You are a miracle worker."

"Well, if you think that was good…"

"Are you flirting again?"

Sydney laughed that low laugh of hers that Jess liked so much. "Maybe a little. Sorry."

"Don't apologize," Jess said. "I was just making sure."

The look that Sydney gave her was all the cure Jess needed.

CHAPTER SIXTEEN

Sydney loitered next to Rachel's desk. "I've been thinking."

"Uh-oh. That can be dangerous."

"Ha ha." Sydney held her hands up. "Hear me out. Though it might mean some hard work for us."

Rachel's face dropped. She swung her chair away from her laptop to face Sydney. "See what I mean? Dangerous. Tell me anyway."

"I think we need some new scents to release in the spring. And maybe a new theme."

"So, an entire new line basically." Rachel moved her head from side to side. "Could do. Spring, though? That doesn't leave us a lot of time. We're already well into January."

"I'll work extra. I want to keep busy."

Rachel looked at her like a penny had just dropped. "I see. This is a Jess distraction."

"No…" Sydney said, dragging the word out. "This is me wanting to focus my mind on other things. Healthier, more productive things."

"Really? So, you're forgetting about Jess? Moving on?"

Sydney shook her head. "I didn't say that. If anything, things are looking up on that front. But instead of obsessing over it like I have been, I'm trying to let things happen organically. And in order for me to do that, I need to keep busy."

"Ooh. How are things looking up? Has something happened?"

"No. It's just a feeling. We've got closer lately. It feels like Jess is finally catching up." The uncrossable line still existed, but Sydney felt like it had slowly started to move. Jess's guard was coming down and she was beginning to let Sydney in.

"Do you really want to be with someone that has to *catch up*?"

Sydney jumped straight to Jess's defence. "Give her a break. Not everyone is good with change, and these are some pretty major changes for her. Don't forget Jess has just got out of a long-term relationship with a guy who's the only person she's ever really dated. She deserves some time to figure things out. I'm fine with being patient."

"Look, I like her, okay? And when I saw you two together at Christmas, I could see it. There's a connection. But you're my sister and I worry about you."

"Well, stop worrying about me and keep me busy instead. Say yes to a spring line."

Rachel glared at her, then relented. "What's this theme you were thinking of?"

Sydney beamed. She panned her hand across the room. "Picture it. *A Day at...* Soaps that smell like your favourite places. For example, A Day at the Fair could be sweet, like a cotton candy kind of scent. A Day at the Park. More natural, floral. A Day at the Beach, fresh, clean. Ooh, with a hint of sunscreen." She flopped her hand. "I'll work on it."

"Has this got anything to do with that Day We Met soap you made for Jess at Christmas?"

"It might have been inspired by that."

Rachel pretended to be sick.

Sydney swatted her arm. "That doesn't matter. Do you like it? Do you think they would sell?"

Rachel sighed. "I have to admit, it's a pretty good concept."

"Is that a yes?"

"Yes," Rachel said grudgingly. "Let's make ourselves incredibly busy when we just got over our busiest period. Why the hell not?"

"Yay!" Sydney threw her arms around Rachel. "Thank you. And you'll not be so grumpy when they sell like hotcakes." She gasped as she straightened. "A Day at the Spa." She shook her head. "Don't know. We'll brainstorm."

"Now?" Rachel looked at her laptop in panic.

"No, not now. Relax, you can finish your emails. We can start tomorrow. I'm taking your son to get his hair cut today." Sydney checked the time. "Soon."

"I wonder where," Rachel deadpanned.

❖

"Here comes your four o'clock," Pam said as she peered out the window.

Jess had been looking forward to her four o'clock appointment all day. She had a quick look outside where Sydney and Ben were approaching Thairapy, deep in conversation. Well, Ben was talking very animatedly about something, and Sydney looked like she was trying her hardest to keep up. She did look really good, though, in her tight jeans and a black sweater. Jess couldn't help but smile. She stopped when she caught Pam studying her. "What?"

"Oh, nothing. I smile at all my friends like I want to rip their clothes off too."

"Pam!" Jess said just as the bell above the door jingled. "Please behave yourself," she muttered before she plastered on a smile for Ben and Sydney. "Hey, you two."

As had become a custom, Ben ran at her immediately. "Jess! Is this where you work?"

Jess laughed and threw her arms around him. "It sure is, kiddo. Ready for a haircut?"

"Oh, you better believe he is. He's changed his mind three times already about what he wants done." Sydney gave her a staggered look that softened into a smile as they held eye contact. "Hey you."

"Hey yourself," Jess replied.

After a few seconds, Pam cleared her throat. "Are you two going to stand around making eyes at each other all day, or is someone going to introduce me to this handsome young man?"

Ben scrunched his nose up. "What does making eyes at each other mean?"

"It's what two people do when they like each other," Pam explained to him.

He nodded like that made total sense. "In that case, Aunt Sydney makes eyes at Jess *alll the time.*"

"Something tells me it's not so one sided," Pam murmured.

Jess nudged her in the ribs. "What did I tell you?" She risked a look at Sydney, who looked rather pleased at the comment.

Violet approached from the storeroom, mixing a tub of dye for her client. "Sydney. How nice to see you again." She looked down and beamed. "And this must be the famous Ben."

"Hi," Ben said quietly.

The phone rang and Pam exhaled loudly. "Duty calls. Just when I was having fun."

Jess laughed as she hurried to the reception desk to take the call. She refocussed her attention on Sydney. "Sorry about her. How's your day been?"

"Quite interesting, as it happens. I'll explain everything."

"I'm intrigued."

Sydney leaned closer. "You should be."

"Is anybody going to cut my hair?" Ben asked impatiently.

Jess started to laugh. "Sorry, Ben. Follow me." She led him to the chair she had set up and held up his gown, which had a Batman logo on the back. "Only my special clients get to wear this one."

His eyes lit up. "Cool."

Jess draped it round his shoulders and got him settled into his chair. "What are we doing today? Fade? Buzz cut? Mohawk? Shaving it all off?" She grinned at Sydney, who was standing behind them with her arms folded and a horrified look on her face.

"I think we'll just go for a trim today so his mum doesn't wring my neck when I take him home," Sydney said.

Jess tutted. "Fine." She leaned in closer to Ben. "Your Aunt Sydney's no fun sometimes."

"Tell me about it," Ben agreed.

"You know I can hear both of you?"

Jess laughed and grabbed her scissors. "How was school today?" she asked, trying hard to keep her focus on Ben. It wasn't easy. Anytime Sydney was in the same room, Jess found it difficult to focus on anything but her.

"I did good at my spellings and not so good at my sums." Ben shrugged. "I don't like sums anyway."

Jess made a face. "I never liked sums either." Sydney gave her a pointed look and she rallied, putting on her most serious expression. "But it's still very important that we learn how to do them."

Sydney rolled her lips in to stop herself from smiling and gave her a subtle nod. *Phew.*

"I suppose so," Ben said quietly. "Aunt Sydney's good at sums."

"Yeah?"

Ben nodded. "Aunt Sydney's good at everything."

Sydney laughed. "Maybe not everything, buddy." She lowered her voice to Jess. "But there are some things I excel at."

Jess almost caught her finger in her scissors. She threw Sydney a look.

"What? I was talking about math."

Jess glared at her in disbelief. "Sure you were."

Sydney lowered her voice. "Maybe it was biology I was thinking of. I was always good with the human body."

Jess gulped.

"Vi, shall I put the air conditioning on?" Pam said, clearly finished with her call and listening in.

"It's January, Pam. Why on earth would you want the air conditioning on? I was about to go look for my second cardigan."

"Just thought our Jess was looking a little flushed is all."

Sydney burst out laughing. "Funny, I noticed that too."

Now they were ganging up on her. "Then you are both imagining things. I'm not flushed, am I, Ben?"

"Your cheeks went red a minute ago when we were talking about school subjects."

Great, she couldn't even get the kid on her side.

That only made Sydney laugh harder.

Pam grinned. "We can't all be wrong, Jess."

"I feel like there's some kind of a joke here that I've missed out on," Violet said in confusion.

"I wish I had missed out on it." Jess made sure to stick to safe topics for the rest of Sydney's visit. Even when Pam's next appointment arrived, Jess suspected Pam would be keeping one ear open.

When Jess was all done with Ben's hair, Sydney went to lift her purse out of her bag, and Jess put a hand on her arm to stop her. "Don't even think about it."

Sydney sighed. "Fine. But I'm cooking you dinner tonight to say thank you."

"Deal. I'll never say no to that. See you in an hour or so?"

"Looking forward to it."

Jess smiled. "Me too."

"Bye, Jess! Thanks again for the haircut," Ben shouted as they left the shop.

Jess waved them off, then turned around to find Pam and Violet both standing staring at her with their arms crossed. "What?"

"Looking forward to dinner, eh?" Pam said.

"Don't you start. You were extra mischievous today." Jess strode over to where she had been cutting Ben's hair and began to tidy. Pam and Violet both followed.

"Do you want to tell her, or shall I?" Pam asked Violet.

"Tell me what?" Jess asked.

"How happy you looked today when you were with Sydney," Violet said kindly. "You light up when you're with her."

Out of habit, Jess downplayed it. "She's my friend. We get along well."

"Is there no chance it could become something more than friends?" Violet asked.

Jess gave in, mainly because she really needed to say it out loud. Keeping her feelings bottled up was stifling her. And who better to offload to than Violet and Pam? "I don't know. I like Sydney. Okay? I really like her. She's funny, and sweet, and kind, and thoughtful, and she makes me feel so comfortable when I'm with her, but on the other hand, she makes me feel excited and alive and like I can't breathe."

"She's also very beautiful," Violet added.

"Oh my God. I could look at her all day." Jess blinked. "And how the hell is that possible? I've never been interested in women. But at the same time, I have never been so attracted to another human being in my entire life. How can both those things be true?"

Violet waved a hand. "Who cares? Don't get caught up in the details. All that matters is how you feel."

Pam clapped her hands together. "Can I just say, I called this."

"We both did," Violet reminded her. "So, what's stopping you? Sydney clearly feels the same."

"I don't know, you guys. We're in such a good place right now as friends. I don't want to mess that up."

Pam blew a raspberry. "Oh, come on. You two are more than friends."

Jess lifted a shoulder. "We flirt a little, yeah. But it doesn't go any further than that. And maybe it's better that way."

"Maybe it's not," Violet countered.

"Just bloody go for it already," Pam said.

Violet scowled at her. "No one's going to rush you or force your hand. Take your time. Figure it all out. From what I saw today, Sydney isn't going anywhere anytime soon. She seems very taken with you."

Jess sighed. "I'm scared. I want to do things right, you know? I would rather have Sydney as a friend than take a chance on more and ruin it."

"Sometimes we have to take a chance." Violet put an arm around her shoulders. "Don't worry. Whatever happens, everything will work out."

"Just don't wait too long," Pam said. "I like the happiness that Sydney brings out in you."

Jess had to admit, she really liked it too.

Chapter Seventeen

"Ben brought home three Valentine's cards from school today, Sydney. Three. I think my son's a lothario," Rachel said.

Sydney laughed, balancing the phone between her ear and her shoulder as she opened the front door with one hand and tried not to drop the bag of take-out food that she was holding under her other arm. "Well, you did say that he takes after me."

"Uh-huh, because your big Valentine's plans don't involve sitting in alone, watching soppy films, and eating junk food. Such a lothario."

"Nope. I was planning on reading a book while I eat my junk food. So there."

Rachel laughed down the phone. "The Fletcher sisters, huh? Could we be any more single?"

"At least you're single by choice. I'm just sad, lonely, and unloved." Sydney stopped in her tracks when she spied Jess walking down the stairs. "You know, I think I might try to change that. Gotta go."

"Wait. What do you me—" Sydney hung up before Rachel could finish.

"Hey," Sydney said, pocketing the phone.

"Hey." Jess eyed her suspiciously. "Why are you looking at me like that?"

"Like what?"

"Like you're surprised to see me."

Sydney shrugged. "I just thought you might have some big Valentine's plans."

"Ha ha. You're very funny. The only plan I have is doing a big load of nothing." Jess stood up on her tiptoes and peeked inside Sydney's bag of food. "Though I could make an exception if you feel like sharing some of that food. I'm sure I could spare the time."

Sydney glanced down at the bag under her arm. She wasn't going to waste this golden opportunity. Why hadn't she thought of it before? "I've got a better idea. Let's go out."

"Out? You and me? On Valentine's Day?" At least Jess didn't sound uninterested—cautious, rather.

"We can call it a mate-date if it makes you feel better."

Jess looked down at her outfit—grey leggings and a navy hoodie. "I don't think I'm presentable enough for any type of date. Mates or otherwise."

Yeah right. Like Jess could ever look anything other than beautiful. Sydney smiled at her. "You look perfect. Especially for what I've got planned."

"Considering you didn't know I was home two minutes ago, you've planned this very quickly," Jess said warily.

"Guess you'll just have to trust my planning skills. Are you coming or not?"

Jess jutted her chin. "That's no way to ask a lady out on Valentine's Day."

Sydney stepped forward. "Jess Black, will you please do me the honour of being my platonic date this Valentine's Eve?"

"Overkill." Jess grabbed her coat and scarf. "But yeah, I'll go."

Sydney laughed. She went and dumped the food on the kitchen table—she could reheat it later or tomorrow. "Is Chloe home? Maybe we should invite her too. Make it a roomie thing." Plus, it might stop Sydney from getting carried away about the fact that she was about to spend Valentine's Day with Jess. On a friend-date. But still.

"I haven't seen her today," Jess said. "Guess she's still working."

"Should we wait on her?"

"Gee, you really know how to make a girl feel special. Would it really be so bad to be stuck with me?"

Sydney softened. "You already know the answer to that."

"Then let's go."

February in London was cold. Bitterly cold. But at least it wasn't raining. Sydney saying that she had a plan might have been a little bit of a stretch, but she knew the city well enough to be able to improvise. She was thinking street food and romantic walk along the Thames. Scratch that. Just a walk. But if it felt romantic, so be it. Not her fault.

"How was the world of hairdressing today?" Sydney asked. "Did Pam behave?"

Jess chuckled. "Luckily, she seems to save the majority of her naughtiness for when you're there."

"Are you saying I'm a bad influence?"

"It's a possibility."

Sydney laughed. "Perhaps I better stay away, then."

"Please don't. I like it when you visit" Jess playfully nudged her arm. "And hairdressing was…busy today. Biggest date day of the year, so a lot of women wanting to make a big impression. Fancy hairstyles for fancy dinners. Fresh new cuts to surprise the other half. That kind of thing. How was soap making?"

"Also busy, but probably less high maintenance. The new scents are coming along nicely, and Rachel's designed some amazing new packaging."

"Are you going to tell me what scents you've chosen yet?"

Sydney glanced sideways at Jess. "That's super top-secret." Translation: Rachel would kill her if she spilled.

"Oh, come on. Can you tell me one?" Jess fluttered her eyelashes. "That can be my Valentine's present."

"My company isn't enough?"

Jess laughed. "More than enough. But I like to be in the know. It makes me feel powerful."

"Well, I wouldn't want to hinder your power. I'll tell you one." Sydney picked one that she had specifically made with Jess in mind. "A Day at the Bakery."

Jess's eyes brightened with interest. "Ooh. Does it smell like cake?"

"Kind of," Sydney said. "It's very similar to the Freshly Baked Scones scent that you said made you want to eat me. Remember?" She made sure to keep her face straight.

Jess's cheeks began to turn pink, right on cue.

"I had to tweak it a little bit to fit the theme, but I hope it will still have the same desired effect." Sydney studied her. "You've gone quiet."

"Because you're a menace."

"Me? You're the one who made the comment in the first place. In front of my innocent nephew, no less. Scandalous."

"You knew what I meant. I was complimenting your soap-making ability, only you have a dirty mind."

"So, you don't want to eat me?"

"I didn't say that I—" Jess's eyes widened, and she stopped speaking.

Sydney burst out laughing. "And there was me thinking my Valentine's Day was going to be dull."

Jess smiled and shook her head. "Crossing so many lines."

"Did you not know? The lines get moved slightly on Valentine's Day. It's a rule."

"Funny, I've never heard of this rule."

"It's new."

"Hmm. And what do you mean by slightly? To allow what, exactly?"

Sydney pondered what she could possibly get away with. "Innuendos and light flirtation."

"I might be able to live with that. Within reason."

"I knew you were a rule follower." Sydney chuckled. "Speaking of dirty…how do you feel about dirty burgers?"

Jess touched her stomach. "I feel excellent about them. Where can I find one of these dirty burgers?"

"You can follow me."

Sydney led Jess to an outdoor market she knew that did all kinds of street food. Japanese, Mexican, Italian, Spanish—you name it, they had it. They had a walk around, looking the various options available. Sydney stopped when they reached the burger stall. She had never actually tried anything from it before, but she'd seen some of their photos posted online and their food looked amazing.

Sydney opted for a burger with bacon, cheese, and chipotle coleslaw. Jess got a little bit more adventurous and added cheese, beetroot, and hot sauce. They both ordered a glass of white wine that didn't really come in a glass, but a clear plastic cup instead.

The dirty burgers were that—dirty and loaded with toppings. Things were going to get messy. Sydney led them over to a wall where they had some space to eat.

"How's yours?" she asked Jess after they were a few bites in.

Jess closed her eyes and moaned in obvious pleasure, which made Sydney tingle right to her core. "Soo good. How about yours?"

Sydney cleared her throat, trying to recover. "Also good, but not as good as that face you just made."

"I'm surprised you aren't making orgasm faces too. This is hands down the best burger I've ever had."

"An orgasm face? Is that what that was?"

Jess shrugged. "That's what I predict it would look like. I've never watched myself to find out."

It was Sydney's turn to blush.

Jess continued. "Besides, I got beetroot in mine. And you know what that means."

"Huh? What's so special about beetroot?"

"You don't know?"

Sydney shook her head.

"Beetroot's an aphrodisiac." Jess made a point of popping another piece of beetroot into her mouth and grinned. "Watch out."

Sydney gaped back at her, and Jess burst out laughing. Oh, she was so enjoying getting her own back.

"Did you just make that up?" Sydney asked.

"No, it really is true. But it might take more than a piece of beetroot to turn me on. Just FYI." Jess giggled again. "Your face was priceless, though—possibly the same colour as the beetroot."

"And you called *me* a menace."

"Beware of moving the lines, Sydney. Very dangerous."

Sydney gulped. Who was flirting now? "So I can see. Come on, trouble. Let's finish these and take a walk by the river." Maybe that would help her cool off a little. Jess had a knack for raising Sydney's thermostat.

"Good idea. Wait." Jess started fidgeting in her pocket. "We should take a photo before we go."

"A photo?"

Jess nodded. "I want to remember this. And we don't have many photos together."

Sydney was sure she would remember their date vividly even without a photo, but she agreed it would be nice to have one. "That's true we don't. Let's fix that." She looked around for a good spot. They could have the river in the background with the distant lights behind. That would make a nice backdrop. "Do you want me to take it?" She was a few inches taller, after all.

"Unless you want a photo of me with your neck, that would probably be best."

"Depends how much you like my neck."

Jess glanced at it. "I like it, but not as much as I like your face."

"Why, Ms Black, I think that might have been a compliment."

Jess feigned surprise. "You know, I think it might have been."

Sydney laughed. "For the record, I like your face too." She held Jess's phone up and flipped the screen for a selfie. Jess slid in beside her, and they both smiled. Sydney pressed the button three or four times to make sure she got a good shot, then passed the phone back.

"Thanks." Jess flicked through them and turned the phone around to Sydney. "I like this one best."

Sydney looked at it. They both looked so happy. Sydney wasn't surprised that she did—she felt happy—but it was nice to see that Jess looked the same way. "Me too."

"I'll send it to you." Jess tapped on her phone.

They finished up their burgers and threw the wrappers into the nearest rubbish bin. They both still had some wine left, so they took it with them and settled into a comfortable stroll along the river, side by side. Every so often, their arms brushed against each other. There might as well have been a defibrillator sending shocks straight to Sydney's heart. When she had woken up that morning, she had never imagined that she would have been spending Valentine's evening wandering around London with the woman she loved.

Because there was no question in her mind that she was unequivocally in love with Jess. This wasn't some crush or frivolous infatuation. She didn't have feelings that were going to fade away in a few weeks. Sydney had been falling ever since she met Jess on that train, and now she was in deep. If only Jess could find the courage to let herself fall too. Sydney was right there to catch her.

"You okay? You've gone very quiet," Jess said.

Sydney forced herself to smile like she wasn't having the epiphany of a lifetime. "I'm fine. Just enjoying the evening."

"I am too. I'm having a really nice time." Jess bumped her hip into Sydney. "You sure know how to pull off last minute mate-dates. I should never have doubted you."

Mate-date, right. Sydney was so screwed. She swallowed and tried to play it cool. "You should see me when I'm prepared. It would blow your mind."

"I hope I get the chance to," Jess said, turning her head to face her. And that look they shared, the one where their eyes connected, and the rest of the world stopped. That's how Sydney knew that she wasn't in this alone.

"Anytime," she said quietly.

"And what if I wanted a real date?" Jess asked after a few seconds.

Sydney immediately stopped walking. Because had she heard that right? She didn't quite trust her brain not to be playing tricks on her. "You mean, not just as friends?"

"No. Not friends."

"So, like a date-date?"

Jess nodded. "Exactly like that."

Sydney's heart rate doubled. She searched Jess's face for any signs that Jess could be teasing, or that perhaps she was misunderstanding, but all she could see was sincerity—and maybe a touch of nervousness. "Then I would jump at the chance," she said with zero hesitation. "Is... is that what you want?" She couldn't take the chance that Jess was talking in hypotheticals right now.

"I don't think I've ever wanted anything so much," Jess said softly, and just like that, all Sydney's dreams came true with that one single sentence.

She threw up a silent prayer of thanks to St Valentine or whoever the hell was responsible for Jess's sudden declaration. There was no stopping the smile that spread across her face. "Do you have any idea how long I've wanted to hear you say that?"

Jess took Sydney's hand in hers. "Honestly? Probably as long as I've wanted to say it." She laced their fingers together in a simple move that made Sydney's knees go weak, because seriously—this was really happening!

They stood lost in each other's eyes and smiles, basking in this new revelation until they almost got run over by a teen on an electric scooter yelling at them to move out of the way. Unfortunately, a typical occurrence in city life. Sydney rolled her eyes and reluctantly pulled her gaze away from Jess as they continued to walk slowly along the path. Jess didn't let go of her hand, which Sydney didn't mind one bit.

Dare she say that their so-called mate-date was shaping up to be rather romantic after all? Even when Sydney had suggested it, she had never expected this outcome. "A proper date, then," she said. "You know, I don't want to state the obvious, but it is Valentine's Day."

"Wow. So it is," Jess replied playfully.

Sydney chuckled, trying to sound casual when all she really wanted to do was jump and squeal with excitement. "And we're out. Together."

"We are…"

"There's handholding." Sydney lifted their hands up to showcase it.

Jess laughed softly. "That is happening, yes." She gave Sydney a quizzical look, so she got to her point.

"I was just thinking that tonight already feels like a date-date to me. That's all."

"You know, I think you're right," Jess paused. "If we are on a real date, maybe this is the part where you take me home."

Sydney turned her head to find Jess watching her intently. "Take you home because you think that we should end the date now, or…?" She left the question hanging, but Sydney had a feeling she already knew the answer. There was no mistaking the look of desire on Jess's face. A look that Sydney was sure she now mirrored on her own.

"No," Jess said, holding Sydney's gaze unwaveringly. "I want you to take me home so we can be alone."

Sydney didn't need to be told twice. "Let's go, then."

❖

Jess was done with waiting.

What had she been waiting for? The perfect time? The perfect place? Well, a romantic date on Valentine's Day certainly fitted the bill.

And those things were great. But the reason why they were so great was all down to the person. To Sydney. Because, the truth was, Sydney made everything great. And Jess realized that the time and place didn't really matter—all that mattered was her. The perfect person had been right in front of Jess this whole time, patiently waiting for her to come to her senses.

And at last, she had.

Jess couldn't ignore her feelings for a second longer. She didn't want to ignore them. She wanted Sydney. She wanted her in every way possible, and it felt so good to admit it. To herself and out loud.

That didn't mean she wasn't still scared or nervous, she was both, but Sydney made Jess feel safe and cared for—and that was enough to quash any lingering doubts or worries running through Jess's head.

They both remained quiet as they walked toward home. Not because Jess didn't want to speak to Sydney, but because she wanted to do so much more. And it was all she could think about.

Jess walked ahead into the house, shedding her coat and hanging it up as Sydney clicked the door shut behind them and did the same.

Jess checked the bowl. Chloe's keys were gone. She listened anyway for any signs of Chloe being home to make sure, but the house was silent except for the jingling of Sydney's keys. When she heard them hit the bowl with a clink, Jess turned around. She closed the gap between Sydney and her in two small steps.

As Jess looked up into Sydney's soft, questioning gaze, her heart felt like it was going to burst out of her chest. This was it. There were no more obstacles. She was removing the lines.

She lowered her gaze to Sydney's lips, lips that Jess had only been able to touch for brief seconds before. But now the shackles were gone, and there was no reason to stop. So she allowed herself to look freely, to indulge, not caring that her intention was vividly on display for Sydney to see. Because Jess *wanted* Sydney to see how much she wanted her.

Jess reached up and gently ran her thumb across Sydney's bottom lip. "I love your lips. Did you know that?" she asked with a smile, mimicking the moment she had admitted that to Sydney on New Year's Eve.

Jess watched Sydney's throat move as she swallowed. She looked at Jess with recognition. "You remember that?" Her voice was husky. Jess loved it when she made Sydney's voice go like that.

"Of course I remember. It's the truth. I meant it."

Sydney's brow furrowed, as if Jess's admission hit deep. She let out a heavy sigh and dropped her gaze to Jess's lips, like she finally dared to hope. How much restraint must Sydney have had while she was free, yet Jess remained untouchable? How had she been able to wait for so long to do this?

Jess couldn't wait for another minute. She leaned forward and pressed her lips against Sydney's, much like she had on Christmas. Only this time, Jess didn't pull away. Like before, she took a few seconds to revel in the softness of Sydney's lips against hers, but then she needed more. Jess deepened the kiss, their lips moving slowly and softly brushing against one another in what felt like perfectly rehearsed choreography. Only they didn't need to rehearse, because this thing between them was the most natural thing in the world. They were made to do this.

Sydney moaned and pushed Jess up against the nearest wall, only breaking their kiss for a second to look at Jess with sheer hunger in her eyes. If Sydney was hungry, Jess was starving. She grabbed Sydney's top and pulled her back in. This time Sydney's mouth crashed against hers, and it was Jess's turn to moan. She pushed her tongue into the inviting warmth of Sydney's mouth, and Sydney's tongue met it with its own gentle caress and expert movement.

Then Jess's mind became an evocative blur. She was hyper-aware of every move, every touch, and every breath she gasped for before she dived right back into Sydney again. But in that moment, if someone had asked her what her name was, she wouldn't have had a clue. All Jess knew was Sydney, and how Sydney was making her feel. How had she ever thought that she wouldn't want this? That she might not enjoy it? Jess could kiss Sydney forever.

She wanted to touch Sydney everywhere. She ran her hands up Sydney's back. Held the back of Sydney's neck. Cupped Sydney's cheek. She grabbed Sydney's hair, burying her fingers in it. At one point, she even reached down and grabbed Sydney's hips. Jess pulled and Sydney pushed, both of them in desperation for their bodies to touch. To become so close that they were practically one.

Sydney's hands were everywhere too. Frantic, yet sure in their exploration of Jess's body. Like Sydney didn't know where she wanted to touch first, but everywhere she did, she touched with masterful skill.

Jess needed more. She needed to touch all of Sydney, without the barrier of clothes. Only she couldn't do it in the middle of the entrance hall of their house—as much as she was tempted to guide Sydney down onto her back right there on the staircase, climb on top of her, and slide her hand straight inside her pants.

Not for their first time.

Jess pulled Sydney's bottom lip into her mouth, giving it one final, gentle nip before she let it go, eliciting a deep moan from Sydney which sent shockwaves right to Jess's centre. Reluctantly, she pulled away, surprised by her own panting breaths, the result of one kiss. One passionate, amazing, sexy kiss. "Sydney, maybe we should—"

"Please don't say anything," Sydney said, through her own heavy breathing.

"But I—"

"Just wait until tomorrow. Tomorrow you can tell me about how much you regret kissing me, about how you can't be with a woman, and about how none of it was real. All of those things. But tonight, please don't say anything. I just had one of the best nights of my life with you. I know that maybe it was different for you, but for me, tonight was perfect."

Why would Sydney possibly think Jess would regret kissing her? Had Jess's actions not told her the complete opposite? "Sydney—"

But Sydney stopped her again. "Nope. I'm going to leave on this amazing note and go to my room now. And tonight, I'm going to tell myself that you kissing me was the best decision you've ever made in your life. Because for me it was *everything.*" Sydney smiled. "I just got to spend Valentine's Day with the woman that I love. And I'm going to pretend that all of it was real, because for me it was."

"Love?" Jess repeated. Sydney loved her?

Sydney leaned forward and placed a soft kiss on Jess's cheek with swollen lips. "You can give me my reality check in the morning. Goodnight, Jess."

Jess watched, stunned, as Sydney retreated from her and walked up the stairs. She heard the bedroom door close as Sydney shut herself away from Jess and the rest of the world. What had just happened? How could Sydney have misunderstood everything so much?

To hell with this. Jess was not going to wait until morning to put things right. She marched up the stairs and right toward Sydney's bedroom. Not bothering to knock, she twisted the handle and pushed the door, so it opened with a bang.

Sydney visibly jumped. She was perched on the edge of her bed, staring at Jess in surprise. "Okay, so we're going to do this now, then." She sighed and shuffled herself round to face Jess. "Look, you don't have to explain. I know you probably weren't thinking—"

In a moment of either madness or bravery, Jess reached and pulled her hoodie over her head. She threw it down on the floor and stood in front of Sydney in her leggings and bra. Thank God she'd decided on black that day, and not one of her grey bras that used to be white. "You know, Sydney, you think about an awful lot of things that aren't true."

If Sydney had looked surprised when Jess had burst through her bedroom door, she was downright flabbergasted now. "What are you doing?"

"What do you think I'm doing? I'm picking up where we left off."

Sydney frowned in confusion. "But downstairs you said, 'Sydney, maybe we should stop.'"

"No. Downstairs, I was about to say, 'Sydney, maybe we should *move this upstairs*.' But you interrupted me and went off on a tangent about a bunch of regrets which I don't have."

"I…" Sydney closed her eyes and winced as the realisation settled in that she had jumped the gun. "You don't?"

"No. None. I get that I've freaked out in the past, so I can't blame you for expecting me to do it again, but let me be clear so there aren't any more mix-ups. I know exactly what I want. I've wanted you ever since we first met, and it feels good to finally say that out loud. I don't want to hide from this anymore. I've denied us both for long enough to let myself come to terms with you and me, and I have. I don't care that you're a woman—I might be nervous because I have no idea what I'm doing, but that's okay. I want you, Sydney. Believe me, I have no doubts about it." Jess took another step forward. "Now, can I keep removing my clothes, or do you want to talk about this some more?"

Sydney basically scrambled off the bed to rush over to her. "No." She reached out and ran her hands down Jess's sides, gazing at her with darkened eyes. "Let me." Keeping hold of Jess's waist with one hand, she reached behind her with the other and pushed the door closed.

This time, neither of them jumped at the bang.

Jess wasn't sure what turned her on more. The way Sydney was touching her so delicately, or the way Sydney was looking at her like she was about to devour her.

"Are you seriously standing in my bedroom in your bra right now?" Sydney whispered in wonderment. She ran her fingertips up Jess's arms and trailed them across the top of her breasts. A shiver ran right through Jess's body, and that was with her bra still on.

Jess had never got all the fuss about breasts. She had never craved any attention there. Austin hadn't really known what he was doing with them anyway. But a simple touch from Sydney elicited a pulsing between Jess's legs, and now all she could think about was Sydney's hot mouth wrapped around her nipples. She yearned for it. "I would prefer to be standing in your bedroom without it," she replied, almost straining to speak.

Sydney didn't hesitate. Without taking her eyes off Jess's, she reached round with both hands and unhooked Jess's bra with expert finesse. She slowly trailed the straps down Jess's arms and dropped it on the ground beside her discarded top.

It was only then that Sydney allowed her eyes to drift downward. Jess's heart pounded under her fervent gaze. Every look felt like a touch, every touch delicious. As Sydney's eyes trailed across Jess's exposed chest, her lips parted in response. Jess watched, entranced, as Sydney ran her hands up her body, and as she gently cupped her breasts. Sydney was taking her time, and it was like excruciating, delectable torture.

Sydney squeezed gently, then a little harder, like she was sussing out how much pressure Jess would enjoy. As Sydney tightened her grasp a little more, Jess let out an appreciative groan, the pulse between her legs intensifying to confirm her own point of pleasure. Had anything ever felt so good?

The sensation of Sydney touching her was everything, yet it still wasn't enough. Jess needed to feel Sydney's skin beneath her own fingers. She had thought about this moment so many times in the recent months. About her inexperience and lack of knowledge about how to pleasure another woman's body. It both excited her and terrified her. But now that the moment had finally arrived, Jess knew exactly what to do and where she longed to touch. It was the strongest, most instinctive feeling she had ever had. "I want to see you too."

Without waiting for the permission that she already knew she had,

Jess grabbed Sydney's top and pulled it off over her head. She smiled as she caught a whiff of their The Day We Met scent. It was fitting that Sydney had used it today.

She reached around and unhooked Sydney's bra, cursing herself that she fumbled for a few seconds until she released the clasps. Jess would learn—she planned on getting in plenty of practise.

Unlike Sydney, Jess didn't take her time. She reached for Sydney immediately, in awe of the feel of the soft, squashy breasts in her hands—a stark contrast to Austin's hard, hairy chest. So much better. She ran her thumb over Sydney's nipple, marvelling at how it hardened under her touch. "You are so beautiful."

Sydney smiled. "You're one to talk." She ran her hands up and down Jess's back. "Is all of this okay? We don't have to do anything if you don't want to."

"I want to do everything," Jess said. "Don't you?"

Sydney gave her an incredulous look. "Of course I do." She paused. "But if you change your mind at any point, you know you can tell me, right? No big deal."

Jess smiled at Sydney for being considerate as always. "I do know, but I won't. And thank you for checking in, but can you please kiss me now?"

Sydney grinned and leaned forward, connecting their lips once more, this time with so much more purpose knowing that they wouldn't have to stop. She pulled Jess close, and their bodies pressed together. The feeling of her breasts against another woman's, against Sydney's, ignited a further spark inside Jess.

As Sydney slid her tongue against hers, Jess trailed her hands down and grabbed Sydney's bum. She pulled Sydney's hips tight against her own, desperate to feel more, right in the spot where she craved it most.

Sydney gasped at the increase in friction, and they both sank even deeper into the kiss. It was no longer gentle, instead a fight for dominance with neither of them really caring who won or lost. It was all about the battle.

Jess decided there and then that she had never felt anything as wonderful as the feeling of Sydney's mouth consuming hers. Their tongues clashing together. Their bodies intertwined. Sydney's hands running through Jess's hair, grabbing on tight for the ride.

Jess felt a flood of warm fluid release inside her underwear, and she almost cried out in response. When had she ever been so unbelievably turned on from just a kiss? Albeit a passionate, topless kiss with a woman who she hadn't realized was her ultimate fantasy until a few short months ago.

"Bed," Jess managed to say roughly.

Sydney, obliging as always, led Jess straight over to her bed and eased her down on top of it. Sydney covered Jess's body with her own, continuing their heated kiss that was too good to stop.

But after a few minutes, Sydney did stop. She pushed herself off Jess and then off the bed. Jess took in the sight as Sydney looked down at her with fire in her eyes. She had never seen anything so sexy. Sydney's hair, messy and tousled from Jess's frenzied fingers. Her lips, pink and swollen from their overindulgent kissing. Her flawless body with her full breasts on display for Jess to appreciate—which she did, openly.

Suddenly, the heat went from high to scorching. Sydney unbuttoned her jeans and pushed them down her long legs, taking her underwear with them. She stepped out of them, and Jess only had seconds to savour Sydney's naked form before Sydney leaned forward grabbed the waistband of her leggings.

"Can these come off?" Sydney asked.

Unable to speak, Jess nodded.

Sydney guided them down Jess's legs with ease. After she threw them behind her, Sydney ran her hands back up Jess's legs until she reached the waistband of her underwear. She hooked her fingers underneath and Jess lifted her hips to allow her to slide them off. Jess lay in front of Sydney, naked, exposed, yet she had never felt so at ease. To think that she had ever doubted that she wanted this. Doubted who she was. Jess had never felt more like her true self than she did in that very moment.

Sydney stared, taking in Jess's body with sheer, unadulterated lust in her eyes. Sydney wanted her. *Bad.* And that knowledge made Jess feel like the most confident, powerful woman in the world. "Touch me."

Sydney climbed back on the bed. She slowly lowered her body down on top of Jess. This time when their lips met, Sydney kissed her tenderly and with care. That was the thing—not only did Sydney make Jess feel wanted, but she also made her feel safe and loved.

As they kissed, Jess pushed her hips up to meet Sydney's, and

Sydney ground down against her. Touching each other so intimately with their clothes still on was one thing, but the feeling of Sydney's naked body grinding against hers was on a whole other level. They found their perfect rhythm as they became desperate for more pressure, their kisses turning frenzied and wild as they moved as one.

Sydney pulled her lips away, only to press them onto Jess's neck. Jess moaned as Sydney sucked on the tender skin and tugged on it lightly with her teeth. She buried her hands in Sydney's hair as Sydney kissed and nipped her way down to Jess's collarbone, where she ran her tongue even further south toward Jess's breasts.

Sydney pulled her mouth away and looked up at her as she covered Jess's breasts with her hands. She squeezed, just like she had before, this time knowing precisely what Jess enjoyed. Jess gasped as waves of pleasure shot right to her centre. Sydney kept watching her and moved her fingers to focus on Jess's nipples, once again gripping them lightly then adding more pressure until she found Jess's sweet spot. She grinned when Jess cried out. Then Sydney dipped her head and took one of Jess's nipples into her mouth. Jess let her head fall back as she felt Sydney's tongue swirling around before she sucked it right into her mouth. Sydney repeated that a few times, then lavished the same attention on her other nipple. By the time Sydney continued her trail down Jess's body, Jess's breaths were coming in short, shallow gasps.

Sydney placed open-mouthed kisses along Jess's stomach. She shuffled further down the bed and placed her hands on Jess's knees to ease her legs apart. As the air hit Jess's centre and Sydney studied her with an insatiable gaze, Jess's clit began to throb before it was even touched.

"Oh my God," Sydney said as she reached forward and gently ran a fingertip along the length of Jess's slit. "You're drenched."

Even the light contact made Jess lift her hips. "Is that okay?"

"Oh, Jess. It's more than okay." Sydney's face settled into a seductive smile as she repeated the move. "It's amazing."

Jess sucked in a breath as she jerked her hips again. "More," she begged. Jess had never begged for anything in her life, but in that moment, she needed Sydney like she needed oxygen.

Sydney added more pressure, rubbing her fingers slowly up and down. Jess could hear the sound of her own desire as Sydney's fingers moved through it. Then Sydney homed her focus in on Jess's clit. She swirled her fingers around in slow, teasing circles. Every time she skated a finger over Jess's clit, waves of pleasure shot right through Jess's core.

Jess could come from this alone.

"Look at me," Sydney said softly.

Jess opened her eyes. As their gazes connected, Sydney moved her hand and slowly pushed one finger inside her wet opening. Jess gasped with pleasure as she felt Sydney inside her.

Sydney moved her finger in and out before adding another, slowly pushing deeper inside. Jess had to force herself to keep her eyes open, to not break that contact with Sydney. Watching Sydney while she had Jess in her rawest, purest form was like a drug—addictive and intoxicating.

The waves that ran through Jess's body built up in intensity with every pump of Sydney's fingers. "I'm so close," she told Sydney through panting breaths.

Sydney increased her rhythm, thrusting harder in and out of Jess with purpose.

Jess threw her head back and closed her eyes, unable to hold back any longer. As she did, she felt Sydney's warm tongue press against her clit. She cried out in overwhelming gratification.

Jess rocked her hips as Sydney fucked her with her fingers and devoured her with her tongue. Then, when Sydney sucked her clit into her mouth and curled her fingers inside her, Jess saw stars. Her mouth fell open in ecstasy as the most intense of orgasms shot through her body in what felt like never-ending waves. Jess wasn't sure how long it actually lasted, but it wasn't quick, like her body was holding on to every drop of pleasure Sydney was giving. She had never known anything like it.

Sydney didn't stop touching her until Jess eventually came down from her high. Sydney placed a final kiss on Jess's clit and slid her fingers slowly out of her before she climbed back up the bed. She wiped her glistening chin on her shoulder and grinned.

Jess lazily lifted a finger. "I need a minute."

Sydney chuckled, clearly pleased with herself—as she should be. She propped herself up on her elbow and drew lazy circles on Jess's shoulder while Jess got her breath back.

Jess turned to face her. "That was...I don't have words."

"For me too." Sydney leaned down and kissed her softly. "I'm glad you enjoyed it."

Could Jess make Sydney feel as good? All she knew was that she wanted to try. She pushed Sydney to lie down onto the bed and rolled on top of her. "Hi."

Sydney smiled. "Hi."

"I think it's my turn."

"Don't feel like you have to. I know this is all new for you."

Jess covered Sydney's mouth with her finger. "I've been dying to touch you since I met you."

Sydney blew out a breath. "Then I need to warn you, I'm already so close from making you come."

"The first one might be quick, then."

"The first one?"

"We have all night, don't we?"

Sydney practically growled as she pulled Jess's mouth to hers, the passion from before kicking back in right away. Jess could taste herself on Sydney's tongue as they kissed. She didn't know where to touch first. She wanted to feel every inch of Sydney. To taste every part of her. It was a good job they had all night.

She allowed herself to get lost in Sydney's lips for a few minutes. Kissing Sydney would never get old. When they broke for breath, Jess lowered herself so that she was eye level with Sydney's breasts. She took them in her hands, enjoying the familiar yet unfamiliar feel as she rubbed them. Obviously, Jess had touched her own, but touching someone else's was a whole new experience. Then she lowered her mouth and teased Sydney's nipple with the flick of her tongue. She gently pinched the other nipple between her fingers at the same time, in a move that Sydney must have enjoyed, judging by her groan.

Growing in confidence, she took Sydney's nipple fully into her mouth and sucked on it as Sydney squirmed beneath her. Sydney let out a sharp hiss as Jess sucked harder. She stopped and glanced up. "Too hard?"

Sydney shook her head and gave Jess a look that urged her to continue.

So she did. Jess licked, and sucked, and even dared to bite on Sydney's nipple while Sydney writhed below her in pleasure. Who knew breasts could be so much fun?

When she moved across to shower Sydney's other breast with the same attention, Jess reached her hand down between Sydney's legs. She gasped, stunned at how wet Sydney was already. Was Jess the cause of that? She began to move her fingers up and down through Sydney's wetness, loving the feel of arousal beneath her touch.

"Fuck," Sydney said, jerking her hips.

Jess smiled at the knowledge that she could turn Sydney on so much. She was determined to make Sydney feel as good as she had minutes before.

Without taking her hand away, Jess moved up and claimed Sydney's mouth with her own. As they kissed, Jess moved her fingers up and down, and she felt Sydney's clit harden against her touch. Jess added more pressure and Sydney gasped into her mouth. Her nails dug into the skin on Jess's back.

"I need you inside," Sydney gasped.

Jess instantly went where Sydney wanted and pushed two fingers inside. If she thought breasts felt good, nothing compared to the feel of Sydney's wet warmth engulfing her fingers. Jess loved the feeling as she pushed her fingers in and out of Sydney. When she added a third, Sydney let out a guttural moan, and Jess knew she was close. She thrust in and out of Sydney hard and fast, and at the same time she used her thumb to rub Sydney's clit.

Sydney's pants and moans got quicker, and a few seconds later she let out a loud cry. Jess watched in astonishment as Sydney's orgasm shot through her, both delighted and amazed that she had been the one to cause it.

When Sydney sank down into the bed, Jess collapsed beside her. She rested her head on Sydney's chest and Sydney wrapped her arms around her as they both tried to catch their breath.

"I could get used to this," Sydney said after a few minutes.

"Me too." Jess had no idea why she had stalled for so long. Lying in bed with Sydney's arms wrapped around her was the happiest Jess had felt in as long as she could remember.

"Yeah? So, you're happy with your experiment?"

Jess hummed her approval. "Very positive results." She lifted her head to look at Sydney. "I think tests should be ongoing, though."

"You do?"

Jess grinned. "Yeah. I like to be thorough."

Sydney laughed and leaned down to kiss her softly. "In that case, would you like to stay over in my room tonight?"

"Of course. I'm not going anywhere." Jess turned over and climbed on top of Sydney again. "Remember I told you you're good enough to eat? I think it's about time I had a taste, don't you?"

CHAPTER EIGHTEEN

Sydney woke up in her darkened bedroom, but she might as well have been on cloud nine. She lifted her arms above her head and stretched out, feeling every part of her body ache in the most wonderful way. She felt bruised with satisfaction.

Sydney turned her head sideways and smiled as she caught a glimpse of Jess still asleep next to her. Jess was curled up on her side, the covers draped over most of her naked body. Sydney resisted the urge to lean over and place a kiss on her bare shoulder. She didn't want to wake Jess up too early—they needed plenty of rest after a night filled with activity.

Sydney had heard of wishes coming true on birthdays. Maybe Christmas. She had never expected her biggest wish to come true on Valentine's Day. But that's what had happened on their impromptu date, where they had gone out as friends and returned as lovers.

She replayed the night in her head. How she had almost blown things.

When Jess pulled away, Sydney had been so sure that Jess was backing off, regretting their kiss immediately. She let out a quiet laugh. How wrong she had been.

Jess began to shift beside her, slowly coming round as she woke up. She looked at Sydney and gave her a lazy smile.

Any apprehension Sydney had about whether Jess would have any regrets that morning quickly faded away with that smile. "Good morning," Sydney said quietly.

Jess flung her arm around Sydney's naked torso and pulled

herself closer. She rested her head on Sydney's chest. "Morning," she mumbled, still sounding sleepy. "Can we stay like this all day?"

Sydney wrapped her arms tightly around Jess and placed a kiss on top of her head. "I wish we could, but I think my sister, and Pam and Violet might have an issue with it."

Jess groaned. "But I like it here."

"You can come back later if you want to."

"I'll have to think about it." Jess turned her head and looked mischievously at Sydney. "I've thought about it, and yes, I want to."

"Me too." She leaned her head down and kissed Jess gently. "How are you feeling this morning?"

Jess turned herself over to lie on her front. She rested her arms on Sydney's chest and leaned her head down. "Tired, a little sore in the best way. But also, extremely happy and incredibly satisfied." She grinned up at Sydney. "That seems like a good assessment. How about you? If you could bottle this morning, what would you call it?"

Sydney narrowed her eyes in thought. "Five and a half orgasms later."

Jess playfully tapped her. "A half?"

"That was a compliment. Some people don't even manage one."

"A half, though?"

Sydney laughed. "We can count it if you want to."

"No, don't pity me. I'll just have to make the next one count as one and a half."

"Next time. That sounds good." Sydney smiled at the thought of being with Jess again. Hopefully many times. "And as for how I'm feeling, I'm much the same as you. Really happy, obviously. And surprised in the best possible way. I really didn't expect last night to happen."

"What? You didn't expect me to walk into your room and start taking off my clothes?"

Sydney chuckled. "No, but I want it on the record that I'm more than happy for that to happen any time."

"Yeah?" Jess placed a kiss on Sydney's collarbone. Another further up. "I'm sure that can be arranged."

Sydney closed her eyes as Jess continued to kiss her way up her neck. She continued all the way up until she captured Sydney's mouth in a searing kiss. Sydney pulled Jess closer so that she was right on top of her as the kiss picked up the same sizzling heat as the night before. Even Sydney's lips felt bruised from overuse, but she didn't care, she could kiss Jess forever.

"How much time have we got before we have to get up?"

"Enough," Sydney said breathlessly.

"Let's fix that half now, then." Jess slid her tongue against hers in a deep kiss and she pushed her hips down to grind against Sydney. That's all it took for the throb between Sydney's legs to start back up again. Jess must have noticed how quickly Sydney was affected, and she slid down the bed and buried her face between Sydney's legs.

Sydney sucked in a sharp breath as Jess's tongue connected with her aching clit. There were no warmup acts this morning. Jess pressed her tongue firmly against Sydney and licked her as hard as she could. Sydney rolled her hips, desperate for release, completely aroused by the sound and feel of Jess's tongue devouring her. Then Jess pushed her tongue inside Sydney as deep as she could go, and Sydney almost yelled right out. She reached out and held on to Jess's head as Jess moved in and out of her.

"So good," Sydney managed to breathe out.

Jess pulled out and replaced her tongue with her fingers as she sucked Sydney's clit hard into her mouth.

Sydney squeezed her eyes closed as a powerful orgasm crashed right through her body, wave after wave. Jess kept up with every single one. By the time she finished she could hardly breathe. Her heartbeat felt like a drum, pounding in her ears.

Jess climbed back up the bed and pulled Sydney into her arms.

Sydney waited a couple of minutes for her breathing to return to normal. "I can't believe you had never done that before last night."

"I'm a quick learner," Jess said cockily. "One and a half?"

You can say that again. Jess had every right to be cocky after that. "Maybe one and three-quarters. You're amazing." Sydney checked the clock, hoping she had time to return the favour.

As if reading her mind, Jess said, "We have to get up, but you can make it up to me later."

Sydney groaned. "Not fair."

Jess smiled. "Trust me, doing that to you brings me a lot of pleasure. I'm good."

"Do we at least have time for one more kiss before we have to get up?"

"Always."

Always sounded good. Sydney claimed Jess's lips again, allowing herself to get lost in their warmth and softness. She barely even registered the sound of her bedroom door opening until Jess threw herself off her like a shot.

"Hey, Sydney, do you mind if I borrow—"

Chloe.

Sydney urged her brain to catch up with the situation. Chloe was standing in her doorway looking stunned, and frankly, furious. Jess was sitting up in the bed, gripping onto the sheets to cover herself up. She looked like she had just been caught burying a body. Her face had turned white as a sheet.

"Chloe," Jess said in a pleading tone.

"Don't, Jess," Chloe said. "Just don't." She took one final look at them and scoffed in clear disgust. "Unbelievable." With that she turned and slammed out of the room, almost taking the door off its hinges.

A few seconds later, the front door of the house slammed too.

Jess remained silent, staring at the bedroom door in shock.

Sydney should do something. Say something. "Hey," she said softly. "It'll be fine. I think she was just a bit surprised."

Jess didn't turn round to look at her. "I think that was more than surprise."

Sydney had to agree. Chloe looked downright annoyed. "I don't understand. Why would she react that way?"

"Because I've hurt her. I'm supposed to be her best friend, and I've gone and fucked her over."

"How?" Sydney frowned. "Because she didn't know about us? There wasn't even an us to know about before last night. Not really."

"That's only part of it." Jess ran her hand through her hair. "Chloe has feelings for you, Sydney."

It took a moment for that to sink in. Sydney had questioned Chloe's intentions a few times, sure. But Sydney thought that Chloe was just flirting with her. That she fancied her, maybe. Sydney had never for one second thought that Chloe had proper feelings for her. "Feelings? She told you that?"

Jess nodded. "Several times."

"And when she said this, you never mentioned anything about us?"

"Nope." *That's not good.*

"But Chloe's in love with Dana." How could Chloe have feelings for her too? Sydney didn't buy it.

"She said that she's in the process of getting over Dana, and she's focussing on her feelings for you." Jess winced. "But she thinks you're still hung up on your ex, so she hasn't made a move."

Sydney recalled the conversation that would have led Chloe to think that. She sighed. "Still, I'm pretty sure it's still Dana she's crazy about, not me."

"Maybe that's true," Jess said, her tone sounding numb. "But even if she only thinks her feelings are real, she still confided in me about them. I still lied to her. I still kept secrets from her. And now, I've betrayed her."

Sydney reached out and took Jess's hand. "Jess. This'll be okay. We'll explain everything. I'm sure that Chloe will understand."

"I don't know that she will. Did you see that reaction? I've been a terrible friend. I hadn't realized just how terrible until now." A tear ran down Jess's cheek.

Sydney reached out and wiped it away. "What can I do? I could talk to Chloe."

Jess gave her hand a squeeze. "Thanks, but I'm not sure what good it would do. It's me she's angry with." She let go of Sydney's hand and swung her legs out of bed. "I need to get ready for work."

Sydney got up too. She found Jess's leggings and underwear on the floor where she had discarded them the night before. Sydney picked them up and passed them to her. "I'll go make us some coffee. Well, tea for you."

Jess didn't waste any time getting dressed. She quickly pulled her leggings up and walked over to grab her hoodie. "I don't think I have time today."

Jess always made time for a tea or coffee in the mornings. She was freaking out. Sydney could see it. "Are we okay?"

"Huh?" Jess asked as she pulled her top on. "Oh, yeah. We're fine." She didn't sound too convincing.

Sydney could feel Jess pulling further and further away by the second and she didn't know how to stop it. The mood had changed so drastically in the blink of an eye. "So, I'll see you tonight, then?" She hated how needy she sounded.

"Uh, yeah. Maybe." *Maybe?* "I should probably try to speak to Chloe before…anything else."

Sydney nodded. "I get that." And she did. Sydney didn't want to come between two people who had been friends for years. But she also didn't want Jess to run from her, which was exactly what it felt like she was about to do. "Are you regretting this? Us?"

Jess looked at her and softened, which made Sydney feel slightly better. "No. Of course not." She walked over and placed a quick kiss on Sydney's lips. "But I need to think. To sort some things out."

I need to think. Because that's what every woman wants to hear after spending the night together. Arguing seemed futile, so Sydney nodded again. "Well, whatever you need from me, just say."

"Thanks." Jess flashed a smile, but it faded just as fast. "I'll see you later."

"Yeah, I'll see you later," Sydney replied, but Jess had already left the room before she had finished her sentence. "I had a great time with you last night," she mumbled, knowing only she could hear it.

Sydney threw herself back down on top of her bed and let out a long sigh. She had woken up in that bed less than an hour ago feeling on top of the world. Now all she wanted to do was pull the covers up over her head and pretend the world didn't exist at all.

Sydney didn't know how to feel. On one hand she was happy, excited, totally in love with Jess. Even more so after the night they had spent together. On the other she was dejected, and terrified of losing Jess when she had only just got her. And mainly, she felt helpless, like it was all out of her control.

She forced herself back up again.

If there was one person whose advice she trusted, it was her sister's. Rachel would know what to do.

"I take it back. Maybe you are a lothario." Rachel snapped her laptop closed and turned to give Sydney her full attention.

"Wow. Even the laptop's out of action. You really must think this is serious."

"To be honest, I'm still digesting how it went from us being single, lonely spinsters on Valentine's Day to you ending up with multiple orgasms and a hickey on your neck."

Sydney self-consciously lifted a hand to cover it. "Let's not forget how I've possibly ruined an almost lifelong friendship, and my multiple orgasms may never be repeated as there's a good chance Jess might move to Timbuktu in order to avoid me forever." She slumped down in her office chair and winced in discomfort.

Rachel pouted in pretend sympathy. "Aww. What's wrong? Sore from all the mind-blowing sex?"

Sydney glared at her. "A tad tender, yes." She blew out a breath. "Maybe I should have remained a single, lonely spinster."

"It has its perks," Rachel said. "None of this drama, for one."

Sydney groaned and held her head in her hands. "You know I don't like drama. I don't know what to do, Rach."

"Okay, here's what I think," Rachel said in the authoritative tone that she used when she meant business. It made Sydney sit up straight and listen. "First off, you've done nothing wrong. This is all on Jess."

"But it's partly my fault too."

"What part?" Rachel said in disagreement. "It's not your fault that Jess didn't want to tell Chloe that you two knew already each other when you moved in. Or that Jess didn't tell Chloe that she likes you. And it's not your fault that Chloe may or may not have developed feelings for you. You didn't lead her on."

When Rachel put it like that, maybe it wasn't Sydney's fault. "Maybe Jess felt like she couldn't tell Chloe *because* she knew that Chloe liked me."

"All the more reason to tell her, in my opinion." Rachel paused. "Look, I know you're all protective of Jess because you love her and blah blah blah. And that's sweet. But she's a big girl who should have been more honest with her best friend. Fact."

"Jess would never want to hurt Chloe."

"I'm sure she didn't do it intentionally. We all dig holes for ourselves sometimes, and some can be very hard to get out of."

Sydney sighed. "So, what are you saying?"

"That this is Jess's mess and not yours. Even if Chloe's a bit pissed at you now, she can't really stay mad. She had no claim to you, and you were barely even aware of her feelings."

"What should I do?" Sydney asked. "Should I do nothing?"

Rachel tilted her head. "You could. You could do nothing and hope that things go your way. Or you could take matters into your own hands and talk to Chloe yourself, regardless of what Jess wants. But if you're going to do that, you should do it soon. Don't let it drag out."

"And what about Jess? What if she starts avoiding me again? She couldn't get out of my bedroom fast enough this morning."

Rachel looked away.

"What? Just say whatever you're thinking."

"I mean, this seems to be her process, doesn't it? As soon as she gives an inch, she disappears and overthinks it. She'll probably come round, but…"

"But what?"

Rachel regarded her seriously. "But I think you need to find out whether she's in or out, once and for all. This can't be your life, Sydney. You have to be prepared that it might be you that has to be the one to pull away from this if she can't commit to you."

The thought of walking away and giving up on Jess made Sydney's heart physically ache. But deep down, Sydney knew that what Rachel was saying was true. Sydney couldn't stay on the emotional roller coaster forever. "I hate it when you're right."

Rachel smiled. "No, you don't. That's why you asked me— because you knew I would give it to you straight. It's just not fun hearing the hard stuff."

"Do you think there's any hope?" Sydney asked. "For Jess and me?"

"Of course. I just hope she doesn't take too long to do the right thing." Rachel swivelled her chair back around and opened her laptop again.

"Or she'll have you to answer to?" Sydney grinned. "What are you going to do? Email her to death?"

"Don't underestimate the power of a good email. Now, stop moping and get soapmaking. We need another batch of A Day in the Woods ready for quality testing."

"So, I'm not out of the woods yet, then?"

Rachel closed her eyes. "That was bad, even for you. Maybe Jess should avoid you after all."

Sydney laughed. At least she knew no matter what happened, the Fletcher sisters always had each other.

❖

There were no lights on when Sydney got home, but Chloe's keys were there. Jess didn't seem to be back yet, but for once Sydney was glad about that.

She went upstairs and knocked on Chloe's bedroom door. No answer.

"Chloe? It's Sydney. Do you think we could talk?"

Still no answer, but Sydney was sure she heard some movement.

She couldn't just burst into the room. It felt wrong to invade Chloe's space. And she didn't want to be too pushy with persistent knocking either.

Sydney decided on a different approach. "Chlo, I'm going to go downstairs and fire Beanie up. Come on down if you want some coffee and we can talk about this. Okay? I'll make the good stuff. Oh, and it's only me here," she added to reassure Chloe that she wasn't about to be ambushed by her *and* Jess.

Sydney went downstairs and flicked the power switch on Beanie to let her heat up for a few minutes. She listened but still didn't hear any movement from upstairs. Maybe this was going to be harder than she thought.

Keeping the faith, Sydney lifted two cups out of the cupboard and added some freshly roasted beans into Beanie.

Lo and behold, a couple of minutes later, Chloe appeared at the kitchen door. Her blond hair looked damp and was hanging down round her face, like she'd showered but hadn't been bothered to dry it.

"Hey," Sydney said, remaining cautiously quiet, like she was dealing with a shy animal that was going to scurry away if there were any loud noises or sudden movements.

Chloe stayed by the door. "Hi," she replied, devoid of any emotion. "You wanted to talk?"

"If that's okay? Like I said, I'm making coffee. You want some?"

"Sure."

Sydney went ahead and filled their cups before she spoke again.

"Can we sit?" She set the two cups on the table and slid a chair out for herself.

Chloe was hesitant but she pulled out the seat opposite.

"I don't really know what to say," Sydney admitted.

"Well, you're the one who wanted to talk," Chloe said sharply. She immediately looked away like she hadn't meant to snap.

"Have you spoken to Jess today?" Sydney asked.

"Nope. And I don't intend to."

Sydney nodded slowly. "Maybe I could explain some things. About Jess and me. If you'll let me."

"The two of you naked in bed together served as a pretty good explanation to me, but knock yourself out. Add to my misery."

"That's the last thing I want to do. I didn't even know you liked me before this morning."

"Oh, come on, Sydney. I think I made it pretty obvious. On several occasions."

"Yes, I realized you were a bit flirty at times. But I thought that's all it was. Harmless flirting."

"Well, now you know different. Apparently, Jess *is* capable of telling people things when she wants to. How interesting."

Sydney needed to be delicate. "Well, I am flattered that you like me. And none of this is any reflection on you, I think you're amazing. And I know it's not what you want to hear right now, but your friendship means the world to me." Sydney put her hand up to her heart because she meant it, even though she hated delivering the line. "But like I told you before—I'm already hung up on someone else. Now you know who."

"You led me to believe that you were still hung up on your ex."

"I said I was hung up on *someone*," Sydney explained. "But I'm sorry if I misled you."

"Misled me?" Chloe let out a bitter laugh. "You and Jess have humiliated me. Sleeping together behind my back? And you've both probably been laughing at me this whole time, haven't you? About how stupid I am that I didn't catch on."

"That's not how it is. We would never laugh at you. And Jess and I only slept together last night. That was the first time."

"Yeah, right. Like I'm going to believe that after all the lies."

"It's true. We've liked each other for a lot longer, yeah. But nothing happened between us until yesterday."

Sydney didn't know whether Chloe believed her or not. Her face wasn't giving much away other than the fact that she really wasn't happy. "Even if you are telling the truth, do you not think it would have been the decent thing to do, to tell me that you were hot for my best friend? Especially if you knew that I was flirting with you?"

"I couldn't."

"Why not?"

There was only one way to explain, and that was to start at the beginning. "Do you remember the woman that Jess met on the train? The one you told me that she was attracted to?"

Chloe frowned like she was trying to work out the relevance. "Yeah?"

Sydney raised her eyebrows and stared at Chloe until it clicked. "Hi."

"Oh my God. It was you?"

"Guilty."

"Well, that I was not expecting," Chloe said after a few beats. "Wait, is that why you moved in?"

"No. I had no idea Jess lived here. It was a total surprise to both of us."

"Okay…but why didn't either of you tell me?" Then Chloe closed her eyes and let out a sigh like she knew why. "Jess freaked out, didn't she?"

"Pretty much."

"And she didn't want me to link it. So she asked you not to tell me." It was a statement rather than a question.

Sydney stayed quiet. She didn't want to make things any worse for Jess. Her hope was to make things better.

"I know how Jess's brain works, so I can kind of get why she didn't tell me in the beginning." Chloe shook her head. "But she had so many chances after that to tell me what was going on. Especially, considering she knew…what she knew." She shifted uncomfortably.

"About that." They might as well address the elephant in the room. "I thought you were in love with Dana," Sydney said softly.

Chloe shrugged, but her face confirmed that Sydney was right.

"Come on. If Dana walked in here right now and said that she wanted to spend the rest of her life with you, you'd jump at it."

Chloe glared at her. "Well, I don't see that happening. Way to kick me when I'm down, Sydney."

Sydney held up a finger. "I have a point."

"Then please, make it."

"Do you think that maybe I was a distraction? Another woman moves in: me. We get along really well. Perhaps you thought...Sydney might be an option if things don't work out with Dana."

Chloe stared at her for a few seconds. Then she burst out laughing. "I don't know if that's more offensive to me or you."

Sydney laughed too. "A little of both, probably. I have a knack for putting my foot in it." It was a relief to see Chloe smile—like the tension in the room had begun to lift.

"Maybe. God, I don't know. I just know that this is a mess and that you and Jess suck."

Sydney took a sip of coffee from her cup. It had started to go cold. "If it helps at all, I'm not sure that there is a me and Jess. I can't remember a woman ever wanting to get away from my bedroom as fast as Jess did this morning."

Chloe frowned. "Look, I might be pissed at you guys for lying to me, but I would never get in the way of anyone's happiness."

"I really am sorry that we lied, Chloe."

"Yeah." Chloe put her head down. "Do you want to be with her?"

Sydney didn't hesitate. She had nothing to hide. "I do. I've wanted to ever since we first met."

"And do you think Jess feels the same way about you?"

"I did think so, but I don't know. Things have been...up and down." *To say the least.* "Jess runs away from me more than she runs *to* me." She bit her lip. "But I do know that she never meant to hurt you. She was devastated this morning after you left."

Chloe rolled her eyes.

"Will you at least talk to her? Let her explain?"

"Don't push it, Sydney. Jess has done major damage here."

"Please? Just a conversation. I can't explain all of her thinking. Only Jess can do that."

"I'll think about it."

They both took a sip of now lukewarm coffee, and each of them screwed their faces up. They started laughing.

"Are we going to be okay?" Sydney asked when they stopped.

Chloe gave her a relenting nod. "Yeah. We'll be fine."

Sydney felt some of the weight she had been carrying on her shoulders all day begin to ease. She smiled. "Can I hug you?"

Chloe tutted. "If you must." But Sydney noticed the slight upturn of the corners of her mouth. She held an arm out.

Sydney rounded the table and threw her arms around her. "It'll never happen again. The secrets."

She felt Chloe hug her back. "It better not."

Chloe gave Sydney a funny look after she sat down again. "What?" Sydney asked.

"I just can't believe you managed to turn Jess onto women. Jess! All that soap must give you superpowers."

Sydney chuckled. "I'm hoping it can bring best friends back together too."

"Yeah, yeah, yeah. Then it better be some pretty strong magic soap." But at least Chloe didn't sound angry anymore, so Sydney considered that a win.

CHAPTER NINETEEN

V iolet looked at Jess with those kindly eyes of hers. "Anything yet?"
"Is she checking that phone *again*?" Pam asked teasingly.
It was a fair comment. Jess had been checking it around every five
minutes.

She locked it and put it back into her pocket. "Yes, I'm checking
it again. And no, still nothing. Well, not from Chloe anyway." She *had*
received four missed calls from her dad and a text saying he really
needed to speak to her—which could only mean that Gretchen had
done something wrong.

"How about Sydney? Have you spoken to her?" Violet asked.

Jess felt a twinge of guilt. She hadn't handled things well with
Sydney, and she knew that. But in order for her and Sydney to move
forward, Jess needed to fix her friendship with Chloe first.

How could Jess face Sydney and act like everything was okay
when her best friend hated her for the very reason of her being with
Sydney? She couldn't. Nor could she risk hurting Chloe any further
either.

So Jess had stayed away, opting to stay at Violet's place the
previous night. She had sent a text to Sydney to let her know where she
was, so it wasn't like she had gone MIA or anything. Besides, it made
sense to give Chloe some space. The three of them in a house together
when Chloe's anger was raw and fresh—bad idea. Jess knew Chloe
well enough to realize that she needed some time.

What Jess *had* done was sent umpteen text messages to apologize.
And she had made it clear that when Chloe was ready to talk, Jess

would be there. So, for now, the ball was in Chloe's court. The only thing Jess could do was wait and hope for a chance to explain and show Chloe how sorry she was.

Then maybe she and Sydney could finally stand a chance to be together with nothing in their way.

"Yeah, I've messaged Sydney a couple of times." Jess shrugged. "I don't really know what to say to her right now."

"I'm sure she will understand," Violet reassured her.

Jess hoped that she would. She lifted her phone out and quickly fired off a love heart emoji to Sydney. At least she would know Jess was thinking about her. That had to be better than nothing.

"Have you contacted Chloe again?" Pam asked.

Jess clicked into her messages and turned the phone around to show her.

"What does that mean? Looks like double-Dutch to me."

"I forgot you're allergic to iPhones," Jess said. "It's about twenty messages from me to Chloe. Every single one of them unanswered."

"Has she read them?" Violet asked.

"How would she know if she's read them if Chloe hasn't replied?" Pam asked as if Violet was being stupid.

"Blue ticks," Jess said.

Pam stuck her hands on her hips and frowned. "Blue ticks?" She shook her head and stomped off across the salon. "You've lost me now."

Jess and Violet shared a giggle, the first one that Jess had had all day. It didn't last long before she started to feel guilty about that too. She had no right to smile right now.

"You know," Violet said. "I know you need to sort things out with Chloe, but I don't think that means that you have to shut Sydney out."

"I'm not shutting her out as such," Jess said. She looked down and fidgeted with her fingernail.

"Does she know that you want to be with her?" Pam asked from across the room. For once, Thairapy was empty except for the three of them, and they had finished up with all their clients for the day. That meant that they could have a rare, private conversation.

"I think she knows."

"How? Have you told her?" Pam asked.

"I'm pretty sure I showed her in other ways." Surely, Sydney couldn't be in any doubt about Jess's feelings after the night they spent together.

"Jess!" Pam covered her ears. "Too much information."

Jess snickered. Finally, she had discovered a way to get Pam off her back.

"But have you said the words?" Violet pushed. "Sometimes we need to hear something to know it's true."

"Of course. Sydney knows that I have feelings for her. She's known that for a long time."

Pam blew out an impatient sigh. "But does she know that you love her? L. O. V. E."

Jess stared at her. Did Sydney know? "I might not have said those exact words," she admitted.

Pam scowled at her. "I could really shake you sometimes."

Jess looked at Violet for support, but Violet gave her a pointed look. "For once, I'm with Pam."

"Are you telling me off right now? Both of you?"

"You bet your butt we are."

"Not exactly," Violet said, giving Pam a look telling her to back down. "No one's telling you off. But we hope you'll take a bit of advice from a couple of old dears who have been around the block a few times."

"What advice?" Jess asked.

"That communication is key," Violet said.

"And what does that mean?"

"It means that you stop hiding out in Violet's living room, and you go and talk to Chloe. And Sydney," Pam said. "Tonight."

"But Chloe doesn't want to speak to me," Jess said exasperatedly. "How many times do I have to tell you?"

"I wouldn't be so sure about that," Violet said quietly. Just then, the bell above the door jingled.

Jess whipped her head round as Chloe walked in. "Hey," she said. She could hear the surprised tone in her own voice.

Chloe shuffled from one foot to the other. "You said you wanted to talk."

Jess nodded quickly. "Yeah, I do. I definitely do. I...I'll be done here soon."

"Chloe, it's so good to see you," Violet said warmly, glancing up from the appointment book that she had only shifted her attention to moments before. "Pam, did you not say that the kitchen needed cleaned?"

Pam seemed confused for a second, then realized what Violet was doing. "I did. I've never seen it so filthy in all my life."

"Oh, deary me. We better do it now, then," Violet said. "Duty calls, girls. Don't mind us."

It was a good job neither of them had gone into acting.

They made themselves scarce, disappearing into the kitchen. Oh yeah, they could give Jess space when they wanted to.

Jess folded her arms and slowly approached the reception desk where Chloe stood. She leaned her hip against it, then straightened again, not even sure what way she should stand. Jess could never remember a time when things had been awkward between Chloe and her. She hated it.

"Sydney was the woman from the train," Chloe said straight away.

"Yes," Jess replied. That meant that Sydney and Chloe must have talked already.

"And you didn't tell me."

"No."

"I'm supposed to be your best friend, and you didn't tell me." Chloe kept her gaze fixed on the tiled floor.

Jess ran a hand through her hair. "Chloe, you know me. Better than anyone. I panicked. When I told you about meeting Sydney that day, I never expected her to show up in our bloody living room. Not for one second."

"I know. I get that," Chloe said. "I hate that you would keep it a secret from me, but I kind of understand you freaking out in the moment. But how about the rest of the times that you kept it from me? The times when I was confiding in you about me liking Sydney. And you never said a word. You just let me prattle on and embarrass myself."

"Hey, you don't have anything to be embarrassed about. It's me who's embarrassed and ashamed. Because, yes, that was wrong," Jess admitted. "I wish I could say something to make it better, but all I can tell you was that I was having a massive internal battle with myself the whole time. I was hoping that my feelings for Sydney would just disappear."

"But they didn't?"

Jess shook her head. "Not even close. The complete opposite happened."

Chloe frowned. "I don't know if I'm more angry that you didn't tell me or more hurt that you didn't. I'm supposed to be your best friend. If you can't tell me, who can you tell?"

"I didn't feel like I could talk to anyone about it," Jess said. "There were so many factors at play. Austin. The fact that I've never dated a woman. I was already so confused. And then you told me that you liked Sydney too, and that made it even harder to come clean."

"No, that's exactly when you should have told me."

Jess looked down at her hands and nodded. "You're right. I should have." She was in the wrong and she knew it. None of her explanations were good enough, but she owed Chloe the truth. "I really didn't think anything was ever going to happen between Sydney and me. I tried to get over how I felt—especially when you told me that you liked Sydney too. But somehow, things still progressed between Sydney and me, and the secret started to get bigger, and became so big that it was almost impossible to tell. I knew if I told you after keeping it from you for so long it would cause a rift between us. And now here we are. The rift happened anyway."

"Here we are." Chloe rolled her lips in. "Difficult or not, I would rather have heard it from you than to find out the way that I did."

"God, I know." Jess closed her eyes, trying to block out the previous morning when Chloe had walked in on her with Sydney. "I messed up. But I didn't do any of it to hurt you, Chlo."

Chloe glanced at her. Was it Jess's imagination, or had her frown softened a little? "I know you didn't mean to. But you did. I still stand by the fact that there were so many times you could have told me, Jess. So many times you *should* have."

"How could I tell you when I couldn't even admit it to myself?"

Chloe threw her hands out. "But why did you have to make it such a big deal? It's not the end of the world, Jess."

"But it was the end of my world as I knew it. And I needed to get my head around that." Jess felt her eyes begin to well up. "I'm sorry."

Chloe closed her eyes. "Don't cry. If you cry, then I'm going to cry, and I really don't want to cry."

Jess started to cry anyway. There was no way of stopping it.

When Chloe opened her eyes, her tears started to fall too. She let out a growl. "You know I'm a sucker for criers."

"I'm not doing it on purpose."

"I know." Chloe sighed. "You aren't ever allowed to lie to me again. Even about the hard stuff."

Was Chloe backing down? "Never," Jess said immediately.

Chloe glared at her, but without malice. "You're such a fucking idiot. Do you know that?"

Jess let out a laugh through her sobs. "I do know. I'm a complete idiot." She grabbed two tissues from the counter and passed one to Chloe. She dabbed her own eyes with the other. "Does the fact that you're calling me names right now mean that you might be able to find a way to forgive me?"

"I might continue to call you names for a while, but yes. I half forgive you. Sort of." Chloe shrugged. "I'm working on it."

"Oh, thank God." Jess lunged forward and threw her arms around Chloe. She squeezed her as hard as she could. "I'm sorry, Chlo. I'll never keep a secret from you again. Never. I swear it."

"I know you won't," Chloe said, squeezing her back.

A loud whooping noise came from the kitchen, which could only mean that Pam had been listening in.

Chloe must have heard it too. She let out a chuckle as she stepped back from their hug. "Anyway, you can thank your girlfriend. If she hadn't been so persistent in trying to clear everything up, it probably would have taken me a lot longer to get here."

"She's not my girlfriend," Jess said. "Not yet anyway."

"But you want her to be?"

Jess gritted her teeth. "Am I going to get in trouble if I answer that? I know you like her."

"Only if you lie to me."

"Well, yes. I do want to be with Sydney. I'm crazy about her, Chlo." Jess let out a nervous laugh. "Me? Crazy about a woman. Fancy that."

"We all come into ourselves at different times," Chloe said. "Does this mean you're a lesbian now?"

"I've been working that part out, and I think I'm bisexual."

Chloe smiled. An honest to God smile. It was a relief to see it. "Cool."

"Yeah." Jess felt good saying it out loud to her best friend. At least, she hoped they would still be best friends after what she'd done. "Are you going to be okay about Sydney and me?"

"I talked to Sydney last night. She suggested that my feelings might not be quite as strong as I thought they were. She thinks that I've been trying to distract myself from Dana." Chloe shrugged. "She might be right."

"Yeah?"

"Maybe." She started to grin. "Don't get me wrong. I still think your woman is hot and everything."

Jess smiled. "I can now openly confirm that I agree."

"So, I'll be okay. I don't think I was heartbroken about the pair of you together. I was more upset that you both lied to me. And pretty fucking shocked, if I'm honest."

"Believe me, I've been in shock about it for months," Jess said. "I never saw Sydney coming. Either time."

"And you love her? Like, really, truly can't live without her, love her?"

"Yes." That was a good assessment of how Jess felt.

Chloe held her hands out by her sides. "Well, are you ever going to tell her?"

Jess frowned. "She knows."

"No, she doesn't. Sydney has no idea. And you hightailing it out of her bedroom yesterday morning and never looking back really didn't help matters. How do you think that looked to Sydney?"

Okay, that did sound bad. Jess cringed. "She told you that?"

"Yes. We've talked. Extensively. And I still stand by the opinion that you're an idiot."

"But Sydney knew that I was upset."

"Jess. You've been playing Sydney hot and cold for months." Chloe stepped forward and flicked Jess on the forehead.

"Ow! What was that for?"

"That was for being flaky as hell." Chloe shook her head. "Idiot," she mumbled again.

Jess held her hands up. "Okay, I get it. I'm an idiot."

"Don't just admit it. Do something about it!"

"I wasn't blowing Sydney off or anything. I just wanted to work things out with you first."

"Well, you've done that."

"Yeah? We're okay?" Jess asked. She needed to make sure.

"We'll be fine," Chloe said.

Jess beamed with relief.

"Now. About Sydney. Are you all in or not?"

"I'm all in."

"Both feet?" Chloe asked.

Jess gave a nod. "Both feet."

"Okay. Then you're going to have to show her." Chloe regarded her seriously. "And you're going to have to really prove it, Jess, because she doesn't trust that you're solid. And from what I've learned, I don't blame her."

Jess went to grab her coat. "I'll go home and tell her right now."

Chloe put a hand out to stop her. "She's not home. She said she was going to stay with Rachel and Ben tonight to give us a chance to sort things out." Of course she was. Because Sydney was the most considerate person in the world. "Besides, telling her isn't going to cut it. You have to *show* her, Jess."

Jess didn't have a lot of experience showing someone that she wanted to be with them. She had spent most of her life in a relationship with a guy who naturally assumed that everybody wanted to be with him. "How?"

Pam burst out of the kitchen. "You need some kind of grand gesture."

Jess put a hand on her hip. "Have you been listening in this whole time?"

"It wasn't just me." Pam jerked her head. "She has been too."

Violet sheepishly followed Pam out of the kitchen. She plastered on that grandmotherly smile of hers. "I'm so glad you two managed to sort things out."

Jess shook her head at them both but couldn't contain her own smile. "Nothing's private in this place."

Pam grinned. "What would be the fun in that?"

Jess and Chloe both laughed. "Okay, nosy parkers, what do you mean by a grand gesture?" Jess asked. "Like a public announcement?" She made a face. "I don't think Sydney would like that."

"It doesn't have to be showy or in-your-face. It can just be something that's personal to you and Sydney," Violet said. "Have you got any special places you could take her to?"

Jess didn't need to consider it for very long before an idea popped into her head. "I think I know a way to show Sydney that I'm all in." She glanced at Pam and Violet, then at Chloe. "But I'm going to need help from you guys."

All three of them looked around at each other excitedly.

Pam rubbed her hands together. "We're in. Tell us what you need."

"Are you all free tomorrow?" Jess just hoped her plan would work.

CHAPTER TWENTY

"Sydney! You're home." Chloe bounded toward her the second Sydney set one foot through the front door. "Did you have a good time at your sister's?"

She slowly closed the door behind her. "Yeah, it was fine." Sydney tilted her head at Chloe and smiled. "You seem chirpier." Sydney was relieved to see it. Knowing that she had contributed to Chloe's pain had been eating away at her, even after they had sorted things.

"I am," Chloe said. "I spoke to Jess."

That made one of them. "Oh. Good," Sydney said as she shrugged her overnight bag off her shoulder. "How did it go?" She assumed it went well given that Chloe seemed like she was back to her old self again.

Sydney led the way to the kitchen and Chloe followed.

"We sorted a lot of things out. The bottom line is that Jess wasn't intentionally trying to hurt me, you know? I think she just lost control of the situation." Chloe shrugged. "She fucked up, basically."

Sydney nodded in agreement. "But you're right. Jess would never hurt you on purpose. I'm glad you were able to see that."

"Don't get me wrong. I could still shake her so hard. But I think we'll be okay."

"That's great." Sydney smiled but it faltered.

Chloe caught it. "What's wrong? I thought you would be happy that things were okay now. It's a good thing for all of us, right?"

"Oh, I am. I'm thrilled that you and Jess made up. Truly."

Chloe frowned. "But?"

"But." Sydney dropped her head down. "I still haven't heard from her. Not really."

"You haven't?"

"No." Sydney sighed. "And it's frustrating because I don't have any idea where we stand." She scrunched her nose up. "I've been thinking a lot about it over the past twenty-four hours, and maybe…" She hesitated because it wasn't easy to say. "Maybe I should take a step back from this thing with Jess."

"A step back?"

"Yeah," Sydney said. Her heart felt heavy even thinking about it, but that same heart needed some protection. She didn't know how many more disappearing acts from Jess it could take. "If Jess wanted to be with me, she would be."

"She does," Chloe squeaked out. "She does want to be with you. You can't give up on her."

"She hasn't spoken to me, Chlo. I get that she wanted to fix things with you, but she's done that, and look. Still not a peep. I can't be with someone who walks in and out of my life whenever they feel like it. Or vanishes when the going gets tough."

"She won't," Chloe said, her face panic-stricken. "That's not what she's doing."

"Maybe that's what Jess told you, but the evidence speaks for itself." Sydney hadn't even had a text message from Jess since she sent her a love heart the day before. Sydney had tried to check in, but her messages had gone unanswered.

Chloe lifted her phone out of her pocket and checked it. She winced. "I'm not supposed to do this for another twenty minutes, but you're leaving me no choice."

"Do what? What are you talking about?"

"Okay. Where would you find stones inside the house?"

"Stones in the house?" Sydney studied her. "Have you been drinking gin?"

"No." Chloe swatted her arm. "Think about it. Where would you find *stones* inside the house?"

Sydney frowned. "I have no idea what's going on right now."

"Think of it as a riddle."

"Why am I doing riddles?"

"Will you please just do it? It's supposed to be fun and you're ruining it."

"Okay, okay." Sydney repeated the phrase in her head. *Stones. Inside the house.* Maybe a fruit? Some fruit had stones inside. Did any of the plant pots have stones? "Should I be thinking about fruit or plants?"

Chloe shook her head. "Focus on the *stones*."

Sydney concentrated. Stones. Rocks. Rock music? Rocking chair? She disregarded both of those because she wasn't aware of any rocking chairs or rock CDs in the house. Stones as in weight measurement? "Is it weighing scales?"

Chloe held her head in her hands. "You're bad at this."

Sydney gave her a look. "Sorry, I wasn't expecting a puzzle this morning." Gravel. Grit. Pebbles. *Hold on...* "I think I know. Is it Pebbles? As in the penguin?"

Chloe shrugged but breathed out a sigh of relief. "I guess you'll have to go and look. My job was only to point you in the right direction." She shot Sydney a smile. "Good luck."

With that, she turned on her heel.

Cryptic. Sydney gaped after her. What was going on? Sydney guessed there was only one way to find out.

She took the stairs two at a time and went toward Jess's room. Sydney assumed Jess wasn't in there, but she knocked just in case. No answer. She turned the handle and slowly entered Jess's bedroom.

Sure enough, Pebbles was perched in the middle of the bed. The stuffed animal was holding some sort of box. When Sydney got closer, she recognized it. She lifted Pebbles and pulled the box out. It was for The Day We Met soap that Sydney had made for Jess. And there was some kind of note attached to it. Sydney didn't waste any time in unfolding the pink paper to read it.

Sydney,

You're confused. I know. But all will be revealed very soon, so please go with me on this.

The fact that you're reading this means you solved your first clue (and that Chloe didn't forget what to say, phew!)

I've spent a while now wishing that I could turn back

the clock and do things a lot differently. Unfortunately, I know that isn't possible.

But what if we kind of could? If we could return to a moment for a second time and choose a completely different path. The path we should have taken the first time. A do-over.

To do that, we would have to go back to the same places as before, starting at the very beginning.

Are you holding the box? If you are, then I trust you'll know where to begin. Noon would be a good time to be there, don't you think? ;)

Jess x
PS. Bring Pebbles.

So, Jess had done this. This was Jess's puzzle. One that was specifically for Sydney. Sydney started to smile. Okay, she would play along. She looked at the box in her hand, and it gave her a fairly good idea where to begin.

It had to be the train, didn't it? Sydney had met Jess on the train.

She checked the time. She could easily make it there by twelve o'clock. That must have been what Chloe had meant by saying she was early. Though in Sydney's experience, it was better to be early than to miss the train—she had already missed an important one once before. She considered that a lesson learned.

Sydney didn't know what exactly Jess was planning, but she had to admit she was intrigued to find out. Without further thought, she grabbed Pebbles and headed straight for the station.

There was still plenty of time to spare when Sydney arrived. She could have caught an earlier train headed in the same direction, but something told her to wait until noon. Jess hadn't specified a time for no reason. Would she be on that train waiting for her?

When it made its approach into the station, Sydney cast her eye on each of the compartments as they passed by. There was no sign of Jess in any of them from what she could see, so she chose a compartment at random and got on. Her usual seat was free, so she took it. She wondered if the seat she picked was important to Jess's plan or not. Sydney supposed it wasn't because the train began to move and Jess still hadn't appeared anywhere.

A couple of stops along the way, the ticket clerk approached. Sydney got her phone out to pay him.

"Sydney?" he asked when he reached her seat. He was an older gentleman, with grey hair and a kindly smile.

"That's me." Sydney squinted, trying to figure out if she recognized him, but she had no recollection. "I'm so sorry if I'm blanking, but do we know each other?"

His smile grew making his eyes crinkle at the sides. "No, but I was told to look out for the penguin." He gestured Pebbles with his head.

So that was why Jess wanted her to bring Pebbles. Clever.

"Your friend told me to give you this." He reached into his pocket of his navy blazer and pulled out another note. It was on the same pink notepaper as the one she found in Jess's bedroom.

Sydney smiled back at him. "Thank you."

"I hope you find what you're looking for." He shot Sydney a wink and went to continue up the carriage.

"Wait, I need to pay you," Sydney called after him.

He held a hand up and kept walking. "Your friend already did. Said she owed you a train fare."

Sydney watched him as he walked away to the next passenger. She unfolded the note, unable to shake the feeling of excitement as she read it. Apparently, *her friend* had been busier than Sydney had realized.

> *You made it :)*
>
> *This is when I start to get sappy, so bear with me.*
>
> *When I met you on this train all those months ago, I felt my life change. At the time I didn't understand it, but I think that's because I didn't truly understand myself.*
>
> *Even when we were stuck in the darkest of tunnels, your smile and your kindness shone bright. And you have been my light ever since.*
>
> *You helped me conquer my fears that day, but instead of doing the same, I became yours—because I've been a clown to wait so long to be with you.*
>
> *I know I've made mistakes, but if you're willing to overlook them, then go to the bench where you first saw the*

red dress (just in case you hadn't worked out where to get off yet.)

    Jess x

PS. Before we even spoke that day, I thought that your smile was the prettiest thing I had ever seen. I don't want to go another day without it.

It felt like a whirlwind of butterflies were swarming around Sydney's stomach. She couldn't keep the smile off her face as she read the letter once, twice, three times.

Sydney sighed. Could she overlook Jess's mistakes? Yes. There was no question that she could. Nobody was perfect. As far as Sydney was concerned, she and Jess were just two ordinarily flawed human beings. Perfection was an unreasonable expectation to put on anyone. And Sydney was in love with Jess, unconditionally. So, it was a given that she could overlook just about anything.

But *should* she overlook the mistakes? Or were they warnings? Because mistakes and flaws were one thing, but someone who might never be able to commit was a whole different ball game. And as much as it pained Sydney, she knew that she needed that commitment.

Would Jess be able to give her that? If not now, then ever? So far, there was zero evidence to say that she would. Was that about to change? Did Sydney want to take the risk and find out? Knowing that she could get her heart broken like never before if it all went wrong?

Sydney came to the conclusion that some things were worth the risk, and Jess was one of them.

So, when the train pulled up at the same station where she and Jess had got off together months before, Sydney stepped off the train.

She took a few seconds to get her bearings and pinpoint which bench they had stopped at before. Sydney remembered looking after Jess's bags while she had changed in the ladies' toilets, and the bench hadn't been far away from there. She wandered along the platform until she found right one.

"You found me," said a woman's voice.

Sydney whipped her head round. "Pam," she said, surprised to see Jess's colleague standing beside the bench and not Jess. "What are you doing here?"

Pam leaned forward. "I'm a messenger," she said gleefully. She opened her brown clutch handbag and pulled out a piece of paper. A pink piece of paper. She passed it to Sydney. "I'm only supposed to give you this, but you know I can't help but give my input."

Sydney chuckled. "I'd be happy to hear it."

Pam beamed. "You're a sweet girl, Sydney. I knew that the very first time you came by Thairapy to see Jess. That was also the day that I knew Jess was smitten with you. She wasn't ready to admit it then." She reached forward and took Sydney's hand, giving it a pat. "I think she's ready now."

Sydney took in the words Pam was saying and nodded her understanding. "That's good to know, Pam. Thank you."

"Good luck," she said sweetly, before disappearing into the crowd in the busy station.

Sydney was so eager to unfold Jess's latest letter she almost ripped it in two. She plonked herself down on the bench to read it.

I hope that Pam behaved herself. You know how she likes to meddle.

This means that you've made it to the station. Yay. I'm so happy that you've stuck with me. I hope you can continue to do so for a little longer.

I'm guessing you're a little confused that I'm not at the train station, considering that's the last place we saw each other on the day we met.

The thing is, that although my feelings for you started that day, they've been growing ever since. That might be the first time I've ever told you that, but I promise that I plan to be totally transparent about my feelings from this day forward.

Speaking of forward, let's keep going.

There's an emergency! And you're needed at work. Not at Makes Scents, the soap is fine, don't worry. I mean your other job.

Jess x

PS. Maybe it won't only be the monkeys flirting today.

Sydney grinned, thinking back to the game she and Jess had played on the train. She stood from the bench and headed for the station exit—the one people took when they were going in the direction of the zoo.

As she walked, Sydney thought back to the day that she had gone to the zoo with Ben and Jess—Jess was taking her down memory lane, and Sydney was sure that had been her intention with all of this.

She remembered Jess waiting for her and Ben that day, looking a million bucks standing by the metal gates. Was that where she would find Jess today? She rushed along the path to find out.

The zoo was surprisingly busy for a cold Sunday in February. Sydney had to look through a sea of people to try and find Jess. She scanned the spot where Jess had waited for her before, but nothing. Sydney frowned as she stopped beside the fence and looked around. What was she supposed to be looking for?

"Cooee." Suddenly, not Jess, but Violet came walking toward Sydney waving a piece of paper. White this time, not pink.

Sydney smiled at her. "You're in on this too?"

"I wouldn't have missed it for the world." Violet pulled Sydney in for a hug. "I'm so glad you came. Jess was worried that you wouldn't, you know."

"She was?"

"She said she wouldn't blame you if you didn't. But I knew you would."

Sydney cocked her head. "How did you know?"

"When you've been around for this long, you can spot when two people are meant to be together. You and Jess are a shining example. I'm just so happy that Jess was finally able to see it too." She passed the white piece of paper to Sydney. "This is your ticket."

"Thanks." Sydney put it into her pocket. Where would she go when she entered the zoo? "Do you have anything else for me? A note maybe?"

"Oh." Violet's eyes widened. She reached into her handbag and pulled out, lo and behold, a pink note. "I can't believe I almost forgot that part. Well, enjoy the zoo, dear."

"Thank you so much, Violet." Sydney waved as she walked away.

She wondered whether to read the note outside the gates or if she should wait until she went in. Impatience won out and she opened it.

Here we are, back at the zoo again. It's funny how things

naturally link together. We talked about this place when we first met, and it was also the first place we went together. It seemed significant that we return.

Do you remember when I held that baby chick? I held its fragile little body in the palm of my hand and cradled it as gently as I could in order to keep it safe.

The thing is—that's what you do for me. You have done ever since we were stuck in that tunnel. You said that day that you were my protector, and you've been my safe place ever since. I want to be your safe place too.

You know, our relationship is kind of like that baby chick. Cute, delicate, and in need of a lot of care. Its new life symbolizing our new beginning.

Seems like a good place to start, doesn't it?

Jess x

PS. I can't wait to see you.

That could only mean one thing—Jess would be waiting for her at the farm.

Sydney joined the queue of people waiting to get in through the zoo gates. When she got to the front after a few minutes, Sydney flashed the ticket that Jess had left for her to get inside and was handed a map. She unfolded it and had a quick glance to check that she was headed the right way. It didn't take her very long to get to the farm.

"Aunt Sydney!" Before she even stepped through the farm entrance, Ben came hurtling toward her with the biggest smile on his face.

"Ben," Sydney said in confusion. "What are you doing here, buddy? And who are you here with?" She looked around.

"Mummy," Ben said as if it was obvious. He gestured to Rachel, who was walking behind to catch up with him. "We're on a secret mission," he said excitedly.

"You are?" Sydney asked. "What kind of secret mission?"

"This kind," Rachel said as she approached her waving a piece of pink paper.

Sydney dropped her jaw open. "You're involved in this? How? Since when?"

Rachel looked at her sheepishly. "Last night."

"But I was with you last night! You never said a word."

"That's because I was sworn to secrecy."

Ben tugged on Sydney's sleeve. "I only found out this morning, Aunt Sydney."

Rachel smiled down at him. "Yes, that's because you're a chatterbox and you would have told."

He stuck his nose in the air. "Would not."

Sydney laughed. Ben definitely would have told. "But how?" she asked Rachel again.

"Jess texted me and asked if me and Ben would help. Said she got my number off the fridge."

That made sense. Sydney always kept a note with important numbers on it in case something ever went wrong with her phone. "I'm still a little surprised you're in on this. You're not exactly the biggest Jess and Sydney supporter."

"I am if Jess gets her act together and starts to treat you right. But don't worry, I've already got her well warned."

"No." Sydney stared at her. "You didn't?"

"Oh, I did."

"Seriously?" Sydney winced. "The whole *if you mess with my sister, you'll have me to answer to* talk?"

Rachel squared her shoulders. "Yep. And don't forget the *what are your intentions with my sister* part as well."

"There's a part of me that kind of wants to shake you, but the other part really wants to know what she said."

"She said she wants to be with you. For real." Rachel lifted a shoulder. "That's good enough for me. Besides, it seems like all the obstacles have disappeared now. If you two are going to work out, now's the time."

"So, you think I should give her a chance?"

"Yeah, I do. And you're here, so obviously you think so too." Rachel smiled. "You know I'll support you in anything. You've got this." She passed Sydney the note. "That's my part done."

"What do you mean? There's more?"

"Yeah. It's my turn," Ben said. He put his shoulders back and stood up straight. "Do you remember I asked Jess why she wasn't your girlfriend? And you said I shouldn't ask those kinds of questions?"

"I remember," Sydney said.

"Well, Jess told me I'm allowed to ask that question again one more time. Only this time I have to ask you instead of her." He cleared his throat. "Aunt Sydney, why are you not Jess's girlfriend?" He was so serious and sincere.

Sydney started to giggle. "You know what, Ben? I don't know why I'm not Jess's girlfriend. I want to be."

He smiled. "Then I think you should go and sort that out."

Rachel put an arm on Ben's shoulder. "Come on, you. Let's go and look at some more animals and leave Sydney to the rest of her Jess hunt."

They said their goodbyes and left Sydney to open her next note.

> *Did Ben ask you a question?*
>
> *I think it's a pretty good one, don't you?*
>
> *Obviously, I know a lot of the reason why is down to me—but I want to change that. I'm ready to change it, Sydney. I'm sorry it took me so long to get here, but I am here now.*
>
> *Do you remember when I told you that I liked you too much to let you be my experiment? I was wrong. Because you've never been an experiment. You are my solution. I'm sorry that it took me so long to come up with the right hypothesis.*
>
> *So, to ask Ben's question again, why aren't you my girlfriend, Sydney?*
>
> *Maybe we can come up with a new answer to that question together. If you want to, then come and find me.*
>
> *If you don't know where to look, I'm sure Pebbles can help.*
>
> *Jess x*
>
> *PS. The only thing left to say is, I love you.*

That was all Sydney needed to know.

"What do you say, Pebbles? Want to go visit your friends?" Sydney ignored the strange looks she was getting from a passing couple. She probably deserved them—after all, she was talking to a stuffed penguin. But in that moment, Sydney didn't care. Because the woman she loved, loved her back.

Jess's note had said to come and find her. That had to mean that Jess would finally be waiting at the next location, didn't it? And it probably meant that Sydney was supposed to go to the underwater viewing tank when she got to the penguin enclosure. She knew how much Jess loved watching the penguins swim around underwater. Beautiful, she had called it.

But there was nothing as beautiful as what Sydney saw the second that she entered the exhibit. Jess was sitting on top of a rock, watching the penguins swim around in the tank. Her long, dark hair was blowing gently in the breeze. She was hugging her knees into her chest, her arms wrapped around them as she waited.

Then, as if she somehow sensed Sydney standing there, Jess turned to face her, immediately catching her gaze. Her face softened into a smile. "Hi." She pushed herself up off the rock and walked toward her.

Sydney walked forward to meet her, not breaking eye contact for a second. "Hi yourself. Sorry if I kept you waiting for long."

"Funny, that's exactly what I was going to say to you," Jess said. "Only I don't just mean today."

Sydney nodded. "It's been quite the journey. Both today, and over the last few months."

"You can say that again." She gestured her head. "Come sit with me. The penguins are showing off."

They both took a seat on one of the window ledges of the viewing tank. Sydney set Pebbles up beside them, and Jess grinned. "Was Pebbles helpful?"

"Oh, very." Sydney chuckled. "You're lucky I managed to work out the first clue, though, or you might have been sitting here for a lot longer."

"Did Chloe not help? She was supposed to help you if you struggled."

"I'm sure she would have told me if I hadn't worked it out." Sydney smiled. "I'm glad you two worked things out."

"Me too," Jess said, her tone relieved. "I hear I've got you to thank for getting her to talk to me in the first place."

Sydney shrugged. "I think she would have come round anyway."

"Still. Thank you," Jess said. She took a deep breath and let it out slowly. "So, I know you've read my letters because you're here. But I have a few things to add, if that's okay?" Jess swallowed, clearly more nervous than she was letting on.

"Please, add away," Sydney said.

Jess shuffled round to fully face Sydney. "I grew up with a pretty poor example of how a couple should be. And I always vowed never to be like my parents. That's why I thought, when I was in a relationship, I had to stay in it and find some way of making it work no matter what." Jess huffed out a laugh. "With Austin and me, that was by us leading separate lives." She looked down at the ground. "The thing is, I was wrong. Not in the fact that I should have to work at a relationship. I still think that's true. But now I know that I should be working at the *right* relationship. And I didn't know what that relationship looked like until I met you."

Sydney's heart started to race faster, and she reached out and took Jess's hand.

Jess continued, automatically lacing her fingers through Sydney's. "I know it wasn't smooth sailing for us to get here. But I am in no doubt that you're the person who I want to be with. I'm sorry it took me so long."

"I'm so scared that you'll change your mind," Sydney whispered. "That you'll run from me again."

Jess nodded in understanding. "I think the word that Chloe used was *flaky*. But I'm hoping you'll give me the chance to prove to you that I'm not. There's no Austin. Chloe's okay about us. And I think we've established that I have no issues when it comes to being with another woman. In fact, I very much enjoyed it."

Sydney laughed.

Jess squeezed her hand. "And there's the fact that I'm so in love with you it's unbelievable."

Sydney couldn't hold back her smile. "Yeah?" She had longed to hear those words from Jess for so long.

"You've got no idea. But you will." Jess turned to look at the tank where the penguins were swimming around in circles. "Do you remember how penguins show their commitment to one another?"

"If I remember correctly, they look for the biggest, smoothest pebble they can find, and present it to the penguin they want to be with," Sydney replied.

Jess suddenly reached into her bag and pulled out a large oval shaped stone. It was so smooth that it almost shined. She handed it to Sydney. "We may not be penguins, but I hope that the same rules can apply for us."

Sydney turned the rock around in her hands and smiled. "You're penguin wooing me right now?"

Jess laughed. "If that's what you want to call it, sure. Though I like to think of it as me committing to you. For life. Or for as long as you can put up with me." She bit her lip. "What do you say?"

Sydney didn't even need to think about it. "I say…why aren't you my girlfriend yet, Jess?"

"I thought you'd never ask." Jess leaned forward and captured Sydney's lips with her own, kissing her for the whole world to see.

After a minute, Sydney pulled back. "You know that I'm completely in love with you too, right?"

Jess smiled. "I had hoped you were. I'd sort of been banking on it."

"Well, I am. Now you know for certain." Sydney had never been so sure of anything in all her life.

"You'll still tell me, though?" Jess asked.

Sydney smiled and leaned forward to kiss her again. "Every. Single. Day," she said before pressing her lips against Jess's, right where they belonged.

"Should we go now?" Sydney asked when they eventually pulled back.

"Let's." Jess kissed her again quickly. "Your place or mine?"

"That's kind of the perk to falling for your roommate, isn't it?"

"In that case, let's go home," Jess said, grabbing Sydney by the hand and pulling her up from the ledge. "Don't forget Pebbles."

"Do you think Pebbles would like some company? Maybe we should buy Pebbles a friend on our way out?" Sydney suggested as they strolled hand in hand toward the exit.

"You mean like a mate?" Jess asked.

"Exactly. And you know that penguins mate for life, don't you?"

"I'm counting on it."

EPILOGUE

Eighteen months later

Jess hated weddings. At least, she used to hate them. Something about this one didn't fill her full of dread as much as all of the previous ones had. For starters, her date was so much better this time round. Sydney was sitting by Jess's side, squeezing her hand for support as Jess's dad's latest bride walked up the aisle.

After her dad and Gretchen had inevitably decided to divorce a year and a half ago, he had gone on a singles cruise to lick his wounds, and there he met Karen. A receptionist. Age appropriate, down to earth, kind, and pretty. Jess had named her Karen the Keeper. Fingers crossed she lived up to the nickname. The fact that Gretchen had dragged out the divorce—holding out for more money, what else?—meant that Karen and her dad had spent time getting to know one another before jumping straight into marriage. He was happier than Jess could ever remember seeing him, and Jess was happy that he had done things the right way for a change.

The ceremony and the meal were both very relaxed and pleasant affairs, but Jess couldn't wait to get home. The rest of the evening would only consist of drunk dancing and bad karaoke, and her dad was blissfully preoccupied with his new wife anyway.

As soon as they had finished their dessert, Jess leaned into Sydney. "Do you think it would look bad if we left?" she whispered.

"Now? Do you not want to stay a while longer?" Sydney asked.

"Not really." Jess ran her foot up Sydney's leg. "Did I forget to tell you that we've got the house to ourselves tonight?"

Sydney eye's widened with interest. "Do we? So, Chloe and Dana—"

"Are away to stay in a fancy hotel for the night for their one year anniversary. And they won't be back until tomorrow afternoon. At the earliest." Jess made a show of looking around her. "But if you would rather stay here—"

"No, no." Sydney set her napkin on the table with purpose. "Let's go."

Jess laughed and quickly gathered her things. She and Sydney didn't have as many nights to themselves since Chloe had Dana had become a couple.

A late-night office kiss had given Chloe the courage to finally call Dana out for her hot and cold behaviour. Chloe had told Dana that if she wanted to be with her, it would be then or never. Luckily, Dana was no fool. Who knew that mega-rich and powerful women struggled with their feelings sometimes too?

The downside—neither of them had to make excuses to stay late at the office to spend time together anymore. Which meant that Jess and Sydney didn't have nearly as much alone time as they wanted. But the upside made up for it. Chloe was disgustingly happy all the time, and Dana had turned out to be a good addition to the group. Though she was just as high maintenance about her morning coffee as Sydney was. Beanie was working extra hard these days.

Jess and Sydney gave their hugs and said their goodbyes. When they stepped outside, Sydney laced her fingers through Jess's. "Do you have to be up early for work in the morning?"

Jess shook her head. "Violet and Pam told me to take the day off. I think they're feeling guilty for working me so hard lately."

"Are they still going to hire another stylist to help out?"

"They want me to choose someone," Jess said. "They said if they're going to be taking a step back, it will be me who will be working with them the most, therefore it should be my decision."

"I'm sure Pam will still make her feelings known," Sydney said with a grin.

Jess chuckled. "I have no doubt about that."

"The first step to becoming the big boss, huh?"

The Thairapy Room was still going to be Violet and Pam's baby, but they both thought it was time to cut back on their hours a little. As

Violet had put it, they weren't getting any younger. What they wanted was for Jess to sit in the driving seat, and eventually, take over officially.

"It's a nice idea, but I don't think I would ever be able to afford to buy this place," Jess had said when Violet suggested it.

"Who said anything about buying? We aren't selling, we're giving."

"Eventually," Pam had interjected. "We won't be easy to get rid of."

"I never want to be rid of either of you," Jess had said. "You have plenty of haircuts left in you before either of you need to think about retirement."

"We do. But maybe a few less than we used to. And eventually, we will just want to be here to watch you succeed," Violet had told her.

"I would never be able to accept it. You could sell up and get loads of money when the time comes."

Violet had given her that kindly smile that she was so good at. "Jess. We've made our money—we've got more than enough. Why would we want to sell to a stranger when we could leave our life's work in the hands of someone we love and trust?"

"Yeah," Pam had said sassily. "So, stop your arguing, young lady. You won't win this one."

Jess sighed. "I can't say I'm happy about it. You know I like things the way they are."

Sydney bumped her with her hip. "Some change is good, remember?"

That made Jess smile. "I can't argue with that."

To think that Jess had ever worried about changing her life before. That she would have stayed with a guy who she didn't love, just because she was so scared of something different. It seemed incomprehensible to her now.

"So, we have tonight *and* tomorrow morning," Sydney said with a suggestive smile.

"And you know what that means."

Sydney laughed. "It's a good job I made up a fresh batch of The Day We Met."

Since discovering her love for the female body—and specifically, for Sydney's female body—Jess had taken to joining Sydney in her morning shower when the opportunity arose. Opportunity meaning anytime they were home alone. If they ever got their own place, Jess planned on starting every morning with shower sex.

"Speaking of my favourite soap, how has the new range been selling this week?" Jess asked. After the Days Out line had been such a roaring success, Sydney and Rachel had created a Nights Out line to follow it up.

Sydney beamed. "Brilliantly. Who knew so many people wanted to smell like a piña colada?"

"That's because everything you make smells amazing. You're a genius."

"Don't forget to remind my sister of that fact. Speaking of Rachel, Ben's off school next week and has requested a two-night sleepover instead of one. Would you mind?"

"Of course not," Jess said right away. "He has his own room now. He can use it whenever he wants to."

Naturally, since Jess and Sydney had got together, they hadn't spent many nights sleeping in separate rooms. None, to be exact. They had tried out each other's bedrooms, eventually opting for Jess's, which was a little bigger. It had only taken Sydney one afternoon to move all her stuff from one room to the other. Falling in love with your roommate was rather convenient.

When Jess's bedroom had become *their* bedroom, Ben had quickly laid claim to Sydney's old room when he came over for sleepovers.

"Is Rachel going to do anything fun with her free time?" Jess asked.

Sydney gave her a knowing look. "I've been trying to get her to download a dating app or something, but she's having none of it."

"She's content on her own. There's nothing wrong with that."

"No, I know. I just worry sometimes that she'll get lonely," Sydney said. "But the course she's been taking keeps her busy. Between that, Ben, and Makes Scents, I don't think Rachel has time for much else."

Rachel had decided to do a course on marketing to help her and Sydney take Makes Scents to the next level.

"Maybe she'll meet a marketing whizz who will sweep her off her feet with a romantic email."

Sydney grinned. "The way to Rachel's heart."

Speaking of hearts, Jess's was full as they walked down the steps to the train station. She sighed with happiness. Trains had that effect on her these days. Who knew one journey would completely change the entire outlook of her life?

Ever since Jess had presented Sydney with that pebble, her life had felt like a fairy tale, every day filled with love and happiness. Penguin rituals really did work, apparently.

As they waited for the train, Jess glanced down at the rock that Sydney had given her in return. It sparkled on her finger as the light reflected off it. Sydney had proposed on the one-year anniversary of the day they met. Jess had said yes before she even finished asking the question. Naturally, Sydney had proposed to her on the train. Then she had taken Jess for a romantic dinner and surprise night away.

They still hadn't set a date yet, but what was the rush? They had the rest of their lives together.

As the train pulled in, Jess looked up at Sydney and smiled. She leaned up and kissed her softly on the cheek.

"What was that for?" Sydney asked.

"Just because I love you."

That made Sydney smile back. "For life?"

Jess nodded. "And even after."

The train stopped and the doors opened. "I love you too," Sydney said. "Let's go home. I've got a nice bottle of wine chilling in the fridge that we can take up to bed with us."

"Best. Roommate. Ever."

About the Author

Claire Forsythe lives in Belfast, Northern Ireland, with her partner, son, and pets.

Claire enjoys cooking and experimenting with new recipes in the kitchen, sipping coffee and red wine (not at the same time), traveling and exploring new places, reading a variety of novels—from romance to crime, playing poker even though she's a terrible bluffer, and binge-watching box sets. She's a big football fan and loves cheering on her favorite team, Liverpool FC. She loves to spend as much time as she can with her family and friends, who mean the world to her. Claire and her partner get beaten by two of their best friends in doubles badminton weekly, though they turn up every week in the hope that their luck will change. It hasn't yet, though there was that one draw…

Claire has loved words and books ever since she was little, and it has always been her ambition to write. After finding herself with some unexpected free time on her hands in lockdown during the pandemic, she decided to follow her dream and start writing. Now that she's started, she never wants to stop.

Her previous book, *We Met in a Bar*, was a finalist in the 2024 Goldie Awards.

About the Author

Books Available From Bold Strokes Books

All For Her: Forbidden Romance Novellas by Gun Brooke, J.J. Hale & Aurora Rey. Explore the angst and excitement of forbidden love few would dare in this heart-stopping novella collection. (978-1-63679-713-7)

Finding Harmony by CF Frizzell. Rock star Harper Cushing has to rearrange her grandmother's future and sell the family store out from under her, but she reassesses everything because Gram's helper, Frankie, could be offering the harmony her heart has been missing. (978-1-63679-741-0)

Gaze by Kris Bryant. Love at first sight is for dreamers, but the more time Lucky and Brianna spend together, the more they realize the chemistry of a gaze can make anything possible. (978-1-63679-711-3)

Laying of Hands by Patricia Evans. The mysterious new writing instructor at camp makes Grace Waters brave enough to wonder what would happen if she dared to write her own story. (978-1-63679-782-3)

The Naked Truth by Sandy Lowe. How far are Rowan and Genevieve willing to go and how much will they risk to make their most captivating and forbidden fantasies a reality? (978-1-63679-426-6)

The Roommate by Claire Forsythe. Jess Black's boyfriend is handsome and successful. That's why it comes as a shock when she meets a woman on the train who makes her pulse race. (978-1-63679-757-1)

Seducing the Widow by Jane Walsh. Former rival debutantes have a second chance at love after fifteen years apart when a spinster persuades her ex-lover to help save her family business. (978-1-63679-747-2)

Close to Home by Allisa Bahney. Eli Thomas has to decide if avoiding her hometown forever is worth losing the people who used to mean the most to her, especially Aracely Hernandez, the girl who got away. (978-1-63679-661-1)

Innis Harbor by Patricia Evans. When Amir Farzaneh meets and falls in love with Loch, a dark secret lurking in her past reappears, threatening the happiness she'd just started to believe could be hers. (978-1-63679-781-6)

The Blessed by Anne Shade. Layla and Suri are brought together by fate to defeat the darkness threatening to tear their world apart. What they don't expect to discover is a love that might set them free. (978-1-63679-715-1)

The Guardians by Sheri Lewis Wohl. Dogs, devotion, and determination are all that stand between darkness and light. (978-1-63679-681-9)

The Mogul Meets Her Match by Julia Underwood. When CEO Claire Beauchamp goes undercover as a customer of Abby Pita's café to help seal a deal that will solidify her career, she doesn't expect to be so drawn to her. When the truth is revealed, will she break Abby's heart? (978-1-63679-784-7)

Trial Run by Carsen Taite. When Reggie Knoll and Brooke Dawson wind up serving on a jury together, their one task—reaching a unanimous verdict—is derailed by the fiery clash of their personalities, the intensity of their attraction, and a secret that could threaten Brooke's life. (978-1-63555-865-4)

Waterlogged by Nance Sparks. When conservation warden Jordan Pearce discovers a body floating in the flowage, the serenity of the Northwoods is rocked. (978-1-63679-699-4)

Accidentally in Love by Kimberly Cooper Griffin. Nic and Lee have good reasons for keeping their distance. So why does their growing attraction seem more like a love-hate relationship? (978-1-63679-759-5)

Frosted by the Girl Next Door by Aurora Rey and Jaime Clevenger. When heartbroken Casey Stevens opens a sex shop next door to uptight cupcake baker Tara McCoy, things get a little frosty. (978-1-63679-723-6)

Ghost of the Heart by Catherine Friend. Being possessed by a ghost was not on Gwen's bucket list, but she must admit that ghosts might be real, and one is obviously trying to send her a message. (978-1-63555-112-9)

Hot Honey Love by Nan Campbell. When chef Stef Lombardozzi puts her cooking career into the hands of filmmaker Mallory Radowski—the pickiest eater alive—she doesn't anticipate how hard she'll fall for her. (978-1-63679-743-4)